The
Spider
King

LAWRENCE SCHOONOVER

The
Spider
King

A BIOGRAPHICAL NOVEL
OF LOUIS XI OF FRANCE

New York

THE MACMILLAN COMPANY

Book One

Chapter One

Between the slow-flowing rivers of Auron and Yèvre in the fertile plain which constitutes the rich heartland of France, there rises an unexpected hillock on which has stood since Roman times the fortified city of Bourges. Imperial legions with an eye to the natural advantages of the place once camped there; imperial engineers first girdled the eminence with a heavy ring of watchtowers and walls to dominate the surrounding flatlands.

But the Roman legions had long since departed, marching into legend, by the year 1423. Such a year, indeed, would have sounded alien to Roman ears, reckoned as it was according to a chronology that began in an obscure Syrian province of the Empire. Nor would a Roman legionnaire have understood the French language now spoken in Bourges, though it was descended from the Latin it had replaced during the course of the centuries that separated this world from his. The buildings too belong to a new and later age. The squat and functional Roman arch had achieved a soaring point in a beautiful temple—the legionnaire would with difficulty have construed the Christian word *cathedral*—which an army of masons was busily rearing above the town to honor St. Steven. The very name of saint would have stirred no chord of memory, though stoning, the manner of the protomartyr's death, would have been familiar.

Nor would the day of the week have been intelligible to Roman ears. It was Sabbaidi, a name that smacked of the Sabbath of the East and bore no resemblance to Roman *Saturni dies*.

Saturday. Saturday of an alien week, 1423 in an alien calendar. But before such a legionnaire departed from the changed and disorderly land of France, he might have observed with a sense of ironical pride that this new and lawless race of men still honored the great name of Julius, first of the Caesars. It was the third of July.

It was also a holiday, not because it was Saturday but because of a painful event that was taking place with agonizing slowness in the château. Peasants coming to town with produce to sell from their farms in the countryside beyond the walls found the market deserted Stonemasons

3

climbing the unfinished tower of the cathedral to go about their daily tasks were told to lay down their chisels and make no noise. Superstitiously they turned the sharp edges away from the direction of the royal residence and tiptoed into the crowded church.

The Duke-Archbishop of Reims was saying a Mass for the queen of France. He prayed for a quick termination of her long labor, an end to her pain, and the healthy birth of another soul to serve God. As a peer of the realm he prayed that the royal child might be male, a prince strong enough to restore dignity to the tarnished crown and wise enough to bring peace to a kingdom torn apart and brutalized by eighty years of disastrous war. At the *Memento* he called to mind the other infants the young queen had borne in a series of recurrent pregnancies; they were dead now, the royal children, every one, and all in infancy. Breathing the beautiful words *in somno pacis*, the sleep of peace, his priestly heart wished them well in a better world; but his stout ducal heart wished that they were still alive in this one, the princes to fight, the princesses to marry for France. Nay, perhaps they were better dead. He strove not to let his thoughts wander beyond the sacred precincts of the altar, above all not to question the inscrutable wisdom of God—but why were the royal children so strange, and why did they die so young?

Outside, in the brilliant sunlight, a monk with a grave, intelligent face paced slowly to and fro across the cathedral steps, his hands clasped behind his back. He was stationed there to listen for the cannon report from the château which would signalize a successful birth, or, if the cannon missed fire, gunpowder being a new and unreliable invention, to watch for the raising of the royal standard, which would convey the same message.

Suddenly he was startled to hear the clatter of a workman's wooden shoes on the pavement behind him and a frightened voice calling, "Friar Jean, Friar Jean, unclasp your hands!"

The man ran down the steps, his work-worn jacket flapping in the wind of his own precipitate running, to do what he thought he had to do. The monk recognized him: a competent artisan from the south, skilled and sober, adept in the laying of tiles. He halted before a large pile of them; they were sorted and tied into bundles according to size, ready to be taken inside and laid in the cathedral floor. Frantically the man untied all the bundles.

"I should hate the poor queen to be suffering on my account," he said. "Nothing must be knotted or shut or tight today." Then, noting that the friar's hands were still clasped, he said, "Will you bless me, Friar Jean?"

"Your heart is sound," the monk said sternly but not unkindly, signing the cross over him. "God bless you and give you a less superstitious head."

"Thank you, Your Reverence," the man said, grinning a slyly satisfied smile.

The monk too smiled, a little ruefully, watching the workman's leather-

4

clad figure retreat into the shadows of the cathedral and disappear among the kneeling throng. "The well meaning rascal tricked me!"

To sign the cross, of course, Friar Jean had been forced to unclasp his hands.

In the château, in a bedroom of the royal apartments, while the whole city pitied and prayed for her, the young queen lay suffering. She was slender; the birth was difficult. It was the unanimous opinion of her doctors that she would die. It was not, of course, the doctors' duty to attend her. Conversing gravely in Latin, they stood in their long black academic robes before a roaring fire into which, from time to time, an apprentice surgeon threw handfuls of medicinal herbs to purify the stale air. All the windows, as usual at a birth, were shut tight. The ebbing strength of the queen, the doctors feared, would soon be exhausted. They based their conclusion on reports from the attending midwife, who kept them apprised of the queen's condition: she no longer bit her tongue to keep from screaming; she no longer wept; her face was turning blue.

It would not have been fitting, nor would the fastidious sufferer have permitted, that they part the bedcurtains behind which she stifled to examine her. Birth was a woman's business; the midwife was one of the best. The function of attending surgeons was to deliberate and advise, to congratulate the king if all went well, to call for the clergy if things went wrong. The doctors performed the only duty the critical situation still demanded of them. King Charles was hunting, but they now sent a runner to the cathedral. Breathless and all but inarticulate at the enormity of his message, the page knelt before the duke-archbishop in the sacristy.

"I shall come at once," the great prelate said. He was saddened at the curse that seemed to hang over the royal house. It was to be, after all, a day of disaster for France. Shortly he appeared in the anteroom where the surgeons, having no further business in the birth chamber, now mingled among the nobles of the realm who had gathered to greet or bury the new prince or princess.

Immediately upon the retirement of the learned doctors, a bevy of women, hitherto silent and respectful, took over the management of the queen. The midwife, a woman of the people with a healthy odor of onions and cookery clinging to her clothes, put off the cumbersome lace headdress which was fashionable among ladies of the court and which she had assumed for the occasion. She wrapped a peasant kerchief around her hair, being careful to tie no knots. She rolled up her sleeves and called loudly for someone to open the windows. "The best calves are dropped in the open fields," she snapped. "Fresh air! Fetch me a bucket of hot water from the kitchens. Another, icy cold from the wine cellar. And while you're there, bring me a bottle of brandy, the strongest you can find, brandy from Armagnac. And in the name of all the saints, put out that stinking fire!"

There was a flurry of activity among the women in the chamber as

5

her commands were obeyed. The blazing fire on the hearth was drowned and stamped out. The casements were thrown open. Opened too were all the cupboards, chests, and drawers. Even the glass stoppers in several bottles of *eau de mélisse*, a balm-mint decoction that the doctors had prescribed to soothe the hot brow of the queen, were carefully removed. Nothing must be knotted or shut or tight today.

A refreshing breeze swept into the apartment, and presently the queen could breathe again. "Now we shall go about this business," the midwife said confidently, planting two small round stones under the pillow, lest the child be a girl, and coaxing a draught of brandy into the parched mouth of the queen. "Drink this," she murmured, "thou gentle, thou royal, thou sweeting. It will give you strength. I am going to hurt you terribly."

Chapter Two

In the crucial moments while the newborn child hovered between the blackness of the womb and the shadows of the grave, before his mouth opened to cry or his eyes to see, no previous worldly experience could inform him that the murmurs which filled the chamber were the voices of his ancestors, who advanced to the bedside to bring him the gifts which so strangely and terribly mingled in his blood.

They were shadowy nameless figures at first, uncouth barbarians speaking a Teutonic tongue and dressed in furs against the frigid winters of the north. Yet one of them, carrying the sword of a leader among the pikemen and archers of the rabble, stepped boldly to the bedside and said: "I am Widukind, the Saxon. Many royal houses will seek to establish descent from me. I plundered the border territories and drove out the Frankish priests. But in the end I was beaten, and so I accepted baptism. My blood runs thin in you, or I might linger and explain my gift of the quick retreat, the sudden turnabout."

Then there stepped to the bedside the towering figure of Charlemagne, carrying the scepter and orb. "My empire extended from the Pyrenees to the Vistula, from Brittany to Belgrade. The islands of the Mediterranean were mine, and in Italy even the States of the Church looked to me for protection. Never since the Romans, were there united under a single monarch such vast territories or so many peoples. Little prince, thirty-third of my blood, I give you the vision to recognize strong natural frontiers and a hunger for territorial integrity. And I promise that one

6

day you shall be styled 'Majesty,' a title that I alone of all the kings of France have ever borne."

There followed the puppet shades of Charlemagne's sons, quarreling among themselves and fighting for the crown, which presently burst into many fragments, signifying the disemberment of the empire.

Then Robert the Strong: "I married a daughter of one of those petty kings and wrested the crown from the rightful heir of Charlemagne, which I was too shrewd to wear, though my sons wore it. I give you personal courage in battle; I give you guile to prefer the substance to the show of power—and the knack of marrying profitably."

Not all the great ancestors bearing gifts were men. There was Blanche of Castile, a magnificent woman, regent of France during the minority of her famous son. "I give you the gift of patience to frustrate your enemies, who will plot against you as mine plotted against me."

The son of Blanche of Castile advanced to the bedside. His countenance was illuminated by an aureole of pure light that circled his head. "I give you my name," he said simply, "and the love of God." It was Louis the Saint, who built in Paris the beautiful chapel that shelters the Crown of Thorns.

There followed a stately procession of other kings whose blood now coursed in the veins of the infant prince, bringing their dominant traits, many good, many bad, some strengthening and some nullifying others, a complex and bewildering whole, miscible yet inharmonious. And all the while, under the rule of the heirs of St. Louis, France prospered and grew.

Then a shadow oppressed the chamber, and a specter that never had been alive hobbled across the room: the Black Death. "You kings!" the monster hissed, and its breath filled the place with a horrid stench of the charnel house. "My gift to this prince is something you kings never dreamed of. In a few short years I slaughtered more nobles and knights than were slain in all the Crusades together. With their decay decayed the old order, chivalry, feudalism, authority. Henceforth the power of the nobility shall be reduced. The people, the villains and serfs you counted among your chattels, have begun to think, to dream of governing themselves. One day they shall, but that day is not yet. My gift is anarchy, in a changing world."

To emphasize his words there was a clap of thunder and a flash of coruscating brilliance. The smell of death was gone, and in its place there was smoke and the smell of gunpowder; and through the smoke the ghostly wail of an Englishman, Roger Bacon, crying to the little prince (who as yet had not opened his eyes): "Would God I had never set down that diabolical formula, even in an anagram! How was I to know it would be deciphered or to what uses it would be put? I thought it so pleasant to dabble in the natural sciences!"

Then arose the swarthy and low-browed ghost of Philip IV. "I give you," he said to his decendant, who was now opening his eyes, "the gift of superstition. In my reign a sorcerer, coveting my throne, made a wax

7

image of my son and set it in the hot sunlight. Had I not rescued it before it melted, my son would have died and the sorcerer would have been king, for he was married to my sister. I invited him to my palace and, when he least expected treachery, had him set upon and killed. Judicial murder of this sort is often necessary; do not accept all the precepts of Louis the Saint. Be practical. I must add," warned Philip IV, "that this murder of mine involved me in embarrassing consequences. The sorcerer happened to be friendly with Edward of England, a cousin of sorts, royalty being the most interbred institution in the world. England and I fell out; beware of English Edwards. As a consequence, I give you another gift: the Hundred Years' War. It has already been going on for eighty years, and exhibits enormous vitality. In your prosecution of this war, look well to the new invention of gunpowder. I wish I had had it."

Hurriedly now, because the child was opening its eyes, there followed King John the Good, so called because he was better if only by a little than his father; and King Charles V, *durement subtil et sage*, so called because he was able to impart the gift of diplomacy, of which the child already had enough and to spare.

And last of all a furtive, pathetic figure with vacant, rheumy eyes and a wild, unkempt white beard, King Charles VI, the child's grandfather. "I bestow upon you," he said, mouthing the words indistinctly and with difficulty, extending a tremulous forefinger to touch the head of the child, "madness."

Louis the dauphin screamed. The shades disappeared, and the successful midwife settled back to receive the applause of the women.

"It was that monstrous cabbage of a head," she explained pridefully. "To extract *that* without damage, and without killing the mother, is an art. Now a warming pan, quick, a big one, for the queen."

A page came running with a warming pan, but before he was permitted to enter the chamber Bernard d'Armagnac, one of the king's advisers, stopped him in the anteroom and insisted on opening the lid, poking among the embers with his dagger. Noting that the duke-archbishop, who had arrived to administer the last rites, was eyeing him oddly, Armagnac protested, "My reverend lord duke, I have known warming pans of this size to be put to extraordinary uses."

"But the queen has already given birth!" cried the page. "It is a prince, a dauphin!"

"Thank God," murmured the duke-archbishop. He was glad it was to be a baptism, not a burial. "Thank God for France."

It would have been pleasant at that hour, the queen thought, if King Charles had been willing to forgo the amusement of his hunt to be with her to see their son, the first of the royal children to cry so loudly and show such signs of vitality. This one would live.

Chapter Three

The royal infant lived, as the shades of his ancestors, with their broader vision of space and time, had known he would, else they would never have returned to earth to make him their several and not all desirable gifts. But in the narrowly circumscribed experience of the living who tended him, no one could be sure. The first vigorous cries gave way to an ominous lethargy. The young wet nurse, who unlaced her bodice, against which strained a brace of white and ready breasts, exciting a concert of lusty admiration among the male peers in the birth chamber, wept with chagrin when the dauphin refused to suck. His promising activity had lapsed into a dull and silent stupor. Never was a human being more in need of nourishment; only the head was large, even too large. The rest of the dauphin's body was scrawny and weak, particularly his bowed little legs. Yet he turned his too quiet face away from the breast and would not feed.

"A man of no taste," said Count Jean d'Armagnac. "A cold and fireless sprig, as you might expect." Count Jean was the sovereign head of the great House of Armagnac. He was addressing his uncle, Bernard d'Armagnac, the man who had poked so suspiciously with his dagger among the embers of the warming pan. "I could show the dauphin a thing or two."

"I dare say you could," Bernard observed distastefully. There was no love lost between them.

Another wet nurse was tried, with no better success, and when, toward morning, the lethargy of the dauphin continued, and it appeared that the child might perish of weakness, the duke-archbishop determined on immediate baptism.

"I conceive it no sin to warm baptismal water," he said to Friar Jean. "Let it be put on the fire until, when you stick your finger into it, you can feel neither hot nor cold. It has been my lot to christen other infants who exhibited symptoms of this sort."

Friar Jean was an apothecary. "Does Your Ladyship fear convulsions, swallowing of the tongue? It happens in the falling sickness."

"God knows," replied the duke-archbishop. "When they are so frail, I never know. But in any case, how would you like a flood of cold water doused unexpectedly on *your* cranium?"

"*Libera nos, Domine!*" he answered. Friar Jean Majoris had a cranium shaved naked and shiny as a child's. Cold bath water applied to his shivering body always gave him the horrors, which he humbly dedicated to God for the benefit of parochial sinners who happily were not required to bathe. It would have distressed him to see cold water applied to the soft and visibly throbbing head of the newborn child.

The dauphin was christened Louis. And whether the remarkable change that followed was a result of the sacrament, as Friar Jean believed, or the passage of time during which some physical change took place, or whether, as the midwife was convinced, it was the salt with which his tongue had been touched during the ceremony that gave him the thirst, the infant began to bawl lustily again, opening his pink mouth, beating his fists against the round white breast, and nursing ravenously. The wet nurse clucked and smiled; her reputation was saved, her fortune made. Now she would be in demand among all the fashionable young matrons of the court as long as her peasant husband, who was in excellent health, continued to discharge his marital duties.

The duke-archbishop now directed his attention to Queen Marie, whose hair had been dressed, whose color was better, and who rested easily under her coverlet of golden brocaded fleurs-de-lis. "Your Highness will be gratified at this happy turn of events," he said, "and so will His Highness the King, who should soon be here. He has been notified of his blessing by a speedy courier, a lad of great endurance, with a knack for accomplishing the unlikely."

"He will need it to find the king. My poor husband always gets lost when he goes hunting, and he never bags anything."

"His companions will see that the royal arrows find their mark." Everyone always laughed at King Charles, who inevitably returned with a noble stag or a wagonload of fat pheasants, though his aim was so poor that his shots always went wild. History would call him Charles the Well Served.

Count Jean d'Armagnac had left the room on the spoor of the first and discredited but cheaply seductive wet nurse. The duke-archbishop now turned to Bernard, knowing him free to speak.

"If I know my nephew," the elder Armagnac frowned, "he intends to do this night exactly what he suggested. Jean always makes me feel as if I had eaten a fish that died of natural causes and lay too long in the sun. I propose to retire to my room and order up the best bottle of Hippocras the king's cellar affords. Will Your Lordship join me?"

"I am somewhat fatigued," the prelate said. "A light wine would be most refreshing." He did not care to admit that Jean d'Armagnac produced exactly the same effect upon him. Moreover, he wanted to know why Bernard, usually so open and trusting, had been at such pains to examine the contents of the warming pan.

Over their wine he inquired. But Bernard, flushing the roots of his hair, said, "I will not tell a duke!"

As a diplomat, charged with great missions, and an intimate of high councils, it was the duke-archbishop's duty to know the secret springs that motivated peers of France. As a friend he was well aware that only a deep sense of shame could bring so red a flush to Bernard of Armagnac's cheeks.

In the private room to which they retired he said, "You can tell a friend, Bernard."

"Neither a duke nor a friend! It is a shameful story."

The guile of a diplomatic peer, the pride of the great prelate who occupied the archiepiscopal see of Reims, dissolved into the common humanity of a simple priest. It was not in his heart to sit complacently by while a good man suffered under a sense of guilt.

"Can you tell a priest?"

"Under the Seal?"

"If you wish." The duke-archbishop pushed away his wine and passed a wrinkled stole, which he always carried, around his neck.

"You can tell me now."

Armagnac spoke hesitantly at first, the iron reticence of family pride fettering his words. Then the words came freely, as if divulging the secret were a positive relief.

"You know young Henri, the lad who rode to seek the king?"

"A strapping youngster," the duke-archbishop replied, "newly attached to the suite of the Comte de Comminges. Courtly, well spoken, and one day I venture to say the ladies will find him attractive."

"They already do."

"I saw nothing unusual about him, except that perhaps I was surprised to hear him conversing in Latin with Brother Jean Majoris."

"He is my—" Bernard d'Armagnac could not go on.

"If by any chance," said the duke-archbishop, "the lad is your natural son, I shall not be severe in my censure. Many honorable careers are open to such men. Indeed, all Europe is full of them."

"I only wish he were!"

"Bastardy does not necessarily reflect dishonor upon the father."

"It does on the mother," Armagnac said bitterly.

"Unfortunately that is true. But after all, among the people—" He shrugged his shoulders helplessly. "Perhaps they are too close to the beasts among which they live. Formerly I used to shrive many of the farm girls. I do not say they cannot be attractive or capable of inflaming the passions of a young man; and I came to understand how heavily they labor in the fields, how barren their lives are, and how eagerly they embrace a young lord, or even an old one."

"I have a niece, Your Reverence. Henri's mother is not a peasant wench."

The duke-archbishop looked at him in pity and dismay, painfully aware of the cost to the pride of the man who was making such an astonishing avowal.

"I find myself distressed and amazed. The Lady Isabelle! I cannot understand how so shocking a thing could have occurred. You—you are the lad's father? But an uncle and a niece! It is incest!"

"When I said I wished Henri were my son, I did not think of that. Do not make the thing worse than it already is. This is not my confession. I have long since confessed to a priest the part I played in the affair."

"Then why—" The duke-archbishop fingered his stole impatiently.

"I was ashamed; I trusted only the secrecy of the Seal."

"If you do not care to trust the word of a friend and a peer of France," the duke-archbishop said stiffly, "we had better drop this subject at once." He removed his stole, thrust it into his girdle, and reached for his glass.

Armagnac, who had already blurted out the worst and involved his niece, had no choice except to continue.

"I will tell you as my friend then, and as a peer who would not wittingly dishonor a Family of the Lilies."

"I would not wittingly dishonor anyone."

"And as a brave man who will not wish my savage nephew to murder young Henri."

"I did not think he disliked the lad. I did not think he so much as glanced at him when he brought the warming pan. I was under the impression that Count Jean's attention was exclusively occupied with the *allaitement* of the dauphin."

"The nursing your reverence alludes to," Armagnac said, smiling at the clerical euphemism, "necessitated, as everyone seems to have noticed but you, the baring of an uncommonly high and exciting breast. Jean instantly took fire, and in his passion, which is deeper than most men's, and twisted, I saw his eye light on Henri. Jean scowled frightfully and drew in his breath. In that second, inflamed as he was, I am certain he caught the resemblance to his beloved, his too beloved sister."

"A sister cannot be too beloved, my friend."

"Can she not, sir? *Can she not!*"

Chapter Four

"It has perhaps escaped the attention of Your Lordship, Your Lordship being a celibate, how effectively the styles of a dozen years ago, the voluminous skirts especially, could conceal a woman's condition." Bernard d'Armagnac spoke bitterly.

"Do not lose your temper, Bernard, and do not cram your worldly knowledge down my celibate throat. Perhaps it has escaped your attention that a churchman is doomed to sit for a lifetime listening to the dreary confession of human frailties. I am neither totally unaware of certain bodily changes that accompany a pregnancy nor of the artifices a lady can adopt to conceal them."

"Henri should never have been born!"

"It would appear that God has decreed otherwise."

"To my shame, and the shame of the House of Armagnac."

"Young Henri appears to reflect credit, not shame, on your house. Though I see how his existence might be awkward for the Lady Isabelle."

"She does not even know he exists."

"Is it possible that you are telling me that a mother does not know her own son?"

"It is true. Isabelle does not know she has a son."

"Such a situation is perhaps not unprecedented, though in my experience I have never heard of it before." The duke-archbishop's eyes narrowed. "I know why you did it. Tell me how. The warming pan?"

Bernard d'Armagnac told him how.

In the welter of warring principalities that divided and tortured the face of France, the neighboring provinces of Armagnac and Foix held ancient enmities. There had often been war between them. In a more stable realm it would have been designated civil war and promptly put down as a local nuisance, but such was the weakness of the king, to whom they both owed nominal allegiance, that Count Gaston of Foix and Count Jean of Armagnac could battle each other and devastate each other's towns without interference from any central authority. There was no central authority.

From time to time, however, the perpetual threat that the English invaders would break out of the provinces they had held in uneasy subjection for four generations and swallow up the whole of France would force a truce upon the French. In any area immediately threatened, this most unruly of Europe's nobility would temporarily unite to save their own skins.

It was at one such perilous time, a time of common danger when the English of Guienne, which bordered on both Armagnac and Foix, had begun to kidnap peasant French girls and press into involuntary servitude any peasant Frenchmen who carelessly crossed the debatable frontier, that Gaston of Foix, astride a white charger with a pedigree as long as his own, appeared under the walls of Lectoure and sought entry into the capital of his "cousin," Count Jean d'Armagnac. Confronted with the menace of the English, Armagnac had remembered that both he and Foix were *royaux de France*, sovereign heads of Families of the Lilies.

"But he has come with altogether too numerous a retinue," Armagnac said sourly. Armagnac had solicited the ally; he was prepared for the parley. But he was not prepared for such a show of friendly strength.

Behind the iron spikes that guarded a narrow window-slit high over the drawbridge, he glowered down on the smartly formed ranks of knights and men-at-arms whose friendship he had sought and whose formidable appearance he now feared. "What words did you put in my mouth when you sent him that letter, good Uncle Bernard?"

It was galling for the elder Armagnac to take orders from his nephew, but an accident of birth had made the nephew, not the uncle, head of the house. Bernard had sworn fealty on his knees, like any other liege-man, between the palms of his nephew and overlord. "I wrote what you asked me to, Jean. If you had troubled to learn your letters, you might have read it for yourself."

"I asked you to write that he is a scoundrel, but that the English are at our gates and I am willing to forget our differences for the moment. You wrote him that?"

"In somewhat different words I wrote him that."

"Then why did he bring his army?"

"I think he shows uncommonly good sense," Isabelle laughed. No one but Isabelle dared laugh in the presence of Jean d'Armagnac. It was whispered among the kitchen staff of the castle that the count had no appetite unless his sister sat at the table with him and that his mood was gloomy and perverse when, occasionally, she rode out for pleasure beyond the walls, depriving him of her company.

"No doubt you also think he cuts a dashing figure on that Arab horse of his! No doubt you feast your eyes lasciviously on that handsome pair of legs and that padded doublet to give him the shoulders of a giant! Oh, I know what you are thinking, my dear sister. You can hide nothing from me." Jean's face was puffy and flushed.

Isabelle lowered her glance, confused, unable to explain such an outburst. "I thought no such thing, my lord brother."

Bernard interjected, "Your sister scarcely has reached an age to harbor such fancies."

"And why not, why not, why not?" The words tumbled out all breathless and hot. "Many women her age, nay younger, are mothers of families and chatelaines of castles."

"You have forbidden me to marry."

"Why should I not forbid you? Any likely hulk of a male that comes along—"

"Remember yourself, Jean," the uncle interposed.

"Anyhow, I do not forbid her. I merely suggested"—he waggled his head from side to side—"that she wait a few years till she is more mature, till her judgment is formed, till an advantageous union can be arranged."

It was not a moment to assure a possessive brother that his sister was already mature and that the doublet of the Count of Foix, waiting in the courtyard with his men on a friendly mission, was not padded.

"Unless you would care to see the prince face about and march back

14

to Foix with all his men, whose services you can ill afford to lose, you will order the drawbridge lowered at once. The discipline he imposes on his men he does not extend to himself. If my eyes do not deceive me, he is already biting his lip with impatience."

"I will never allow so many armed men within the walls of Lectoure."

"Then give them a feast and send them home. I guess that this startling array is only a super-bodyguard, such as the times require. With the aspect of the English so threatening, would *you* travel from Lectoure to Foix without an adequate force?"

That was something Jean d'Armagnac could understand. In a sudden reversal of mood he grasped his sister's hand and said: "My dear, our Uncle Bernard is quite right. You must be very polite to the Count of Foix."

"I hope you will never have cause to reproach me with forgetting my manners."

"But in this case you must be exceptionally charming."

She said she would try. Bernard, eyeing her covertly, caught the sparkle of her smile, and glanced again at the Comte de Foix. Jean missed it, engrossed as he was in his scheme to get rid of the count's retinue.

"Remember to address him as 'my lord prince.' Remember that he alone, of all the *royaux de France*, is possessed of the title 'Prince by the Grace of God.' I have never understood," Jean added peevishly, "why the Holy Father made an exception in favor of his House."

"It dates back to the Crusades," Bernard reminded him. "The counts of Foix wrought prodigies in the Holy Land."

"So did the Armagnacs. It was only the luck of battle that caused so many Armagnacs to be taken prisoner by the infidel during the Crusades. Nobody ever heard of *our* prodigies."

"I have always tried to console myself with the same excuse."

"Remember, Isabelle, that he is the only peer of France, except the king, who still has the right to strike his own coinage."

"I'm sure I appreciate his qualities, Brother."

Bernard glanced at her.

Jean said, "Wear your prettiest gown—I have always liked the green chartreuse velvet, the way it matches your eyes."

Isabelle curtsied and smiled archly in a manner that should have informed him that all his fussy advice was quite unnecessary.

"Shall we use the Italian forks? Yes, yes, we shall use the Italian forks at supper. Do you think you can manage?"

"She taught you to use them," Bernard said.

"She did? Oh, so she did. It's a foolish new custom. But I hear that Foix eats with a fork every day. I am only a bit apprehensive lest some little contretemps strike a jarring note in the entertainment of our guest."

"If you do not lower the drawbridge quickly," Isabelle said, "we shan't have a guest."

15

Jean bawled an order. Two tensed men-at-arms in bull-hide jackets thick enough to turn an arrow kicked out the wooden stops, jumped aside for their lives. The mighty iron chain that supported the drawbridge leapt like a serpent, its heavy links striking sparks against the opening in the masonry of the tower wall through which it passed as through a hawsehole on a ship. The ponderous drawbridge thundered down, raising a cloud of dust in the face of the guest. Jean of Armagnac was extending his welcome. He was secretly annoyed that the prince's mount did not rear and that the prince did not wince as the drawbridge fell.

"In heaven's name why didn't you use the windlass?" Bernard asked. "A moment ago you were warning Isabelle to watch her manners. Is that the sort of welcome for a prince of the Lilies?"

"I was only trying to please Isabelle. She told me to hurry. Well, I hurried. And incidentally, it will do no harm for Foix to observe that my fortifications are sound and my drawbridges do not shatter for a trifle."

Bernard shook his head at the indignity of the gesture. Besides being bad manners, it put a wholly unnecessary strain on the structure of the bridge.

Isabelle said: "You had best raise the *sarrasine*, Brother. Having looked so long at the waters of a moat, our guest will not take it kindly that you still block his way with iron bars."

But Jean would not raise the portcullis. "His men must not come in."

"Then you should go out and greet him."

"Beyond the *sarrasine*? And put myself in his power? Not I!"

"Then I will," Isabelle said.

"That you shall not, Sister. I would clap you into a dungeon first."

Bernard knew that his nephew was perfectly capable of carrying out his threat. "I will go out," he said wearily. "This is a sorry welcome you extend to our neighbor of Foix."

"It was my intention to parley through the bars," Jean said.

"Isabelle can show herself behind the bars; it does not befit a man. I shall put the best face I can on this miserable business."

"Do not heedlessly expose yourself, Isabelle!" her brother pleaded. "I will stay here and see personally that the archers cover you," and indeed he would have liked to remain behind the thick castle walls. But when he saw Isabelle standing at the open grating of the portcullis, envisioning in his mind's eye her slender body transfixed with a hundred arrows and bleeding from a hundred wounds inflicted with razor-sharp swords, he began to sweat, drew in his breath, and rushed trembling down the tower steps and placed himself in front of her to shield her with his body. His impulsive gesture effectively blocked her sight of the Comte de Foix and his of her. Nothing more lethal than glances was flying through the air at that moment.

"Are you safe, Isabelle?"

"Good heavens, Jean, how you startled me! Of course I'm safe. You look as if you had seen a ghost. What is the matter with you?"

Jean wiped his clammy brow with the back of his hand. "I cannot endure even a fancied threat where you are concerned. I saw you all maimed and bleeding."

"Dear Jean! It is time you married and worried about a wife. The Prince of Foix does not slay women." She laughed and said she was going to her chamber to change for supper.

The forces that would one day change him into a monster were still young in the Count of Armagnac. With Isabelle's withdrawal her slain and tortured image faded. He found himself picturing the glowing shoulders of the bakery wench who labored half naked in the bowels of the castle kitchen in front of an oven from which, as the browning loaves swelled and baked, there issued fragrant billows of moist and hungry heat.

Meanwhile the portcullis had inched up and quickly shut again after Bernard had gone out to greet the Count of Foix.

The churlishness of this welcome, Bernard explained diplomatically, was only on the surface, a deplorable necessity dictated by the hazards of the times. The fact that His Grace of Foix appeared not in belligerent armor but in peaceful doublet and hose had recommended itself to be friendly recognizance of Count Jean d'Armagnac. The whole city, Bernard said, was impatient to do honor to an ally against the English, so nobly represented in the presence and person of Gaston, by the Grace of God, Prince, Count of Foix. But this retinue, this army, this horde of allies! Count Jean was chagrined by their numbers and dubious whether the resources of all Lectoure would prove sufficient for their proper entertainment.

"My men?" Foix said amiably. "It was represented to me that the passes were full of skulking Englishmen, and I had hoped to teach them a lesson; but in two days' march we have not seen hide nor hair of a single one of the rascals."

Count Jean would be vastly relieved, Bernard thought privately; but aloud he said: "The rumors of enemy activity, however exaggerated, may have some basis in fact. Here in Armagnac your illustrious person will be safe. Would it not therefore be prudent to send your men back to Foix?"

The prince's face darkened, and Bernard instantly shifted his ground. An appeal to personal safety was not the way to influence Gaston of Foix. "I was only thinking of the possibility of a sudden descent on your towns while Your Grace is our guest."

Appeased, Foix said: "Perhaps you are right. Very well, I shall send them home."

From the shadows of a battlemented area on the walls outside his private apartments, Jean peered down on the parley, scratching an itch in his scalp. He saw with intense satisfaction all but a handful of Foix's

17

retinue wheel about and march away. He heard the portcullis grind up to admit the visitor and rattle down again, and the ponderous clanking of the chain as the drawbridge was hoisted. Once again iron bars and the wide waters of the moat isolated the castle.

"You are singularly cautious here in Armagnac," Foix observed.

"Of your safety, my lord prince."

Foix shrugged it off and let it pass.

"I thought I saw a lady at the *sarrasine*."

"The Lady Isabelle, my niece, sister to Count Jean. Like us all, she is impatient to welcome Your Grace at supper."

Isabelle would lighten an otherwise dull and gloomy meal, Foix thought, for his first impression of the garbage-strewn courtyard, in which pigs rooted and stank, was uninviting.

Meanwhile the itch continued unabated in Jean's scalp, and his major-domo, a privileged old servant, noting his master's fingernails, ventured to suggest: "I have heard that a total bath is often effective in drowning the creatures. That is how the Lady Isabelle—"

Armagnac's face flushed red as blood. "Prurient, spying, filthy old man, how do you know my sister bathes every day?" He looked wildly around the room for something to throw. The major-domo winced and trembled.

"My lord, it is common knowledge, I wasn't spying. All the maids talk—I heard it in the kitchens—the custom is so bizarre. Do not beat an old man, a father and a grandfather—" He caught himself up short, biting his tongue. Armagnac always took offense at any remark that seemed to reproach him with childlessness and celibacy almost as complete as a priest's.

"Send up that bakery girl. She shall comb them out. Bathing is for babes and women."

The old man shuffled out of the apartment, surprised not to receive a blow, and delighted at the unprecedented demand. Count Jean would have no truck with bathing, and when he itched he bawled for a kitchen wench, like everybody else. There was hope for him yet.

Chapter Five

In the days that followed the conclusion of the alliance, Isabelle and Foix saw much of each other, but never alone. Isabelle had never been alone with any man except her brother; and Jean d'Armagnac, casting his eye on the person of his guest, resolved that the Comte de Foix was of all men the last in whose presence he dared trust his budding and inexperienced sister.

An event occurred, however, that forced his hand. An Armagnac spy, sent out to observe the activities of the prince's men, returned with the news that they had not marched back to Foix but had broken up into inconspicuous companies and lodged themselves in nearby towns. They made no secret of their intention to remain in the vicinity until their master should emerge—"was released," as they put it—from behind the formidable walls of Lectoure.

"They say," Bernard commented, "that they do not trust you, and suspect you will hold your own guest to ransom, an unpardonable breach of hospitality."

"Well, why shouldn't I?" Jean asked.

"The English."

"I will see for myself whether the English or Foix's men present the greater hazard."

"The prince might take it amiss if you absent yourself to spy on his men."

"Who is going to tell him where I am? You?"

"No, Jean, not I. I am loyal to my House."

But Jean knew the prince would not easily be deceived. While he rode out to reconnoiter his potential as well as his avowed enemies, some strong distraction would have to be provided to snare the attention of the prince. Behind Foix's prepossessing exterior, the intelligent face, the candid eyes, the mobile mouth full of courtly phrases, Jean d'Armagnac recognized a certain sensuousness as only a supremely sensuous man could. The surest snare was Isabelle.

"I am not sure I approve," said Bernard when his nephew told him what he had in mind. "For once your solicitude may not be misplaced. Are you sure it would be wise to throw them together?"

Jean's face twitched unpleasantly. "Do you stand there and tell me that you doubt my sister's virtue? Do you imply any weakness on her part for this fop of a prince?"

"I shouldn't call him a fop."

"Any lack of devotion to me?"

"I am simply suggesting that Isabelle has led a very sheltered life, and the prince is a handsome man."

"Isabelle is used to having handsome men around," Jean said with such utter conviction that the elder Armagnac smiled.

"A brother isn't quite the same thing, Jean."

That night when the supper board was cleared, when the Italian forks were taken to the kitchens to be washed, marveled at, and experimented with by the servants, when Isabelle was preparing to retire as usual and leave the men to their wine, Jean motioned her not to rise.

19

"Nay, Sister, sit with us a while. You too shall have a cup of wine; I am in a mellow mood tonight. Sit and charm us with the music of your voice and the beauty of your countenance. Has it not struck you, my lord prince, that when Isabelle leaves the room the candles lose their glow and the fire its heat?" He lifted a languid forefinger a fraction of an inch; the major-domo set a goblet for Isabelle and reluctantly filled it, his mouth a thin line of disapproval.

But Foix's face glowed with pleasure. "When a brother speaks like a lover," he said, "he leaves naught for the lover to say but that he is honored beyond his expectations or due, and doomed to a thankless suit."

It was the harmless flowery talk of the time, and Bernard did not know why it should make him uncomfortable. Isabelle too knew the convention of high flattery and overpraise, but it had never before been directed to her. It was new and it was heady, as was the strong sweet wine. Her answer, as she knew very well, should have been that, though she was a maid who as yet knew nothing of love, she was well able to distinguish between a brother's devotion and a lover's passion; and that, though the lover had so styled himself too soon and too impetuously, yet his suit was not necessarily doomed to fruitlessness.

Instead she whispered an answer that gave far, far too much, and demanded nothing at all in return: "My lord prince, when one is loved, he is wrong to say he loves unless he truly does."

During the murmured reply the major-domo, whose ears were as sharp as his stern old mouth was grim, intentionally made a great clatter with the decanter against Jean's cup, filling it to the brim and a little more.

"Curse you for a clumsy, palsied old fool! Don't spill on me! Isabelle, what did you say? Our guest reproaches me as a rival! Ha! How did you answer him?" And to Foix: "My little sister still falters when she attempts a courtly reply. What did she say?"

Foix said casually, "She cautioned me to hold my tongue, as well she ought." But Bernard did not like the fire in his face. It was high time to change the subject, and tomorrow's plans also.

"My nephew the count," Bernard said, "has a foolish notion that the English are lurking this side of the border, and plans to go out tomorrow and string up a few of the brigands on some tall trees as a warning. Would not a raiding party accomplish the same mission, Jean? Is it mannerly to leave your guest?"

"Am I not invited on the English manhunt?" Foix asked.

Armagnac reddened. "My uncle misinterprets to annoy me. I did not say there were English around. I merely said I had heard a rumor. I intend to go out and see for myself. This is not a punitive expedition; just a minor reconnaissance."

"Then I shall go with you," Foix said emphatically.

"The truth is," Jean said, glaring at his uncle, "my guest would only be in the way. I am taking a few picked scouts, only three or four. We shall glide through the woods"—it was amazing how serpentine the pudgy hand that made the gesture could appear—"silent as snakes. In such an undertaking, surely you agree, the smaller the party, the better."

Foix hesitated, looking at Isabelle.

Count Jean suggested: "My sister is fond of riding beyond the walls and trying an arrow or two at a pheasant or quail. Recently we have kept much to the castle, and it has struck me that the roses bloom a trifle less red in her cheeks. The open country east of the town is safe. But safe or no, if she hunts tomorrow—and I do not forbid her—I should feel more at ease if I knew that she was protected personally by the Prince of Foix, Armagnac's new friend and ally."

Foix said: "I should count it an honor. Will you hunt tomorrow, Isabelle? You are not afraid?"

"I am not afraid."

Bernard was.

Chapter Six

"And so it was," said the duke-archbishop, who had listened attentively, "that they hunted to the east while Count Jean beat the bushes to the west of Lectoure spying on the forces of his guest? And they found themselves in a sylvan glade? And the Prince of Foix begat on the body of Isabelle of Armagnac, who asked too little and gave too much, this personable young page, Henri! It always happens."

"Your Reverence puts it biblically," Bernard said, "but brutally. It might have been a sylvan glade."

It was dark when they returned, Bernard continued, or at least as dark as a spectacular moon would permit a night to be. Count Jean raged and cursed at the moon. He had found no trace either of Englishmen or of Foix's men. He routed the major-domo out of bed and sent him to the kitchens to examine the pheasants Isabelle had shot; the major-domo called the saints to witness that the pheasants were freshly killed; they could not have been purchased from a farmer; she and the prince had assuredly spent their time hunting. Armagnac kicked him savagely and sent him to the cellar for wine and to the bakery for the bakery wench; but the moon set and morning came, and the wine had not made him drunk and the girl had given him no pleasure. Though Foix obviously wished to speak to him, he sulked all day, supervising the drawing of some chickens for supper, watching with great attention the slaughtering of a pig. He astonished the kitchen staff by personally throwing all the pheasants into the castle moat, and only when some carrion crows swooped down to feed on the floating carcasses did his mood seem to lighten.

Isabelle kept to her rooms, pleading a headache, and did not come down for supper.

"I should think her head would ache," Count Jean said, avoiding Foix's glance. "When I trusted my little sister to you, I did not intend your protection to extend through the space of an entire night."

Foix shrugged slightly; this was not a moment to quarrel over a detail. He and Isabelle had indeed returned long after the hour deemed proper by convention, but what was an hour compared with a lifetime?

"I love your sister, Jean. It is my intention, if you approve, to take her to wife."

Bernard had never heard him speak so directly and simply; his face was purged, almost transfigured; the proposal was from the heart.

Politically the proposal was momentous. An alliance of Foix-Armagnac, cemented by marriage, might well result in an independent kingdom in the south of France. More than a temporary union against the English, this might signal the birth of a new principality, greater than Aragon and Navarre, as great indeed as the realm of France itself. It was almost incredible to Bernard, as he sat watching the conflicting emotions on Jean's face, that Jean should hesitate.

Foix, puzzled and vexed, retired. Bernard too left the room, fearful of antagonizing his perverse nephew. He could not help saying however: "Think well before you refuse, Jean. I know a king who would give a province for such an offer."

Jean nodded, his chin sinking lower and lower upon his chest. He knew the king too: King John of Aragon and Navarre had dangled his daughter Leonora before the Prince of Foix for two years, and the dowry was a royal crown.

In the back of his mind, pushed down and unacknowledged, Jean had always known that he would one day lose Isabelle to a husband. In the same manner he had always known that one day he would die.

He raised his hand to call for brandy, but the major-domo was already there with it, looking down at him with compassion as he might have looked at a sick dog suffering from some queer and painful disease.

"Thou'rt a good rogue," Armagnac muttered, staring at the brandy.

He drank the flagonful at a draught, without taking a breath; it went down tastelessly as water; he no more felt its searing sting in his throat than he would have felt an arrow in a limb already severed by a sword. Losing Isabelle would be like losing a part of himself.

The brandy seeped into his brain, which suddenly began to race like clockwork that has lost its balance wheel. All at once everything seemed bright again, and crystal clear. Why had he not seen it before? If kings wanted a union with Foix, and if Foix wanted a union with Armagnac, then it must follow, not as a matter of personal preference but as a matter of cold logic, that kings, *kings*, would soon propose a union with Armagnac! Therefore Isabelle must not throw herself away on the first prince to propose marriage. He persuaded himself that others, a swarm of others, each more glorious than the last, would present themselves. Meanwhile he could keep his sister by him, and everything would be as it had always been.

His sister however was infuriatingly unmoved by the alcoholic arguments that delighted him so with their apparent cogency. Against his brandy-born tour de force of logic Isabelle could oppose only three stubborn, illogical words, "I love him."

Then he threatened; and Isabelle, cringing before his too lucid description of what he would do to the Prince of Foix, who was powerless in his hands behind the castle walls, experienced a horrid suspicion that perhaps her brother actually liked to witness the drawing of chickens and the slaughter of animals. It was a complicated suspicion, and required an effort of imagination which she instinctively put from her. But the conviction remained that momentarily, at least, her brother was insanely jealous and capable of carrying out his threats. Nor was she quite easy in her mind, wondering how much Jean knew of all there was to know, and how much he suspected. For everyone concerned, until this savage mood passed, the sooner Foix left Lectoure, the safer she would feel, both for herself and for the prince, who had styled himself too impulsively, but only a little too soon, her lover.

"You must be the one to refuse him, Isabelle."

"I could not. Does it please you to torture me, Jean?"

Armagnac recoiled in genuine horror and astonishment. "Sweet sister, I had rather be thrown into a pit of adders, nay, racked for eternity till every joint tore loose, than cause you an instant's pain. I do not care to live unless I can see you happy every hour of the day."

"Then spare me the pain of refusing him, and refuse him yourself."

"But my dear, he will never believe it from me."

He did not believe it from Isabelle either; not at first. Not until she played a part, in an effort to make him detest her.

"I had thought," Foix said as directly as he dared in Jean's presence, "that the Lady Isabelle gave me some indication that I might hope for a favorable answer."

"Oh, that!" Isabelle managed to laugh. "That was nothing."

"What was it!" Jean demanded.

"I—I permitted him to kiss me."

"Was that all?" Jean glared at Foix.

"If you do not believe your sister, how can I expect you to believe me?"

"Do not impertinently suppose that I doubt my sister, sir!" Then, more smoothly, because the prince's color was rising and he did not wish to endanger the alliance: "I myself am perhaps to blame. I mentioned to my sister how highly Armagnac values the friendship of Foix. I spoke of the obligation on all of us to show our gratitude. Isabelle is very young, and perhaps stretched a point in allowing the liberty of a kiss. It is nothing."

Foix glanced at her for confirmation.

"Nothing at all," she said.

Foix covered the hurt to his pride with a wry smile. "Not 'nothing at all,' my dear count, my *dear* Isabelle. Be assured, I have been royally entertained."

Next morning he left. A few months later King John of Aragon and Navarre had the pleasure of witnessing the betrothal of his daughter Leonora to Gaston, fourth of his name, by the Grace of God, Prince, Count of Foix.

But by that time Isabelle had come to her uncle, the only man she still could trust, with her secret, her terror, and her shame.

Chapter Seven

"I had been away too long," Bernard said, "from my city of Auch, which I hold in fief from my nephew; but the alliance with Foix held firm in spite of all that had passed at Lectoure. The English retired behind their borders, and I was able to remain near Isabelle."

"Yet it must have been necessary to take her away very soon," said the duke-archbishop, "before Jean's suspicions were aroused."

On the contrary, Bernard assured the prelate, Jean was not suspicious until the very last moment. The quirk of feminine fashion conspired to keep Isabelle's secret. Never in the history of women's dress had skirts been so full. It was not Isabelle's figure but her drawn and anxious face that finally aroused Jean's apprehension. He fretted himself that she was listless and pale and poor company at table.

She begged him to allow her to go with her uncle to Auch. Bernard, fearful that the child might be born in Lectoure, vehemently reminded him that Auch was noted for its clear and salubrious air. Even a short visit to High Armagnac, Bernard said, would be beneficial.

Jean sullenly refused to let her go.

It was a time for desperate measures. That night Bernard wrote late in his room, composing a letter to Foix.

"What did you write to the prince?" Jean demanded next morning, dangling the intercepted letter triumphantly in front of him. "Did you think my man would carry this without telling me?"

Bernard had thought so. The courier had been willing to accept a gold piece for holding his tongue. But Jean's men feared their master more than they loved gold.

"Read it yourself," Bernard said, "or get your chaplain to read it. I do not expect you to trust me to read it to you."

The chaplain had already read it aloud to Jean and, under threat of a beating, sealed it up again.

"Read it to me," Jean said.

Bernard broke the seal and read:

"Jean, Comte d'Armagnac, to our cousin Gaston, by the Grace of God, Prince, Comte de Foix, *greeting*: We rejoice in the happiness vouchsafed of God to your Grace in the betrothal of Leonora, Lady of Aragon and Navarre. May Divine Providence heap blessings upon you; and should you travel this way again, fail not to seek out your good friend and ally,

"Armagnac

"*Post scriptum*: The English continue quiet."

Jean muttered, "That is exactly how my chaplain read it."

"He could hardly do otherwise. That is all it says."

"I myself should have thought to congratulate the prince," Jean said. "I am extremely glad he is married."

Bernard said, "I took it upon myself to congratulate him in your name. It is a detail."

Jean sent the courier off. The letter seemed harmless enough. When, in a few days, Foix's courier returned with an answer, Jean gave it directly to Bernard to read to him.

It read:

Divine Providence already heaps a blessing upon me, which temporarily interdicts the pleasure of travel to the Princess de Foix; so that, should the necessity arise, I must come alone.

Post scriptum: If the English were not quiet I should already be there.

"What does he say?" Jean asked.

Bernard tossed the letter aside. "A mere formal acknowledgment. He may visit you, but he says he won't bring his bride."

"So that is how it is, eh? Hm-m-m!"

Jean was gloomy at supper that night. "There was more to the prince's letter than was apparent, my uncle."

"Oh, I don't know. He would naturally want to revisit his ally at his earliest opportunity. I see no harm in that."

"I see infinite harm in it. Married less than a year, and already the wretch deserts his bride! Does that mean nothing to you? Can you not read between the lines? Do you not see who is the object of his lascivious scheming?"

Bernard did not answer, letting the suspicion run its course.

After a while Jean said: "My uncle, I have reconsidered your suggestion. The air of Auch will do Isabelle good. I want you to leave tonight."

To travel from Lectoure to Auch one must pass from Low to High Armagnac on a road that winds south through increasingly difficult and ever less fertile country where swift little streams, which rise in the Spanish Pyrenees and are fed by their snows, cut into the Plateau of Gers. From these snows High Armagnac is also called White Armagnac. The distance is not great; a courier could easily traverse it from sunrise to sunset.

But Bernard took two days, to the great amusement of the guard that Jean had provided. They were instructed to accompany him and Isabelle all the way to Auch. But at the border of his own estates Bernard ordered them back to Lectoure, and since in his own domain his word was law, superseding even that of his overlord—a situation perfectly consistent with his subordinate position and well understood by Count Jean's men—they had no choice except to turn about and return to Lectoure. There would be no reprisals. Jean would assume that Bernard no more wanted his men in High Armagnac than he had wanted Foix's men in Low Armagnac. Customs, costumes, dialects, weights, measures, laws, everything changed with the crossing of each petty boundary. Such was the chaotic legacy of generations of war and the Black Death, and such was the misery of France. Men drew apart from their neighbors, trusting only the power of some local lord to protect them in times of danger, and danger was constant, behind the walls of some provincial capital. The polity was six hundred years old; the oldest man alive could remember nothing different; and only in ancient parchments in monastery libraries did literate monks read and marvel at a France that had once stretched from Flanders to Spain, blessed with one king and one law, and pray for its speedy return. It was an act of faith that they could envision its return at all. The Kingdom of God seemed scarcely less near at hand.

A body of his own men who were stationed at the border greeted him with cheers and quickly rounded up a presentable guard of honor to escort him to Auch, dispatching a flying herald ahead with the news that their lord had returned after his long sojourn in Low (which by constrast with their own province they derisively called "Black") Armagnac.

"I have spared you all I could," Bernard said sadly, "dallying along at a pace that would shame a snail. But there may have been prying eyes in your brother's escort. Now we shall get you into a litter, as I should have done from the start if I have dared."

Isabelle understood. "It was wise of you, dear uncle. I know how necessary it was for me to seem able to ride." Nevertheless the incessant

26

motion of the horse had been a cruel torture, and near the end of the first day she whispered to Bernard that it seemed as if the burden she carried had shifted a little lower down.

Bernard was worried. So soon? But he patted her shoulder encouragingly. "There is plenty of time, even after that happens. You will be comfortable tomorrow."

They stopped at a border inn for the night. Before dawn Isabelle knocked at her uncle's door. She had slept ill, she said, troubled by bad dreams, and she felt a strange anxiety. Would it be possible to start at once?

Bernard instantly routed the innkeeper out of bed, and the party resumed its march so hurriedly that some of the laggards had to finish their breakfast on horseback.

In her litter, slung between two horses, Isabelle dozed fitfully the greater part of the day, exhausted from her sleepless night and the previous day's painful ride. Toward evening she opened her eyes and looked up at her uncle.

"I feel queer," she said, "and a moment ago there was a terrible pain, though the horses did not stumble."

Bernard sighed. They would never reach Auch in time.

He knew his lands like the palm of his hand. A little to the east, off the beaten path, rose a terraced hill round which were planted the hardy vines from which the best brandy in France was distilled, L'Eau de Vie Hault Armagnac. Crowning the hill, which the natives called Mount Saint-Michel, rose a castle-like structure with an ancient keep, squat and square, from the top of which, however, no guards kept watch and no engines of war bristled. A slow and peaceful bell rang out the hours from the ivied tower of the Monastery of St. Michael of Peril. Here, if anywhere, there would be safety and secrecy for Isabelle.

He turned to his niece and said: "It is not necessary to go any farther. You will be well cared for here."

He sent his guard on to Auch, ordering the captain to take them to his residence and bid his steward set them a good supper with wines of their choice to make up for the breakfast they had missed. They left him and Isabelle at the door of the monastery, raising such a shout of thanks that a bewildered lay brother slammed the gate against them and rushed to the prior with the startling news that the place was attacked by a howling horde of wild Englishmen.

The prior appeared at the gate, a crystal reliquary in his hand.

"Seigneur Bernard! God be praised it is you!" Somewhat shamefacedly he attempted to hide the reliquary under his cassock, but Bernard saw it.

"Did you take me for the Devil?"

"*Peccavi, Domine!*" the flustered prior replied. "I was going to confront the invader. I was quite prepared to swear that this is the right hand of the Archangel Michael, and rout them with it. You have saved me the sin of pretending, even to a foreigner, that angels have bodies."

Bernard laughed in spite of himself. "Don't they? Didn't somebody wrestle an angel and wrench his thigh out of joint?"

"Oh, no, my lord. That was Jacob's thigh." Then, soberly lifting the lantern in the gathering dusk, noting that the litter was unattended, "Is this something of a confidential nature in which I can be of service?"

"The person in the litter is about to give birth," Bernard said, lowering his glance. It was impossible for him to pronounce the name of his niece. "Tonight, perhaps."

"I see," said the prior. "Of course. Rest assured that every care shall be given her. It is like you, sir, not to abandon her. If she is a woman of the people," he added practically, "I suggest that the brother apothecary handle the business."

"She is my niece," Bernard said miserably.

"Nay, all the saints forbid."

"It is true, however."

"If it is true, then it is true; and of course no man must attend a lady of Armagnac. Would you care to tell me about it? Perhaps there are extenuating circumstances."

"When I do," Bernard said grimly, "At least you won't think what you are thinking!"

"I do not know what I was thinking. I must be a very wicked old man. I beg you to forgive my unworthy thoughts!"

"Forget it, old friend. In view of the circumstances, they were probably natural enough. Come! Let us get her into the house."

On the order of the prior, the canonical hour of Matins was skipped and the monks were not called to the chapel for their midnight devotions, to the great delight of most of them, to whom the hour when Paul and Silas sang in prison was the least popular of all their religious observances, especially at a time when their work in the fields was most exhausting. Thus the community was silent when Marthe, a widowed lay sister with a vast heart and vast experience, approached the wing of the monastery buildings set apart for those occasions when women travelers sought shelter of the house.

She examined the patient and clucked her tongue knowledgeably. It would be tonight of a certainty. An hour, two hours at the most.

Bernard lowered his voice to a whisper, though the prior was now out of earshot. Her face altered and she directed a look of reproach toward Bernard. But as he continued speaking for several minutes, her expression softened. "It is a kindly act, my lord. I will do it, and no one will ever be the wiser. The warming pan will be simple to procure, though there are none in this house. I shall have to go and get one. As for the other thing, that too, alas, I know where to find. So many are born dead. It is lying in a poor home awaiting burial. For a gold piece the bereaved

28

parents may be persuaded to part with it for a few hours. They will demand that it be returned, however."

"That I promise."

"They will naturally be suspicious; the request is so unusual. Can I tell them why it is necessary?"

"Without mentioning names, you may tell them."

"They will ask no names when they know why it is necessary. They are good and honest people. They will be glad the poor little thing did one good deed, though he never drew a breath."

While Marthe was away for an hour on her mission, Bernard sat by Isabelle's bedside, counting the bell strokes that sounded the quarter-hours from the tower with a slowness that caused him to wonder whether some demon had not severed the bell rope; and all the while Isabelle's pains came on at shorter and shorter intervals.

The midwife returned, a satchel in her hand and a large brass warming pan under her arm.

"Lest the lady suspect," she whispered, "I have also brought with me a phial of a soothing potion that I employ to make them comfortable. It has the added advantage that a slight overdose addles their senses."

"Is it poison?"

"Far from poison, it is something that often is drunk for pleasure. And in excess, far more than I shall use, condemned criminals have known to lie for hours on the rack, happy as on a featherbed, singing ballades and smiling while their executioners turned the wheels in vain. No, my lord; it is the very thing we need if your plan is not to miscarry. That—and this."

But Bernard could not look into the satchel. He left Isabelle to the midwife, hearing her murmur as he left the room: "Sip this, thou weary child. You have suffered enough for one night." Then he sought out the prior, who was praying alone in the chapel, and poured out the story on his knees. "Assuredly the act you perpetrate is deception of a high order," the prior said. "What retribution will be visited upon the mother and father, God only knows. My fear is especially for Isabelle. It is the nature of man to be vile, a woman less vile. Old Adam was only clay, common and coarse, when God formed him; but Eve was already flesh, formed in the image of the Everlasting before she ever drew breath. The brandy we double distill is of finer quality than that which is distilled but once."

There was a menace in the prior's parable, however generally he put it.

"Let us hope that your gloomy prediction will never come to pass," Bernard said, and hurried back to Isabelle.

She lay in a semi-stupor, conscious but fuzzy in her thoughts, her sense of time all askew. She knew when the babe was born, for the pain knifed through the fog of the midwife's drugs; but before she heard her uncle speak the bell in the tower had sounded twice, tolling another quarter of an hour into eternity. To Isabelle it was only an instant, the space between two grateful sighs that the ordeal was over.

Time passed at a different rate for the midwife and for Bernard; and for the brother apothecary who, since the child was male, had been summoned to take charge of him. This was a foundling, he was told, abandoned on the monastery doorstep. Life, the brother apothecary marveled, was a chaotic concatenation of unlikelihoods. One moment he was sleeping in his cell, excused from Matins; and the next, behold! he was called upon like the Magi to minister to a newborn child.

Marthe had done what was necessary, and when the brother apothecary saw the child it was swaddled and clean, like any other unwanted but well cared-for foundling. There was nothing to do but to feed it and place it in a room where a makeshift crib had been prepared.

"Thou'rt a greedy young man," said the brother apothecary. The child was sucking avidly on a sop of sponge that he dipped in a bowl of goat's milk. "Thou'rt not one to take kindly to fasting and the subjugation of the flesh. I doubt if you will ever make a churchman. Easy now, thou glutton, not so fast!"

Having turned the infant over to the brother apothecary, Bernard said, "Treat him kindly, Friar Jean Majoris," and went back to the birth chamber, where the midwife whispered: "She is coming to. It is time to tell her."

Bernard retired to the rear of the room and stood in the shadows. Marthe knelt by the bedside and drew something small and still from her satchel and transferred it to the warming pan. Then she stood up and slipped it into the bed, and for a moment her hands were busy. "It is nearly over, Madame," she said cheerfully. "The worst is already passed —ah!"

Then she said softly, "Alas, Madame, what a dreadful misfortune!"

"What is amiss, Midwife?" Bernard asked loudly, so that Isabelle would be sure to hear and remember.

"I have done everything I could, my lord. But it is dead."

There was a long silence. Then Isabelle murmured, "Was—it a boy?"

"A girl," Bernard answered. He did not know why he lied.

Isabelle spoke very slowly and indistinctly, as if she were muttering something out of a nightmare. Bernard thought she said, "Let me hold her for a while." He shook his head in alarm toward Marthe; but Marthe, more knowing, complied with the request and placed the babe against her.

The unnatural chill of Death against her breast caused Isabelle to draw back with an instinctive shudder. "Take it away!"

The tears did not come yet. Later, at her uncle's château, she wept deliriously and tried to pray, but the only prayer that would come was, "Pray for us sinners now and at the hour of our death." At that time she wanted desperately to die.

30

Chapter Eight

"You doubtless saved the honor of your House," the duke-archbishop said, "and it may be that you saved Isabelle's life also. Count Jean might have murdered her. It is true, as you said in the beginning, that a sister can be too beloved. It would have been wiser, however, my friend, to have married her to someone at once."

"That was beyond my power. She returned to Lectoure. Her brother showered her with fussy little favors. Now she completely filled his life, the more so because she seldom left the castle even to go hunting, and never once did she mention the name of the Prince of Foix or of any other man. I think she loathes all men."

"You Armagnacs are a stubborn and single-minded race," the duke-archbishop said. "Often such a trait is a great virtue. Sometimes it is not. And young Henri?"

Bernard's eyes softened. "How I have schemed for that lad! I visited the monastery of St. Michael of Peril as often as I dared."

The duke-archbishop smiled. "To make personally sure that the science of distillery was being properly taught to your vineyardmen?"

Bernard shrugged. "It was my only excuse. Brandy is my principal revenue. My visits caused no comment, and I always saw Henri. Friar Jean educated him far beyond his duty; he loves the lad like a father. I think he would have liked to make him a priest."

"That would be natural and fitting."

"But Henri preferred horses, the mechanics of the wine presses, and the alchemical mysteries of the great distilling apparatus, which even I do not understand. After the woeful defeat of Agincourt, my revenues leapt, since people appear to consume more brandy when war is at its most violent, and I was able to provide a school building for the monastery so that Henri could grow up among other boys. Unfortunately, most of his schoolfellows were orphans like himself— or as he thinks he is."

"Who knows what blood runs in the veins of his schoolfellows?"

"It is true," Bernard admitted, "that they looked like any other group of likely youths. Perhaps it was Friar Jean's way with them."

"I shall look into the qualifications of this remarkable monk. I do not forget that a dauphin was born this night, and that one day he will need a tutor."

Bernard nodded absently, thinking only of Henri. "When he was old enough to emerge from ecclesiastical surroundings, Friar Jean having justly observed that he had no aptitude for the sheltered life, I planned at first to recommend him to Duke Philip the Good of Burgundy, thinking Henri would make a better career in the service of that great prince than under King Charles of France, our weak-kneed son of a madman, who barely reigns and cannot rule."

"His ministers rule very competently," the duke-archbishop said sternly, "and Burgundy is a traitor. Have a care lest your tongue betray you into treason."

"At the time Burgundy was loyal, as Your Reverence very well knows."

But an ominous change occurred which upset the balance of power in the shifting loyalties of the all but independent heads of the Families of the Lilies, who always forgot their feudal vows except when reminded of them by self-interest, so weak was the Crown of France and so decrepit the dying institution of feudalism. In this change France's greatest hope against the English became overnight France's greatest peril.

In one of Burgundy's fairest provinces in the Netherlands, on a night when a heavy storm was surging against the dikes, the ocean burst through in a titanic flood. Seventy-two populous towns, not only along the coast but on either bank of the river Meuse, vanished forever beneath the waters of a broad estuary which formed between sunset and sunrise.

The English promptly dispatched a fleet to rescue the miserable remnant of the population, who clung to the church steeples to escape drowning. For a week the English ships cruised over the flooded fields and city streets among the ruins of cross-topped belfries, which daily crumbled and crashed into the sea as the water weakened their foundations. Sometimes in the darkness of the hideous nights that followed this mighty convulsion of nature, the rescue ships would be guided by screams of women and children fighting off pet dogs which they had sought to save and which now, maddened by hunger and thirst, turned upon them. Sometimes the ships were guided by ghostly bells, ringing weirdly under water, set in motion by action of the waves till their trunnions broke and they sank to rest, forever silent upon the floor of the newly formed inland sea, among the drowned bodies of ninety thousand Burgundians who a week before had answered the call to prayer of the same silent bells.

"The prompt humanity of the English cannot be too highly commended," Bernard said grudgingly, "but it was quite impossible for the wily islanders not to notice that the inundation had created a near and excellent harbor, capable of sheltering their entire navy, from which they could either threaten or trade. They elected to trade, as less hazardous and more profitable. They offered Burgundy attractive terms for his Flemish wool. Burgundy, always in debt to support the magnificent vanity of his court, and now deprived of the revenues of seventy-two towns, also elected to trade. Naturally, I did not send Henri to Burgundy. It is never possible to be at peace at the same time with both England and France."

"So young Henri remained at the monastery?"

Bernard nodded. "Somewhat against his will, I am afraid. He was more often on his knees peering into the intricacies of the distilling machinery than on his knees in the chapel."

"How did Friar Jean take that? I have a special reason for asking."

Bernard feared some ecclesiastical discipline, and sought to excuse the monk. "No one is more zealous than Friar Jean Majoris, Your Reverence—"

"Encouraged the lad, eh?"

"He was not overly severe."

"Good!"

Bernard looked relieved, and the duke-archbishop smiled. "There is a psalm which goes, 'The stone which the builders rejected is become the head stone of the corner!' The Lord uses us all, Bernard, in our several capacities. Not everyone is cut out for a churchman; Friar Jean seems to have recognized that. This southern monk of yours interests me. Did he come north with Henri?"

"When word reached us in the southern provinces that the queen would soon be brought to bed of a child, many loyal nobles came up to Bourges. Comminges is a neighbor, needy but loyal, and as we rode north I suggested to him that, at little expense, he might attach a handsome page and a chaplain-apothecary to boot to his suite. It was not difficult to arrange."

One should leave a share of the credit also to God, thought the duke-archbishop, that the chaplain who assisted in the christening of the dauphin was an apothecary. Confining his remark to the subject that interested Bernard most, he asked, "What did you really hope for Henri when you brought him north?"

Bernard sighed. "A miracle, I suppose, but it did not happen."

"They don't, when you demand them."

"I hoped Foix would recognize his son."

"And instead Jean d'Armagnac recognized his sister's bastard?"

"There can be no doubt of it."

Delicate balances weighed and counterweighed in the mind of the Duke-Archbishop of Reims, who at this moment was pure statesman; the possibility that Foix *would* recognize his son existed; such fathers often did. In Henri's face there was at least as much resemblance to the handsome features of the House of Foix as to the dark and rather eerie beauty of Isabelle of Armagnac. Foix might legitimize him, a worthy but not always safe procedure, since wives never take kindly to it. Leonora of Aragon and Navarre, daughter of a king and heiress to a double crown, would have something to say about her husband's romance of twelve years ago; and if she said the wrong thing, as was likely, what would become of France's good relations with Aragon and Navarre?

33

Henri would not be the first of illegitimate birth who had severed alliances simply by reason of his unfortunate existence. What was one life against the possible loss of a powerful ally, at a time when France needed allies as never before? A less scrupulous statesman would have settled the matter with a poignard: Henri would have turned up in a gutter, and no questions asked.

"It is a heavy responsibility," Bernard heard him say.

"You see how the lad is in danger. Jean will find a way to blot him out."

The duke-archbishop snorted. Bernard d'Armagnac must be naïve, or love had spoiled him. "Good heavens, man! I am tempted to blot him out myself! I think, in a way, I must. You should have left him in the south, where he could cause no trouble. Fortunately, Count Jean is busy tonight with that trollop of a nurse that the dauphin refused. You say Henri has a mechanical bent? Splendid! I know a gun founder who can put such a trait to good use, and for France."

Bernard no longer hoped for a career for Henri, since a career, even in the suite of the petty Comte de Comminges, threatened only danger for the lad and shame for the House of Armagnac. Bernard now wanted only one thing. "My young kinsman—he will be safe?"

"The obscure are always safe."

That was not true, and the duke-archbishop knew it. Ninety thousand obscure Burgundians had not been safe when the sea burst in. But it was what Bernard d'Armagnac wanted to hear; and obscurity for a lifetime was what the good of the realm of France seemed to demand of Henri.

Chapter Nine

The duke-archbishop had set his heart on a goal that would culminate his long and honorable career—the marriage of Louis the dauphin to an enemy of England and an ally of France. But for two years after the dauphin's birth, no likely princess presented herself.

Then there was born to James Stuart, King of Scotland, a daughter Margaret. From the moment of her birth the duke-archbishop determined that she should be Louis's queen when he came to reign. Margaret and Louis had nothing to say in the matter, naturally. It was not to be expected that the bridegroom, who was still in his teens, was as wise as the statesmen who guided the destinies of the realm; and as for Margaret, being a princess, she was consulted even less. It was felt in the court at Edinburgh that the alliance was advantageous. Nothing more should be expected by a princess.

She was a sensitive child, full of gay, romantic notions, but silent and sullen when crossed, a legacy, as many believed, from her father, who had to appear much in public but to whom public appearances were an ordeal. A sprawling amethyst-colored birthmark disfigured full half of his face. Whenever he could he would escape to the privacy of his apartments to write poetry long into the night.

The marriage, attractive as it was, was not easily accomplished. The duke-archbishop worked at it for eight years to no avail. In the penultimate decades of the interminable war which men were already calling the War of a Hundred Years, everything went against the French. Why, asked the canny Scots king, throw his princess away? The English advanced to the gates of Paris, burst in, occupied the ancient capital, and surged beyond, till even the distant southern provinces seemed threatened. It seemed to be a tide that nothing could stop. France was doomed.

But it was only a wave on the crest of a tide that had already begun to ebb, like an opponent bearing his adversary down by the accumulated momentum of his attack long after a mortal disease had struck at his heart. No one on either side was aware of the English weakness at the height of their success; but an English poet, writing in the clear afterlight of a later age, put his finger on the cause: "No treachery, but want of men and money! Amongst the soldiers there is muttered that you maintain several factions." England was already victim of the internal disunity that would drag her into the civil Wars of the Roses, and the poet's lament continues: "Cropped are the flower-de-luces in your arms. Of England's coat one half is cut away." England's loss, when the tide turned, was France's gain.

The Duke-Archbishop of Reims had told Bernard d'Armagnac, who had wanted a miracle for his young and unacknowledged kinsman, "They never happen when you demand them." No one demanded the miracle of Joan of Arc. When she appeared before King Charles, the dauphin's father, he refused to receive her; and when, in spite of him, she infused a spirit of fanatic resistance into his armies and hurled back the English, he sat idly by and let her, a girl of nineteen, do the fighting. One day, in the forefront of a fierce melee, she was captured. The English, desperately in need of a victory, burnt her at the stake; and from that moment the tide turned and the flood of invaders began to recede. There were other engagements, and the massive withdrawal, like any other tide, was slow. But the English never won another victory in the Hundred Years' War.

King James of Scotland, with a poet's insight, sensed the aura of coming change. If an eighteen-year-old maid could rally the French, what must be the secret weakness of the English! Promptly he dispatched his daughter in a ship to France with a chaperon, a band of bagpipes, and his hasty blessing. "He is a Frenchman, my dear, and Frenchmen are always in a hurry. Do not be alarmed. A child in the first year of your marriage is just what Scotland needs to cement the alliance—if you are old enough. I really do not know." He really did not, for his poetical activities occupied a great deal of his time.

"I am not afraid," Margaret said proudly. "I am older than some of my ladies in waiting. Is the dauphin handsome?"

"I hope so," James said, touching his cheek in an involuntary gesture of concealment that was habitual with him. "He shall have to be handsome," Margaret said definitely. "I cannot abide ugliness." She spoke with the unreasonable and demanding idealism of her youth, which had been warped and exaggerated by the flattery of court minstrels who always knew how to sing for their supper.

"There are other virtues," her father said, his hand never leaving his cheek. "The dauphin has many." But there was no time to teach the little princess what they were. Off she went to France.

Her dowry was not in money, for that would have been contrary to Scotch custom, but in something France needed even more: an army of ten thousand Scots soldiers under command of Archibald, Earl of Douglas, who had hated and fought the English for fifty years, not always with success. Before he died next year at the battle of Verneuil his persistent ill luck won him the title of Tyneman, "the loser." But at this time he was welcomed enthusiastically in France. Charles made him lieutenant general of all the French armies, and gave him a French peerage. Douglas of Douglas found himself styled "Duke of Touraine," though to make him a duke the king, with few provinces and few titles to bestow, had had to take one away from his own queen. Until that time Queen Marie had been Duchess of Touraine.

"If you remain the duchess and Douglas becomes the duke," King Charles said, roaring fatuously at the only sort of joke his sluggish wit knew how to contrive, "all the world will say that I have personally bedded you two!" The queen let it pass. He had never been polished, and with the passage of time he had grown more and more gross and remote, though he showed up regularly in her bedchamber like a rutting animal whenever nothing better was available.

The queen found Margaret a spoiled child, but as things turned out she was much in her company partly because Charles's court followed the royal example and neglected her and partly by reason of the tragedy of Margaret's marriage, for from her nuptial night Margaret was to be neglected also.

No one suspected a tragedy when Margaret, her soldiers, and her suite made a triumphant entry into Tours on the brilliant June day of the wedding. Douglas drew up his Highlanders on one side of the street; the French soldiery smiled at them across the flower-strewn cobbles from the other. And how they smiled! Full-grown men with big muscular knees peeking coyly out from under queer short skirts! What the Gallic love of the ludicrous did with that! A few violent altercations in taverns, however, quickly taught the French to respect the Scots national dress, and from laughing at the outlandish garb they soon found themselves hard put to defend their own. "Was it exactly manly," the Scotsmen asked, "to wear skin-tight hose from hip to toe? Why were one Frenchman's legs striped and another's embroidered with flowers? For that matter, why was it that often, on the same Frenchman, one leg would be pink and the other blue?" It was a holiday, said the Frenchmen. One had to honor the dauphin and dauphiness, did one not? Ordinarily one wore leather leggings, except among the gentry.

And were French legs so tender that "one" had to protect them with bull hide? the Scotsmen retorted. The Scots, as the French soon learned, could argue like demons.

The markets were closed, and trade was suspended except in the taverns. In the streets there was merrymaking: hawkers selling their sugar fruits and roasted melon seeds and salted eels; acrobats dancing on ropes for pennies thrown them by the holiday crowds, dancing-bear men, exhibiting their forlorn and weary beasts for dogs to snap at, and ragged beggars from the slums to torment with stones. Here was something poorer than the poorest, sillier than the most ignorant, lower even than they. Among the crowds were many maimed and crippled veterans of the perpetual war, brutalized by poverty, unemployable and forgotten, begging their lives away on the streets before old wounds killed them.

In a more prosperous realm, in Burgundy, for instance, there would have been a tournament to celebrate the wedding, knights shattering lances against each other in the lists, silver trumpets pealing, and silken awnings to shade the ladies. But in France there was no money to build the stands or pay for the heralds' costumes. Excitement and blood spilled in anger was still to be had, however, at the cockfights.

Bells rang from the church of Notre Dame la Riche, from St. Saturnin, and the basilica of St. Martin, adding their lesser tongues to the chiming carillon and solemn booming that burst in waves from the twin towers of St. Gatien's cathedral. The day was fine and clear and flooded with the music of laughter and joyous bells.

A cannon had been set up on the walls of the château. An artilleryman was lashing it firmly down. It was to be fired at sunset, or whenever the dauphin and his bride retired, and the booming report would serve as a signal for every good Frenchman to drink the dauphin's health and wish him and the dauphiness happy issue. If the cannon should misfire, a husky man-at-arms would beat a huge drum.

But the artilleryman, running his hand through the powder to test its dryness, finding it dry and seeing no threat of rain in the sky, nodded his head as if he were satisfied that the elements would not conspire to spoil the dauphin's salute. He wanted a good one, a thunderous one with a double charge of powder. He was irked that artillerymen should

37

rank lower than the engineers who manned the cumbrous old-fashioned catapults. They could, of course, be terribly effective at times, hurling a 500-pound stone against a castle wall. But he had faith in the future of his neat little engine of war. When working well it could eat away the masonry of a fortification bit by bit, scattering shards of high-velocity stone fragments, so that the very walls that were supposed to protect the enemy became the means of their destruction. Loaded with scraps of iron, it would work havoc among troops no matter how heavily covered with plate mail. Yes, the day would come, the artilleryman was sure, when the lightness and mobility of guns would replace the battering rams and catapults that armies had used since the times of the Romans. Louis the dauphin and his bride would have a salute like thunder tonight!

Louis looked forward to his wedding with pride and excitement, and no more misgiving than many a man far older than he in age and experience. He had not been consulted in the choice of his bride, a thing he considered quite natural since he realized that his grip of foreign affairs was still immature. But he had seen the Scottish princess, and he was overjoyed that the international experts had chosen her. It was the duty of some princes, and he considered them wrong and selfish if they protested, to marry dumpy, pock-marked simpletons. Margaret was slender, her mouth mobile and full, and her skin, when he should come to touch it, would doubtless be soft and smooth as his dreams had always led him to believe a maiden's skin would be.

King James had sent him a ruby-hilted sword as a wedding gift. Louis wore it into his father's presence the night before the wedding.

"Oh, ho! The bridegroom parades his trenchant weapon already! Save your posturing for your bride, my young braggart."

Speaking in the transparent clichés that youth always thinks will fall weightily on an elder's ears, the dauphin said, "My lord sire and king, I want to talk to you as man to man."

The king had had a little wine and was planning an evening out for himself with a tavern wench in Amboise. "So you want to know how a bridegroom behaves, eh? The tutors haven't taught you? No, I suppose not. Friar Jean doesn't know, and Bernard d'Armagnac is too prudish. Well, what d'ye want *me* to do, show you how? By God, with that lassie it would be a pleasure!"

The dauphin colored to the roots of his mouse-colored hair, his dark features flushed brick red. It shamed him that his father should make a cheap joke of betraying his mother; it infuriated him that his own bride should be mentioned as taking part. He drew himself up and thrust out his barrel chest. It and his head were a little out of proportion—he was proud of the chest but he wore a larger-than-fashionable hat to conceal his head.

"I shall certainly require no lessons," he replied with more confidence than he actually felt. "I merely wished to ask whether the Scots alliance is deemed sufficiently permanent to admit of an early pregnancy

38

when the princess becomes my wife." He listened attentively for an answer, a great resentment in his heart against Friar Jean Majoris and the Lord of High Armagnac. Why had his tutors not taken him out to a tavern one night and let him find out for himself about these things, like other noble boys? It would have been easy, it would have been exciting and, muffled up with cloaks about their faces, the adventure could have been accomplished incognito. He almost hoped his father would answer that the international situation required no pregnancy at the moment. "Should the alliance have to be abrogated," Louis suggested, "a child would complicate matters exceedingly."

King Charles stared with heavy-lidded eyes at the prince who was questioning him with all the gravity of a privy counselor. It was on the tip of his tongue to retort: "How the devil should I know? My advisers never tell *me* anything." But he would not admit such ignorance in front of the dauphin, and his answer, when his slow wit found one, was brutally sarcastic: "Louis, my boy, why don't you invite the *conseil du roy* into your bedchamber tomorrow night and debate the matter with them? They will be delighted to oblige. Several, indeed, will want to revive the old privilege of witnessing the authentication of the blood royal." Charles slapped a saffron chamois-shod thigh and shouted with laughter. "Old Dunois d'Orléans watching you and Margaret naked in bed! You might have to fight him for your lassie, old as he is."

Even in his ire and confusion Louis noted his father's riding attire, which no occasion that he knew of seemed to demand that night. His eyes flashed, but partly their glint was tears of doubt, for he had had no answer. "Do I have your permission to retire?" he said curtly. He stood waiting. It was the request demanded by custom when leaving the presence of the king.

Louis's head was pounding—it often did under stress of emotion—and up and down his spine he felt a chill like eerie puffs of icy breath, though the candles burned with a steady, undisturbed flame. This was sometimes a warning that tomorrow he would be ill. Sometimes, however, if he ate very little next day, he would be perfectly well. Bernard d'Armagnac knew nothing of the dauphin's idiosyncrasy; to Louis it seemed an unmanly weakness. But not a sin, so Friar Jean had not heard of it either, not even in confession. It would have disturbed the apothecary in Friar Jean, who sometimes remembered how he had queried the duke-archbishop about the falling sickness when the dauphin was christened.

King Charles exercised his long-established right to say the stupid thing. "Retire, my boy? By all means retire and get a good rest. You will need all your strength tomorrow night." He thought he was being devil-may-care, and he nudged the dauphin in the ribs. "There's one thing to be said for those bandy legs of yours. No mount has ever been able to throw you no matter how high they reared. Hold fast when she tries to get away!"

Louis flinched. The fear had often occurred to him that a woman would look with disgust at his thin, deeply bowed legs, which the tight hose that were fashionable exaggerated almost into a deformity. That was one of the reasons he was shy before women. On horseback his legs were not noticeable; that was one of the reasons he was a superb horseman. On a charger he felt confident, exhilarated, proud, and his legs helped him keep a firm seat. He was jealous of all tall straight men on whom the ladies always smiled even though they were not dauphins, and the prospect of besting them was one of the reasons he had always been a fiery antagonist in the passages of arms that had constituted an important segment of his education, till Bernard d'Armagnac expressed himself satisfied that France would never be ashamed of him, and Friar Jean Majoris marveled, "He turns even his disabilities into assets, his weakness into strength."

That a bride might look askance at his body he had long steeled himself to endure, and the challenge stimulated his agile brain into a stratagem and a ruse: he would extinguish the candles and tell her that the moment required the shrouding decency of darkness. Then he would woo her with words; his voice was exceptionally deep and melodious, a natural product of his abnormally developed chest and throat. He studiously learned the tenderest ballades the minstrels could devise, and practiced on the lute to accompany his singing, till the minstrels conceded among themselves that the prince sang well. "When a prince sings it is to be expected that the ladies will melt into languorous smiles," they muttered. "But the closing of the eyes, as in a sensuous dream—he has an art!" Others would say, "If you were a woman, wouldn't you close your eyes instead of looking at Monseigneur le Dauphin?"

But that a bride might actually refuse him was a terrifying possibility, unsuspected until King Charles suggested it. The dauphin retired from his presence ashamed and unnerved, his heavy head bowed, his large shoulders slumping, and slept not at all, keeping vigil till sunup as he had not done since the ceremony of his knighting, trying to pray now as he had prayed then.

It was difficult to pray. No saint in the entire hagiarchy—at least not as taught by Friar Jean—had a special care for the hideous. Yet perhaps St. Lazarus would listen.

"Blessed St. Lazarus," he prayed again and again, "who lay four days in the tomb, dead and rotting, four days thou wert not handsome either. I do not beg for the miracle of beauty, since that would be too obvious and astonish everyone, but only for the little boon that tomorrow you blind the princess to my legs and head"—he had better include the chest—"and my chest also, which is sharp like a pigeon's in front, though nobody knows it because my doublet, like a pigeon's feathers, conceals it. This can be very easily accomplished," he prayed earnestly, anxious to convince the saint that the affair was practicable, "for I will see to it that the chamber is dark, and I shall sing ballades to distract her attention." Bernard d'Armagnac had taught him that when one asks a favor, a favor is expected in return. "Blessed St. Lazarus, if you grant me this, I will wear your image in gold on my cap as long as I live!" The dauphin recollected that he had no gold; his father, the King of France, had precious little, and had had to hire the napery for the wedding feast tomorrow from a local guild of drapers. "In silver, if I cannot in gold," he amended. "In lead, at least. And when I am king I will found a leprosarium in your name, to your glory and for the help of all the sick and afflicted."

It was daylight when he rose from his knees, mysteriously refreshed. The creeping chill was gone from his spine. His body glowed with warmth, his cheeks were flushed. He was not going to be sick today. St. Lazarus had heard him. He felt like singing. He did sing. His groom of the chamber, dressing him in a doublet of blue-gray velvet embroidered with leaves of gold and girding on the ruby-hilted sword, congratulated him on his appearance. Touching cautiously on the good sleep he must have enjoyed, and taking advantage of his high spirits, the groom hinted slyly that tonight's sleep was likely to be less uninterrupted.

Louis swore his favorite oath, *Pasque Dieu*, By the Passover! It was a mild oath, oddly at variance with the fulsome curses of most men, but the letter of the third Commandment was easy to obey, and the thought that the wrath of God might be conjured away and pass over him struck the dauphin as an irresistible bargain. "Sleep tonight? Pasque Dieu, not a wink!" He was a man in the lists, he was a man at the lute. Could he be less than a man with a woman—with the help of God and St. Lazarus?

It seemed natural enough to the groom that the dauphin should sing and strut a bit as he looked forward to his wedding night. True, Louis had never confided any amorous adventures, and the groom considered his position intimate enough to have shared some of them; but since he had not, the groom merely concluded that the young heir to the throne was more secretive than everyone already knew him to be.

At noon St. Gatien's cathedral was thronged to the doors with humanity. Over the city the chorus of pealing bells soared to a climactic height and then, at the hour, suddenly fell silent so that the duke-archbishop's words might be heard when he read the nuptial service. In the Lady Chapel the queen in an azure velvet gown powdered with silver fleurs-de-lis spoke quietly to Margaret, "It would be unseemly for the service to begin without the king."

"Where is the king?"

The queen replied, "His Highness had business of a confidential nature at Amboise. Some affair of state. I do not know. Queens do not inquire too closely into these matters, my dear."

"I shall when I am queen!"

The queen sighed. It was understandable that the girl who in a few minutes would become the dauphin's bride was anxious to display her wedding gown, richer and finer by far than the queen's. During the solemn rites she would be the center of attraction for thousands of admiring eyes. There would be reason to admire her. In spite of her youth she was taller than the queen; her gown of velvet and cloth of gold nipped in at her tiny waist and cascaded into a billowy skirt that hid her delicate satin-slippered feet. Over her jet-black hair she wore a diadem of gold studded with lapis lazuli that matched the blue, the deep incongruous blue, of her eyes. The combination of black hair and blue eyes was not unusual in Scotland, where the Caledonian blood played strange tricks, but it was startlingly rare in France. The diadem was the queen's own, an Angevin treasure that she had worn when she married Charles of France. Yesterday Charles had said, pinching Margaret's cheeks familiarly: "Let us give your old crown to this pretty princess when she marries our son. The treasury could not afford anything half so fine." The queen had not demurred. Perhaps a pretty princess in the royal family was just what the royal family needed to reunite it. If King Charles should become a grandfather next year, the new dignity might change him completely, lessen the tension between him and the dauphin, and above all put a stop to these nights away from home.

"When you are queen, dear Margaret, you shall do as you please. But that will not be at once. King Charles is not old—"

"I meant to imply no such thing."

"—though of course he looks old to you. Please God he shall live and reign many years."

"Naturally, Madame, that is my prayer also."

"Meanwhile, dear child, cleave close to my son. I know him better than anyone; he loves you, though he is too shy to say so. You are beautiful, Margaret; a prince more handsome than the dauphin might easily be shy before you. But he has great vision, penetrating intelligence, and boundless ambition for France. And he has a great heart—open it, lest it turn inward and feed upon itself!"

Margaret's eyes were calm and a little empty. "Surely I know my duty, Madame. Do you know my father?"

"I know King James only by report of his valor and statesmanship." She had heard of, but did not mention, the monarch's unfortunate disfigurement.

Margaret said, "He also told me that the dauphin has many virtues."

It seemed to the queen that the love was all on one side.

In the sacristy the duke-archbishop awaited impatiently the arrival of the king. Mitered, vested, and uncomfortably warm under his heavy robes, he watched the hourglass, which a sacristan had turned at noon. The sand in the nether globe had already reached the first of four dividing lines: A quarter of an hour had passed. He stole a glance around the sacristy door. Perhaps the hourglass was wrong; perhaps the old sacristan had turned it too soon in his anxiety to do everything smartly today. But the hourglass was right, for the sun, which at high noon had shone through the windows of the northern transept, was creeping round to the windows of the nave, flooding the body of the great church with color and light.

Most of the throngs who crowded the cathedral were common people. On one pretext or another, almost to a man, the heads of the great seignorial Families of the Lilies had stayed away, among them Gaston of Foix and Count Jean d'Armagnac. To appear at the dauphin's wedding implied a little more loyalty to the king than the great nobles cared to display. They wanted to keep their hands free. Many of them took it for granted that Louis would never be their sovereign, since King Henry of England, whose armies occupied so many provinces, was a grandson of mad old King Charles VI of France no less than Louis himself, and as such had a remarkably good claim to the French throne. Conspicuously absent was Duke Philip the Good of Burgundy, though he had been invited more urgently than any of the others. He sat peacefully in his castle at Genappe in Flanders, sending magnificent presents to everyone on both sides, pleading his illness and age, watching how the wind of battle blew. Margaret's father, though far away in a foggy isle, saw more clearly; his faith was in France; he was wagering his kingdom that France would win the Hundred Years' War, and his daughter was his hostage to fortune.

In the forefront of the cathedral congregation the duke-archbishop saw only Monseigneur d'Anjou, the queen's loyal brother; the Comte de Vendôme, Bernard d'Armagnac, and Pierre de Brézé. The duke-archbishop did not approve of De Brézé, but for once he was glad to see him. Charles the Well Served was incapable of finding even pleasure without help. If De Brézé, his boon drinking and wenching companion, was in the cathedral, the king could not be very far away.

Meanwhile, in the chapel adjoining the sacristy, alone except for his groom, the dauphin waited, while the sand in the duke-archbishop's hourglass crept upward: the second mark, half an hour. Louis was impatient. He was not at all embarrassed by the staring eyes today. The mantle of state that he wore as dauphin reached to his ankles.

The people in the great public spaces of the cathedral, where there were no benches to sit on and where, since nobility was present they could not have sat anyhow, shuffled nervously and began to murmur. It was long past the hour when they ate their biggest meal of the day. Never too well fed, their mood grew surly. Here and there someone would draw a chunk of bread from some dark recess in his jerkin and began to munch upon it, though it was blacker now than when freshly baked by reason of contact with clothing and skin, and the good Lord knew that even freshly baked it was always coarse and black enough. It was significant that these men, more provident or more cynical than the others, did not share their bread with anyone except their wives and families. Bread was precious.

The holiday mood had evaporated. Today they had seen large tables set up in the market place, they had heard promises in the king's name that after the wedding everyone could eat his fill and drink himself drunk at the king's expense. But the least pang of hunger reminded them how often they had starved in the past, how often the king had failed to keep his word, and how full of insecurity their lives were. Thus, on the lower levels also, each man drew apart from his neighbor, thinking only of himself, trusting no one. Perhaps the Scottish marriage had been canceled. Perhaps there was a new alliance in the making with some other country. Scotland might now be an enemy. It would go hard with the ordinary man if this army of ten thousand foreigners which had penetrated to the heart of France should suddenly prove to be a covert horde of invaders. Betrayals and sudden reversals of role, from enemy to ally and back to enemy again, were so commonplace that every Frenchman, particularly in the towns, accepted them as a normal way of life. He might not know why such things happened, but he had seen them happen so often that there was no longer anything shocking in them. Ignorant and illiterate a man might be, but he could sense and fear the onset of these perpetual shifts. Perhaps it was significant that the king was late.

Shortly before the sand in the hourglass reached the third division, there was a clatter of hoofs outside and a trumpet blast. In the Lady Chapel the queen started and blushed, glancing at Margaret. But the fanfares in Scotland were different, and Margaret simply looked happy and relieved that the king's confidential business at Amboise had kept him no longer than it had.

"That was a brave trumpet," she said. "His Highness has finally come to the wedding?"

"His Highness has come to the wedding," the queen answered, her lips tight, her face under perfect control.

The trumpet call was a lusty trill taken from a popular hunting song, "The Quarry Is Brought to Bay," and Charles, exercising his right to do the stupid thing, had had his trumpeter sound it for his son, with an obvious and not too subtle allusion to the bridal night. It was unregal and indelicate, but it tickled the fancy of the people, who thrust their black bread into their jerkins and forgot all their vague apprehensions and greeted King Charles with understanding snickers. He strode into the sanctuary, shook hands with Douglas of Douglas, and motioned with his riding crop in the direction of the high altar. He was thirsty from his dusty ride of fifteen miles. Let the wedding begin, by all means so that he could get at the wedding feast. In this at least, King Charles and his good people in the cathedral were of one mind.

The pageantry of the nuptials, which ordinarily the people would have enjoyed, was hustled through with indecent haste, for the king kept snapping his riding crop against his thigh. Louis and Margaret knelt, exchanged vows, and were united in wedlock in less time when the king had taken to ride from his assignation in Amboise. Then the cathedral cleared as if the populace were afraid the roof would fall in on their heads, and the tables in the market place were filled with a hungry but now good-natured crowd that ate the free food and drank the free wine, toasting King Charles, praising Margaret's beauty, wishing they were dauphins, and more than once breaking into the song "The Quarry Is Brought to Bay."

If the wedding feast had been held in one of the banqueting halls of the palace in Paris, the inadequate staff of servants, the poverty of the plate, and the smallness of the king's retinue would have been dramatically apparent. The entire court would scarcely have filled one room. Here in Tours, however, in this small château, things were more intimate and more in proportion. Margaret blushed when the king chucked her under the chin, and even contrived to smile prettily when he reached over with his hunting knife and skewered a great cut of smoking beef and thumped it down in front of the dauphin, calling on him loudly to build up his strength against the coming *combat d'amour* for France.

It happened that the dauphin had been extraordinarily hungry since his chill of the preceding night. Usually his eating habits were abstemious to such a degree that the queen was concerned with the state of his digestion. His good appetite today, his odd sense of well-being and the curious lack of fatigue that had come upon him after his sleepless all-night vigil the dauphin attributed to the efficacy of his prayers and the intercession of St. Lazarus. He wolfed down quantities of food and matched his royal father glass for glass in wine.

Following the example of the king and the dauphin, everyone else did the same, and Margaret remembered her father's words, "Frenchmen, my dear, are always in a hurry." She could get used to such table manners, she supposed. After all, the men here were only a little worse than the men in Edinburgh, where they scorned the new-fangled Italian forks also. She noticed that the queen was using hers, however. And the French food was decidedly superior to the Scottish. It was a pity, though, that the handsome equerry standing so straight behind the dauphin's chair was not the dauphin and the dauphin the handsome equerry.

In her mind's eye they changed places. The equerry lost a foot of stature, his chestnut hair went mouse-colored, his livery sagged, and his eyes, which had carefully avoided her glance, stared straight into hers with fanatical steadiness. She had not been especially conscious of the dauphin's head until now, when an optical accident happened to place it and the equerry's directly in line of sight, almost superimposing the two.

It was the dauphin staring at her. "Is something amiss, my dear?" Margaret dared not answer, but she whispered to the queen, "Do the servants always stand so close?"

Margaret now learned for the first time that her husband was gifted with extraordinarily keen ears. He said, "It is a relic of the time when princes had to protect their backs."

"Huh?" grunted the king through a mouthful of meat.

"The servants, sir. I was explaining that they stand close because at one time a prince's back was always in danger."

"Still is," muttered the king. "Wait'll you're king. You'll see."

"Now they just push chairs in and out," the dauphin continued to Margaret, "and hold the fingerbowls for us after we've eaten." The fingerbowls were full-sized basins in which the whole hand was dipped, since hands got greasy if one did not use the Italian forks. "If the servants annoy you, the custom can easily be changed."

"I am not annoyed, my lord husband." There was an earnestness in her tone that pleased everyone. She felt guilty at the mental betrayal which had substituted in her mind the image of the equerry for the image of the dauphin. She did not think she had willed it, but her husband was still staring at her. "Are you displeased with me, my lord?"

"Nonsense," the king grunted again. "Louis always looks like that when he eats too fast. Always does. Hasn't got my stomach."

The dauphin lowered his eyes; it was true enough that he did not enjoy his father's superb digestion. But he had quite put out of his mind the apprehension which the chill of the preceding night would ordinarily have caused him. He was confident that he was not going to be ill.

Shortly after sundown the artilleryman saw the dauphin and his bride walking arm in arm upon the ramparts outside the bridal chamber. The dauphiness, as Margaret was now entitled to be styled, had put off her formal wedding gown and the Angevin crown of gold. She wore a heather-blue robe and the rays that still lingered from the sunset glinted her hair with dark flashes of color. Such brilliance from such darkness the artilleryman had never before seen save in the smoky flame of gunpowder when samples were tested by burning.

The dauphin still wore a cloak, though not the cloak of state. A lute was slung over his shoulders by a ribbon, and other ribbons, pink and blue and gold and green, fluttered gaily from the turning screws, tied in love knots like a minstrel's.

In such a light, at such a time, with such a bride, the dauphin looked a king and the girl a queen, both very much in love. The artilleryman smiled a little slyly, wishing them well in his heart, and blew up his slow match. It was high time to send this handsome high-born couple to bed with a rousing salute so that the bonfires could be illuminated.

But the young people seemed in no hurry to retire. They continued to walk in his direction, talking and smiling into each other's eyes, until the cannon and the artilleryman blocked their path and they were forced to recognize his existence or actually to collide with him.

"Pasque Dieu!" Louis exclaimed. "And who are you?"

"I am Henri, Your Highness."

"Henri what?"

46

"I—am sometimes called Henri LeClercq."

"Well, Henri LeClercq, what are you doing with this engine of yours so close to my chambers?"

"It is the best place, Your Highness. The parapet is strong enough to block the recoil; the piece will not hurl itself into the courtyard; the carriage is roped fast to iron bolts, the only ones to be found for twenty paces either side of this spot. Observe also that it is pointed through a crenel away from other buildings, so that the concussion will break no windows and injure no innocent people—"

Margaret laughed gaily. "It would seem that you are answered, my lord husband, and at length."

"Hang it all, man, why were you stationed here in the first place? To spy on me?"

For an instant the absurdity of the accusation nettled the artilleryman. Why in the name of all the saints would anybody spy on the dauphin? What useful or unusual knowledge could anybody gleam by spying on a bride and groom! "Monseigneur le dauphin," Henri smiled, "I am stationed here by order of Jean Bureau, governor of the castle, to fire a salute in your honor when you and your lady retire."

"What is humorous about that? Why are you laughing, Henri Le-Clercq?"

"My dear lord, the man is not laughing."

"I do not like to be laughed at. Never laugh at me, Margaret."

"No, my lord husband." It seemed to Margaret that the dauphin's mood had suddenly altered.

He was, in fact, extremely irritated because a moment before he had experienced a feeling of giddiness on looking over the wall, but it passed. "What will happen when you fire the salute, Henri LeClercq?"

"I do not understand Your Highness. The powder will explode, of course, with a terrific roar—"

"No, no. It is a signal for something. What does it signify?"

"Monseigneur, as soon as I have the honor to touch this match to the vent, everyone in Tours will drink your health and the health"—he bowed to the dauphiness—"of your bride, who will one day be our queen. That is what the salute signifies."

"He is well spoken," Margaret said.

Entirely too well, the dauphin thought. They must educate artillerymen better than he had imagined, or a higher type was becoming attracted to the craft. Most artillerymen were powder-smeared brutes like the catapult engineers and the miners who tunneled under castle walls during a siege. Henri was also too tall for comfort, and Margaret had been too quick to defend him.

But Louis knew intuitively that he would not gain stature in Margaret's eyes by revealing the twinge of jealousy he felt. Here was another straight-legged man to best, or at least to equal. The situation offered no legitimate area of challenge except in the artilleryman's own special field.

"Guns burst from time to time, do they not, Henri?" His voice was friendlier, and he called the artilleryman by his first name.

"Often Monseigneur. But this one will not."

"How do you know?"

"I cast it myself." He made the statement without insolence, but with the confident pride of a master craftsman who knows his own handiwork.

It did not suit the dauphin's little stratagem to have the gun too safe. "Perhaps you have also charged it with only half a charge. Since it is only a salute, that would be a commendable economy of powder I should say."

"On the contrary, Monseigneur, it is charged with a double charge. I want a good salute."

"Did you ever double charge it before?"

"Well, no—but I am sure—"

Before he could go on to say that it was safe, Louis interrupted him. "I am going to fire the piece."

Margaret drew back. "Do not, Louis! I beg you, let the artilleryman do it."

"Then if it bursts it will kill Henri. Wouldn't you care?"

"The artilleryman is not Louis of France, and he is not my husband."

Henri had a notion what the young man was up to, and decided to help him with his bride. "I have every confidence in my ordnance, Madame, but it is unquestionably true that there is always a certain element of danger, and I should not like to take the responsibility of permitting Monseigneur le Dauphin to fire this gun." Margaret thought he looked very grim and severe. Actually, the tight set of his mouth was an effort to keep from laughing. If the thing did blow up, which it would not, there would be nobody left to take the responsibility, neither Henri, the dauphin, nor Margaret herself. They would all be blasted to bits, together with several square yards of the wall.

"Give me the match, Henri. If the people want to drink my health, they must not be kept waiting."

Henri blew on the smoldering slow fire till it flared up into a glowing head of flame, and handed it to Louis. "It would be well if Madame were to retire to the safety of her chamber," he said ominously.

Margaret hesitated, but the dauphin agreed emphatically and she obeyed.

"Keep your head well to one side, Monseigneur. The backfire leaps up three feet from the vent."

Louis nodded. "I have no intention of blinding myself. I know."

"Also, stand on tiptoe and open your mouth, if you please."

"Pasque Dieu, why?"

"That's how it's done."

48

"Suppose I don't?"

"The concussion is unpleasant."

"I shall look a fool! Are *you* going to?"

"Certainly, Monseigneur."

"Then go ahead!"

If Margaret was watching, as very likely she was, let her see Henri LeClercq stand on tiptoe and open his mouth like an idiot, but not her husband. A wedding night was not a night to look ridiculous. Louis thrust the slow fire against the vent, his laughter lost in the roar of the cannon as it leapt backward against the lashings and belched a long red tongue of fire and smoke over the city.

He smiled proudly and looked in the direction of his chamber where Margaret stood at the casement. "How did I fire your gun, Master Henri?"

"Like a veteran, Monseigneur! It was magnificent. It was epic. It took me years to achieve such skill. Such a hand, such steadiness, such technique—"

"Tut, tut, man. She can't hear us. How did I really do?"

"Fairly well. But you should have opened your mouth."

"I think you know why I did not. Thank you for helping me, Master Henri. I shall remember you." He picked up his lute, which lay beside the gun carriage. "Pasque Dieu, it is cracked! I set it against the wheels."

It was a beautiful and costly instrument. "I blame myself, sir," Henri said. "I should have noticed. I was so intent on watching Your Highness—"

"Nonsense. It isn't your fault. Take it; there may be music in it still." He tossed it, all fluttering ribbons and love knots, to Henri. "I think I shan't need it after all."

He strode rather jauntily to the casement, which opened like a door on the battlement, and entered the chamber where Margaret leaned her head against his breast for a moment. "My dear lord, I was terrified when you did that."

Louis laughed. "Did you see how foolish that artilleryman looked with his mouth wide open?"

"I was not looking at him."

Louis glanced at the candles.

"They make it very warm," Margaret said shyly.

"I was going to sing to you, but I broke my lute."

"It does not matter."

From the battlements Henri saw the light in the dauphin's chamber fade, as one by one the candles were extinguished. In the streets below bonfires were beginning to glow, and he could hear laughter and singing. His work was done. He secured his cannon for the night, thrust in the tampion, put on the vent cover against the dew, and went to report to his commander that, since he was no longer needed on the battlement, he would like to join his friends and drink the dauphin's health.

In her chamber, on this night for which she had been sent to France, Margaret mused that it would be her lot to bear children to a royal but unprepossessing husband. She thought of the handsome equerry who had stood behind his chair during the wedding feast. She thought of the artilleryman to whom they had just spoken. It would have been pleasant if the dauphin had looked like them. But in that case perhaps he would not have been a dauphin, and her children would not be kings and queens. Perhaps there was something in blood royal that set it apart from common blood. She remembered her father's nervous habit of hiding his disfigurement with his hand. She loved her father and she was never conscious of his birthmark; no doubt she would learn to love her husband too. She knew now what they meant when they said that the marriages of princesses were not quite like the marriages of other people. She remembered her father's high sense of duty, how he would receive ministers from foreign powers and comport himself with dignity. What these interviews must have cost him she realized now.

Therefore she smiled when Louis smiled at her, reaching up to extinguish the last of the candles.

But she was not prepared for the horror of the next few minutes. No one on earth could have warned her, for no one knew, no one but the shades of the dauphin's ancestors, and they were not of this world. The thing that now happened had never happened before.

Louis made some inconsequential remark about his lost lute; she made some light rejoinder, something to the effect that there would be plenty of time tomorrow for singing.

The intimacy of the compliment, its promise, its warmth, pleased Louis.

His smile broadened.

It broadened far too far.

It broadened into a hideous grin, like a death's head, all his teeth showing. His arm, upraised to snuff the candle, froze motionless, and his eyes rolled back in his head, showing nothing but the whites. His head jerked to one side, as heads jerk at a hanging, and one whole side of his body began to twitch as if an invisible monster were clawing at each separate muscle. She thought he gasped, "Blessed St. Lazarus!" and, "Give me room to fall!" but she could not be sure, for the words were uttered backward as it were, not with an expulsion but with a great intake of breath. Then all the breath that filled his large chest and lungs burst outward in a cry like nothing she had ever heard, like nothing most people have ever heard; and the unfortunate man who did not want to be laughed at, who did not wish to appear ridiculous on his wedding night, and who had eaten too heavily in spite of the warning chill, secure in a conviction that he would not be sick, fell awkwardly to the floor, jerking and twisting grotesquely, all his motor functions out of control, his stomach and bladder and bowels incontinently voiding as if an enormous weight had fallen upon him and crushed the contents out of his body.

Margaret recoiled from him in pity and terror.

The secret was kept. A royal dauphiness did not reveal an illness in her husband, and Margaret's loyalty was involved, for great pressure was brought upon her not to reveal it by the only two men who knew.

Friar Jean Majoris, as confessor to the dauphin, as a former apothecary, and now a full-fledged surgeon, was summoned by the guards, who heard the cry but dared not enter the bridal chamber. He handled the situation with humanity and discretion; to Margaret he was open, frank, and encouraging. Not only would the dauphin remember nothing when he recovered consciousness, he assured her, but the prognosis was actually far from bad. He had feared the falling sickness from the moment of the dauphin's birth, at which he had been present. But these violent symptoms were not always repeated, and every hour, every day, that went by without a recurrence made a recurrence less likely. Hundreds of sufferers experienced only one such seizure throughout their entire lives, and were in every respect like other men, healthy, intelligent, brave, gentle, and lived to great age. Caesar himself in the antiquity of the Romans had once had such a spasm.

Next morning the dauphin, when he woke, had no memory of what had happened. One moment he was snuffing a candle; the next he was waking, normal and refreshed, in a bed. But it was a separate bed, and in Margaret's face there was nothing of the brightness of a bride.

The king, of course, had to be informed. "Louis is a queer one," he shrugged. "Forget him. Come to your father-in-law when you want company, or get yourself a nice-looking guard and go hunting. I myself am a great one for hunting. You mustn't tell anyone about this, however. I cannot afford to have your father snatch you back to Scotland and lose ten thousand soldiers. And you would never be Queen of France."

"Is that all I am supposed to feel, Your Highness?"

He patted her young round hips, taking advantage of his privilege as a father-in-law. "Such a solemn child! Royal marriages have their little drawbacks, but you get used to them; and what is to prevent you from enjoying life—in a discreet manner?"

She began to weep. "He terrifies me."

"Friar Jean says he'll be all right. It's *my* opinion that he simply ate too much. Hasn't got my stomach. Just act as if nothing had happened."

"It will be very hard to bring myself to do my wifely duty."

"Oh, I think you had better do *that*. I am almost certain the *conseil du roy* will insist."

"Please, please don't tell all those men."

"I won't. If you promise."

"I shall try. I shall truly try."

She did try. But the dauphin soon deserted her. Between him and his bride he knew there was something terribly wrong; but Margaret was too proud and too ashamed to make mention of their wedding night, and Friar Jean was too good a surgeon to go into detail. As for the king, he avoided the subject altogether, as he avoided everything difficult or distasteful, particularly anything that reminded him of the last mad days of his father, King Charles VI, and he was glad that Louis had never been close enough to him as a son to bring him his troubles and ask for advice. Inevitably, however, over a period of months, under constant questioning by the dauphin, Friar Jean disclosed bits of data which Louis put together in his agile, retentive mind: Margaret's frightened expression, which she tried to control and could not whenever he approached her, led him inescapably to the conviction that he was an object of indifference, if not of loathing to her.

A compensatory rage to distinguish himself began to burn within him. It burned for nine years, with important consequences to France, till Margaret died.

Book Two

Chapter Ten

Louis threw himself into war, not like his father loftily brooding over generalities with commanders in the rear, but in hazardous bodily contact with the enemy and with a fury like the fury of love. It would happen that an opponent, misjudging the firmness of his seat by the slenderness of his legs, would assume him easy to unhorse, only to find himself unhorsed instead; the dauphin's legs welded him to his mount. Many a confident chevalier miscalculated the distance from which the dauphin could strike, and lived just long enough to see a sword flash through an astonishing space, wielded by an unnaturally long and over-developed arm.

It was not wise, it would never be wise, to miscalculate the distance from which Louis could strike.

Margaret was left alone in Tours with no duties except her embroidery, no amusement except the itinerant minstrels, and no company except the queen, who had grown used to being alone. The separation was easy, even welcome, at first, since it seemed to solve many problems. But it became painful after the first year. "Where," King James wrote to her from Scotland, "are my grandchildren?" The war against England was going exceedingly well, he said; let his daughter have no scruples against strengthening the French alliance. By now even King James knew that she was old enough.

"Is this to be my life?" Margaret asked.

The queen replied, "It has been mine."

"No, Madame," Margaret smiled. The queen had borne King Charles a daughter and was about to bear him another. "Your husband comes home at least occasionally. Mine only writes me letters."

"I used to think I understood my son. Now I cannot be sure. One thing comforts me, however. He has not deserted you for"—the words came with unaccustomed sharpness—"for a tavern wench! Gossip travels faster then the heralds, my dear, and we should have heard if *that* were the trouble. By all reports Louis is making a splendid name for himself in battle, fighting like a Charlemagne." The queen's eyes shone with pride.

One day a happy idea struck her. It would lighten Margaret's tedium and it would consume many weary hours. "I am sure it would please my son if you were to learn to read his letters and answer them in your own hand. I shall find you a tutor."

Margaret asked a curiously irrelevant question. "Madame, can artillery-men read and write?"

The queen laughed. "Good gracious, no. At least I never heard of one who could. Why do you ask?"

Lest evil tongues start wagging, the queen engaged a tutor who was neither so handsome as to cause comment nor so ugly that there was danger of his proving fascinating. He was Jean d'Estoutville, Sieur de Blainville et Torey, a gentle and proper man, well known for his slight lisp and great erudition. Under him Margaret learned to read.

Presently, reading became a passion. She shared the guilty love of Héloïse for Abelard; with *la belle Aude* she fell dead at Charlemagne's feet on the news that her Roland was slain by the Moors; her eyes grew wide in the candlelight at night, spellbound by the gallantries of Queen Constance of the South, *sans foy, sans loy, et sans pudeur.*

"I am not at all sure you are reading the right things," the queen said, troubled. The Sieur de Blainville et Torey somewhat stiffly rejected the criticism, reassuring her, "Madame la Reine, the dauphiness is wonder-fully apt, and there is nothing improper in the old poems of France save perhaps that they deal with a time when ladies engaged in political mat-ters instead of remaining securely behind castle walls, which is infinitely more cultured." They also led to daydreaming and dangerous fantasy, as the queen remembered from reading them herself. It would be her pleas-ure, she instructed the tutor, if Margaret should devote more time to composition.

Shortly thereafter the dauphin began to receive dutiful answers to his letters, and King James in Scotland began to read tentative, tender little ballades in his daughter's own hand. He wrote her his congratulations with fatherly pride. But as he penned the letters, cupping his chin in his palm, hiding a side of his face out of habit, he wondered. His last letter betrayed the anxiety he felt for her: he suggested a visit home to Scot-land. One poet in the family, he quipped playfully, was quite enough.

But Margaret did not go home. The same courier brought word of a tragedy. King James had been stabbed to death by the Earl of Perth, and King James II, Margaret's brother, now sat on the Scottish throne. In Scotland the times were troubled, her brother wrote. Stay. It was safer in France.

Margaret remained in Tours, lonelier than ever before, while in the northern provinces the English armies slowly withdrew, leaving a vacuum in their wake of misery, desolation, and the plague.

Into this vacuum now flowed the French armies, sufficiently powerful to block a return but powerless to hasten the retreat, though every minor engagement was astutely magnified by report. Every herald riding into Tours brought official news of another great victory. The king's extremely sagacious ministers could now for the first time represent their sovereign as a great general, a father of his people, a man who, as it were, had grown in office. Louis was also mentioned, but only as a dutiful son, loyally upholding his liege lord the king. France desperately needed unity; unity demanded a single head, even if the ministers knew it to be only a figurehead. Moreover, the tension between Charles and Louis was already suspected. It would never do to divide the honors.

But although the heralds officially minimized Louis's activities, nothing could prevent the common people from reporting what they had actually seen. Peasants who had witnessed the battles from behind haystacks, carters who had gone to and fro with provisions for the army, and the wounded debris of humanity perpetually straggling back to towns in the rear related tales of the dauphin's conduct that fell on the ear of the listener like something out of an old French epic, just as brilliant, just as brave, but, a growing element in modern war, ingeniously unprincipled.

He fought like a maniac, asking and giving no quarter. Once, it was said, he unhorsed an old-fashioned chevalier with a crest on his helm, who yielded and sought to save his life by shouting, "A ransom! A ransom!" Louis found a chink in his armor and stabbed him where he lay. Once, outfought by a huge antagonist, Louis slit the throat of the opposing *horse*, and as the hapless rider fell, slew him. The dauphin would, it was said, win fairly if he could, and usually did, thanks to his long arm and amazing seat. But if he could not win fairly, he did not care how he won, so long as he won.

Some of the older nobility affected to deplore the dauphin's behavior. He was fighting contrary to all the rules. Where were the ideals of chivalry?

From time to time a member of their own class would supply the answer by dying miserably of a bullet no surgeon knew how to extract, some deep-seated fragment of iron aimed by a base-born engineer and shot from a blindly impersonal gun that the chevalier had not even seen, mortally wounded through Milanese armor that offered no more protection than if it had been eggshell. Where had the rules of chivalry been ever since gunpowder was brought into war?

The common people did not condemn the dauphin. For weary years without number no rules had applied to them. A generation of brutalized and degenerate soldiery, sometimes their own, had burned their homes, stolen their possessions, driven off their cattle, insulted their wives, and ravished their daughters. Louis was merely modern, like gunpowder.

Reform of these abuses became so clamant that the king, on the advice of his ministers, resorted to a desperate expedient: he convoked the States General of France. That august and seldom consulted body of representatives acted with rash and excessive courage, which hastened the end of the Hundred Years' War and all but plunged France into civil conflict as fatal as the English Wars of the Roses. The States General decreed the Ordonnances of 1439.

In accordance with this reformatory legislation, the king himself henceforth was to be known as commander in chief of all the French armies, and a perpetual tax of 1,200,000 pounds was imposed to give him the means to pay their wages. The army paraded before the palace, shouting their joy and loyalty to King Charles. No longer need they rely on their feudal lords, who had so often defaulted and sometimes failed even to provide fodder for the horses. The result of the Ordonnances was a massive shift of loyalty and a concentration of power into the sovereign's hands. There was more. Merchants, laborers, churchmen, the bourgeois of the towns and even the peasants henceforth came under the king's protection, with right of appeal to the royal courts of justice if any noble wronged them. Worst of all, from the nobles' point of view, no great lord was permitted to levy taxes in his own domain except those which could be proved to date from antiquity so remote that the records had long since been lost.

The great lords saw in the Ordonnances of 1439 a mortal blow at their privilege. In the States General they fought the measure with all the eloquence at their command. But they were only one of the three estates; the clergy and the commons overruled them. When words availed them nothing, they strutted out of the assembly, their hands on their swords, muttering dark threats against the gorgeously mitered churchmen and soberly garbed representatives of the bourgeoisie who dared restrict their independence. This, they said, was the overturning of all the old order; this was a revolution. From this time forward they would have nothing to do with words, those snaring devices of prelates and presumptuous commoners. They would trust to their swords, as always before in troubled times. And they knew a leader to lead them!

Louis listened. Distinguished statesmen of the realm approached him, noblemen with great appanages, old titles, and reputations for bravery. Two of them were *royaux de France*, senior heads of Families of the Lilies: Charles, Duke of Bourbon, and John, Duke of Brittany. Two others also had royal blood in their veins, illegitimate but honored: Alexander, Bastard of Bourbon, and Dunois, Bastard of Orléans. They were bastards so called to their faces, and proud to be. Two others were famous generals, Antoine de Chabannes and Jean de la Roche.

The Bastard of Bourbon was especially successful in winning Louis over to the coalition. He knew how to play on the dauphin's youthful vanity and make much of his battle successes. He referred constantly to the slighting references in the official accounts of the fighting as reported by the heralds. Sensing a lack of worldly experience in the young heir, the Bastard produced a dimpled, ambitious little wench, with whom Louis spent some instructive nights and then, overwhelmed with remorse, never looked at again, nor would he suffer her name to be spoken in his presence. About that time Margaret received the first tender letters from her husband, making no mention of the war, stating that he had been away too long from home and from her.

Sensing this emotional turnabout, the Bastard struck a high moral tone:

58

Did the dauphin know that King Charles had abandoned his clandestine amours, to which, after all, any king was entitled, and taken up recently with a woman of Fromanteau whom he proposed to bring to court and flaunt in the face of his mother, the queen herself? Such a thing, the Bastard said, had never been known in all the long history of France, and indeed it had not. Would Louis permit this affront to his mother? Were not the noblest lords of France entitled, nay, were they not in conscience bound to curb the excesses of their king, especially with the king's son at their head? Such a leader, the Bastard craftily insinuated, would purge the revolt of all taint of disloyalty, since if the king refused to be curbed, Louis himself would be king. A legitimate undertaking.

Ambition, pride, lust, remorse, the great love he bore his mother, nothing in the dauphin's heart was spared. Alexander, Bastard of Bourbon, played like a skilled harper on every string.

It was heady stuff for a young man already successful in war and ambitious to rule.

Louis said: "I learned from Bernard d'Armagnac that a favor is never asked unless a favor is expected in return. What are your conditions?"

The Bastard waved the conditions aside as if he were brushing away a fly. "There are no conditions, Monseigneur. These new Ordonnances, of course—we should expect you to revoke them, that is all."

"The Ordonnances seem to me very wise—in part, at least." Louis saw fierce scowls on the faces of all the great nobles. "Surely," he pleaded, "the peasants and people have a right to look to someone for protection. I have seen terrible things."

They had indeed such a right, the conspirators agreed; and what better protection could be asked than the protection of their own immediate lords, who were always closer than the king's justice and who had redressed the wrongs of vassals for six hundred years? The terrible things the dauphin had seen must have been done by the English. "The insidiousness of the Ordonnances, Monseigneur, is that they strike against the strongest upholders of the throne, the ancient nobility of France. To whom shall a king look for help if he alienates his natural friends?"

Louis looked into the rebellious faces of his father's great vassals. One and all they had knelt before their king in honorable obedience. One and all they had sworn the ancient oaths of fealty, promising on their faith to be loyal to King Charles, "observing homage to him completely, between his hands bound together with a kiss, against all persons, in good faith and without deceit," repeating the oath on holy relics of the saints. Yet here they stood forsworn, his "natural friends." To whom indeed could a king look for help!

"We shall need artillery," he said. "Why is Jean Bureau not among you?"

Bureau was a commoner, they said, and all artillerymen were hairy brutes and engineers.

"I knew one who wasn't," Louis murmured. "His cannon fired a noble

59

salute." But the incident was painful to recall; he did not press the matter and he let himself be overruled. Brave hearts, the Bastard assured him, were more dependable than a mechanical novelty.

"I believe you, Bastard," the dauphin said. "Brave, loyal hearts!" None of them caught the tinge of irony in his tone. Louis was learning to school his tongue.

"Your Highness gives us hope!" said the Bastard, kneeling on two knees, as before a king. "Sire!"

"Not yet," the dauphin answered.

Not yet, nor for quite a while. In the Bourbonnais, in Auvergne, in Poitou, the people shut the gates of their cities against the coalition of rebels, though they were the most brilliant nobility of Europe, sometimes in the face of their own liege lord. They declared themselves for the king. The lesson of the power of the people was not lost on the dauphin.

From Burgundy, Duke Philip the Good sent messages of good cheer and financial help to both sides, then quietly hanged a score or two of impulsive Burgundians who had expressed a desire to enlist in the dauphin's army. "The man has no guns," the duke grumbled. "Damned young fool." He liked Louis.

Then, one by one, the rebellious nobles deserted the coalition and one another and threw themselves at Charles's feet asking pardon.

Charles swore he would hang them all, beginning with the dauphin. The queen intervened and was thrust rudely aside. Margaret intervened and was heard at greater length, for she threatened spiritedly, "If you hang my husband I shall go home with my ten thousand Scotsmen." Charles recalled that his armies were winning the war against the English, and replied, "I no longer need your ten thousand Scotsmen."

But the *conseil du roy* intervened with ponderous authority, which Charles always heeded. It was impossible to hang the dauphin, they reasoned. It would be grossly impolitic to destroy a young prince whom everyone praised for his valor, who reflected the spirit of the times, and who, above all, had somehow managed to unite into a powerful coalition, if only for a time, so many fractious and dissident nobles. Five times before, they reminded King Charles, he had pardoned the Duke of Bourbon for similar and bloodier revolts when the French armies were losing. Could he do less than pardon his own son this once at a time when the French armies were winning? Such a pardon, from the plenitude of power, from the inexhaustible treasure of fatherly love, would endear him to the people, and the people backed the Ordonnances. Every pulpit in France would ring with the story of the Prodigal Son. Charles the Well Served agreed. "But give me at least one traitor to hang."

The ministers tossed him the least dangerous of the lot, the unfortunate Bastard of Bourbon.

The dauphin was pardoned with a good deal of calculated and well publicized festivity. On a pleasant greensward by the river Seine, while a band of music softly played and some fireworks were shot off to amuse a great crowd of influential townspeople who were invited to a feast to celebrate the event, King Charles ostentatiously threw his arm across his son's broad shoulders, graciously welcoming him home, and gently recalling him to his duty in a long speech, ending with an affectionate, "Remember thou."

Margaret stood faithfully by his side; his mother the queen smiled tearfully. Deeply moved, the dauphin made a motion as if to kneel and embrace his father's knees, but the king restrained him. "Wait," he said pleasantly. "Let me show you something."

A man came leading an ape by a chain; another came leading a gaunt and hungry dog, apparently starved for the occasion. A third, with a squad of pikemen, came leading Alexander, Bastard of Bourbon. His chain was painted gold to mock him, and he was clad in the violet cloak of mourning permitted a prince of the blood. He was comely, and the lineaments of his features were strikingly like those of the royal Valois. He walked unsteadily and stared straight ahead of him with dull, unseeing eyes. Near the fringe of the crowd some of the people began to mutter that they were being cheated, that the traitor had been drugged.

"I think I shall retire," the queen said. "I never find this amusing. Margaret, I should advise you to come with me."

The pikemen seized the animals and the man and tied them all together by their chains and sewed them up in a huge sack and heaved it into the river. The music fell silent until the screams, both brute and human, grew faint as the current carried the sack some little distance downstream. Then it sank, and the water mercifully strangled the cries.

"You may be assured I shall remember," the dauphin said. He had learned a lesson in kingcraft. But he no longer wished to embrace his father's knees.

Chapter Eleven

The speech of pardon which the king had memorized and so adequately delivered by no means reflected his private feelings. Vaguely, as if by instinct, he had begun to fear the dauphin. "I did not like the look on Louis's face when he witnessed my justice. *He* should have been in that sack."

To a degree the *conseil du roy* were also uneasy about the dauphin. It was contrary to their cherished policy of a single head for France that he should become too popular with the people, who were the power behind the Ordonnances and who constituted the king's only real strength. But to punish him would only make him a martyr and further disrupt a realm already torn by faction.

Then in a darkly inspired moment the king's chamberlain, Pierre de Brézé, whispered a suggestion into the king's ear. De Brézé had a triple claim to Charles's favor. He had spent many years fighting the English. He held thoroughly opportunistic views of the functions of a statesman. And he considered no avenue devious, no device obscene, so long as it ministered to the king's pleasure. It was De Brézé who had seen in the woman of Fromanteau a means of advancing himself. Now he saw in the Bible a device to get rid of the dauphin.

In the days of King David, De Brézé said, Uriah the Hittite stood in a king's way. Had King Charles heard of King David? Assuredly, the king replied, but he could not quite remember Uriah the Hittite. De Brézé shook his head sanctimoniously. Uriah was a great problem, he said, just like the dauphin. This was how King David handled the matter; he sent Uriah to fight in the forefront of battle, and Uriah had the misfortune to be slain.

The aging duke-archbishop was not present to warn the king that the devil can cite Scripture to his purpose or to supply the end of the story, which was ominous: the Lord arose in His wrath and thundered, Behold, I will raise up evil against thee out of thine own house. *Out of thine own house* would have been stressed by the duke-archbishop.

Lest the king do worse, the council agreed that the dauphin, now older and proven in battle, might well be sent away as nominal head of an army which was about to depart for the southern provinces, where a threatening situation was developing.

Those who dwell by the sea and are conversant with the behavior of tides have sometimes noted that the water does not everywhere ebb at a uniform rate, that indeed crosscurrents can be set up which temporarily inundate a section of beach at a time when from all other beaches the ocean is receding.

So it was now. A backwash of the English invaders welled out of Guienne and threatened Count Jean in the province of Black Armagnac.

Louis greeted his appointment as a challenge and rose to meet it with the febrile enthusiasm that had marked all his military activities and with the vigor of a man still young but learning fast. This was his first command. Now he could enlarge his sphere of action. Now he could grasp other means of distinguishing himself in the eyes of the world—and of his wife.

It would mean another separation, of course. But by now he had almost come to welcome them. Since the personal disaster of their wedding night, Margaret had never quite been able to hide the fear in her eyes whenever he approached her, though she was dutiful and submissive. That only made the situation more difficult and kept the shame

62

green in the dauphin's memory. He had hoped a few years would erase the tragedy; seven had not. He had counted on a child; there was no child yet, and Margaret no longer mentioned the possibility.

She had gathered a little library of books and had set up a writing desk with paper and pens and other monkish paraphernalia in a pleasant room adjoining their bedchamber, an astonishing thing for a lady to do and a source of considerable lifting of eyebrows among the court.

One day Louis fretted, "When I am away you write for me to return, but when I return you sit up till dawn and write poetry."

"My dear lord," the dauphiness replied, looking down. "I will toss all my books into the moat if that would please you."

"No," Louis said, helpless before such submission, "No. Never mind." Later he quipped good-naturedly, "It would seem that to compete with your epics I shall have to be epic too, eh?"

She did not understand, and he did not press the point.

On the eve of the dauphin's departure for the south, De Brézé gave a sumptuous banquet to honor the event. He spoke disparagingly of the English intrusion into Armagnac, calling it a minor disturbance that would crumble before the victorious advance of the dauphin.

De Brézé had been a great favorite with the ladies of the last generation, and was still renowned for his wit. He wore a beard, the only man at court who did, beards having lately fallen out of fashion. De Brézé's, as some fading belles of the late king's reign could have told you, hid a singularly receding chin, no more prominent than a trout's, but he tinted it flaming red and trained it into a neat little fork, and it gave him a certain satanic air of distinction.

The meats were rich, the wines were strong, and the guests were gay. Near the end of the festivities De Brézé toasted, praised, and overpraised the dauphin to his face, calling him redoubtable, victorious, and "peerless peer of France." "Peerless peer" was a graceful tribute and well deserved, but De Brézé, sustaining his reputation as a wit, gave it a twist possible only to his own sly tongue and the infinite subtleties of the French language: a certain intonation, little more than a breathing at the end of a word, gave it the double meaning of both "father-forsaken bastard," at which Charles exploded with laughter, and, far worse, "Prince Gelding," a lewd and sneering jibe at the dauphin's childlessness.

Margaret fortunately missed the allusion, which required more knowledge of the gutter speech of Paris than she possessed. Louis's jaw muscles tensed as he controlled his resentment; he would only make himself more ridiculous by showing his anger and hurt. King Charles, as the broad implication of the jest penetrated his slow wits, tossed down a great draught of wine, wiped his rather pendulous mouth with the back of his hand, and shook with coarse laughter. "*Pair sans pair, pair sans père*, but especially *pair sans paire!* My lords, let us hope that the dauphin returns to us better equipped than he leaves!"

Louis glanced round at the wine-flushed leering faces. They did not impress him as particularly formidable; merely foolish. He was sober and they were tipsy. It would be an effort to join in laughter at his own expense, but by doing so he saw a way to blunt the edge of the ridicule and gain, perhaps, something that the expedition sorely needed. For the first time in his life he understood how the street entertainers, the jongleurs and mummers whose antics had always made him cringe, were able to make fools of themselves in public: the more the crowds laughed, the more tangible were the benefits to the performers. Pricked by challenge, his genius for turning his weaknesses into strength was growing.

He put on a wonderfully ingenuous and convincing smile. "My lords," he said, "I have been at some pains to examine my equipment—"

They roared and pounded the table, shouting with laughter.

"—which, as you know, came from my father and is the best, I suppose, that can be expected—"

"Good lad!" Bernard d'Armagnac muttered. "He deserved that."

Now they all turned their laughter toward the king. The king looked accusingly at De Brézé. "What is funny?"

"Nothing is funny," De Brézé quickly said. It was time to bring the repartee out of the realm of the abstract. "His Highness seems to have some complaint about the expedition's equipment."

"You said it was fully equipped."

"And so it is, Your Highness."

"Then what's he complaining about?"

"The men are good," Louis said, knowing that his words would be quoted, "stout-hearted and bold."

The king asked, "What more do you want?"

"I want guns." The dauphin nodded toward Jean Bureau at the foot of the table. "And an engineer to command them. There is not a single piece of ordnance in the entire expedition."

"Bureau is needed here," the king said. De Brézé said that artillery was not necessary against a few marauding bands of English longbowmen, who would flee at the dauphin's approach. He tried to imply that there was something unchivalrous in gunpowder. But he dared not go on record as publicly refusing guns. He turned to Bernard. "My lord d'Armagnac, you come from the south. Are your cities not proof against a handful of Englishmen?"

"The city of Auch is safe," Bernard asserted confidently. But as he recalled the unstable character of his nephew, Jean, his instinct warned him to add, "It would be prudent, however, to supply a few guns to my kinsman's capital, which is closer to the border than mine." Bernard was uneasy at reports that the English were openly exposing themselves in the vicinity of Lectoure. Such deep penetration into Black Armagnac implied either lethargy on the part of Count Jean or something worse, perhaps some tacit understanding between his nephew and the English. Jean d'Armagnac would not have been the first to have intrigued with

64

them. But Bernard was loyal to his House and kept his own counsel. There would be time enough to sound the dark currents of his nephew's mind when the expedition arrived in the south.

"If I supplied guns to every vassal who demanded them," the king said, "there would be none left to protect Paris. Nevertheless, we shall find some artillery, shan't we, De Brézé?"

"Assuredly, Sire," De Brézé replied. He knew the very gun.

"And Jean Bureau?" the dauphin persisted.

The king shook his head. "I cannot spare him. How about young Henri LeClercq?"

Louis was satisfied. "He will do admirably."

"Oh, no!" Bernard shook his head with more vehemence than the wholly reasonable suggestion seemed to justify.

"Why not?" De Brézé demanded suspiciously.

"Henri LeClercq is a thoroughly competent engineer," Jean Bureau spoke up from the foot of the table. "A deadly marksman and a capable strategist, he also speaks Latin and plays the lute with great skill." Bureau was proud of his engineers. Not many men in the corps could meet the gentry on a level of cultural equality; he was glad to advance the name of one of the few who could.

The dauphin smiled. "I know about the lute. But I do not envisage an expedition encumbered with women." Margaret lowered her eyes.

"You're missing the best part," chuckled the king.

Friar Jean Majoris and Bernard d'Armagnac exchanged glances. The two former tutors, now permanently attached to the dauphin's suite, understood and respected each other. Friar Jean was telling Bernard that he had got himself into an ambush and had better get himself out. De Brézé was staring at them, his little forked beard jittering inquisitively like the antennae of an insect. He sensed a secret here.

Once before Bernard d'Armagnac had intervened in the life of Henri LeClercq, wishing him well but forcibly removing recognition from his path, thrusting him back into obscurity. Now he must do so again. Henri and Jean d'Armagnac face to face, as would inevitably happen if Henri joined the expedition, presented a picture to his mind's eye so fraught with unpleasant possibilities that it could not be entertained.

To exclude Henri LeClercq while the jovial mood still prevailed at the banquet required merely one more joviality: "Jean Bureau must have another engineer just as able, at least as far as fighting ability is concerned. The dauphin has indicated that skill with a cannon against an enemy is preferable to skill with a lute against the ladies."

King Charles toasted the ladies thickly, "May the pretty little things never be enemies!"

"If you choose me a good marksman," Louis said, "I do not care who he is." He was content to have turned aside the ridicule and to have procured some artillery for his small forces.

Bernard d'Armagnac was content to have played the guardian angel, unseen and unsuspected, for his unknown and distant relative.

Pierre de Brézé was never content with anything. He had never scrupled to advance himself by playing the pimp for King Charles. The ingenious idea now struck him that Margaret was likely to be lonely during the dauphin's absence. She had a loyal personal circle of friends at court; she was popular with both the king and the queen. A tall and personable lute-playing engineer might provide just the proper touch of scandal to ruin her, divide the dauphin's friends, and sully his memory with the people when word came, as word would come, that the dauphin had been blown to bits by a piece of artillery that his generous father had provided against the English.

Chapter Twelve

Early in June, in a month of dry, good fighting weather, the dauphin departed. There appeared in his train one of the largest, shiniest cannon ever seen in France. It was mounted on a carriage of four wheels; the muzzle was so wide a man could put his head into it; it was polished till it shone like gold. Louis would have preferred a wagonload of rapid-firing, breech-loading small-caliber cannon of wrought iron; but this theatrical brass monster was all he could get. The people of Paris, lining the streets to cheer the departing expedition, were awed by its size. The dauphin's own soldiers, mistaking its dimensions for efficiency, patted its smooth flanks affectionately and boasted to their wives and wenches that with such a weapon they would not be long away from home. Perforce, Louis expressed himself satisfied. The cumbersome piece could only be fired three times an hour, but since it contributed to the morale of his men it performed a valuable function.

Margaret stood on the battlements above the gate of the Hôtel des Tournelles, surrounded by her maids and matrons of honor, all dressed in gay holiday gowns, waving brightly colored wisps of handkerchiefs as so often in the past when he had ridden away. Through her mind there flashed a doggerel couplet from one of those catch tunes that were forever working up from anonymous song writers of the slums, irreverent and cynical but breathing the disillusionment of the day:

> I never love my love so dear
> As when my love is nowhere near.

A vagabond by the name of François Villon was said to have written it, and a great many more. No one really cared who wrote them; everybody sang them. They were spicy and tickling to a jaded taste. From the quiet of his archiepiscopal palace, the Duke-Archbishop of Reims wrote elegant Latin letters to the Holy Father deploring the impudence of secular ballades and suggesting curbs on poets like François Villon. The Holy Father replied in a gorgeously engrossed but wearily worded scroll that greater issues were at stake: Eastern Christendom was tottering to its fall, the Turks might threaten Europe itself, and his venerable brother of the Gallic Church would better serve mankind by uniting France in a Crusade against the Infidel than by frittering away his energy in complaints against one beggarly balladeer. In a spirited passage the pope declared that King Charles, whom he blessed with conspicuous restraint, might make a worthy contribution to unity by repealing the iniquitous Pragmatic of Bourges, an ordinance which threatened to infect the French Church with the same chaos as now infected the French nobility. Nothing came of this correspondence. Villon continued to scribble his witty little scatologies, and Margaret, sitting alone in her library, penned lonesome, tender missives to the dauphin. This time, for some reason, he did not reply.

De Brézé observed her closely as a week and then a month went by, watching the play of her mood. Margaret would never achieve the patient resignation of the queen. In a larger setting her sensitive nature might have dedicated itself to some great ideal. In a convent she might have become a saint. Born a commoner, she might have become another Jeanne d'Arc. But in the narrowly circumscribed sphere of a dauphiness, dutiless, childless, and much alone, ardent, overflowing with vitality and nothing to spend it on, her temper was erratic and unpredictable. Reading could still charm her, but where as a bride little more than a child the romances had read like some hazy and golden dream, they now painted pictures in her mind that were sharply human. Her poetry too had grown up. One day the queen was alarmed to read a verse in which a lover was described as sweating.

"Sweating!" murmured the queen. "My dear, what a horrid word."

"Men do," she retorted. "That's how God created them."

"He created women to ignore it, or gently to wipe it away without a word."

Margaret's volatile spirit instantly shifted to the other extreme. She tore up the poem and flung the scraps from the window, tears in her eyes. "I am vile, vile, vile!"

The queen put her arm comfortingly around her shoulder. "You are sweet. And the sweetest thing in your heart is a love big enough to embrace and understand the duty of a queen, which is sixteen million times as heavy as other women's. That is the population of this great land of France. That will be the splendid multitude of your subjects, who will look to you and love you and expect you to be more than a woman easily can be because you are queen."

"I shall never be queen."

"Nonsense. King Charles will not live forever."

"Neither, thank God, shall I."

In one such forlorn and lonely mood, when the emptiness of her life seemed to hem her in like a wall, exerting a palpable force, setting her apart from the rest of the world, De Brézé presented her with a mirror like nothing she had ever seen before. Till now, like every other lady of quality, she had seen her face only in a handsome, but small, hand mirror of polished metal, from which every day one of her ladies would remove the tarnish. De Brézé's gift was a full-length sheet of flawless Venetian crystal, clear as the air she breathed, so wonderfully transparent that she touched it hesitantly, fearful of magic, half suspecting to feel the warm flesh of her own image. "Oh," she said, laughing like a child, "I thought my finger would go in, like water!" Then she blushed. "But it shows me all the way down!"

"That is how men see you," De Brézé said. "It would be folly for a charming woman to hide from herself what charms everyone else."

"It is beautiful, Monsieur de Brézé."

"It is beautiful when it reflects beauty, Madame la Dauphine." Presently he left her, to let the mirror work its magic. She must be very unlike other women if the wonderful Venetian invention did not fan the spark of vanity. He mentioned casually in parting: "I must inspect a cannon foundry this afternoon. It might amuse Your Highness to accompany me and see how artillery is made."

Alone, she looked at herself in the glass. The dauphiness had two maids of honor, whose Christian names by a pretty chance happened to be the same as her own, Marguerite de Salignac and Marguerite de Hacqueville. She had often complimented Mademoiselle de Hacqueville on the beauty of her hair, shrugging aside the answer that her own was more beautiful still. She had put her thoughts into a playful verse:

> If I were a man I'd boldly steal
> A tress of the lady of Hacqueville,
> And wear it on my helm of steel.

Mademoiselle de Salignac, who wore clothes superbly, wanted a poem too. Margaret laughed, "Your charms, *mon amie*, are more intimate. I really do not know how to do you justice and still phrase it politely."

She wrote:

> If I were a man I'd pick the lock
> Of her door when the lady of Salignac
> Slips into bed without her frock.

68

"What a dreadfully obvious person I must be!" Marguerite de Salignac had replied, pretending to be shocked. "If you were a man, Madame la Dauphine, you would not find my door locked against you."

The clear Venetian mirror, sitting in judgment upon the flattery, pronounced it valid. Her black hair was as pretty as Mademoiselle de Hacqueville's, and far more interesting, since she had blue eyes and Mademoiselle de Hacqueville's were only brown. As for Mademoiselle de Salignac's figure, which caused so much comment, the candid eye of the great glass mirror saw nothing wrong with her own—perhaps her gown was a little more formal and less revealing. Margaret had always dressed quietly, like the queen.

What in the world did one wear to a cannon foundry? Something light—the place was sure to be hot; something not too long—the floor was probably littered with gunpowder and brimstone. Gunpowder in her skirts! How would she explain that to the dauphin? But what a fascinating conceit, what a refrain for a ballade à la Villon:

> Beware the thralldom of the flirt
> With eyes of blue and gorge ungirt,
> And gunpowder in her skirt!

She would not unlace the points of her bodice like a flower girl in the streets, and she never played the flirt. How was it a mirror could put such ideas into her head? "Thou'rt a sorcering piece of glass. Why does more come out than goes into thee?" Her image stood before her, life-sized and frighteningly like another person in the room, asking her the same question.

She chose a bare-armed gown with a lacy bodice and cool silk skirt. It exposed her ankles, which was daring for a dauphiness, and some elderly eyebrows would probably be lifted disapprovingly, but it would not drag on the foundry floor. She hesitated whether she ought to drape something over the mirror when she changed. The absurdity of the notion made her smile. "Shy of yourself, Madame la Dauphine, when Marguerite de Hacqueville dresses you and Marguerite de Salignac bathes you and you are not shy of them? This is *yourself!*"

She watched herself slip into the gown. The mirror pronounced her adorable. She drew very close, and all at once she shyly kissed the image on its lips.

"Me!"

A strange little thing happened. The imprint of her lips remained visible as if suspended in the air for a misty moment, and vanished. Ghostly kisses etched in breath that disappear in an instant set too many memories to stirring. She wondered what it meant, and decided it meant nothing, but she wished she had not seen it. She would kiss no more mirrors.

The gun-founding establishment of Jean Bureau was a squat, ugly building begrimed with smoke and age, built as a fortress beside the Seine in the days before Paris had outgrown its river isles. Now it lay within the metropolitan walls, but its own stout walls had never been torn down, and found themselves for the first time in centuries repaired and stood watch upon. Heavy barges pulled by long mule teams from a towpath on the bank inched their way against the current and came to a halt by the quayside, where a gang of leather-clad longshoremen made them fast. The barges rode low in the water under the weight of enormously heavy cargoes. Some of them were easily recognizable: ingots of brass and iron, black lumps of coal, which grunting, sweating workmen heaved into carts and wheeled into the foundry. Some cargoes were carefully sacked, and one was carried into a separate building.

"Niter and Sicilian sulphur," De Brézé said with an air of authority. "For gunpowder."

Margaret nodded intelligently; niter and sulphur had a grim and warlike sound. Sicily was notorious for its bloody revolutions; probably Sicilian sulphur was more explosive than most.

"But what is *that* barge—with Bacchus at the helm?" She laughed in spite of herself. A smaller barge was drawing up to the quay with a monstrous fat man at the steering sweep. He had cast off all his clothes in the heat, retaining only his drawers, the drawstring of which was straining hard against his pendulous abdomen, threatening to give way at any moment. In his ragged hat he had stuck a crown of dogwood leaves to shade him from the sun, and with one hand he waved a wand, apparently cut from a weeping willow tree, to scare away the flies, who seemed to like him. From time to time he refreshed himself from a jug of wine with a spout. He held it a foot above his open inviting mouth; the thin red stream arched down in a graceful parabola; swallowing would have insulted it; it flowed home without a pause. The barge was laden with freshly peeled logs.

"I'm afraid I don't know," De Brézé said. "The manufacture of gunpowder is a closely guarded secret. Perhaps Maître LeClercq will tell you."

"Henri LeClercq?"

"You know him?" De Brézé had not expected a first-name acquaintanceship.

"An artilleryman of that name is known to the dauphin."

"Rather tall? Rather handsome—for a bastard?"

"I'm sure I don't know. It was on my wedding night."

Pierre de Brézé hid a wry grin in his flame-colored adder's tongue of a beard. So the dauphiness remembered somebody from her wedding night, somebody who wasn't her husband! This might be easier than he had thought.

"Captain LeClercq is in charge of the arsenal today. A highly respected engineer. I have asked him to show us around. From no one else could you learn so much."

70

At the entrance two sentries challenged them. De Brézé's beard twitched angrily. *"Mort de Dieu!* Don't you know us?" It looked for a moment as if he were about to shoulder them aside, but he changed his mind when they crossed their pikes and barred the way. He glanced up at the portcullis. The ancient ironwork had been replaced by a new steel grille with polished spikes at the bottom. The guide-way was freshly greased. He had a notion that the touch of a hidden lever would send it crashing down at a moment's notice. From the dark interior of the building they heard the sound of hammering; a wave of heat heavy with strange metallic smells issued from the gate; inside they could see fires burning.

"Of course we know you, Monsieur de Brézé," one of the sentries replied, "and Madame la Dauphine." It was something of a comedy to see them both bow low without uncrossing their pikes, which still barred the way. "Captain LeClercq will be here at once; he is expecting you. Perhaps he is changing his shirt. There was a little accident."

"To the captain?"

"One of the powdermen, Madame la Dauphine. There was a regrettable conflagration in the mixing room. The captain refused to let him burn to death, though it was the man's own fault, and got dirty dragging him away from the flames. It is a pity this had to happen today when Your Highness honors us with a visit."

"We shall wait for the captain," Margaret said. The grim low gate of the ancient structure, with its acrid smells and glimpses of sultry flames, where regrettable conflagrations occurred, reminded her strongly of Dante's description of the gates of Hell. De Brézé heard her murmur, *"Lasciate ogni speranza voi ch'entrate!* This is a fearsome place."

As she spoke the pikes uncrossed, the sentries stood back, and the captain greeted them. He dropped to one knee and kissed the hand she extended. "On the contrary, Madame la Dauphine, those who enter here should gain new hope for France, not abandon it. My tutor taught me that Dante also said, *Fecemi la divina potestate, la somma sapienza.* Power and wisdom have a place here."

Margaret smiled, "Did your tutor go on, Maître Henri? *E il primo amore?"*

"As for love, Madame, I cannot say. Love and cannon do not mix."

De Brézé thought perhaps they did and perhaps they didn't. The Italian exchange had eluded him, but it pleased him to see Henri LeClercq and the dauphiness already on common ground. "Show us this Inferno of yours, Captain LeClercq. How does it happen that your guards are armed only with pikes on the very spot where the deadliest weapons in the world are manufactured? I expected muskets."

"Oh, that," Henri said.

"The dauphin often mentions the military mind," Margaret said. "You are reputed to be a conservative folk."

"It would never do, Madame la Dauphine, for English spies to kidnap these fellows and steal their firearms and copy the design. So we give them pikes."

He led them through the gate and into what had once been the great hall of the ancient château. Forges blazed on every side, with husky varlets working enormous bellows; steady flames roared up the flues; heating ingots, turned like roasting meat by half naked, sweating workmen with long-handled wicked-looking tongs, slowly came to a white glow on the coals. Brawny smiths with massive hammers, bodies protected from flying sparks by thick leather aprons, pounded and shaped the ingots into slender rods on anvils of enormous dimensions. No blacksmith ever saw such anvils. As the iron rods slowly changed from the size of a man's arm to the size of a man's thumb, lengthening proportionately as the diameter diminished, a technician snipped them to a cannon length. "We braze them together into a cylinder and reinforce them with annular bands of tempered steel," Henri explained. He had to raise his voice to be heard above the din and speak close to her ear. She bent her head toward him to listen. "Much stronger and lighter than castings. These are the small rapid-fire pieces."

The fire and heat and noise and novelty of the place excited her, though all seemed chaos and disorder, and nowhere in her romances had she encountered such terms as "brazing" and "annular bands." But in another room, where the pieces were being assembled and mounted, she recognized the finished product. They were trim little cannon, small and light enough for half a dozen to be carried on an ordinary farm wagon. This was the sort of ordnance the dauphin had asked for and been refused. In battle it was deadly against personnel, wreaking a havoc and causing a dread like no military invention since in ancient days some genius had hit on the idea of fixing long scythes to the hubs of war chariots. These gun wagons possessed the mobility of ships, thundering into the ranks of the enemy, showering them with armor-piercing missiles of iron, pronouncing with foul gunpowder breath the doom of the cataphract and the end of the age of chivalry. No shining knight ever threw down his glove in stately *défi* at a cannon's muzzle. Battles were noisier now; the shining knight could not have made himself heard. Nor would the base-born engineer with his match at the touchhole have withheld his fire. A new generation of warriors, proud of their wonderful weapons, contemptuous of the old rules and, like the dauphin, dedicated solely to winning, had changed the art of war. It was impersonal now, soulless, incredibly effective.

In another room muskets were being made. "Some day," Henri said, "we will make them with two barrels. But so far no one has been able to solve the problem of weight." He took a finished piece from a workman and let Margaret feel its weight. She could not have held it if he had not largely supported it with his own hand. It was a tube of wrought iron mounted on a crossbow stock and fired, like a cannon, by applying a slow match to a vent. Strips of red-hot iron were hammered round a form, the seam was brazed shut, and the form withdrawn a little at a time as the brazing progressed. The trick was to keep advancing the form lest the iron being shaped around it contract as it cooled and "freeze" into a solid piece. "If that happened, you would not have the tube necessary for a musket."

"How was the dauphin's big brass cannon made, Maître Henri?"

"That was a casting, Madame." He seemed to hesitate.

"Surely the dauphiness can be trusted with your secrets, Captain," De Brézé said.

"It is not that, Monsieur de Brézé. The casting foundry is—"

"No place for a lady?" De Brézé laughed, waving an elegant hand at the half-stripped gnome-like workmen gleaming with sweat as they labored before their forges, directing all their attention to their exacting work save now and then when one of them wistfully hazarded a fleeting glance, as from another plane of existence, at the delicate creature who had appeared momentarily in their sweltering low-born world. "Madame la Dauphine has given no indication that she finds the men in this place repugnant to her."

"I do not," she said, looking at Henri. She quickly added, "The artificers who equipped my husband's troops I count my friends."

"I did not mean the men," Henri said. "They have to dress that way in this atmosphere. I just meant that we are pouring a cannon today, and there is always the possibility of an accident. Sometimes the metal boils over; once a crucible cracked."

"You can hardly refuse the dauphiness if she commands you."

Margaret did not like to be crossed; she was reluctant to leave the presence of this interesting engineer who was reputed to speak Latin and play the lute and who had just quoted fine Italian verses. "I think I shall be safe; Captain LeClercq seems to be good at everything."

"Stand close to me then, and do not go wandering off toward the big crucible."

"Yes, *Monseigneur* LeClercq," she smiled, and passed her bare arm through the crook of his elbow quite unexpectedly. "Will this do?"

Henri was conscious that soot from the fire might be clinging to his clothes. "I'm afraid you'll get dirty, Madame la Dauphine."

Dirty, dirty, dirty, sang jubilantly in De Brézé's mind. If only he had had the wit to arrange for the king and queen to see them at their first meeting. He had counted on things to take a little longer to run their natural course. If only that proper and garrulous D'Estouteville or gossipy Jamet de Tillay, the most venomous old busybody of the court, could walk in at this moment. How the word would spread! And he would do his part too. How quickly the world would be whispering about this poetry-scribbling, vain, light-minded dauphiness who spent all her time looking at herself in a great glass mirror that she had imported from Venice at fabulous expense to the taxpayers, flirting with a base-born, nay, with a bastard, engineer while her husband was away getting himself killed with a cracked cannon cast by this very bastard!

"Brass casting differs in several important essentials from iron working," Henri said. He led her and De Brézé from the iron foundry to the brass foundry.

"*Tiens, tiens!*" murmured the dauphiness, leaning on his arm and smiling merrily up at him. The little and absolutely untranslatable word was a sly reproof at such solemnity, like "You don't say!" or, "What do I know or care about these technicalities?"

"Is it really true that you play the lute, Maître Henri? It is hard to believe."

"Very seldom any more." There was a new note in his voice, and she sensed that she had touched on a subject that for some reason was painful to him. He was more at ease talking about his beloved cannon.

The brass foundry was another large high-ceilinged room. At the door a strange, unnatural current of air, such as is sometimes encountered at the entrance to caves, blew on their backs and rustled the dauphiness's skirts around her ankles. There was no hammering here, only a steady, deep-throated roaring from the biggest fire yet seen. In a corner a great iron pot, tall as a man, sat on a support of firebrick; the fire underneath was too bright to look at without hurting the eyes. Standing on a platform at the rim of the crucible, which was red-hot, a man reached in with a long iron bar and stirred the brew. An assistant continually dipped a sponge into a bucket of water and dowsed his body against the heat like a cook basting a roast. As the man lifted the stirring rod, testing the viscosity of the melt, liquid brass streamed like self-luminous water from its end. Over the darkly glowing red belly of the crucible pin points of intensely white sparks began to appear, flaring and fading like instantaneous stars, a shimmering effect of weird, dynamic beauty confusing to the eye.

Despite the heat, which beat like a wave against her face, Margaret would have stepped closer to the great red glowing thing that beckoned with hypnotic fascination, but Henri's arm clamped hard on hers and stopped her. "Beyond this point it is not safe to go."

The sparks on the surface of the crucible must have had some technological significance. The foreman beat with a hammer against a long iron bar suspended from the ceiling; it rang like a great bell and filled the room with a warning signal at which all the men scurried out of the way. The man with the stirring rod threw it down and leaped off the platform to safety. The black-faced gnome-like sweaty men all turned their eyes expectantly in Margaret's direction, but she realized they were not looking at her. They were looking to Henri, as if now were time for him to do some habitual thing. She felt herself passed without so much as a by-your-leave from Henri's arm to De Brézé's arm. Henri walked up to the base of the crucible, seized a mallet in his hand, and knocked out a plug that protruded from its base.

74

There was a thump, a heavy splash, and a hissing noise as a jet of liquid fire-colored brass leaped out of the pour-hole of the crucible and cascaded into the sand mold just below. There seemed to be no motion in the fiery arc of metal, since it was too heavy to fall like water; it glowed, as it were, suspended in the air, little blue flames licking at its surface, while all the men watched with fixed, intent faces. It was an anxious moment. The melt in the crucible, though carefully measured, was sometimes scant, and then the cannon was too short, for no one had discovered a way of making a casting in two separate pourings. Sometimes there was too much metal, and then the mold would overflow, with consequent peril to the workmen and detriment to the cannon, since all the extra metal would have to be chipped away after it had cooled and the muzzle was never so strong as if it had annealed naturally in the mold.

This pouring happened to go exactly right; Margaret wondered why the men suddenly cheered, why Henri grinned, pressed his finger and thumb together in a circle in the direction of the foreman, and returned to her and De Brézé so pleased with himself.

"You have brought us luck, Madame la Dauphine!"

The metal in the crucible had run out just as the level in the mold had risen to the brim. A thin sagging string of rapidly darkening brass like a natal cord was all that connected the perfect cast shell of the new cannon with the iron pot that had given it birth and under which the fire could now be allowed to die.

"How do you know it is perfect underneath, Maître Henri? All I see is a ring of metal on the surface of the sand; the rest is hidden. If you have eyes that can see through opacities, a lady has great cause to be uncomfortable in your presence."

"*Tiens!*" De Brézé smiled. With Margaret leading him on at this rate, he had better call the witnesses today.

Henri said: "I could tell by the way it poured, by the absence of bubbles, by the thin crust, by the smooth sound as the mold filled. It will be a beautiful gun!"

"One would think you loved them."

"I do—the perfect ones. Many of them, unfortunately, are not. When the mold is broken, you find weak spots, cracks, blowholes, tiny flaws scarcely visible to the eye—"

"It is extremely hot in here," De Brézé said. "Madame la Dauphine has seen the best; surely she cannot be interested in the flaws."

"On the contrary," Margaret smiled, "I am quite interested in the captain's flaws. I was beginning to think he did not have any. What do you do with the flawed cannon, Maître Henri?"

Henri was conscious of the playful badinage; he would be the butt of many good-natured jokes tomorrow on the conquest he had made, for the men were by no means as stupid or as deaf to the conversation as their perfectly expressionless faces seemed to indicate. It occasionally happened that great ladies would visit the foundry and make such coquettish remarks from the safe height of their other world and exalted birth. He had not expected such play from the dauphiness, whom he had always revered.

He said, rather unimaginatively, "We throw them on the scrap heap and break them up and recast them. Come. I'll show you."

"I am sure Madame la Dauphine has seen enough for one day," De Brézé said quickly.

"I want to see everything."

It was cooler in the courtyard. There, in a mound against a wall, he showed her the defective cannon. The faults in some were obvious deep pockmarks, gaping ragged holes where the metal had not closed. Others looked perfect to the eye. "But even the tiniest crack," Henri said, "would cause a catastrophe."

Suddenly he caught his breath. He knew the scrap pile like the palm of his hand. A gun, a gun like the one the dauphin had taken on the expedition to the south, was missing. The deadly possibilities, the somber implications of its disappearance, flashed through his mind. He glanced at the dauphiness, coquetting so mischievously with him; at De Brézé, who was glaring at him suspiciously; and back again to the pile of worthless pieces of ordnance.

"Well, what are you staring at," De Brézé asked.

Henri's whole manner changed. "Madame la Dauphine must be gathering a woeful impression of the king's engineers, Monsieur de Brézé. All these failures! I can never bring myself to look at them for long. Come. Let me show you the rest of the establishment." He led them out of the courtyard, to De Brézé's immense relief.

At the powder building, however, he paused. "I should not advise your going in today. There was an accident in one of the charcoal kilns. A whole batch took fire and was spoiled. If there are any live sparks still lying about—the possibility of an explosion is remote, of course, nevertheless it would be safer for you, and for Monsieur de Brézé too, to come back at another time. I'll have got some new wood by then, and if you like you can watch the whole process."

"If there is danger of an explosion," De Brézé said, "Madame la Dauphine should definitely not enter."

"I saw a funny man on a barge of wood," Margaret said. "I wondered what it was for."

"It was dogwood and willow, one for fast-burning powder, one for slow. He'll have to go back for more, and I'll probably have to go with him. I like to pick out my own trees."

It seemed to Margaret that Captain Henri LeClercq was churlishly unresponsive to her attentions, actually anxious to get rid of her. But De Brézé spoke up, all smiling white teeth and twitching red beard. "My dear fellow, did you say you were going on the barge too? What a charming excursion it would be for Madame la Dauphine! After all this heat, it would be so cool and refreshing. The river is exquisite, the breezes, the picturesque mule teams on the towpath! I doubt if she has ever experienced anything like it. Why not go with Captain LeClercq, Madame?"

An hour before she would have welcomed the adventure. Now she hesitated. Much of her mirror-evoked mood had vanished. The day was wearing on toward evening, she was fatigued—and floating down the Seine on a barge was a bit unconventional for a dauphiness even though it would be novel and exciting. "You are coming, De Brézé?"

"Alas, Madame, I have an appointment with the king."

"It is a very short trip, Madame," Henri said eagerly. Suddenly he seemed anxious for her to come. "The trees I want grow just below the place where the fireworks were set off."

"Where the Bastard of Bourbon was executed," De Brézé reminded her. "What a superb banquet that was!"

Margaret hated De Brézé for that; the dauphin had been implicated in the same revolt. She said stiffly, "I think I shall find Captain LeClercq's company very welcome."

"That is my hope, Madame. Adieu, Madame; adieu, *mon capitaine*; *joyeuse voyage!* Now I must hurry to my appointment."

The bacchanalian figure of the helmsman, clothed in less pagan a fashion now that the heat of the day was past, welcomed them aboard; he spread a clean mattress of willows for them to sit upon on the little deck in the stern of the barge, volubly regretting that the bulkhead shut off a view of the beauties of the shore and heavily suggesting that the selfsame bulkhead shut off with equal effectiveness the view, from the shore, of the deck. And as if he had not already made his meaning abundantly clear, he confided how an old wound in the head had greatly impaired his eyesight and hearing. On which he hallooed loudly to the muleteers, and the barge pulled away from the quayside.

De Brézé kissed his fingers gaily toward them and instantly went off to fetch the king and queen, revolving sly phrases on his tongue, searching the one best suited to prepare them for the scene which, in his mind's eye, he already pictured in clear and vivid detail: the dauphiness and her lover in a compromising situation. The king would be particularly incensed. Margaret's beauty and inaccessibility had always excited him. He was prudish where she was concerned.

Margaret's light-hearted mood now made a complete turnabout. She was frightened to find herself adrift on the Seine with darkness coming on, a deaf-blind man for a pilot, and for a companion a mannerless engineer who suddenly leaned toward her, grasped her wrist with a grip no woman could break, and thrust his lips so close to her cheek that his hair and hers must have intermingled: "It would be extremely dangerous not to grant me a certain request!"

Chapter Thirteen

The defective piece of ordnance could not have been removed from the scrap heap and issued to the dauphin without connivance on the part of personages high in the government, Henri told her earnestly. Jean Bureau, King Charles's close friend and adviser, had equipped the expedition. De Brézé, King Charles's boon companion, who had exhibited such nervousness when Henri showed Margaret the cracked cannon, was obviously in on the secret. Who else might be conspiring against the dauphin's life, perhaps even the king himself, Henri could only conjecture. "But clearly, Madame, the dauphin has made many jealous and vindictive enemies. It is only because of his great popularity that in order to destroy him they have resorted to trickery—and with my cannon!" he added angrily.

Margaret's face was stricken—fear for her husband, remorse and self-accusation for having enjoyed herself at a time when he was in danger. "My poor Louis! He is always making enemies. He rode away so gaily, so confident of victory. It was his first command; he kissed me when I told him how proud of him I was. Now he is dead!" She sobbed, and the helmsman cocked a curious ear.

"Sh-h!" Henri warned. "My corpulent friend is a sentimental soul, and only pretends to be hard of hearing and dim of sight. I'll prove it. Pierre!" he said in a conversational tone. There was no reply.

Without raising his voice he repeated, "Pierre, you are not listening to me."

"Yes, yes, Captain, I am listening. What are your orders?"

"You should not be listening," Henri said, and to Margaret, "See?"

"I see that no one is to be trusted," she said in a low voice, "save only yourself, and even of you how can I be sure?"

He could have answered that he liked the way the dauphin fought the English, that he admired him for the courage he exhibited when he headed an inadequately manned expedition to put down a revolt with artillery that he knew to be more showy than effective. He could have answered that his gun had fired the salute on the dauphin's wedding night, and the dauphin had given a lute and been friendly to a base-born engineer. He could have answered that Margaret had a lovely face and he would not care to see it veiled in a widow's veil. The answers sounded impertinent and self-seeking.

"For one thing," he said grimly, "I love my cannon and will not have them maligned. And also, if Your Highness were of a more practical turn of mind you would realize that any man who cast the gun that killed the dauphin will be sewn in a sack like the Bastard of Bourbon to appease your husband's friends and clear the reputations of his enemies. In ancient times, I was taught by my tutor, a goat would be solemnly cursed, tied around the neck with a red scarf, which was the color of shame, and chased into the wilderness to die, in the belief that the guilt of a lot of wicked people would perish with it. I would be that scapegoat. But I do not think the expedition is yet a failure or that the dauphin is dead. We should have heard by now. I have a plan, but I shall need help."

He was still whispering into her ear, still grasping her wrist. Margaret passed her hand over his in a gesture which caused the tubby helmsman to whistle a wistful tune at the moon, just rising over the graceful willows of the greensward where the banquet had been held and which they were now approaching. "Thou devoted, thou faithful, thou friend!" Thee-thouing was employed between lovers, or when a princess spoke to a subject she wished to praise warmly—or when anyone prayed for help to God. "A moment ago I was terrified when you said it would be dangerous not to grant you a certain request. I was a feather-witted fool. If you have a plan to save my husband, if he is still alive, tell me how I can be of help."

Henri raised his voice to the helmsman, "Let us off at the embankment." It was close to the palace. "You'll have to gather the wood alone tonight, Pierre."

It would be an honor and a privilege, the helmsman replied, to gather the wood, to be of any assistance. The spot where his passengers had been put ashore, for example—did Captain LeClercq have any suggestion as to what he should say about that, if asked? Monsieur de Brézé had made some mention of going to fetch the king and queen. Perhaps the lady would wish them directed to some more remote area. He knew of a beautiful swamp.

Margaret's eyes blazed. So that was why De Brézé had been so anxious to send her off on an intimate excursion with the artilleryman!

"If you are asked where you put us ashore," she said, "tell the truth!" and she whispered to Henri, "Truth is the one thing De Brézé won't believe."

"Softly, Madame," Henri smiled. But there was guile as well as justice in what Margaret said. De Brézé would probably lead Their Highnesses a weary, brambly chase through a number of sylvan hideaways before he ended up on the well groomed greensward so close to the royal residence. That would gain time, and Henri could use the time.

They took a gravel path that led them from the river, among the clipped hedges and lawns of the garden-like embankment, toward the palace. "Since no word has come of the tragedy that the dauphin's

enemies expect," Henri said, "there may still be time to avert it altogether."

"He should have written me," Margaret said, shaking her head. "He
always wrote before." There were tears in her eyes. "But Louis is subtle
and resourceful. Perhaps there is some reason for his silence."

"What I shall need, Madame, is a good sound horse with a thirty-league
wind to get me to Armagnac in two days! I am going to spike that cannon with my own hands!"

"A horse will be simple to arrange."

Henri struck his first into the palm of his open hand again and again.
"If only, if only I could bring him a gun wagon too! But there isn't time.
And how could I filch it out of the foundry? Who is there to trust if
Jean Bureau cannot be trusted?" He thought, but he did not say, And
King Charles too!

"Won't you need money as well?"

Henri was silent; money would help greatly, but he could not ask for it.

"Of course you'll need money. The dauphin often speaks of its importance." She embarrassed him with a purse which, when he counted its
contents next day, embarrassed him still more. But it bore witness to
the lengths she was willing to go to aid her husband.

She gave him one of the dauphin's hunters, a superb beast with a
magnificent chest. As he was about to depart, she said: "You will be
missed at the foundry. Is there anything I can do? Anything I can say?
Any excuse I can make?"

He shrugged. "It doesn't matter."

"Your home, Maître Henri? Madame your wife? Children, perhaps?"

"Dead, Madame, in the plague that the dirty English left behind when
we took Paris."

She did not meet his level look. She understood something of his pride
in his cannon now.

"Fare safely," she said, "fare swiftly with God; farewell."

Pierre de Brézé, beating the bushes in moonlit romantic spots along
the Seine with the king, the queen, Jamet de Tillay, and the Sieur d'Estouteville, found nothing but nesting thrushes and scurrying baby rabbits
and, after a tedious search, the bacchanalian bargeman chopping down
dogwood and willow trees by torchlight. The dauphiness, Your Excel-
lencies? 'Fore God, he had never seen Her Highness, not to his knowledge, he hadn't. A lady of that description had alighted hours ago at the
embankment and gone straight to the royal residence. Oh, yes, Your Ex-
cellencies, the light was good at that time. It was hardly sunset, 'fore God.

"I think," said the queen, "that you've made a fool of yourself, De
Brézé."

In her apartment again, standing before the mirror, Margaret made a
frightening discovery. The mirror reversed everything. Her wedding ring

was on her right hand, like a virgin nun's. She made the sign of the cross; her image crossed itself from right to left, the backward sign used by necromancers in the Black Mass.

"Thou traitor!" she cried. She would have smashed it—she had already picked up the inkpot from her writing desk—but fear fettered her hand. The cursed thing might take vengeance upon her.

It was to be many weeks before the dauphin returned with Friar Jean, his confessor, and before Friar Jean would explain that the inversion of a mirror is not black magic. The same phenomenon could be observed in woodland springs and natural pools, which God made good, nay, even in a font of holy water.

Meanwhile, however, she could not look in it, and draped it in a violet mourning cloak, and often wept.

In the south Louis pitched his tent and drew up his army before the gates of Lectoure. The gates were closed. This was the first overt act of rebellion the dauphin had encountered during the long march down from Paris through territory nominally loyal to the French crown. Everywhere else, as soon as he made it clear that Lectoure was his goal, that his passage would be rapid, and that nowhere did he plan to tarry, town gates had opened before him and municipal dignitaries had greeted him with speeches of loyalty. Loyal too were the peasants. They were accustomed to seeing their cattle slaughtered, their barns looted of fodder by every passing band of armed men; but now they saw a long line of wagons and sumpter mules accompanying the troops of the dauphin, laden with supplies for man and beast. Here was a prince, they told each other in wonderment, who supplied his own needs.

And the prince, quick to exploit an advantage, made them a series of extemporaneous speeches. Speaking before crowds was a newly discovered skill that he found, quite unexpectedly, he possessed, a skill that would grow in him and give him great sway over the illiterate masses. To himself he admitted: "They would listen as readily to any great lord, De Brézé, say, if he made things simple and stooped a bit to their level. But De Brézé will not stoop. There is value in it." When, therefore, they pulled off their sweaty hats and humbly thanked him for not robbing them, he promised that Louis the dauphin would never rob any man and that Louis the king, when God should see fit to call to Himself his royal father—years hence, they were all adjured to pray—would rob no man either. On the contrary, he would lighten taxes, ensure prosperity, render every man safe in his habitation, and bring about peace at home and abroad. "God helping me," he added, for it was a great deal to promise alone. They cheered him and prayed, but for him, not for his royal father.

Certain immediate results accrued to the expedition. What had not been demanded was freely given. A peasantry whose economy was notorious, who never would eat a fresh fowl if a rotten one might go to waste—inventing the delicious *pot pourri* in the process—loaded the supply wagons with prime beeves and heavy sides of pork and holiday geese that had been stuffed so fat they could hardly waddle to the chopping block.

Musing in his tent before Lectoure, Louis wondered how, without fighting, he could accomplish the mission for which he had traversed the length of France, how bring back the surly and inaccessible Jean d'Armagnac to his feudal duty. The loss of Armagnac would imperil the entire complex of southern provinces, deprive France of the bastion of the Pyrenees, and invite the restless English of Guienne to overrun everything from the Atlantic to the Swiss Confederation.

For the dauphin could not fight. His forces were inadequate for a mass assault on the high walls of Lectoure, and the weapon on which he had counted to awe and subdue the city, his single monstrous gun, was valueless.

Louis himself did not discover the flaw in the cannon, nor did Henri LeClercq, who was still some hours away. The man who pointed out the flaw was a nameless Englishman, the only Englishman Louis ever spared.

During the last days of the expedition's march, ever since crossing the boundary and entering Count Jean's province of Black Armagnac, Louis had been plagued and puzzled by a series of encounters with elusive strangers dressed in a peculiar shade of forest green. They would peer at the long marching line of the dauphin's troops from a distance and fade away behind some clump of trees or bushes or disappear behind some farmhouse; and when the farmer was hustled before the dauphin to explain he would protest in a terrified voice that he had seen no one. One old peasant, confronted with suspicious hoofprints in his field, swore by the saints, "They are the marks of my own plow mare, an ancient nag that would be of no use to your troops."

"Your ancient nag has a magnificent stride," Louis observed, measuring the distance between the hoofprints with a skeptical eye. "Do not fear me, my friend. I do not want your mare. I want the man on the horse that made these prints. Where is he?"

The peasant knitted his work-gnarled hands together in an agony of indecision that the dauphin sensed was rooted in fear. Two sturdy men-at-arms held him fast. "Before God, Monseigneur, I do not know; I did not see him; there was no one; I never see them."

"An interesting concatenation of mutually exclusive impossibilities," Louis said smiling.

The peasant brightened, answering not the words, which he did not understand, but the dauphin's smile. "You are not going to rack me?"

"I do not torture Frenchmen."

"*He* would."

Louis did not question who "he" might be, for he already knew. The terrified peasant was Jean d'Armagnac's vassal.

"Why would he rack you?"

The man stared at the ground.

"For seeing the green strangers?"

"Monseigneur, I would not speak, I could not speak to—" He bit his lip and stopped short.

"Let the poor fellow go," Louis ordered.

The men-at-arms did not immediately release him. "He has told you nothing, Monseigneur," one of them said.

"He has told me enough."

That night Louis ordered a ring of mantraps set at close intervals around the circle of wagons which formed the outer ring of the encampment and which, in the event of a surprise attack, would act as a sheltering wall. In the arsenal of the age, familiar to every lord of a manor, there were two kinds of mantraps. One was a mechanism of steel with spiked jaws for use against poachers, who would spring it by stepping on the hidden trigger. The spikes would meet in his belly as the jaws snapped shut. The other, useful against spies, lesser offenders, and persons who were to be taken alive, was a concealed noose of rope attached to a sturdy sapling; it would string a man up by the heels, affording him an opportunity to howl head down till morning and make a resolve to mend his ways.

Next morning the sentries found the quarry, cut the noose, and brought the Englishman to the dauphin. Louis questioned him, amiably at first, then with increasing severity when the captive's heavy accent betrayed him as an enemy alien and his evasive answers aroused an ugly suspicion: the truculent foreigner actually seemed to think he had a legal right to be five leagues deep inside the French province of Black Armagnac!

"The legalities of the situation were settled eighty-three years ago at the Treaty of Brétigny," Louis said, "and I know of nothing that has altered the boundary since that time."

"Nothing you know of," the man smirked. "That is good. That is good for England."

"And yet," Louis said, grasping quickly at the shred of information, "perhaps some recent detail escapes my memory, perhaps, indeed, some harmless understanding between you and the local lord of these lands. It may be that you and the other green-clad—'foresters,' let us call them—are merely allowed to do a little hunting, *noblesse oblige*, on the estates of our loyal vassal Count Jean d'Armagnac. Might that be the situation?"

"I really couldn't say," the man replied, aping his manner. Then, stoutly: "I know your reputation, Monseigneur. Why not hang me out of hand and have done with it? I will tell you nothing."

Louis's eyes hardened, wholly at variance with the slow soft voice in which he said: "Tut, tut, *mon brave*, for brave you are. Have no fear I shall hang you. You couldn't say much with a noose strangling your windpipe. But I do think, for your own good, unless you want the friar here to shrive you, that you ought to be a bit more communicative. Why are you English skulking through the woods in hunters' garb? Why do you go unarmed, with bows unstrung, as if you feared nothing? Above all, why are you all going in the same direction, though by circuitous routes? To what rendez-vous do you converge and for what purpose?"

The dauphin's men glanced at him as followers glance at a leader who sees what every man sees but finds more meaning in it. To them, simple men, his intuitive mind at work was frighteningly akin to witchcraft.

"Jean d'Armagnac invited you into his province!" Louis's voice rose angrily. "By twos, by threes, by little inconspicuous groups, didn't he? Did he not promise, once you were safely inside his city, to arm you against me?"

"If I were to answer your questions, I should deserve to be hanged," the man said, "by my own commander."

The reluctance of the dauphin to hang Frenchmen did not extend to Englishmen.

"You islanders are a tongue-tied lot," he said unpleasantly. "When William the Conqueror stormed your beaches and taught you the Norman tongue, there was some reasoning with you; since you have lapsed into Saxon again, or whatever English is, there has been continual war. I shall write the dauphiness and suggest that she compose one of her poems on that theme; nay, I shall not write, since it is not romantic and therefore not ladylike. Meanwhile, yonder is a brazen open mouth. Stand against it, English spy, and let it teach you to open yours, for Pasque Dieu! if it speaks first there will be nothing left of you to speak again in this world."

Now the prisoner began to struggle in the vise-like grip of the men-at-arms. "Well?" Louis snapped at them. "Do your duty!"

"Monseigneur," one of them said vacantly, "we do not clearly understand our duty."

Dolts and *muttonheads!* leaped to the tip of the dauphin's tongue, but he conquered the impulse to utter the words. The stupidity of the soldiery provided by his father's ministers for this expedition was inconceivable, and ominous. When he should come to the throne, Louis resolved, he would surround himself with penetrating minds, keen intellects, sharper, harder even than his own, whetstones to keep a cutting edge on his wit. He found himself admiring the efficiency of razors. How softly they did their work, slipping feather-light over the skin, and death only paper thickness away from the vein below! How peacefully and unopposed a dangerous instrument could function if only the edge were fine enough! As the function of a razor was to cut away the dross and cleanse, so, God willing, Louis the king would one day cleanse the face of France.

"Few men know their duty nowadays," was all he permitted himself to say to the men-at-arms who complained that they did not understand theirs. "Truss up that Englishman face to, against the cannon's mouth."

That was more understandable. The men who on holidays relished the spectacle of game cocks pecking out each other's eyes and the dumb agony of dancing bears, which danced only because there was fire under the platform on which they performed and to which they were chained, leaped to this larger amusement with alacrity and gutter jibes: Would he foul his breeches from fright before or behind? Or both? At a hanging it was often both. Some wagered one way, some another. A man began to charge the cannon with powder.

"Half a charge will suffice," Louis said. "We shall need much powder to blow in the gates of Lectoure. And waste no iron shot; a shovelful of dirty Armagnac stones will serve very nicely to hoist our taciturn friend into Paradise."

Another man ran to a campfire and lighted his slow match, and then stood by, waiting for the charging to be finished and for the command that would permit him to apply the match to the vent and shatter to atoms the upper half of this human being. It would be a waste of a handsome green doublet, but perhaps the greater part of a good pair of British woolen hose would remain, and surely, in their entirety, though probably at some distance, those excellent English leather shoes. No one made leather shoes like the English. No wood in them anywhere, not even in the soles. Friar Jean Majoris might insist on burying the legs in them, however. You had to consider that. Friar Jean was looking extremely grim and disapproving just now.

"Let us not be impatient," Louis told the gunner. "Lay a length of your slow match along the barrel so that the Englishman can watch the progress of the fire as it creeps toward the vent. We shall give him time to change his mind. If he decides to speak before the gun blasts him to hell, remove the match. Do you understand, Englishman? I am offering you your life."

The Englishman understood. The lighted match was laid; he watched the slow fire sputter and smoke. Sometimes it would dwindle to a spark as if it were about to go out; sometimes it would burst into vivid flame as it struck a small segment especially well impregnated with sulphur, and then the fire would race a little way toward the vent as if in mercy to put an end to the suffering of the man at the cannon's mouth. "Erratic, temperamental French match!" He tried to make his voice steady; he tried to spit in disgust. "Get an English match!" But his eyes stared at the fire, he tried to turn his face away, his body being lashed motionless; big drops of sweat formed on his brow and ran down his pallid cheeks into his beard, which seemed suddenly to have gone white. The change of color of the beard, however, was caused by some ashes from the slow match that had fallen from the gun barrel and lodged there.

The match soon shortened. All that lay lengthwise along the barrel burned away. Only a small curved segment now remained, forming a stiff arch that rose away from the barrel and descended vertically down into the vent hole. The fire was creeping up the arch; when it reached the top and started to consume the vertical portion there would be danger that a stray spark might drop into the powder chamber and fire the gun several minutes before the last few inches had burned.

Friar Jean kissed the cross on his stole and placed it around his neck. "You failed, Louis. He isn't going to talk. Now he's mine."

85

Louis pointed to the sputtering slow match and gripped the priest's arm. "It's too late. For God's sake don't get close to him now!"

"It is for God's sake that I must. Even for an Englishman. Au revoir—somewhere—Louis." He shook off with astonishing strength the dauphin's iron grip on his arm.

A kind of wondering disbelief calmed the Englishman's contorted features as the priest approached. "Not *you!* Get away!"

"Quickly, man. Make an act of confession. Recall such sins as you can. Under the circumstances God will probably not expect you to remember them all in detail."

"I do not know the French words—"

"Just say in English, 'I am sorry for all my sins,' and I shall absolve you."

"God bless you! Of course I'm sorry. Now run for your life! Isn't there an artilleryman in the suite of your precious dauphin? Or don't French artillerymen know when a cannon is flawed from muzzle to breech? Look, you can see it! Blessed St. Barbara, the breed of engineers in this filthy country! All I fear is that someone will discover it before it blows the dauphin to hell. What a victory! Now run!"

It was a fortunate linguistic accident that Latin was extremely compact; Friar Jean's absolution, which he faithfully pronounced, took only a few seconds; and perhaps St. Barbara, patroness of artillerymen, whose leaden image the Englishman wore on his cap, raised the gentle breeze that whitened his beard with ashes and also wafted the sparks away from the vent hole. Louis always attributed the providential breeze to her, and her image was the first of a line of images of the saints, all in lead, that he wore till he died and that caused such comment.

Friar Jean, the stole still circling his neck after the sacrament he had just administered, now did a mundane, brave, and unsacramental act, burning his hand in his haste. He rushed to the breech of the cannon and tore the hissing stub of the fire match out of the vent hole.

The Englishman, no longer sustained by the certainty of a hero's death, slumped against the cannon's muzzle. The long wait for the blast which did not come had sapped his courage. Weak and limp, the breath of life still sweet in his still whole body, his first thought was a thankful prayer: Blessed St. Barbara, it is good to be alive! He would have kissed her image if the bonds that held him had permitted. His second thought was a feeble curse: The dangerous dauphin of France was still alive also.

Louis ran up to Friar Jean, who was blowing on the burn in his hand. "Why did you save him!"

"Because he saved you, he saved us all." Friar Jean's conscience was troubling him as much as the burn. True, he had acted instinctively, impulsively. Yet he feared that by his action he might have divulged something committed to him under the Seal. Contrariwise, he did not conceive it to have been his priestly duty to stand by and become an accomplice in the murder of a Prince of the Lilies. Would it have benefited the Englishman, would his absolution have been valid, if the Englishman's last knowing

86

wilful act had been murder? Nay, since Friar Jean knew the explosion would kill him also, might he himself not have been guilty of the unpardonable sin of self-destruction? He looked at the living men who would now be dead men but for his action, and decided it had been worth while, remembering no rule that prohibits a priest from acting like a man, and remembering that overscrupulosity is also a sin.

"Did he talk? He must have talked. What did he say?"

"You had better ask him."

Louis nodded. "I understand," and grimly to the Englishman, "Well, fellow?"

The Englishman, still shaken, could not immediately reply; but with his finger he traced a portion of the hair-line flaw that lay within reach of his bound hand and indicated the rest, which extended all the way to the breech of the gun. Louis followed it with his eye, and understood. The understanding deepened. "Pasque Dieu!" he gasped, and crossed himself.

Two tremendous thoughts had burst into his mind. One was simple and uncomplicated: patently he was under special protection. He recognized St. Barbara's image on the Englishman's cap—*her* protection, unquestionably.

The other thought was ominous, complex, incomplete, full of ugly overtones. Why was the cannon cracked? Jean Bureau's foundry was thorough; Henri LeClercq's skill was proved; flawed cannon were not issued to troops. If this flaw was no accident, and it could not be, who besides Jean Bureau and Henri LeClercq had hatched an all but perfect plot to kill him? In the manufacture of highly secret weapons like gunpowder and cannon, the chain of command, which in an "accident" of this sort was a chain of guilt, led directly to the king's ministers, perhaps to his father the king himself.

Insolent English enemies filtering into Armagnac, Armagnac's attitude unknown and probably hostile, intriguers plotting his death at court with the connivance of his own father—the face of the dauphin twitched.

"Calmness, Louis!" Friar Jean was at his elbow. "Quiet; thought! Our success will depend on your keeping your head. Tomorrow you will be before Lectoure. It would not do for you to be unwell."

"Confound it, I am always well. I have not been sick in years." Still, Friar Jean Majoris was his physician as well as his confessor; and something in St. Barbara's wind, which had wafted the sparks from the vent hole, was chillier on his spine than a little wind ought to have been at this time of year. Nor ought the wind to have penetrated his velvet doublet. "You are always telling me not to excite myself, like an old woman." Nevertheless he exerted his will to put down the apprehension and anger, his face moderated, the chill passed, and he felt more himself again.

But he no longer dared destroy the Englishman whom St. Barbara had protected no less than himself, nor did he quite dare steal her image, which he coveted. Anything so powerful would be good to keep on his person.

"I will give you your freedom if you will freely give me St. Barbara there on your cap. She is only lead, I perceive, not very valuable."

"Willingly," the Englishman replied, in whom, with the interminable smoke of the slow match, the martyr mood had long since evaporated.

"Loose him!"

Louis buckled the saint on his own cap. In the cheap little lead stamping she was depicted, as usual, standing beside the tower in which her pagan father imprisoned and tortured her for espousing the new religion, and the bolt of lightning that struck him dead was clearly outlined. Though she lived in the dawn of Christianity, long before cannon or gunpowder were invented, their thunder and lightning reminded artillerymen of her and they had adopted her as their patroness. That she had adopted them also was clear to Louis from today's intervention. "You are free to join my service as well as to go back to Guienne," he suggested. "I would make it worth your while."

"That was not in the bargain, Monseigneur."

"Very well. It is not your fault that you are English and stubborn. I warn you, however, you will feel an arrow in your back if you are found again in the vicinity of Lectoure."

"Monseigneur," the man replied, recovering some of his earlier insolence, "the welcome at Lectoure is a privilege I shall gladly leave to Your Highness . . . if the chief pig lets you into his swinery. It will be a pleasure to breathe again the pure English air of Guienne." He walked away, and he did not once look in the direction of Lectoure.

"English air of Guienne!" Louis muttered. But he could not deny that Guienne, like so much of France, had been occupied by the English for a hundred years.

Friar Jean mused. " 'Chief pig' and 'swinery' are hard and cryptic words."

"I do not understand the words either. But I understood his face. Something in Lectoure outrages his British sense of the proper."

Chapter Fourteen

An artillery captain who knew the closely guarded secrets of making gunpowder also possessed a keen eye for trees and their habit of growth, since healthy trees furnished the charcoal which comprised exactly one-fourth by volume of the powder mix according to the most modern formula yet devised. As the walls of Lectoure rose in the distance in the dusk of his last day's ride, Henri LeClercq found himself in a scrubby woodland that Louis had chosen for his camp.

The aspect of the woodland was not quite normal; there was something curiously wrong with the trees; a larg number of tough saplings had been bent to the ground. For a moment Henri conjectured whether some great wind had not blown them down, then smiled to himself, recognizing the mantraps. "One must walk warily when approaching the dauphin of France," he said half aloud to his tired mount. "*Courage, ma belle!* This is the hand of a man who trusts no one." In justice to Louis, Henri reflected, how could he? It was a great relief to be assured that the dauphin was still alive.

Cautiously he picked his way among the snares, noting the cunning with which they had been concealed. Presently he caught the gleam of a pike point in the bushes, red in the setting sun as if it had already tasted blood.

"Well, you in there?"

The sentry instantly challenged him.

"If you don't expect to be seen first, stick your point in mud to dull its shine." Then he identified himself as Captain Henri LeClercq, and asked to be taken to the prince.

The sentry muttered something about orders to keep all weapons razor-bright and said, "I don't know if I can take you to the prince."

"Why not? Is the dauphin indisposed? Wounded?" He hesitated. "Dead?"

"I do not know that either."

"Confound it, man, you must know something!"

"All I know is, the dauphin ordered the sentries to bring to him at once anybody caught skulking around the camp; but then Friar Jean came out of his tent and said the dauphin was sleeping, that the order was countermanded, and that tomorrow would be plenty of time to question English spies."

"*Charbieu!* Do you take me for an English spy?"

"No, Captain, you do not talk through your teeth like the English." Also, the sentry recognized the blazonry of one of Jean Bureau's captains of artillery on the tabard that Henri wore over his light steel breastplate, the only armor he had put on for the long fast ride. "And your name is well known. If you are really Captain Henri LeClercq, I advise you to turn around and go back to Paris as fast as you can. For an écu I'd forget I had seen you."

"You shall get no écus from me, Master Sentry. Perhaps, if you take me instantly to the dauphin, I shall forget that an écu can make you forget your duty."

"I meant it in kindness, sir." The sentry struck off hurriedly in the direction of the dauphin's tent, which, situated in a clearing, was somewhat larger but just as plain as the others, and round which guards with dark lanterns had already taken up watch. "The dauphin was heard through

89

the walls of his tent to mention your name in anger. His voice was thick and the soldiers say he's drunk. There was a near accident today." Rapidly the sentry recounted the capture of the Englishman and his torture at the cannon's mouth. "It was good sport till he pointed to the crack. Maybe you'll find yourself in a similar situation tomorrow. You can't say I didn't try to warn you."

"I am not ungrateful. But believe me, it is precisely because of that crack that I am here."

"I hope the dauphin believes you. He suspects everybody."

And well he might, Henri thought grimly.

"Do you still command me to rouse the dauphin? Friar Jean would be more pleasant, and *he* isn't drunk."

"Is this friar a Friar Jean Majoris who used to be an apothecary of Auch?"

"I do not know where he comes from; he has always been Monseigneur's confessor and physician as far as I know; but he speaks with an Armagnac slur and assuredly Majoris is his name. Doubtless it is the same man."

"I have known him since I was a boy! Take me to him."

"Do I not deserve a sol for suggesting it? The pay of a man-at-arms is nominal in the extreme, and we are sternly forbidden to forage among the peasants for anything, even for entertainment, which often would be given freely."

Henri laughed. "The dauphin keeps an orderly house, eh? Here is your écu—for reuniting me with Friar Jean, my old friend. It has been many years."

In a tent close to the dauphin's, Friar Jean greeted Henri affectionately and without reserve, for the climate of his thinking was as gentle as that of the dauphin was stormy. "What a tonic the sight of you will be for His Highness when he wakes up! He thinks the whole world is against him, you, Jean Bureau, De Brézé, nay, even his own father, all combined in some dark scheme to destroy him. Nothing could prove his suspicions so unfounded as your presence. Tell me about yourself, Henri. We shall not be disturbed. I have administered a draught to the prince to quiet his nerves. It made him talkative at first, but sometimes in patients that is a good sign; they talk the silly notions right out of themselves. Now he is sleeping peacefully as a babe. You have done well in the world from the reports I hear of you. You married, did you not? Have you children? One of the joys I pray for in the life to come is that I shall be granted a glimpse, as the centuries roll, of the descendants of my foundlings. They grew to be quite a brood before I left the peaceful cloister of St. Michael. And when I shall see brave men and good women of the House of LeClercq, I shall say: 'These are the progeny of the lad who did not need to be born to a name. He learned Friar Jean's lessons so well that everyone called him LeClercq, the well instructed!' Why is your face so grim, Henri?"

"There may be more to the dauphin's suspicions than you realize, Friar Jean. As for myself, I do not complain. I once had hopes of a career in the suite of the Comte de Comminges, but something I never understood shunted me into the Corps of Engineers."

"I remember how the coils of the distillery used to fascinate you. I cannot say that I approve of these new-fangled cannon, but it is not for me to judge whether artillery or brandy is more destructive. Your career is an honorable one; it should not make your face grim."

"I was remembering my bride, Friar Jean, and my little son. Both died in the plague that the English left when they evacuated Paris. There will be no House of LeClercq."

Friar Jean murmured in Latin, "Eternal rest grant unto them, O Lord, and let perpetual light shine upon them." The loss was perhaps too recent for Henri to take kindly to a suggestion that he was still a young man and would probably marry again.

"When Louis has finished with the English," Friar Jean said with the rancor that any good Frenchman, lay or clerical, might feel, "it is my thought that France will be rid of a brace of plagues!"

A sudden voice said softly, "And so France shall!" They both turned, startled, toward the entrance of the tent, where the dauphin stood muffled in a cowled cloak that rendered him all but invisible in the shadows. His shoes were wet with dew and there were burrs in the hem of the cloak as if he had been walking in the woods.

"I gave Your Highness a sleeping potion!"

"My Highness spat it out. Do you think I leave all the watching to the sentries?" Clinically, Louis's face no longer displayed the signs that always made Friar Jean apprehensive.

"It is good to see you yourself again, Monseigneur," he said, "but it is a careless apothecary who does not look for the swallow when the draught is administered. I shall be more watchful henceforth." He smiled.

"And I shall make a note to swallow visibly, audibly, convincingly in the future, *mon père.*" He was apparently in good humor. "It made me talkative, did it?" Apparently also he had been listening to all their conversation. He laughed and sat down. "Perhaps I did inadvertently swallow a trifle; I held it in my mouth for quite a while. Sit, sit, gentlemen. Do you know what the men are saying behind my back? I know. It is always useful to know." He paused. "You came south on a handsome mare, Henri Le-Clercq."

"Monseigneur, I assure you—"

"Do not explain. I know my own stables. Margaret, at least, is not conspiring against me: therefore you are not. Some things are very simple."

"I rode south, Monseigneur, to inform you that your cannon is cracked."

"I believe you did, now that I've seen the mare. But an Englishman has already given me the same information about the gun."

"It was stolen from the scrap heap in the foundry and issued to your troops—God only knows how."

"I know *why*."

"It is the nature of cannon to be imperfect," Friar Jean sighed. "I cannot believe there is a conspiracy."

Henri said hotly: "I can; and my honor and the honor of the foundry are involved. I intend to find out who stole it!"

"Do you, my friend?" Louis said, tapping his fingers nervously on the table. "Perhaps it would be unwise to push an inquiry like this too far. It is enough that Blessed St. Barbara has thwarted the conspiracy." He rested his forehead against the heel of his hand, his fingers idly stroking her image on his cap. "I have a mind to abandon this Armagnac expedition and retire into the Dauphiny. The Dauphiny is stiflingly small, and I should feel hemmed in, but there at least I shall be secure. A quick retreat is sometimes the best attack; one can always turn about."

"Monseigneur, you must not retire."

"*Must* not, Henri LeClercq? That is a singular tone to take with me."

"Retreat is not necessary, Monseigneur. That flawed cannon is not worthless."

Briefly he outlined a plan, which the dauphin eagerly seized upon and elaborated. It was exactly the sort of stratagem that appealed to him most, for it turned a weakness into a strength.

Friar Jean listened a while and said tonelessly: "With your permission, Monseigneur? I am extremely fatigued."

So many men, so many unsuspecting, unwarned, unshriven men, so soon to become bloody, mangled corpses, unrecognizable as humanity! In former wars with less violent weapons there had always been something left to bury.

Louis answered absently: "Certainly, Friar Jean, retire if you wish. This is not your province. Pleasant dreams."

As the priest rose, the bandaged hand which hitherto he had concealed under the table was exposed. Answering the inquiry on Henri's face, Louis shrugged, "He refuses to physic his own wound," and related how Friar Jean had got it. "Though he's forever bending over the humblest man-at-arms with a pot of soothing unguent. He even treats the English—after the French, of course."

"Naturally," Henri said.

Then they talked more technically about the cracked cannon.

"The lure will have to be manned," Louis said. "It will appear far more convincing that way."

"They would be blown to pieces, Monseigneur!"

"I was not thinking of living men. There are certain to be some French casualties before the cannon comes into play. Part of the sinful waste of war is that nothing is ever done with the corpses."

Henri looked at him across the table; Louis's eyes seemed to reflect more light than could have been generated by the single feeble candle; Captain LeClercq was gaining a new measure of the man.

"I do not think I could have thought of that detail, Monseigneur."

Chapter Fifteen

Next morning, after a refreshing night's sleep, Louis said: "First I shall give him a chance to return to his duty. Friar Jean would approve; also, it would be cheaper."

And that morning he suffered his first casualty. He dispatched a herald, a handsome, noble youth conspicuously without armor, and on a richly caparisoned horse, to the closed gates of Lectoure. The herald carried in a reversed position a gilded lance, holding aloft the butt end so that the fighting end pointed not to the enemy but to the neutral earth; and attached to the butt, unfurled to the breeze and unmistakably visible, was a white banner without device of any kind. Such blank flags had lately come to be known as flags of truce.

No one could possibly misunderstand the message. The dauphin was signifying his willingness to parley.

What the dauphin might have said, what concessions he might have made, what promises he might have given or whether he would have kept the promises was never to be known. Hard realities quashed all speculation; a monstrous breach of faith occurred in a few seconds as soon as the unsuspecting herald rode within bowshot. A shower of arrows slanted down upon him from the walls like a driving rain. Intermingling with the shafts, cutting like bolts of lightning through the rain, whined the iron quarrels of crossbows, deadly missiles with a flatter trajectory and armor-piercing speed. The herald wore no armor. Horse and rider fell. The blood of the beast and the blood of the man mingled in the dust in the ultimate comradeship of death. The flag of truce did not immediately fall; by chance the spear point plunged into the earth and the flag remained fluttering over the bodies. Then a lucky shot, for they continued to shoot at the fallen man, snapped the lance and the flag floated down upon him. Slowly the white silk assumed a brilliant red. From the walls a shout, as if the lucky shot were marksmanship, went up from Jean d'Armagnac's men.

"The person of a herald is privileged!" Louis said, white with fury. "Armagnac is a fool."

Friar Jean said sadly, "Perhaps he is mad."

That night at sundown Louis sent a strong force against a section of the wall. Jean d'Armagnac, observing the engagement from a thick high tower of his castle, sniffed, "The dauphin is reputed to be brilliant, but he chooses a weak low spot. Doesn't he know that there is certain to be a concentration of troops at such a place?" There were many casualties, and Friar Jean was busy all night comforting the dying, whose curses against the dauphin showed that they shared Armagnac's estimate of the dauphin's generalship.

Armagnac retired to the bedchamber of the bakery wench who had borne him several bastards, and then, full of wine, descended into the cellars where he kept his sister prisoner. "Thou gazelle," he whispered thickly, "let me relate a great victory. It may bring again to your lips the soft speech I so loved. Nay, stand close to me, Isabelle." But she drew away.

Isabelle, still regal and erect, still immaculately dressed and fastidiously well cared for, but her hair perfectly white, stared emptily beyond the gilded bars of the cell, beyond her brother, into some calm and distant world that only she could see. She had not spoken since her first horrified recognition of the signs that tokened the pregnancy which followed soon after her brother's visits to her in the dungeon where, angered at her resistance to his advances, he had confined her for more than a year.

In the half-light of the early dawn, before the shape of things had clearly emerged from the shadows that still hovered on their outlines, magnifying and distorting to an old man's vision so that he saw his own fears, Jean d'Armagnac's major-domo limped to his master's bedchamber and pounded on the door.

"My lord count! Wake up, you are needed! We are attacked again!"

There was a drunken grunt inside, then a naked spanking of delicate feet. A pink little urchin of a page slid aside the bolt and opened the door a crack, blinking stupidly into the major-domo's rushlight.

"Go away, old man."

The major-domo's mouth compressed; he scowled at the empty bottle, the two cups, by the bedside. "Get yourself down to the kitchens, child. You'll catch your death of cold." This was the page whose peasant parents had despaired of teaching even women's work, even spinning or churning, because of his simple-mindedness. They had been overjoyed when he found favor as a body servant in Count Jean's eyes.

"Do not wake him, Major-domo. He has only just dropped off to sleep. I must sleep now also; I am tired. If I am ugly tomorrow, he will be cross."

"Out you go!"

The page cringed and began to whimper. "You're cross too!"

"Not at you, lad. There's trouble outside. Go sleep in the dairy where you won't be in the way. And drink some milk."

The boy glanced at the count, who had not wakened, and scampered off, seemingly glad to escape. The major-domo shook his master by the shoulder, wondering whether he would be able to rouse him.

Jean raised his white soft bulk to a sitting position and passed a hand

94

heavy with jeweled rings on every finger through his hair. He looked around for the page, but saw only the faithful ancient face of his major-domo.

"Oh—you. Get out of here, nightmare. Why are you bludgeoning me? I shall be black and blue tomorrow."

"My lord count, we are attacked again."

"Tell the castellan. Tell the English auxiliaries. Louis has shot his bolt. I am very fatigued." The count lay down again, turned over, and shut his eyes.

"The English auxiliaries have been drawing their longbows on the target ever since there was light enough to distinguish it. But the creatures will not die. The English think it is witchcraft."

Quickly but unsteadily Armagnac got out of bed. He was sober enough to grasp the fact that anything the hardheaded English accepted as witchcraft must be desperately out of the ordinary.

He climbed the winding stair to the tower above the gate, resting often against the wall, pausing not only because he was tipsy but because of the fear of what he might see.

From the window slit he looked down. In the gathering light he saw a huge cannon, the mightiest piece of ordnance he had ever beheld, trained point-blank at the closed gates of his city. All around it stood a gun crew, some leaning jauntily against the barrel, one ready with the next shot— a giant, apparently, for he held a three-hundred-pound ball in the crook of his arm as easily as if it were a prize melon at a fair. In spite of the arrows that whistled down at them they did not attempt to take cover. The gunner, with a flaring slow match, continued to swing it idly; the giant with the cannon ball waggled his head from side to side, apparently mocking the inaccuracy of the famed English longbows.

"The attack was a ruse!" Armagnac shouted, cursing the English auxiliaries, calling them cowards unnerved by an obvious trick; cursing also the dauphin, whose trick now seemed clear: the original attack, which had been in strength, had drawn most of Lectoure's defenders to the danger spot on the wall; then during the attack, when the night was darkest, Louis had moved up his heavy artillery unobserved!

"Call off those bungling longbowmen!" Armagnac ordered. "Give the insolents a taste of bolts, lead ones with soft noses!" Leaden crossbow quarrels would not penetrate armor, but there was now light enough to observe that the attackers wore none, having apparently trusted to silence and the dark to cover their movements. Leaden crossbow quarrels would, however, easily penetrate leather jerkins and human bodies, often passing clear through, spreading in the course of the transit, so that the wound on emerging was greater than that made on penetration, a principle that was being taken up by artillery experts with a view to its application to firearms.

Not even dead men could stand up to the impact of the missiles that now whizzed down upon them. One by one they began to fall off their

95

props; the strings that had moved their stiff limbs now jerked them in a semblance of a second death agony. The slow match went out; the cannon ball rolled away.

From sally ports in the big gates a crowd of soldiers with crowbars and ropes now swarmed upon the cannon, for Jean d'Armagnac also had a plan: he would take inside and turn against the dauphin the piece now neutralized by the crossbow quarrels.

The struggling workmen found the gun carriage half buried in the earth.

"Dig it out!"

Obeying his orders, men with picks and shovels now joined the others, hacking at the earth to free the ponderous wheels, encountering enormous rocks jammed between the spokes, stepping on hidden knives.

From a vantage point out of bowshot two pairs of eyes watched in the growing light. "Has your fuse gone out, Maître Henri? I counted heavily on you. It is nearly daylight."

"I measured the slow match very carefully, Monseigneur."

"That is not what I asked."

"It has not gone out."

Suddenly a furious wail went up from the crowd of men. They had discovered the arrows stuck like porcupine quills in the corpses.

The men, suspecting a trap, ceased their work, glanced over their shoulders, saw nothing; but one of them sniffed the air. "*Mort de Dieu!* I could swear I still smell that match!"

"*Dig—out—that—cannon!*" Armagnac screamed from the walls. From the height he could not see the arrows; he could not smell the hidden match.

His voice never reached the men. In that instant a gigantic ball of fire with its nucleus on the cannon burst over the whole scene. A shock like a blow from an invisible fist struck him in the face and hurled him to the floor. Then followed the most awesome volume of sound his ears had ever sustained, and the horrid new stench of war.

The dauphin had been able to procure only one gun, but the king's ministers had not stinted the supply of gunpowder. Louis had crammed his cannon with such a charge as no metal could have withstood even if it had been sound. What remained—and there was much—Henri had buried in the earth beside the gun on the chance that it too might explode by concussion. Under other circumstances the dauphin would have considered so novel an experiment a sinful waste, but since there would be no use for the excess powder after the destruction of the gun, since it would be, in fact, only a dangerous impediment, he permitted the trial.

Thus there were two almost simultaneous explosions. The earth in front of the city gates blew up; the gates burst off their ponderous hinges and fell backward into the High Street, crushing the stalls of shopkeepers, collapsing the roofs of houses. As for the cannon, it fragmented into thousands of jagged brass missiles of all shapes and sizes, from glittering dust that settled on the leaves of trees, gilding them like an autumn wind, to massive chunks that sailed over the walls, knocking down chimney pots and falling into infants' cradles. People died everywhere, defenders on the walls, peaceful citizens at unexpected distances, struck down at haphazard with a queer expression of utter disbelief on their faces.

The horde of soldiers who were attempting to move the cannon when it exploded simply disintegrated. As Friar Jean had foreseen, there was nothing left to bury.

Around the smoking crater formed by the explosion, a double file of the dauphin's men now entered the hapless capital of Black Armagnac.

Chapter Sixteen

Inside the city of Lectoure, more particularly in the cellars of Jean d'Armagnac's castle, there was brought to light a situation which twenty generations of historians would never be able to narrate with detachment. What he saw in the next few hours shook even the monolithic faith of Friar Jean Majoris, as an earthquake can shake the granite of a cathedral foundation. Why had not brimstone and fire from the Lord rained upon Lectoure as it had rained upon Sodom and Gomorrah?

In a sense, perhaps in the sulphurous breath of the dauphin's cannon, it had. Friar Jean prayed for the serene breadth of vision that had brought to the lips of a Thomas Aquinas, "It pertaineth to the infinite goodness of God that even from evil He bringeth forth good." God only knew what good could come out of Lectoure, but perhaps Friar Jean could hazard an answer. Perhaps future generations would read the annals of King Charles's reign and be thankful that no such enormities occurred in their own day, just as no weapon more horrible than gunpowder had been or ever could be suggested by the Devil and invented by man. Surely gunpowder had exhausted both man's ingenuity and the Devil's imagination.

Most of all Friar Jean feared for the dauphin, who had learned the art of war too readily and to trust his fellow man too reluctantly. War had shaped him, he was still young, still impressionable; his character was still forming, like any other young man's who must learn to survive in the tiny fragment of eternity into which he is born; Lectoure would shape him also, with what results in the reign that lay ahead Friar Jean could only wonder and view with foreboding. He knew how Louis's lip would curl, how Louis would fling at him: "What have you *now* to say for the dignity of man? What of Jean d'Armagnac? It will avail you nothing to protest that he is mad. A madman does not try frantically to put his house in order when he is caught red-handed at his crimes. You saw his hands, Friar Jean? I am not employing one of Margaret's poeticisms. It was blood, quite literally human blood, nay, the blood of a priest, which even I have never shed. I always fancied it might look different, but it seems not to."

"The priest, alas, was a criminal too; let us pray that his blood and the Blood that was shed for us all shall wash away the sin for which the unfortunate chaplain was heartily sorry in his last breath."

Friar Jean did not care to discuss the subject of madness with the dauphin, nor to remind him that madmen are often exceedingly cunning, possessed of a clear sense of right and wrong which they will not or cannot apply to themselves.

Trapped, Jean d'Armagnac had tried to put his house in order like a drunkard who has drunk too long alone and, finding no way to dispose of the bottles, shatters them. It was a futile gesture.

There was an interval of some hours after the gates blew in before the castle surrendered, though the English auxiliaries deserted almost at once. They suddenly found the townspeople against them. They banded themselves into a compact little body and shot their way to the postern gate of the city under a hail of French curses, French cobblestones, and French vegetables. Louis observed, "The good people of Lectoure do not like a lord who traffics with the enemy," and permitted the English to escape. He needed all his little force to reduce the castle, for though the townspeople willingly pelted their hereditary enemy they did not yet dare raise their hand against their hereditary lord. The dauphin might march away in a day or two, and they would be left to Count Jean.

One man dared.

A thin, defiant peasant who had been in the van of the mob that routed the English shouldered his way roughly into the dauphin's presence. He seemed to have suffered a slight scratch on his lip.

"Which one of you is Louis?" He looked expectantly at Henri, whose tabard of an artillery captain caught his eye. "You?"

The dauphin advanced to him, ignoring the fellow's manners, who had forgotten to kneel or even to address him properly. "I am Louis," he said.

"Oh," the peasant mumbled, "I thought the prince would be somebody like him."

"Kneel, you fool!" Henri whispered.

Louis frowned. "I am not like anyone. If I were I'd order you horse-whipped. What do you want of your prince?"

Friar Jean bent toward the dauphin's ear and said in a queerly strangled voice: "Bear with him, Monseigneur. The wretch has been kissing blood."

"Pasque Dieu! I thought it was merely a little wound."

98

"There is no wound," said the priest-physician, "save in his mind or in his heart. Both, I suspect."

The peasant's teeth ground in his jaws with a crunching like grist in a mill.

"I want to lead your men into the castle of Jean d'Armagnac and kill him."

Louis nodded encouragingly. "Yes, yes, my good man. Why?"

It seemed to everyone but Friar Jean that the dauphin was wasting time with a curiously idle question. The city was obviously lukewarm in its loyalty to the Comte d'Armagnac. In such an atmosphere there is always someone who comes forward, for a reward, to deliver a stolen key or point out a hidden passage or pass the word to a confederate within the castle; and behold, the walls that faithful hearts might have defended for many days are opened to the besiegers and walked through as easily as one might pass from one room to another.

"If it is a reward that you wish, be assured that yours shall be liberal. Many French lives will be saved on both sides if you know a way to get a force of men into the castle without storming it."

The peasant replied that the only reward he asked was the privilege of killing Jean d'Armagnac with his own hands.

Louis said: "No doubt that can be arranged. But first I must know why you make such an odd request. How can I trust you otherwise? How do I know you are not leading my men into a trap?"

The man looked at the circle of questioning eyes, then lowered his glance and said in a voice that halted and shook with shame: "I had a witless son, but in a poor weak sort of way he was comely. Count Jean took him into his service, to serve at his table and sing, for the lad had a clear sweet voice when he could remember the words. Today was my day to clean the moat; I must give Count Jean three days a week."

It was an abuse of the *corvée*, Louis noted for future use against the lord of Black Armagnac, but he did not interrupt the peasant, who was not complaining about the forced labor. He was only explaining how he happened to be in the moat.

"One place, under the *necessarium* of the Lady Isabelle, I was always instructed to give special care. Count Jean wanted flowers. I must still put flowers there, though nobody has used it for a year. Nobody ever did except the Lady Isabelle. It was just for her, and it had to smell like roses."

Louis and Friar Jean were not smiling, so the others did not smile.

"Today, where the tile conduit empties into the moat, I found my boy. The pipe was big enough for his body to have passed without being dismembered. I wondered why it had been. I was afraid to take him home. I—assembled his body—and hid him in the reeds. I kissed him farewell. Then I saw that one of the wounds was long healed."

"*Miserere nobis, Domine!*" Friar Jean breathed.

The peasant struck his forehead again and again with the heels of his clenched fists. "To geld my daft little boy so his voice would always be

99

sweet and never change into a man's! The swine, the swine! But then to murder him—I do not understand."

"Madness," said Friar Jean.

"Fear," Louis said. "I was at his gates. You shall have your reward."

At sundown a force of Louis's men swarmed up their scaling ladders to attack a section of the castle wall that lay to the west of the main gate, where the rays of the low sun would be in the eyes of the defenders. In spite of the light which favored the dauphin, having experienced one example of his tactics, the defenders suspected another ruse, for the wall was high at that point. They strung themselves out in a thin and wasteful line all along the battlements, trying to be everywhere at once, shouting to one another and peering into the shadows, vainly seeking the real attack. The result, gratifying to Louis, who had expected heavier casualties, was that his troops actually gained a foothold and made their way in considerable numbers into the lofts and upper rooms of the castle.

The real attack was straight through the main gate, behind which presently there was a noise of confused screaming as unsuspecting guardsmen died with poignards in their backs.

The peasant had led well the raiding party that snaked through the conduit of the *necessarium* and entered Isabelle's empty apartments. Her luxurious rooms were dark and dusty; rats squeaked in undisturbed nests in the velvets of her bed. Henri's stature and Louis's position as commander excluded them from the venture; they learned later of the odor of stale perfume and newly spilled blood which the peasant thought he identified as his son's (though there were other murders that night) and which seemed to drive him mad. For several minutes the men had to gag him to keep him from crying out and betraying their presence. He recovered sufficiently to lead them through the lady's rooms and along the shadows of a palisade that stood within the outer court to the gate. Then he disappeared on an errand of his own.

At the gate the raiding party fell upon the sentries and dispatched them. Before the sentries could be reinforced, the portal stood open and the main body of the dauphin's troops swarmed in and spread out through all the length and breadth of the castle, racing up the stairs and joining their comrades in the upper regions, who were now hard pressed.

Jean d'Armagnac's liegemen promptly laid down their arms, though Jean d'Armagnac himself was not at their head, a circumstance which perhaps explained the confused defense of the stronghold. The man who formally surrendered to Louis was the ancient major-domo.

"You will find Count Jean in the cellar," the major-domo said. "He is quiet now. Torches will be required. The presence of a priest is most fortunate. If Monseigneur will follow me?"

There was a finality in his manner and a certain dignity of speech. Friar Jean assumed at first that it was the fearless dignity of age and faithful service to a master who now happened to be vanquished in a fruitless rebellion.

An old servant in the shifting fortunes of civil war would have nothing to fear; neither would the count's liegemen, who had only done what they conceived to be their duty to their immediate lord and would now simply replace one loyalty for another. But then, as the major-domo limped down the stairs that descended into the cellars, Friar Jean saw, with distinct clinical shock, the pin-point pupils of the major-domo's eyes in the smoky light of the torches and smelled on his breath the bitter odor of a plant that was cynically known as the "herb of grace" and of which the major-domo had taken a massive, perhaps fatal, dose. Erring ladies usually drank it. His fearlessness was the fearlessness of imminent death; he must have been in agony, but only his pallor and glistening brow betrayed it.

"You have need of me, *mon vieux*, both as a priest and a physician."

"There will be time for me, *mon père*, after the others."

The dungeon in which Count Jean had immured his sister for a year had once served as a storage room for grain, and as such was dry and reasonably healthful for a human being. The major-domo paused beside the barred and gilded door and drew a massive key from his belt; the bolt clicked and the door swung open.

"I feared that some harm might come to her," the major-domo said, "so I locked her in as usual."

It was as if they were entering a garden, for there were flowers everywhere. Mingling with the scent of the flowers there was an odor of death, of birth, and the smell of the *herbe de grace*.

One by one the torchlight picked out the details. Louis's eyes narrowed, and he felt a chill along his spine. "Holy Mother of God!" he prayed.

"*Ora pro nobis peccatoribus nunc et in hora mortis nostrae*," prayed Friar Jean. Prayer was all that remained to prince, priest, or physician that still might avail the Lady Isabelle of Armagnac. She sat among the flowers in a throne-like chair, the only piece of furniture in the cell, her jewels about her neck, a ruby coronet on her brow, a gentle smile on her lips, nodding slightly as if she had just dozed off after dressing herself in her best gown to greet an important visitor. The mark of the Visitor was upon her eyes, which stared unblinking into the faces of the intruders. At her feet, naked, unwashed, and dead, was the body of a prematurely born infant lying on a bed of flowers. The hardened men who had watched without a tremor the cannon of the dauphin hurtle scores of soldiers into oblivion stood rooted to the ground.

Suddenly Henri advanced to the chair and bent toward her and gently closed her eyes. "I could not help doing that," he said apologetically. "She was looking at me."

Sometimes in moments of great stress, when the chill was on his spine, the dauphin's senses seemed to become preternaturally acute and his mind made fantastic leaps. As Henri leaned over the dead woman, it seemed as if her features were duplicated in his. Louis passed his hand before his eyes, fearful that he would be sick. When he removed his hand, however, the resemblance was still there; it was no hallucination. His Captain LeClercq and the dead woman were startlingly alike. One day it would bear looking into.

The dauphin was the first to rally. "Who is this poor creature?"

"She is Isabelle d'Armagnac, Count Jean's sister, my mistress."

"Who kept her in this loathsome place?"

"Jean d'Armagnac."

"Whose is that babe?"

"Hers—and Jean d'Armagnac's."

There was a silence.

Friar Jean said, "Who gave her the abortive?"

The weary litany went on: "Jean d'Armagnac. But he did not think it would kill her, nor did I. He wanted to hide her shame. He wanted her to live. At his bidding I willingly drank some of the medicine. Now I wish I had drunk it all."

Friar Jean was perilously close to losing control of himself. "Who mixed the savin and rue? Does Jean d'Armagnac number the apothecary's skill also among his accomplishments?"

"Nay, Father, his chaplain did that, the chaplain who married them."

It was at this point that the rock of Friar Jean's faith was shaken. "Where is that priest? Where, fellow, where? I want a word with him. Don't just stand there!"

Louis asked dryly, "My clerical friend, if you had joined in holy wedlock a brother and sister—"

"Nay, God forgive him!"

"—and mixed a brew, hastily and carelessly no doubt, that murdered the sister and their child, where would *you* most likely be at this moment?"

"In hell, before God's holy altar!"

"Well, then, my clerical friend? Go find an altar."

Friar Jean fled from the chamber, his hands shaking.

Louis turned to the major-domo. "Now, old man, before you die, where is Jean d'Armagnac?"

The major-domo leaned sickly against the wall, his voice now thick and his thoughts seeming to run all together. "Your priest will not find the chaplain; he ran away when the count stabbed him; I could have stanched the wound—anybody could—but he ran away like a rabbit to die, and I was glad. He always knew he would be stabbed when people found out what he did. Count Jean had a poignard at his ribs during the marriage ceremony. Count Jean is in a cell—" He indicated the keys at his belt. "The lad who used to sing, his father appeared. I locked up the count before he could kill him."

"Pray, why didn't you let him?"

"Ah, *mon prince*, you are very young. Are there no slower ways to die?"

In that venomous query, the last words the major-domo ever spoke, Louis sensed a depth of hatred that made him dizzy.

In a corner of the chapel Friar Jean found the crouching form of the chaplain, bleeding his life away, afraid to approach the altar.

Louis and his men found Jean d'Armagnac howling behind the locked door of a cell. It became apparent that the major-domo, finding his master beaten unconscious by the peasant, had crept up behind the peasant and slain him, then pushed his master to safety and locked the door, knowing that Louis was now within the walls and would take him into custody.

Louis was sick that night, though no one knew of it but Friar Jean and no one would have attached any importance to it. Many strong men were sick after Lectoure.

All the way up to Paris after quelling the Armagnac revolt, Louis struggled with an almost uncontrollable temptation to halt the column, set up a gallows, and hang Jean d'Armagnac out of hand. But he felt himself on slippery ground. He was returning successful from a venture that highly placed and unknown enemies had hoped would be the death of him. While his father was still king, he dared not preempt the king's justice. Things would be different in time. In a dark and bitter mood he prayed for that time to come swiftly.

Chapter Seventeen

As a dying man breathes more feebly and at greater intervals before death finally takes him, so now the Hundred Years' War lapsed into a period of quiescence before it finally came to an end. The English hastily signed a truce with France, having already lost in the north and discovered in the south no more trustworthy ally than Jean d'Armagnac, who turned their sturdy British stomachs.

The brilliant victory in Armagnac and the subsequent end of hostilities added to the dauphin's popularity among the war-weary people; his popularity added to the annoyance of the king's ministers, always working for a single head for France and seeing in the indestructible crown prince a threat to the king's, and their own, power.

Jean d'Armagnac was accordingly haled before a parliament of the full estates of the realm for them to bent their vengeance upon in the king's name. Public indignation ran high when the stench of Lectoure was disclosed, and King Charles was cheered in the streets of Paris. Louis thoughtfully looked on, learning that justice, well publicized, can be an instrument of politics. But how he would have liked to hang him himself! "Yet in that case it might have been represented to my father that I had usurped his prerogative, perhaps even slain a loyal vassal!" How warily one must walk.

The Estates promptly found Jean d'Armagnac guilty of high treason, murder, and incest, and sentenced him to be hanged at the king's pleasure. At one point during the trial a judge arose with a scarlet face, approached the image of the Saviour that hung behind the bench, and veiled it for pure shame.

"When they hang him," Louis said, "it will be a source of great satisfaction to me, not only because justice will be done, but also because you will be lord of both High and Low Armagnac, a not inconsiderable estate." The dauphin smiled, expecting an expression of content from Bernard d'Armagnac, though he knew that the death of Isabelle had struck his old friend and tutor a stunning and shameful blow.

There was no expression of content. "Perhaps I am not so ambitious as I was in my younger years, Monseigneur." But also, Bernard knew in his heart, closer blood than his own had a better, though illegitimate, claim to the double coronet of the two Armagnacs. It would have eased his conscience if he could have blurted out, "Monseigneur, the son of the lady Isabelle, Henri LeClercq, is the rightful heir." But he could not bring himself to heap further dishonor on his House or sully more than it was already sullied the name of his kinswoman, who had lived so shamefully and died so foully. "There will be time enough for me to think seriously about my advancement when Count Jean is actually hanged. I am as yet aware of no date set for the execution."

"If the king does not hang him, Pasque Dieu, I will!"

"Meanwhile, Monseigneur, Captain Henri LeClercq surely deserves some preferment for the part he played in reducing Lectoure."

Louis sighed, ruefully conscious of how grandly he had just spoken when he said he would hang a great vassal and how nakedly he must now admit his actual lack of power to advance a simple artilleryman. "Captain LeClercq was not well received when he returned after being absent without leave from his duties. Naturally I could not let it be known that we suspect a motive behind the cracked cannon. It was all I could do to get him reinstated with honor."

"Is Henri LeClercq a happy man, Monseigneur?"

"My friend, who is a happy man while Lectoures still exist in France? It is more to my purpose that he is a valuable man. And yet perhaps he is happy. He hates the English, he loves his cannon. One hate, one love, no fear. That should fill a man. I myself should be happy if life were as simple for me as it is for Henri LeClercq."

"Will you take him with you into Switzerland?"

"No," Louis said positively. "We shall want no quick artillery victories. Surely *you* understand the purpose of the Swiss expedition. Henri is back in his precious foundry, struggling with a scheme to construct a twenty-barrel wagon gun. Let him remain there with nothing more dangerous to deal with than gunpowder."

Bernard smiled. "He'll be safer."

Very few knew the purpose of the expedition now about to set out toward the Swiss Alps. It was to be a campaign that would tickle the fancy of Machiavelli in Italy when he should come to write *The Prince*, the most cynical exposition of leadership ever committed to paper.

Like Lectoure, the Swiss campaign also would shape the dauphin.

He spent few days and no nights with the dauphiness, the memory of his recent illness in the south still fresh.

But in this he was little different from most soldiers, who had scant time for their homes or their wives. All was a hubbub of warlike preparation, with an army assembling in Paris, daily swelling in size, terrorizing the streets after dark till the thrifty burghers, viewing their looted shops and consoling their ravished daughters, whispered to one another the same sentiments that King Charles had suggested in council, "France is sick, and ought to be blooded."

The truce with the English had spewed into Paris twenty thousand brawling soldiers, brutal spawn of the weary war, with no skill but the skill of killing, no home but the camp, and no pay since for the moment there was no fighting. It seemed natural to them that they should now be sent away again to exercise their aptitude; they cheered when they were told that King Charles had appointed the dauphin commander general.

"The prince returns from a glorious victory in the south," the heralds shouted to their ragged ranks, reading a scroll that purported to be a speech from the king, though Charles had only suggested it. The wording as usual reflected the mind of his ministers, the cunning of whose speech eluded the ignorant soldiers. "Now we are called upon to free the rich land of Switzerland—"

"Rich in snow, rocks and cheese," Louis muttered.

"—where every loyal Frenchman can make his fortune. The Swiss have wickedly revolted against their liege lord Frederick, the Holy Roman Emperor, anointed of God—"

"A ghost empire!"

"Render to the dauphin the same loyalty you have always shown me—"

"By loyally looting your capital city?"

"—and follow Louis to wealth and victory, for he will ever be in the forefront, leading you onward!"

"That I shall not, Father, not in the forefront."

With a heavy heart Friar Jean accompanied the dauphin, since a physician has an obligation to a patient. He prepared an elixir of potable gold which he had found efficacious recently in the treatment of Louis's secret attack at Lectoure. Sometimes he prayed that God would see fit to reveal to mankind a better medicine for the management of the falling sickness.

Margaret bade Louis adieu; there was a pallor on her cheeks that he too facilely attributed to the normal anxiety she always showed when he departed on a mission from which he might not return. She said: "Dear Louis, are we never to be alone again with a little time to ourselves? Even a little time might suffice to provide you with an heir." He chucked her under the chin. "I think you are coming to love me."

"I have always loved you."

"When the Swiss are subdued," he smiled, "I shall count it a pleasure to concentrate on the venture you suggest, in calmness and seclusion. We shall go on a holiday, you and I alone."

Margaret said, *"Fi des sales Suisses!* Why cannot we go now? You have been away too long."

But the dauphin drank his draught of potable gold and recalled her somewhat sharply to their mutual responsibilities.

The night the expedition marched, she penned a fuzzy ballade on the role that artillery would play in the campaign, but she did not know the technical terms applicable to ordnance and the poem turned on the personality of artillery captains.

Louis did not read the poem. And no artillery was issued to the army that he captained into the Swiss Alps. When the surgeon cups the vein, there is no accompaniment of noise. This was a bloodletting, subtle, cynical, silent, swift. It was a successful operation.

On the French side of the Alps, the valley of the river Doubs lies like an invitation to conquest, fertile and green between two folds of the Jura Mountains. Thither the dauphin led his turbulent band of twenty thousand veterans. Even before they passed the Swiss border, the soldiers, who prided themselves in their savage name, "The Butchers," began to forage and loot for food. The dauphin did not restrain them, knowing for what they were destined, and powerless in any event, provisions being calculatedly low. He pressed on, hoping to confine the depredation as largely as possible to the Swiss side.

Very soon, however, the broad valley gave way to a wild fir-wooded region of waterfalls and limestone chasms as they toiled upward toward the source of the river, which rapidly dwindled into a rocky Alpine stream. There was little to loot in the poverty-stricken mountain hamlets where the peasants, sure-footed and nimble as goats, fled at their approach. Though the Swiss were invisible, their mocking laughter could sometimes be heard above the roar of crashing rocks that would hurtle down unexpectedly from the heights on the heads of the troops.

Snow was already falling in the pass on the flanks of Mount Terrible, where the column turned into the valley of the Birs. Here there were more villages to ravage, for this was the valley that led to the free and imperial city of Basle. Here too, as in High Armagnac, grew a grape that had bred a flourishing brandy industry. It was late in the year, another calculated factor, and the harvest was in. There was no gold, no honor, no food, no clothing, no shelter in Switzerland. But there was brandy; and since they were already dead men Louis let them loot and drink themselves into warmth and stupidity every night before they lay down in the snow, which here, as nowhere in France, whitened the earth eight months out of the year.

Three thousand of the twenty deserted, some to assume Swiss nationality, some to fight their way into Swabia, most to be waylaid and miserably murdered.

The rest, weak and hungry, tramped on to Basle, where, Louis promised them, everything was to be had for the asking.

But under the walls of Basle the Butchers advanced into a forest of Swiss long pikes.

Terrible and effective as this weapon was in the hands of an expert, the Swiss long pike could be neutralized by a classic tactic: a heavy preparatory fire of crossbow bolts in combination with the overwhelming crush of a determined cavalry charge. But the freezing hands of the French could not aim; the cavalry were not determined, and most of the horses had been killed and eaten. The French advanced only to impale themselves. Two thousand Swiss killed four thousand Butchers and perished beside their victims. The dauphin, by no means in the forefront, watched the slaughter in amazement and disbelief as one by one, then by scores and hundreds, the Swiss fell. Not one Swiss left the field alive. No gate opened even a crack to admit a survivor. Over the carnage the walls of Basle loomed grim and impregnable.

Louis counted his casualties. They were sickening. The dead, deserted, and wounded totaled ten thousand, fully half of the force that had marched so raucously out of France up the green valley of the Doubs. No army since Caesar's time had been expected to sustain casualties of more than 20 per cent without prudence dictating withdrawal and honor absolving it from all taint of cowardice.

"I have achieved a masterpiece of misdirection," he said grimly to Friar Jean. "For once my royal father will be pleased with me."

It was no comfort to Friar Jean to remember that most of the Butchers were rogues and scoundrels with long, murderous records. Something had made them so; they had not been born so. No more had Louis. The friar did not answer the dauphin, but he had no doubt that all France, from King Charles and his council down to the lowliest beggar in the slums of Paris, would feel safer at the purging of so much, so bad, and so dangerous blood.

"I think I shall request a truce," Louis said.

He did not have to request the truce. A Swiss herald with a white flag and a spear in the reversed position rode into the French camp and signified that Basle was willing to parley. Instantly Louis's terms stiffened. He demanded indemnity for his losses, food for the remnant of his army, and hostages as a guarantee against attack during his withdrawal.

"Pasque Dieu!" he muttered when all this was granted. "I think I could have taken Basle. But what would I have done with it? This is a frigid country." It had bewildered him how the cold and the thin air had made his head throb. He had worn his hat every night and wrapped his head in a heavy scarf of wool. Cold had never had this effect before. The magnificent country, the grandeur of the gorges, the depth of the chasms, the towering mountains, did not exhilarate him. On the contrary, he felt irritable and depressed. One could fall so far, so dizzily far.

Before he reached France, he learned that he could actually have taken Basle. Every defender had died under its walls. The city had been caught unprepared; the Swiss had made the same response to the challenge as the Spartans at Thermopylae, total, futile, wonderful.

"One day I shall see whether it is possible to hire an army of these Swiss. They are poor and they know how to die. When I am rich—if I am rich—when I am king—if I am king—"

"You will be king," said Friar Jean.

Louis smiled slyly. "My clerical friend, I cannot tell from your tone whether you consider that an unmixed blessing."

His mood was lighter as the mountains and gorges were left behind and he approached the broad plain of France where there was room to fall. He found himself dwelling fondly on the image of the blue eyes and the blue-black hair of the dauphiness.

Louis's return to Paris was a triumph. The plaudits of the people were not new, for they had always demonstrated enthusiasm for a prince who dressed as simply as themselves and was not afraid of demeaning himself by speaking to them, no matter how undistinguished the audience. But the effusive welcome he received from his father surprised and momentarily disarmed him.

"Louis, my dear, dear boy! Not only I but all my council, Dunois, Chabannes, Coeur, Bureau, Xaincoings, De Brézé, everyone sings your praises. Welcome home."

In the face of such warmth the dauphin ventured to touch warily on the subject of the cracked cannon. King Charles professed himself dismayed, but waved the matter aside as an accident; it happened all the time, he said, and he blamed Henri LeClercq, who had cast it. "That is one unregal thing about you, Louis. That disgustingly suspicious nature of yours. Who in the world would want to kill you?"

Louis looked at him. The king quickly spoke of something else.

"I am informed that you could have taken Basle," he said, a hint of reproach in his voice. "Not that you did not do very well, very well indeed. But there are still too many Butchers. I suggest an immediate return to Switzerland."

"There are only half as many Butchers as there were. Surely the slaughter of Frenchmen by a French prince has gone far enough. Give them pensions, give them small farms to cultivate, divide and weaken them, settle some in one province, some in another. In such a manner Caesar solved the problem of *his* veterans."

King Charles looked vague, and Louis sensed that the study of Caesar's polity had never interested his royal father. "No," said the king, "the Butchers are dangerous. My council says so. Dangerous elements must be ruthlessly exterminated."

"*All* dangerous elements, Sire?"

"Oh, yes, Pasque Dieu, as you say. Yes, indeed."

"Have you ever thought of ruling without your council?"

"Good gracious, no. How could I?"

How could he indeed.

"I had looked forward to a holiday with Margaret, Father."

"Oh, that, lad, who would not? So single-minded, so faithful, never fluttering an eyelash at any of her admirers while you are away. I can vouch for that. What a welcome she must have given you; it heats me just to think of it."

Louis's eyes narrowed.

The king continued: "A holiday, by all means. It would be curious if you had a son, would it not—if a dauphin's dauphin should result in the same year that the dauphin gets a brother? You will have heard, of course, that your mother the queen is pregnant again." Charles VII beamed sanctimoniously, dynastically.

Louis had heard. He had also heard that his father's new mistress, an exciting creature named Agnès Sorel, was equally pregnant. It was not an easy situation for a son who adored his middle-aged mother and envied his complacent father, to whom everything seemed to come without effort: sage advice from able ministers, boundless good health, magnificent appetite, superb digestion—and children by anyone with whom he spent a casual night.

"But it must be a short holiday. Your leadership of the Butchers was admirable; you have a genius for killing. Go back to Basle and take it for me; do not waste your time in bed. Breeding is not in your line."

"The killing was not my idea, Sire, and the breeding, as you call it, is in God's hands."

He refused point-blank to lead the Butchers back into Switzerland, convinced that this time he would surely die, probably not even honorably on a Swiss long pike. The forces that had desired his death and managed the cracked cannon would unquestionably desire his death the more fervently now that the queen was about to bear another child which, if it were a son, could replace himself as dauphin and heir. His father was smiling at him, but he experienced an unpleasant illusion that he could see through the skin to the skull: a death's head grinned and mocked.

Though he refused to go to Switzerland, he dared not remain in France. He pointed out that the season was well advanced, that an expedition would perish in the snow. "The Alps are a strong natural frontier," he observed, "placed by God as a wall and a shield on our flank. No further expansion need be made in that direction."

"The council did not mention that. That is very good, a wall and a shield on our flank. Wait till I tell that to the council! Sometimes I think they underestimate you."

"Which of them?"

"No, no, lad. I meant nothing. But something must be done with the Butchers. What would *you* do with them? Besides pensions, which I cannot afford, and little farms for which I have no land?"

Louis proposed an alternative. "There is also a natural frontier to the north, a wall of water, the Rhine!"

"But the Rhine is German."

"Why should it be?"

Charles asked his ministers. De Brézé, acting as spokesman, replied that they knew of no reason why the Rhine should be German if the dauphin wanted it to be French. If he cared to captain the Butchers into the vast Habsburg provinces to the north, they would sanction the expedition, nay, even supply it with artillery of unquestioned soundness, since the venture was as hazardous as an excursion into Switzerland. They commended the dauphin and called him before them, praising him to his face for his daring, indicating that if he could take Kolmar or Strassburg for France he would do something that no one had been able to do since Charlemagne's time. The dauphin pointed out that it would also thoroughly embarrass old Philip of Burgundy by flanking his duchy without actually bringing on war with him.

But at the mention of Strassburg and Kolmar, he had smelled a trap.

His holiday, short as it was, was sweet. On departing he could say to the dauphiness, half in earnest, half in fun: "My father has told me that I am good for nothing but killing. Pen me one of thy pretty poems if it should appear that God has permitted me to make good the loss of at least one of the martyred Frenchmen."

Margaret murmured in his ear, hiding her face against his ungainly head, "*Mon prince*, it were likelier two!" and, clinging to him, "Do thou protect thyself before Kolmar and Strassburg."

One did not confide to one's pale little wife, who would probably put it into a ballade for chattering ladies in waiting to read, that one had no intention of going to Kolmar or Strassburg. He patted her cheek. "And let there be roses here, Margaret, when I return."

"If you promise to return."

"I always return. Tell me, thou Scottish princess, can you find a French rhyme for the German city of Strassburg?" It would be well to leave her with no suspicion of another destination.

"Not for German Strassburg," she answered proudly. "But for Strasbourg, the French city, yes, a beautiful rhyme." It was *l'amour*.

Louis kissed her farewell. He was immensely pleased. One day his Scottish Margaret would make a wonderful queen of France.

Chapter Eighteen

Through the valley of the Marne in the royal demesne the Butchers passed under reasonable restraint and in good order. Beyond the Marne lay Lorraine, a duchy hesitating between allegiance to Burgundy and France, having feudal obligations to each and waiting to see which way the wind of fortune would blow now that the English menace had temporarily abated. In Lorraine Louis hanged one of the Butchers for stealing a chicken. One did not stir up the ire of Burgundy for a chicken, not when an entire province was hanging in the balance, not when one's father would seize on any excuse to reproach one for jeopardizing France's foreign policy, perhaps even for bringing on a Burgundian war.

The Butchers grumbled. Where was the booty Louis had promised them? It lay beyond, Louis answered, and sent a herald with a letter of apology to his "good uncle" Duke Philip the Good of Burgundy, explaining that he was merely traversing the duchy, accompanying the letter with a present of a handsome cross set with amethysts. Duke Philip loved jewels, as he loved everything costly and showy. "A proper young prince," he observed, "with excellent taste." Simultaneously his agents in Lorraine warned the provincials to shut up their castles at the approach of Louis's terrible companions. "He says he intends to keep on going, but take no chances." Privately the duke shook his head—Strassburg, Kolmar, very far, very rash. It was in the direction of these cities that Louis said he was bound.

And so he was, in their general direction.

Beyond Lorraine lay Alsace, a province of that vague, Germanic, chaotic, decrepit, but superstitiously venerated Holy Roman Empire, over which hung the giant imperial shadow of Charlemagne, and to which European chivalry still looked, in its own decline and in wistful awe, as the ancient fountainhead of titles and honors. This did not prevent national princes, or even the burghers of strong cities, from rebelling against their shadowy emperor, and they often did.

Louis had called it a ghost empire, but Louis believed in ghosts like everyone else. Like a ghost, with outlines as ill defined, it brooded over Central Europe, exerting an awesome power yet every year thinner and fainter as national states took shape within its wraithlike substance and the memory of Old Rome faded from men's minds.

As the Butchers passed the eastern versant of the Vosges and entered the dry late-autumn fields of the valley of the Rhine, Louis felt vaguely uneasy at the temerity of his venture. No king, not even the king of France, was entitled to be addressed as "Majesty." That imperial dignity was reserved to the Holy Roman Emperor, into whose territory he now struck.

"Fortunately there is at the moment no Holy Roman Emperor," he grinned. If a thing was not personified, Louis did not fear it very deeply. He felt better in his mind that no pope had as yet seen fit to crown a successor to the late emperor, who had died five years before. Frederick of Habsburg, Louis supposed, would manage to get the imperial crown in time—he was assuredly scheming for it: a pious concession here, a vigorous campaign there, elsewhere a well placed title or two that cost him nothing and made needed friends. There was much to learn in the art of kingcraft, more than one could learn from one's dull and sensual father.

Meanwhile, lacking the cohesion of authority, like curds separating and solidifying in sour milk, the Habsburg possessions, city by city and province by province, drew apart from one another, each trusting only its own mountain or valley or plain, its local language or local lord. Curds, Louis mused, were not necessarily bad; they were better than sour milk. But the process that created them was always ferment, and ferment was intolerable in one's own state, good only to have on one's frontiers.

No imperial ghosts, no academic concepts of national unity troubled the conscience of the Butchers. Here in Alsace, unhindered, they added new terror to their terrible name, looting, ravaging, leaving a trail of fire and murder as village after village was destroyed. They burned barns full of living cattle as an easy way to cook their suppers, and fell upon the smoking carcasses. They burned cottages and haystacks and grain fields, dry and ready for the harvest because, as they said, the flames would light their night marches. Louis, when he struck, struck fast and at night. Inevitably many of them perished, since the beaten Rhinelanders who had witnessed the ruination of their homes, their families, and their livelihood, fought wildly to die avenged. The earth was black after the passage of the dauphin's army. Ahead of his column frightened peasants and wild beasts fled toward the Rhine, the human beings to seek shelter in the Rhine cities and the animals to seek water, as brutes do in a terror of fire and smoke which they cannot understand.

Kolmar and Strassburg flooded their moats, drew up their drawbridges, closed their gates, and prepared for a siege with stolid German phlegm. It was hard to lose the harvest, but they knew their German cannon were as good as the French, and their German powder was better.

Louis turned aside, however, and led the Butchers neither to Kolmar nor Strassburg. Normal wastage of the troops had already reduced their number to a level that he was confident would satisfy even his royal father. Louis might not be able to conquer as far as the Rhine, but the Lilies of France had been unfurled in the Rhine Valley for the first time in hundreds of years; Europe paused and watched; a new and warlike luster glinted on the tarnished arms of France. Now he could accomplish an intensely private object of the expedition: if he could not yet be king he could perhaps make himself rich.

Between Kolmar and Strassburg lay the industrial city of Dambach. It was weakly fortified, trusting to its stronger neighbors, only a day's march in either direction, for protection in times of need. It possessed a thriving guild of merchant drapers who manufactured thick woolens, fine linens, and sumptuous cloth of gold. There was also some goldsmithing, since gold was needed for the textiles. No prince had ever made war on these tradesmen, not because robbing them would have been repugnant to the chivalry of the time, but because of the proximity of Kolmar and Strassburg. There was an even greater deterrent: textiles were bulky, they impeded the march of your army, and when you brought them into your own principality your merchants would be jealous, since if you used them for your court they became unemployed, and if you sold them—an unchivalric gesture in any case—you glutted the market. Either way you lost; textiles were poor as spoils of war.

Louis had weighed these difficulties. He had devised a scheme to side-step them which so outraged a Burgundian diplomat at his father's court that he warned, "Have an eye on the dauphin; he thinks of everything" (*Subtilier jour et nuict diverses pensées, aviser soudainement maintes estrangetés*).

While Kolmar and mighty Strassburg prepared for a siege, an operation that commonly drained the surrounding countryside for many miles, Louis struck with lightning swiftness at Dambach. The city fell in a day. That same night he offered peace in the guildhall to a deputation of merchants who stood quaking before him in their furred cloaks and velvet hose, twisting their hats in their hands.

His aspect was terrifying; he was in an agony of physical pain and spiritual fury; and he was tortured by the thought that the armies of Kolmar and Strassburg might descend upon him and wipe out his force before he could retreat with his booty.

The physical pain was caused by an arrow which had pinned his thigh to the saddle of his horse during the battle. He had not paused to let it be treated till all resistance ceased.

The spiritual fury was directed against St. Odile, the patron of Alsace. Louis had thoughtfully pinned an image of this saint on his hat and prayed for protection, since it was always wise to placate a local authority. St. Odile had not protected him. Louis had angrily trampled on the image, then picked it up and replaced it, asking its pardon.

Now he limped up and down the length of the great table at which the merchants held their weighty German conferences and their heavy

German banquets and shouted his demands in a voice that shook the flames of the torches in their sconces. Pain and excitement heightened his threats. The Germans had seen what Frenchmen were capable of. Would they care to see Dambach treated like the scorched villages? Would they care to be hanged by ropes of their own velevet to the hammer beams of their own guildhall?

The Master of the Goldsmith's Guild tremblingly admitted that there was a certain amount, a certain small amount of the precious metal of his trade in the treasury, regretting that most of it had recently been spun into thread and woven into cloth on an order from the Duke of Burgundy. This gold had already been sent for, he said. It was to be hoped that on its arrival His French Highness would retire and leave the small peaceful merchants of Dambach to their looms.

The gold arrived, little nuggets of uncoined bullion. It was not enough. Four burly Butchers spread-eagled the Master Goldsmith on the table. A pikeman heated the point of his pike red hot in the roaring fire at the end of the hall.

"Let him see it," Louis said. "Let him get a good look at it."

The pikeman thrust it so close to the shrieking merchant that it crisped his beard.

"Well, my squirrelish friend? Is there not some other hoard of precious nuts in some less obvious place?"

There was, there was, the merchant howled, straining away from the pike point. "My wife, let my Gerdrut be brought!"

The woman labored into the assembly, walking with difficulty under the weight of an enormous pregnancy.

"German pig, this is a sorry jest," the dauphin said.

"It's no use," panted the merchant. "He guesses everything. Let him have it."

The pregnancy disappeared; bags of gold nuggets thumped to the floor. A shout of rough laughter went up from the Butchers.

"Madame," Louis said grimly, "I am delighted to have eased you of your burden. This is probably the first time in history that a delivery has been more painful to a husband than to a wife."

Though the tribute was considerable, the dauphin was not satisfied. He would spare Dambach only if they emptied their textile warehouses and lashed the precious stores to the backs of pack animals which they themselves must supply. He gave them three hours.

At the same time he sent back through the ravaged and empty country to the rear a flying herald with a message for Duke Philip of Burgundy that if his good uncle should care to send an emissary into Lorraine he would meet him there with a choice shipment of cloth of gold and other fabrics which he had procured at a most advantageous price and which he had reason to believe his good uncle could use. For the love that he bore his good uncle, he said, he would part with it for far less than the guilds of Dambach would have demanded.

In Burgundy Duke Philip frowned a courtly frown at the lapse into trade of the heir to the throne of France. But Louis's terms were attractive. A Burgundian emissary was waiting in Lorraine for the dauphin, with money, a spectacular suite of retainers, and a gorgeously engrossed parchment assuring Louis that the hospitality of Burgundy and the friendship of his good uncle were perpetually at his disposal.

The emissary, observing the litter in which Louis was traveling, hoped that His Highness was well. Louis answered that his health was never better and, lest gossip start, thrust his wounded thigh under the astonished eyes of the polished Burgundian. Would *he* ride, he demanded, with a leg like that? That quieted the rumors about the dauphin's health for some time.

The emissary said he was also permitted to state verbally that if Louis should come to Burgundy, Duke Philip was in a mood to do him a great honor, and ceremoniously delivered into his hands two cheap leaden images to clip to his hat: St. Andrew and the Blessed Virgin. They were the patron saints of the exclusive Order of the Golden Fleece. Duke Philip had heard of the dauphin's piety, the emissary said, a piety approaching the holy poverty of a monk, else the images had been of gold.

"Tell my good uncle I'm no monk!" Louis snapped from his litter. Nevertheless he felt the great honor of which the leaden images were an earnest. The Virgin was already among the saints on his cap, but Louis now wondered why he had never thought of honoring St. Andrew, who was Scotland's patron saint and who must therefore take personal interest in the husband of Margaret, a Scottish princess. St. Odile was shunted ignominiously far round to the rear of the hat.

Thus honoring the saints in his own fashion, distributing Burgundian gold to his Butchers, and letting his mind dwell on the bourgeois art of trade, which had enabled him to keep a secret hoard for himself (though it rendered the litter painful to rest upon), the dauphin returned to France, where his thigh swelled to the size of a melon.

Chapter Nineteen

"There is no morbidity in the wound," Friar Jean advised him, frankly puzzled. "If Your Highness would only keep off it and rest in bed, perhaps the swelling will disappear. My science teaches me that it should."

"I must walk; I *must* be in motion when I am thinking. How am I made, Friar Jean? How? Why am I not like other men?"

"God knows, Monseigneur; and God knows only good."

"I seem to know only bad."

There was much bad to know. In his sickroom he had learned from gossipy old Jamet de Tillay that Jean d'Armagnac had managed to escape from what was officially described as a "deep and secure dungeon"; but on the exchange of a few pieces of Burgundian gold De Tillay confided the court rumor that the dungeon had consisted of comfortable quarters and that Count Jean's guards had consisted of nothing more substantial than Count Jean's parole. The dauphin listened in anger and apprehension. Jean d'Armagnac had simply forsworn himself, walked out of commodious confinement, and disappeared with the connivance of the king and council. "My mortal enemy, and they let him go!"—perhaps because he *was* his mortal enemy. He did not voice his suspicion aloud, but the pattern was plain: since a cracked cannon could not destroy him perhaps a human agency with a powerful motive would. He cudgeled his brain, searching where to find trustworthy guards for his sickroom. There was no one but Friar Jean, and Friar Jean could not totally neglect his ecclesiastical duties; or the dauphiness, who ought rightly to be confined to a sickroom of her own. The pallor on her cheeks had not diminished with his return, nor had she sent him a pretty poem announcing that he might expect an heir, nor had her mood of gloom lightened when he tried to comfort her. There was no pregnancy, there would never be a pregnancy, she felt a curse upon her; and often she pressed her wet cheek against his, his mouse-colored hair mingling with the brilliance of her blue-black curls. "Jean Boutet says it's because I eat apples, and Father Poictevin says it's because I stay up late writing. Could it be?"

"Everyone eats apples, and you did not stay up late writing—not writing, my dear—before I went away." Jean Boutet was the king's trusted apothecary, Robert Poictevin was the king's own physician; King Charles had always been inordinately fond of Margaret; his medical men were above suspicion as far as she was concerned. The dark fear that he himself might be to blame came to Louis in nightmares.

The envy and fear that he had of his father bordered on something like hatred when he thought of his mother. Frail and aging under the burden of twelve pregnancies in less than twenty-five years of marriage, now heavy with the thirteenth, she hovered in the background of the court, weary and unnoticed. Queen Marie expected the royal babe to die, like the others, with the exception of Louis and his three sisters who had managed to survive. She expected to die too; the thing in her womb was sluggish and dull; she did not much care. King Charles sometimes found time to encourage her. *Courage,* Madame! If she had not achieved quality, she had at least achieved quantity. He thrust out his chest to show where the quality lay. Generously he said that her record was not entirely to be censured. Eight dead, four living—one more prince, Madame, a proper prince this time, with straight legs and a head without room to house so many strange fancies. The ratio would then be less than two to one in favor of the dead, and he would cease making demands on her. A big and beautiful babe, Madame, like the one—

The queen had looked at him so sorrowfully that he left the room in confusion, muttering that she and Louis were equally moody and hard to understand.

The big and beautiful babe to which he referred was a bastard, proudly presented to him recently by Agnès Sorel, cooed over, smiled over, chucked under the chin, and universally caressed by the court, who said the child had her mother's eyes, her mother's peaches-and-cream complexion, and would one day have the spectacular Sorel figure. King Charles said there had been nothing wrong with his own in his day; Agnès Sorel dimpled and said she was very fond of it right now. De Brézé laughed, and said, "As all the world can see." Paris was very gay that winter. France was secure after the decimation of the Butchers, the terror that their slaughter, both inflicted and sustained, had wrought in Alsace, and the continuing abatement of the English menace.

Louis felt neither secure nor gay, and his wound healed slowly.

Some social success attended the dauphin's return. His sudden solvency, a curiosity concerning the whereabouts of his fortune—no one, of course, thought of rummaging through his mattress—and a foresighted desire to be on speaking terms with the heir to the throne attracted a thin stream of courtiers or paid informers to his sickbed, to which he kept long after the condition of his wound would have permitted him to be up and around.

Agnès Sorel herself visited him one day on the arm of Pierre de Brézé, whose adder-tongue beard flamed more brightly than usual, as if she had set a standard of brilliance that the old dandy wished to equal. She inquired after the dauphin's health, she inquired after the health of the dauphiness. She hoped he was resting comfortably, and bent over and smoothed his pillow with a patronizing hand, carelessly exposing a depth of voluptuous white bosom with rouged tips that momentarily took his breath away. She smiled archly when his face betrayed him. "Monseigneur is feeling better."

De Brézé glowered.

Louis put her down as a simple wench who had brazened her way to power and could not be condemned for acting a little giddy in the rarefied atmosphere where she now moved. De Brézé's reaction was more complex; he seemed anxious to lead her away; he seemed positively jealous. The dauphin's mind leaped, and his mouth twisted into a wry smile. There was probably more between these two than anyone guessed, more than De Tillay, even if De Tillay suspected, would dare to divulge.

"Mademoiselle is most accommodating," Louis said. He pointedly referred to her as "Mademoiselle." "You know how to make a bed very comfortable, thank you." The allusion was too broad for even Agnès Sorel to miss. But he did not stop there. "It comes to my ears that you just had a baby. How is the dear little bastard? And the lucky father—if Mademoiselle happens to know which of her host of admirers—"

Agnès Sorel's cheeks flamed under their paint. De Brézé interrupted, "Madame, your good nature is wasted in visiting Monseigneur's bedchamber—"

"Bedchamber, bedchamber, bedchamber," murmured the dauphin. "Surely you cannot intentionally imply, Monseigneur de Brézé, that Mademoiselle's good nature is wasted in a bedchamber. I should have thought that all the evidence points vehemently to the contrary."

"I had hoped to be friends with you," she said. "If you will not receive me, there is nothing I can say. Come, De Brézé." Her velvet train rippled like water over the little irregularities of the stone floor as she walked, tall and superbly self-possessed, out of the room.

Louis got out of bed and strode up and down the length of his apartment, his soft fur slippers padding nervously on the floor, still limping slightly, clicking off on his fingers the possible reasons for her visit. She was too simple to have come to find out where he kept his money, though De Brézé's eyes had searched the dark corners of the room when they were not probing down the deep décolletage of her gown. She was not genuinely interested in the health of the dauphiness, for the king already knew all about that from his medical men. As for his own health, he did not suppose she cared one whit, for hers was not a political cast of mind. Someone, then, had sent her, someone who genuinely wished him and his father's mistress on friendly terms. Poor, good-natured Agnès Sorel had simply said her lines and stalked away in a magnificently feminine pique. No wonder his simple father adored the creature.

Nor was it his father who had sent her. In a very short time the king came storming into the bedchamber. He was not announced, of course. Louis heard and recognized his heavy tread, sensed the overtone of anger in the way the heels snapped upon the floor. There was scarcely time to jump into bed, pull the coverlet up to his chin, and assume an expression of illness.

"Ah, Sire, how good of you to visit me. One gets so lonely on one's bed of pain."

"Why in blazes did you insult Madame de Sorel?"

"*Madame de* Sorel? Oh, yes, of course, Madame de Sorel. How careless of me. Did I insult her? I should have thought that was impossible."

"Have a care, Louis! One day you will carry your impudence too far. I am a terrible man when I am aroused."

Louis said smoothly, "Now all the saints forbid that I should arouse Your Highness," and was about to quip that Mademoiselle Sorel did it better anyhow, but something in his father's face put a tether on his tongue.

"I have warned you, I have warned you," the king muttered over and over again. It seemed to the dauphin that the warning was an easement of conscience for something likely to come.

After that, for a long time, Louis was left pointedly alone. No one dared approach him; the king's displeasure must have been voiced more publicly than ever before. Bits of news filtered through to him, however. He learned from Friar Jean that the Count of Armagnac was again in Lectoure, exercising full power and privilege as usual in his city in spite of the parliament's death sentence. He learned from the dauphiness that the queen could expect to be brought to bed at any time.

One morning he was jarred from sleep by the booming of cannon, the pealing of all the city bells, and the cheering of crowds in the streets. A page rapped sharply on the door, entered unbidden, and announced with the slightest of bows that Louis had a brother.

"And Madame my mother?"

"Who knows, Monseigneur?" the page shrugged impishly.

"Shrug at me, will you, fellow?" Louis clutched the terrified lad by his holiday doublet and struck him a deafening blow on the ear. "Shrug at the name of my mother, will you?" His long arm arched and descended violently upon the other ear. "Shrug at Marie, Princess of Anjou, Princess of Sicily, Queen of France? Do you dare! Who are you, strumpetson? What is your name? Tell me your name, so I shall remember to hang you!"

The youngster ran screaming from the dauphin's presence, holding his palms tightly over both injured ears, which Robert Poictevin treated with sweet oil that day, snapping his fingers at graduated intervals and shaking his head, wondering if the hearing would return.

Later Louis was sorry and sent the boy a small Dambach gold nugget. It was not the page's fault that he had caught and reflected the prevailing attitude of the court. Privately he inquired of Friar Jean whether he had done the lad any harm.

"Less than you did to yourself, Louis. I am informed that he answers the dinner bell regularly again. But one should save arms like yours for smiting the enemies of France."

"Who are the enemies of France, mon père?"

"Monseigneur," Friar Jean smiled sadly, "Pilate asked, 'What is truth?' As I recall the Scriptures, nobody knew, and Our Lord did not answer."

"Neither does anyone know the enemies of France, and I cannot wait for Our Lord to point them out."

In this colloquy Friar Jean recognized a new tone: his former pupil was speaking more authoritatively and more ominously than he could ever remember in the past. The fire of ambition that had started on his wedding night as a necessity to distinguish himself in the eyes of his bride now embraced a vastly greater territory, since it is in the nature of fire to spread. Everywhere in his campaigns the dauphin had found fuel to feed his flame. From High Armagnac at the foot of the Spanish mountains to Dambach in the valley of the German river he had found naught but disunity, treason, degradation and misery, great wealth and grinding poverty. Vaguely and uncertainly a light in this darkness began to shine and beckon him: all might be changed if one strong hand could guide the destiny of this great land of France, if the all-but-sovereign aristocracy could be brought down and the all-but-brutish commoners could be brought up within human reach of each other. The concept of such a polity came to him half formed and obscure because it was contrary to the precepts of his, and every other prince's, feudal education, which presented society not as a plain but as a pyramid.

It was further obscured by his eccentric terror of heights. He knew only that he feared the Alps and loved Touraine, and that he was most at ease among men of the stature of the bourgeoisie, where no one was toweringly independent like Jean d'Armagnac and no one was independent in abasement like the Butchers.

It was further obscured because he was only a prince, not yet a king, no longer even the only prince, and powerless to effect the reforms that he fitfully and imperfectly envisioned. Nor was he yet prepared to go to any and all lengths to achieve them. True, he had obeyed evil orders, like leading the Butchers to their death; but never yet, as Friar Jean knew, who had taught him the purest of feudal ethics (now considered a little old-fashioned), had the dauphin done a premeditated evil deed on the specious excuse that a good end would justify it.

Now he would witness at work that also, that most seductive of fallacies, which the waning voice of the Schoolmen had never ceased to condemn and which the burgeoning Italian Renaissance would exalt into a virtue, especially among princes. It too would shape him. It came in a form so gentle and sweet that even Friar Jean at first detected no sin in it, nor could he foresee from so small a seed the terrifying plant that would spring from it. But in Louis's perpetually harrowed mind seeds grew with great speed to abnormal proportions.

It was his own mother who had been interested in effecting a reconciliation between him and the king, and to that good end she had stooped to employ Agnès Sorel, and worse.

Louis had attempted to visit his mother shortly before the birth of the little prince; guards crossed their pikes in his face at the door of the royal apartments; the queen could see no one, they said. When the royal infant was born, he attempted to visit her again; this time the guards were doubled and he was informed with humiliating shortness that Madame la Reine did not *wish* to see him and that Monseigneur le Prince, Duc de Berri, the newborn infant, had been placed in seclusion against cranks and intruders.

Louis murmured, "Monseigneur le Prince, Monseigneur le Duc; how they wish they could call him Dauphin!" And the gratuitous reference to cranks and intruders . . . as if he were intruding when he tried to get a glimpse of his own brother, as if he were a crank who might do the child harm! That his beloved mother did not wish to see him he could not quite believe, but his heart was heavy at the thought of the influences that might have been brought to bear upon her in her sickness and misery. It might be true.

Margaret was constantly with the queen, however, and she reassured him to some extent, saying that the queen had asked for him every day. He had never doubted Margaret's word, but it was quite conceivable that she might paint a rosy picture of a bleak situation simply to please him. Margaret had also been permitted to view the princeling. She thought Monseigneur le Duc de Berri somewhat moon-faced and lethargic. That, Louis grimly believed.

Then, on a quiet night, his mother crept silently into his bedchamber and whispered that since he would not come to her she must needs come to him. She was unattended, she lighted no candle, but he saw her face in the moonlight and it was old, deathlike. For a moment he sat wildly upright, clapping his hands to his mouth for fear he would scream—this was assuredly one of his nightmares.

Two well known, well beloved hands quieted him, Margaret's on his brow, his mother's on his own. It was real, but what it portended he did not know.

"Your matrons, *Madame ma mère?* Your torchbearer? This eerie hour?"

"Hush, Louis. I need no light to light me to my son, who will not come to me."

"Believe me, dear mother, I have made every effort to see you, and my little brother also."

Margaret said, "Did I not tell you so?"

"I needed to hear it from his own mouth, which has never lied to me. Everyone else lies, some for spite, some like you, Margaret, to console me." She smiled ever so slightly; it was a ghost of a smile in a cold blue light that robbed the lips of all color. "I sent you a witching visitor some time hence. You did not receive her very graciously."

"*You* sent that woman here?"

"She is the only avenue to the king's favor. I was afraid for you." What the employment of such an emissary must have cost her proud spirit furrowed the dauphin's brow. "It was most impolite of you to aggravate your father's displeasure by insulting her. But in my heart I was glad you did. It made it easier to bear your brother; I kept saying to myself, 'This one too may grow up to love me.' But I feared for you the more when the child was a prince and your father took a decisive step. Here is something you should read, for without the evidence of your eyes you will not believe what is in it."

"I will believe you, Mother; and we must not light a light." Now he saw in her hand a parchment of imperial proportions. The red seals looked black in the moonlight, but he could make out the arms of

France upon them. The seals had been broken. He wondered how much money had changed hands to obtain this secret document, which obviously concerned himself. He had never thought of his gentle mother as an intriguer.

"I can tell you in a word. It is a petition to the pope to set you aside in favor of your brother."

Louis drew in his breath sharply. In addition to bribery blood must have been spilled to intercept so privileged and important a thing as a petition to the Holy See.

She sensed his suspicion. "No one was hurt, Louis. It merely cost more. Money will always ransom blood. I do not conceive it my calling to do murder in the twilight of a life spent in creating life—though I cannot say to what lengths I might have gone had not money accomplished my purpose."

"What do you counsel me to do, brave mother? though I already know."

"You must fly."

"I will not leave France."

The queen sighed. "I knew he would not. Margaret, did I not tell you he would not?"

Margaret whispered: "In Scotland we shall be safe. The craggy Highlands would not be to your liking, but the valley of the Tweed is a gentle country with scores of forgotten little fishing places nestling along the river—"

"I do not wish to be forgotten."

"Perhaps it will be only for a short while."

"Till the Duc de Berri dies?"

"Louis, Louis, Louis," murmured his mother.

"They were uncommonly watchful, Madame, that I should not kill him!"

"They do not know you as I know you, my son."

"And what, Margaret, lies south of your precious Scottish river Tweed?"

"Why—England, of course."

"England!" He spat out the name.

"He will not go. Attend me, Margaret. I am sick and heavy in my heart."

Louis said: "Mother, that petition must be sent to the Holy Father, you know. Do you know?"

"I know," she said wearily.

"Every crease in the ribbons exactly as before; the broken seals, somehow they must be replaced—"

"I know. There are duplicate seals; everything is arranged."

"But who could arrange duplicate—"

"Good night, dear Louis." She walked slowly to the door, leaning heavily on Margaret's arm.

Louis paced softly, nervously, swiftly, up and down his chamber. The full import of the sinister parchment now struck him, with all its host of overtones, like a prolonged reverberation of thunder rolling over him, engulfing him, pounding upon his ears after the silent lightning flash which only stuns and blinds.

All at once he was aware that the sensations were physical and real: he was hearing a distant booming, it was coming closer, increasing in volume, mysteriously in step with the beating of his heart; he was having difficulty with his vision, for the blue-white moonlight assumed a darkly purple hue. There was an icy wind upon his spine, colder than the chill that usually meant only a few seconds' extinction of consciousness. He struggled to maintain control of his arms, which wanted to move at their own wild will; he succeeded in detaching the scarf from about his waist, and wrapped it tightly around his mouth to muffle the sounds that he knew would come when he fell.

Outside his heavy, securely bolted door, no one heard anything unusual.

Chapter Twenty

Next morning, when the country people who daily came into Paris to sell their farm produce had scarcely set up their pushcarts, before they had yet disposed of their freshest eggs, a meanly clad man with a shining face smiled his way into the slums. How warm it was for April! How brilliant the sun, how noble the long shadow of his legs cast by its early light upon the rough cobbles of this interesting out-of-the-way sector. How promising the evidence of his own eyes had been when he examined the scarf around his mouth upon waking—what a rosy prognosis for the future—there had been not a fleck of foam. The seizure could not have been severe; it must have merged with the sleep that would have come at that hour anyhow; it must have seemed severe only by reason of its duration.

Supremely confident, almost patronizingly, he resolved to mention nothing to Friar Jean, who would only fret and brew him more potable gold to drink and preach him a homily on the therapeutic benefits of preserving an equable balance in his thinking. Equable balance, forsooth! How could anyone be unbalanced in this best of all friendly worlds where everything was crystal-clear and warm and bright and safe!

He greeted the peasants cheerily as he strode past their carts. They nodded stolidly and warmed their blue fingers over smoky little fires. They took him for some university student coming home after an all-night revel, still cheerful and flushed with wine but too poor to have bought enough to stagger, probably a divinity student, to judge from the saints on his cap.

How clearly his mind was working, how lucidly, how pleasantly! How foolish of his mother to take that pompous parchment seriously! What a ridiculous thought, the Holy Father setting him aside! Popes did not set aside first-born princes and set up their infant brothers in their stead. That would entail dealing with a council of regents; councils were notoriously factious, all popes hated factions, all popes hated councils. The thoughts came flashing fast, too fast to examine critically. His mother must have exaggerated things because she was worried and sick. He was not sick and he was not worried. Never in his life could he remember feeling so warm and happy and friendly.

In the Rue Saint-Jacques he passed a churchyard, noting how prettily the morning sun laid a wash of gold upon the tombstones. It would do no harm to hear a Mass, though he did not think he needed one. Slyly he dropped St. Odile into the poorbox; at last he had thought of a safe way to get rid of him! Maybe there were some Alsatians under those modest tombstones; let St. Odile protect them, since His Blessedness did not seem to care for French princes.

In the gloom of the mean little church, however, when the collection basket came round, he remembered that there were no Alsatians buried in Paris, and slipped a gold crown for St. Odile under the pennies of the workmen who knelt around him. The man with the basket, a man with remarkable eyes, watched him sharply; Louis averted his face, but smiled when he noted out of the corner of his eye that the man seemed satisfied that he had not been stealing. The basket passed on.

He emerged from the church still happy and now hungry. He had walked a long way from the palace, and he now remembered that he had completely forgotten all about breakfast. "Pasque Dieu," he muttered to himself, surveying the tombstones, the charnel house beyond, and the squalor of the surrounding area, "how does one satisfy an appetite in this place?"

"What kind of appetite, Monseigneur?" The voice was amiable and singularly resonant. Louis turned his head; he must have spoken louder than he had realized. He found himself looking into the sharp eyes of the man who had taken up the collection, a man with a face as pale as the dauphiness's.

"Monseigneur, fellow? Who is Monseigneur around here? I am—" He glanced up at the portal of the church. He was still, perhaps, on consecrated ground. "I am a merchant," he said, thinking of Dambach, chuckling at the way he must be discomfiting St. Odile. But it wasn't a lie, and could not be held against him in heaven.

"As you wish. If Monsieur le *marchand* has another gold piece in his pocket, I can show him a place to satisfy all appetites known to man."

Louis assumed that a collection taker must of necessity possess sharp eyes in a district like this. The speech of the man interested him. "You have a curious turn of phrase, my good man."

"So have you, Monsieur, with your lordly 'fellows' and 'my good man's.' "

"Oh, that," Louis said. "A habit I picked up from some of my noble patrons. On a beautiful day like this, I feel almost a king."

"So you should," said the man.

"This magnificent light, this fragrant air—"

"The fragrant air is not at the moment from the direction of my lodgings."

"Where do you lodge, my friend?"

The man pointed to the charnel house.

It was half above, half below ground, like all the other temporary resting places of the deceased who must wait till their graves were dug.

"The custodian of this churchyard is very obliging," the man continued. "For a sol a week he lets me dwell yonder, with silent companions who no longer have appetites of any kind. Was the appetite you mentioned perhaps for food?"

"Pasque Dieu, yes, food." It struck Louis that this pleasant new friend might be starving. "If you know where a man can fill an empty belly, come join me for breakfast. I have many other gold pieces in my purse."

The man glanced at him strangely. "You have?"

"Oh, yes."

They fell in step together. "You are not who I thought you were, Monsieur. He would never have said he had gold on him. In fact, you appear to be singularly guileless, far too guileless for a merchant. Whoever you are, I like you. I like few men; few men like François Villon."

"Are you François Villon?" No wonder the fellow had a curious cast of phrase.

The man nodded. "François Villon, François des Loges, François de Montcorbier, I am known by many names, especially among the sergeants."

"Villon the great poet! I can hardly believe it. The man who wrote,

'De trois sergens pendez-en deux,
Le monde n'en sera que mieux.'

It is a beautiful thought, a delightful thought!" Louis laughed till passersby looked at him suspiciously.

"It is a beautiful thought, Monsieur. I agree heartily with the sentiment, as you seem to too. But it is a vile couplet and I did not write it. Everything vile is attributed to me."

"Tut, tut, man; nothing is vile. Things are simply funny." Louis was still laughing at the meager joke of hanging two out of three of the

Grand Provost's sergeants, those owlish louts who paraded about in their wooden clogs and their cheap fleur-de-lis tunics, performing routine police duties, sometimes making arrests and escorting culprits to jail when they could catch them. They were underpaid and generally held in low esteem.

Villon suggested, "Perhaps my prosperous friend is known to them too by several names." He had an idea Louis might be some amateur cutpurse who had made a lucky snatch during the night.

"Pasque Dieu, François, I am known by dozens of names." It tickled Louis's boundless good humor that he had not told a lie today; the dauphin *was* known by dozens of names.

"And naturally you do not wish to divulge them. I understand. Let me warn you, however, that it would be wise in this district which you find so fragrant to conceal your purse."

"Who would steal from me, François? As for my name, call me Louis, for assuredly Louis I am."

"So is half of France, my merry friend, or Henri, or Jacques, or Philippe, or Charles—"

"Nay, not Charles. Anything but Charles."

Villon led him beyond the charnel house into a tumbledown blind alley strewn with filth, avoiding the wall lest the contents of chamber pots tumble down on their heads. "Still fragrant, friend Louis?"

"A little night soil, that is all. Upon my word, François Villon, you are a most gloomy person."

"And you are most simple-minded. What an idiot I was to take you for a certain crafty, morose, taciturn, secretive—"

"What a monster you are describing! Who is this monster?"

"Nay, let it go. *You* would not know him. Here is our breakfast. If you will not hide your purse, let me carry it for you."

"Certainly, François." He slipped it off his belt. It was the only rich item of all his attire. Louis had many shabby doublets, many patched hose, many shoes with holes in the soles, for he never threw anything away. But he always carried a good purse, for a threadbare one might let money slip through.

Villon examined it swiftly with a practiced eye. He saw a small decoration, the image of a fish, a dolphin, embroidered upon it. With a motion too rapid for the eye to follow, he whisked it into the deep dark sleeve of his academic gown; one would have taken an oath that the purse had never existed.

"*Hohecté, mon brave!* I am beginning to respect you. To have got so close to *him!* How we shall breakfast, oh, how we shall breakfast, my Louis!"

They were now at the door of a gloomy building at the end of the passage, an uncared-for pile of rotting stone that looked as if it dated from the First Crusade. Louis conjectured that it might be a warehouse of some sort. The narrow windows were blocked up with weather-stained boards, and the gate was shut. Villon knocked with the hilt of a dagger which appeared from one of his deep commodious sleeves as suddenly as the dauphin's purse had disappeared; it was an odd knock with a distinct rhythm.

"That was a signal," Louis said brightly.

"Your perspicacity is almost uncanny," Villon said with an ill concealed barb of sarcasm in his voice. "Welcome to the Ass with the Brindled Fell."

At this Louis's face changed slightly.

"Have I offended you, my friend? I meant no offense by my sharp tongue. But naturally it was a signal. This is a tavern—of sorts."

Something was happening to the dauphin. His merry mood was passing swiftly. Decidedly he would speak of last night's seizure to Friar Jean and ask what it portended. Nothing like it had ever happened before.

He could not understand himself. To dismiss the danger of that parchment! To venture unattended into this unsavory district, to strike up an acquaintance with a known though gifted scoundrel—and Pasque Dieu! to have relinquished his purse! He must have been mad. Nay, not with the madness of his grandfather but with something insidious that left his senses unimpaired at the same time that it warped his judgment out of all recognition. He felt less warm—more normally cool for an early morning in spring. And he felt a normal reluctance to enter a place that was at such pains to conceal its whereabouts. But he had come too far to go back now. The door opened, and Villon took his arm and propelled him through. The door grated heavily shut behind them.

It was quite dark inside. A surly voice, unpleasantly close to his face, in a breath offensive with garlic and sour wine, said, "Welcome to you, Master Villon; but who is this?"

"A friend, thou gallows cheat, and see that you serve him like a gentleman."

"If I did I'd serve him with my poignard."

"Perhaps we should take our custom elsewhere, François. Our welcome and our host are equally invisible."

"Good God, another poet!" the voice said resignedly. "Bring him in, bring him in, but see that he pays."

"I shall pay," said Villon. Louis sensed that he was being protected, sensed also that Villon would not mind distributing the coins from the purse in his sleeve with an affluent hand.

Shortly he saw the dim outline of a doorway at the end of the room. To this the host led them, walking before them in ape-like silhouette.

"Walk close to me, warily, Louis. This used to be a stable; one could easily slip into the manure trench and break an ankle."

"I shall attempt to walk warily."

He would also attempt to continue as stupid and simple as, with ample reason, Villon took him to be. There was no time now to speculate why he had wakened this morning so different a person from the person he actually was and always had been.

At the door of the dining room the silhouette of the host turned aside and limped into nothingness, a shadow merging with shadows.

"He is sensitive about his appearance," Villon whispered.

"A veteran of the war?"

"A veteran of one of His Highness the King's prisons."

"What did he do?"

"One day when I know you better perhaps I shall tell you something of the company here. It strikes me you ask more questions in the dark than in the light."

"It was an idle question."

"Do not ask them here if you expect to return. The Ass with the Brindled Fell is a convenient place for 'merchants' like yourself to take refuge in, to dine, to sup, even to stay many weeks in security from the sergeants after, let us say, negotiating a generous commission from a prosperous client."

A number of men and slatternly women looked up from their wooden plates as Villon escorted his guest to a table by the fire where the carcass of a sheep was roasting on a spit. Seeing him with Villon, they accepted him without interest and turned their attention again to their plates. Except for one man they were ragged and dirty. They were not boisterous, however. That would come later, Louis supposed, when they had had a good day's rest and prepared to return to whatever they did at night. The knives with which they cut their meat were sharp and bright, handled with utmost dexterity. Not even among the Butchers could Louis remember such vicious faces. He realized that he was sitting in a conspicuous seat, but he knew it would be bad tactics to slink into a shadowy corner. It was the dark low portion of the wall at Lectoure that the enemy had manned most heavily, and Lectoure had been stormed through the frontal gates.

The only man who was not ragged and dirty sat also at the conspicuous exclusive table by the fire. It was not Friday, but it was April and it was Lent. Like everybody else he was eating meat.

"Good morning, Père Sermoise," Villon said.

"Good morning, Your Reverence," said Louis.

Nothing surprised him any more; he had lost his capacity to be astonished. It was the priest who had said the Mass in the Rue Saint-Jacques.

He stared at Louis quizzically, half frightened. "Who—is—this—man!" Louis's mind pictured the rabbit-like chaplain of Jean d'Armagnac, and his miserable end.

Villon said: "Have no fear, Père Sermoise. I made the same mistake. This is the fortunate sinner who will pay for your meat and mine, for an absolution. He cut the purse of Monseigneur le Dauphin last night!"

128

"I happened to be on the same street," Louis smiled. "Would it be a sin, Père Sermoise, to cut the purse of the dauphin?"

"Monsieur, it would be an impossibility."

"Nevertheless, Master Villon has it in his sleeve for safekeeping."

"That was very wise of you. I do the same thing with my collection basket. The rascals would steal each other's pennies otherwise. I set a thief to catch the thieves, and the parish is not robbed too severely—of course I do not know how much Villon collects for himself."

"Now here is my honor at stake," Villon laughed. "Was there a gold piece in the basket this morning?"

"I thought it was a miracle."

"It was my friend's, and I did not steal it."

"Then that was the miracle." The priest stuffed a great handful of mutton into his mouth and crooked a finger at a barmaid, who brought him more wine. "You are eating no meat, Monsieur," he said, looking reproachfully at the dauphin. "You throw in my face my regrettable weakness. What can I do? When I was young I starved. I resolved to starve no longer. Now I do not starve at the Ass with the Brindled Fell."

"Père Sermoise has appointed himself to do missionary work in this delectable place," Villon said dryly. "Many of the clientele value his absolution."

"Don't you think they need it? Look at the swine," the priest grunted.

"Which he gives for a price in most execrable Latin with a nauseating Italian accent—"

"My accent is perfect. I was educated in Rome, you sentimental scribbler. And I would remind you that the personal peccadillos of a priest do not in the least vitiate the efficacy of his sacerdotal acts."

"My good patron, Guillaume de Villon, thinks there may be some minor diminution of efficacy."

"The chaplain of Bestourné and I move on different planes."

Louis was listening, looking, weighing the best means of retiring quietly from this queer haunt. The faces of the clientele, on closer inspection, were no more formidable than the faces of the Butchers, and he had handled them. The Butchers killed professionally and stole only incidentally; this precious coterie of thieves in the Ass with the Brindled Fell did the same, merely in the reverse order; he felt he could handle them too. They might steal his purse, if François Villon had not already stolen it, but he did not feel that his life was in danger at their hands. He was not comfortable, but he was at least as comfortable as he was with De Brézé or his father or the council.

It was instructive to learn that François Villon was on intimate terms with such dissimilar members of the clergy: this cynical, sensuous pastor of a disreputable parish and equally the erudite chaplain of the Collegiate

Church of St. Benoît-le-Bestourné, through which passed much diplomatic correspondence.

It was instructive to learn that the polished prelate, Guillaume de Villon, was François des Loges's or Montcorbier's patron, and that the poet had changed his name to Villon to honor him. Most of all it was instructive that the patron had not repudiated his protégé, even though the protégé got into endless amorous difficulties with loose women and with the authorities for impudent verses. Why? Why was François not repudiated? Fidelity was always founded on love or on fear. If Guillaume de Villon loved François Villon, there might be something closer than a name that they shared, some secret tie of blood. If, on the other hand, Guillaume de Villon feared François Villon, a certain scheme that was taking shape in the dauphin's mind might stand a good chance of success.

"Not only does he not eat, he doesn't even talk," Père Sermoise muttered.

"I was thinking," Louis said. "I was thinking of the miracle of the dauphin's purse."

"A miracle indeed," Villon answered, testing its weight on his arm. "I wonder it does not rip my threadbare sleeve. How often, when I was a student, proud of my new academic gown, did I not muse on the ancient days that gave it its shape, which was practical then. Students still begged, as students always must, but begging was easy when France was rich and secure. The students stuffed their alms into their sleeves till they bulged with bread and sausages, so generous were the good people of that golden age. Each year the sleeves grew longer and more commodious. Then the English came, Burgundy arose, France was sundered and fragmented. Apocalytic disasters engulfed us; floods came and plague and war and famine—"

"I find no famine here," said Père Sermoise through a mouthful of mutton.

"Till our priests eat stolen sheep in Lent and kings flaunt their strumpets in our teeth—"

Louis clamped his scarlet face under iron control.

"—and our academic sleeves hang like old breasts, sad, flat, full of nothing but wind and memory."

A barmaid leaned over and filled his stone cup with cheap wine. She patted his head familiarly and said to the priest: "Wine heats him at breakfast. What is he composing now?"

"A monologue on the academic gown, my girl, which yours is not." Père Sermoise was boggling at her bodice.

"And would seem to belie his thesis," Louis said slyly.

"Not at all," Villon said, passing his arm around her slender waist. "You too will be empty and flat one day, my Isabeau."

"You didn't talk like that last night."

Villon laughed. "My muse is strangled. Bring me some mutton. It is all right—today I pay for everybody."

Louis had liked the tenor of Villon's words. The poet was a devoted Frenchman, idealistic, vain, poor. He was not so sure of the priest. Contented men with narrow horizons did not throw themselves into hazardous ventures. One might blackmail him, of course, but eating meat in Lent was not serious enough to scare a priest into opening the pope's correspondence, nor was Louis certain that an education in Rome or a chance Italian accent in one's Latin necessarily guaranteed access to the papal reply. The impudent François Villon, so highly connected and irreverent, was a far better instrument for the scheme. It would be a risk to reveal his identity, but Louis had calculated that risk and he deemed it in his favor.

Villon's conversation touched on the barmaid now, but Louis learned nothing that he did not already suspect—a willing wench, a union that sometimes inspired a ballade and always exacted a fee. "But she trusts me when I am temporarily short of funds, Louis."

Père Sermoise yawned and said he must be getting back to his church. He had a better than average funeral and he wished to make some preparations.

When he was gone, Louis lowered his voice to a whisper and said: "I trust you too, François Villon. In trusting you I am trusting God, who has put into my hands a weapon to protect my country from evils greater than those you have described. Yours will be a dangerous mission but it will be profitable. And it will save France from civil war."

Villon caught the tone of authority but looked confused.

"The dauphin's purse was no miracle, nor was it stolen. A man cannot steal from himself. Louis the dauphin has freely given his purse to his friend for help in a mighty enterprise, which will fill your sleeves with gold like the loaves and sausages of the ancient days."

"Monseigneur!"

"It was Monseigneur all the time."

Rapidly he sketched his plan. Villon admitted that his relations with his patron, the chaplain of St. Benoît-le-Bestourné, were strained at the moment because of the girl Isabeau. Louis reminded him that in the ordinary course of events no reply could be expected from Rome for several months; there would be plenty of time to patch it up with his patron. Meanwhile he would keep him in funds; Villon would not be forced to live for a sol a week in a charnel house. The pope's reply, the dauphin stressed, was not to be destroyed, merely intercepted and read and the dauphin apprised of its contents so that he could perfect his plans. He played on all the strings of Villon's heart, a heart he had dissected and studied from the moment his power of judgment returned: Villon's vanity and avarice, his love of France, his love of Isabeau. He promised him favor when he should be king; he found the barmaid worthy of a peerage.

"If the Holy Father sets you aside, Monseigneur, *charbieu!* You should make a revolution! You are strong, respected, trusted; you would have hosts of followers."

"No," said the dauphin simply, "in that case I must retire forever into the Dauphiny and do what I can in a smaller sphere."

"The reply shall be intercepted, Monseigneur! Before God, I will manage it. I have many resources at my disposal. Your Highness may not approve of the vagabonds here, but they are powerful. You shall never be set aside!"

It was in the late morning, shortly before he was hurriedly summoned to his mother's bedside, that he met Friar Jean in the hall of the palace. Friar Jean was full of a sudden excitement that centered around the queen, but he found time to counsel the dauphin, who said that he had experienced a seizure during the night and taken a long walk on awakening, during which time he had felt queerly happy.

Such symptoms were common, Friar Jean told him, and not necessarily alarming. Sometimes a victim of the falling sickness would suffer a temporary aberration on emerging from a serious attack. The world looked better than it ought, as in mild intoxication. One felt a deceptive optimism, a sense of warm well-being for which there was no real cause. It was as if the sickness were trying to cure itself by means of a convulsion and succeeded too well, going a little beyond the cure, purging the mind of darkness and fear so completely that not even the normal residue of prudence and caution remained. The phase always passed quickly. The best thing to do was to keep to one's bed and avoid situations which might not be recognized as dangerous.

"I shall be on my guard," the dauphin said.

Friar Jean said gravely: "Your mother has been calling for you. It would be well to hasten, my son."

Chapter Twenty-one

When the dauphin arrived at the queen's bedside, she was in a coma from which she never awakened. He saw her die.

"It would have been a comfort to your mother if you had taken the trouble to be with her," King Charles observed. "I had every nook and cranny of the city searched for you when she collapsed. Did I not, my lords?"

The entire council had crowded into the death chamber. Scanning their faces for one sympathetic eye, Louis found only high statesmanship, cool and disinterested. De Brézé alone displayed a flicker of emotion, and the emotion was suspicion. He was wondering where the dauphin had disappeared during the space of an entire night. Even in his grief Louis was struck by the fact that the Ass with the Brindled Fell must be an extraordinarily secret place.

With the council gravely nodding assent to the king's statement that no one had been able to find him, Louis bowed his head. His conscience was clear. More pertinently, nothing could be gained now by protesting that he had been repeatedly barred from the queen's presence, and it would have been dangerous to divulge that he had conversed with her in most tender intimacy only last night.

Queen Marie's funeral was conspicuously unostentatious. It was the king's wise decision, said the heralds who read the carefully prepared proclamation, to expend the public monies only on absolute necessities, that taxes might go no higher. In the cathedral Agnès Sorel, sitting beside the king, joined the silent congregation in their sorrow by dabbing at her beautiful eyes with a gossamer handkerchief of black Genoese lace, wearing a new necklace of pearls, appropriately black also, in mourning.

By midsummer she was pregnant again, and at the happy disclosure King Charles let it be known that further mourning for the late queen was distasteful to him. The little Duc de Berri did not cry when the violet draperies that honored his mother were removed from his crib; in fact he seldom cried or even moved. But the dauphin continued to wear the violet cloak of mourning of a Prince of the Lilies. "I will wear it," he said vehemently to Friar Jean, "till the full year is up, though I know how they laugh at me behind my back."

Friar Jean did not want to tell him that his physician's instinct warned him he might wear it even longer.

On Sunday, the 8th of August, as Louis emerged from Notre-Dame, where he had said a prayer for his mother and a shorter one for Margaret, who was suffering from a slight cold, he was rudely jostled by a beggar. It was common for the beggars who crouched and whined on the cathedral steps to be sick or deformed or maimed by the wars or demented, or to pretend to be so that the generosity of the worshipers might be spurred. But this man's face was frightful. He wore a scrap of rag turban-fashion around his head. There was no bulge underneath where the ears should be. His nose was slit into two halves, and the cut, now healed, continued down, severing the lips and exposing fine firm teeth. Louis, who had seen much of war, could not easily reconstruct in his mind what freak series of battle accidents could have caused such wounds. A sword seldom cut off both ears; a dagger seldom wrought such havoc to the center of a face without damaging the teeth.

"Pasque Dieu, thou'rt no veteran. Look how you jostle me, fellow, or you shall not have your penny."

The man held up his hat for the coin with an arm that crooked unnaturally, as if he had two elbows. Someone must have done a sorry job of bone setting. "If you reach into my hat," he said in a whisper, "you may find something worth a crown."

Louis plunged in his hand and clutched a crumpled piece of paper. Without waiting for his coin, the beggar turned his back and hobbled away. His crooked silhouette against the brilliant sunlight on the cathedral steps was remarkably like the host's in the Ass with the Brindled Fell.

Knowing that he might be watched, realizing how odd it would look for him to pause and read a dirty scrap of paper in public, Louis held it tightly against his palm, which grew moist with anxiety. In his apartment, as soon as he was able to bolt the door and look behind the tapestries to be sure he was alone, he opened the paper and read:

> Now Christian men at last foresee
> The end of the late Great Hullabaloo;
> No longer need we count to three
> To number popes, but only two,
> Which almost anyone can do.
> But if there be, among my betters,
> One who cannot, let him come to
> François, to learn the art of letters.

Louis frowned and burned the paper at once. He was not annoyed that the irrepressible poet had penned a satire on the tragic Triple Schism which men still living could remember, when three rival popes claimed the Holy See and solemnly excommunicated one another with most lively side remarks. Nor was he annoyed that Villon impudently referred to a current minor schism caused by a few disgruntled ecclesiastics sitting in Basle, whom nobody took very seriously and who claimed to have elected Amadeus of Savoy as Pope Felix V in opposition to the saintly Eugenius who legitimately, if precariously, reigned in Rome. Villon had composed such verses before, and doubtless if this one had fallen into the hands of the authorities people would merely have laughed and Villon would have been haled before some sturdy Gallican bishop, asked if he were the author of the new impudence, promptly denied it, and been set free with a warning that his inky knuckles would be soundly rapped if he wrote another like it.

No, it was not the substance of the verse that annoyed Louis. It was the covert message in the last three lines. Villon did not care or did not dare come to the dauphin, and the dauphin perforce must go again to the Ass with the Brindled Fell, "to learn the art of letters." Even in his annoyance Louis had to nod approvingly at the cunning way Villon concealed the dangerous intelligence that the Pope's letter had arrived. It was less amusing to search the poem for any hint of what the reply had been; Villon was apparently divulging no information before he had his reward. It was less amusing still to realize that he must go at once, for he had expressly commanded that the letter be only intercepted, not destroyed, on its way to the king and council. If it were unfavorable he would have to act swiftly.

Since the death of his mother Louis had been seen in public only to go to church or to attend the most necessary of court functions. Now that the court had put off their mourning dress, he appeared even less frequently, conscious of the whispers and smirks caused by his violet cloak, which he stubbornly and conspicuously continued to wear. Even Margaret at first had reproached him. "What good does it do the dead?"

"Wife," he had said, "it honors them."

"Aye, so it does," she had replied. "I wonder if they know."

Louis had looked at her sharply. She had lapsed into English for the first time since the early days of their marriage. "Is there something amiss, my dear? You know I cannot abide that tongue."

Tonight, however, his attitude, or at least his attire, struck her as gay. He suddenly appeared in her writing room and said he thought it would be wise for the dauphin and dauphiness to put in an appearance at the king's fireworks. "His Highness and Her Sowship are celebrating the commencement of another litter."

Margaret asked wearily, "Must I go?" Then she smiled at the way he was dressed. "At first I was afraid you might be ill. Such hose! One gorgeous blue leg and one leg all green and white stripes! 'Next he will be twanging the lute,' I said to myself. Then I heard 'Her Sowship,' and I know you for my own dear bittersweet prince. But I do not feel well, Louis."

In that case, he said, he would not go either.

He looked so thoughtful that she instantly changed her mind. "It seems to be important, Louis. Naturally I shall go. Can you tell me why?"

"If they see you they will think they see me, whereas actually I intend to disappear for a short time. I think the Holy Father has sent an answer to the petition to set me aside. I mean to discover what that answer is before the king does."

Margaret shivered slightly. "How? Will it be dangerous?"

"It would be more dangerous to do nothing. Everybody will be watching Captain LeClercq's new pyrotechnics; they say he has invented a gunpowder rocket that propels itself like a comet over the cathedral and bursts into a thousand shooting stars. There will be immense crowds in all the streets."

"You will be recognized, Louis. Send someone else."

"There is no one I can trust. And—look at me, my dear. What do I look like?"

"Like my lord and husband, Monseigneur le Dauphin."

"And in this garb exactly like a street performer also. All I need is a dancing bear. It is the sweetest thing about you, Margaret, that you do not know how spectacularly mediocre my appearance is; or if you know, that you hide your knowledge from me, which is charity close to holiness. God bless you—and take care of your cold. Do not fear for me. I shall be back before Pierre de Brézé begins to stagger with wine. That fast."

In the pleasant park by the Seine-side, where the Bastard of Bourbon had been sewn into a sack for the edification of the king's enemies, King Charles commanded and honored by his presence a sumptuous entertainment to celebrate the happy condition of Agnès Sorel. There were dancing bears, talking birds, fighting cocks, mummers, minstrels, wrestlers, and, the great novelty of the evening, a display of fireworks saved for the last.

The great world, the half-world, and the underworld, disposed in that order from the king's person outward to the fringes of the park, crowded to witness the performance and view the fiery display.

Near the center of things among the great world, Louis and Margaret moved and were seen by everyone; rumors that they had withdrawn from public life died. The dauphin made a point of speaking to the soberly dressed ascetic nuncio of His Holiness Pope Eugenius IV. "In the pyrotechnic display that we shall soon see, does it not strike Your Eminence that the new invention of gunpowder can be put to peaceful uses?"

At the same time De Brézé was speaking to the nuncio of His Holiness, the anti-pope Felix V, for both were invited in the king's name, the ministers deeming it statesmanlike to prolong the schism and play one off against the other. Here was an invention, De Brézé said, which, for a price, might be the means of securing the papal tiara to Felix in actual fact rather than in shadowy claim. How much would His Holiness, Grandpa Amadeus of Savoy, be willing to pay for a good corps of artillerymen? The nuncio, in spectacular ermine, said that his master was rich beyond anyone's knowledge and would pay anything, but that help would have to come fast, for the cause was daily losing ground.

The dauphin also spoke pleasantly to Jamet de Tillay, who instantly went chattering off like a herald with a proclamation, to spread the word that Monseigneur wore no mourning and planned to remain till the last rocket, and that Madame la Dauphine must be using paint on her face like Agnès Sorel, so high was the color on her cheeks.

To Margaret, Louis pointed out M. de Charmay, the Burgundian ambassador, with the Golden Fleece hanging from his neck on a chain of braided gold. M. de Charmay was accompanied by a servant, himself a man of noble birth, so imposing was the figure Burgundy cut in the world. The servant held the ambassadorial cloak, and was forever dancing to the rear of M. de Charmay lest he inadvertently obstruct the ambassadorial view.

Louis did not approach the Burgundian, who at the moment was talking to an English diplomat, but when the Englishman sauntered off to speak to a small dark man M. de Charmay instantly came up to the dauphin. He bowed amiably, lower than anyone had yet bowed that evening, oblivious of the fact that De Brézé was looking squarely at him —or perhaps for that reason. It would serve Burgundian diplomacy, Louis supposed, to pay court both to the king and to the heir of the throne of France, making capital of their differences, just as the council were polite to the nuncios of both the pope and the anti-pope. *Divide et impera,* divide and rule, play both ends against the middle. The Romans had done it and conquered the world. No one seemed to have been able to make the rule work since then. Politicians could now only divide, as the face of France was witness, pockmarked with independent principalities. The genius of statesmanship, if God granted it to him, would be to unite.

"Monseigneur, Madame," said the Burgundian. "This is an honor you accord all too seldom to your friends." He made a courtly reference to Margaret's high color and bright eyes. Privately Louis thought her color too high and her eyes too bright, as if her cold had given her a fever. He wished the evening were over.

Margaret could see, with M. de Charmay standing so close to them, that the emblem of the Order of the Golden Fleece was a little figure of a dead lamb, magnificently wrought in pure gold, hanging limp and pathetic from the middle. The significance of the emblem was a secret known only to initiates of the Order, who would smilingly say that it symbolized the wool trade of Burgundy. Most people guessed that, like the emblems of the Templars and the Hospitalers, it had also a religious significance. The collar from which it hung was of furisons and double steels, interlinked with gold, cunningly contrived to form a chain of B's, the initial letter of Burgundy. The gold, the steel, and the fire stones blazed like one great jewel. The ambassador caught the admiration in Margaret's glance.

"Le Roy Dauphin seems to value it less highly than Madame," he said playfully. "He had only to take a little trip, like Jason of old, but to a country much closer and far more hospitable, to gain one of his own. My master feels affection warmer than fatherly love for Le Roy Dauphin."

Louis could see why M. de Charmay was an ambassador. Not only had he publicly paid court to him when others hesitated, he had also artfully resurrected an ancient title, ostensibly to honor him, but partly, no doubt, to spur his ambition to be king. In former times there had been dauphins of Auvergne, heirs to the throne of that duchy, called *princes dauphins* to distinguish them from the heir to the throne of France, who was called *le roy dauphin.* He had also reminded Louis that a Burgundian "good uncle" could feel greater affection than a French father. All in all, M. de Charmay was an exceedingly brilliant diplomat.

"The death of the queen, my mother, will keep me in France at least throughout my year of mourning," Louis said.

"Will it? But if it should not—ah, who knows what is before any of us? Who knows indeed what is behind?"

Louis felt a persistent plucking at the hem of his cloak, and spun on his heel.

The ambassador smiled and bowed himself away. "Your servant, Madame; Monseigneur, your servant. I must go to the rescue of Burgundy's wool trade. The Englishman and the Portuguese are whispering. When England whispers, keep an eye on your commerce."

Louis found himself facing the page whose ears he had boxed. Some time ago the lad had gambled away his Dambach nugget and more, and come to the dauphin to make up the difference. Louis had doled out a small subsidy at weekly intervals till the debt was paid, with many good words of advice on the evils of gambling. The friendly help had gained the lad's affection, or at least his service, which tonight Louis had used.

"Monseigneur, your horse, it is ready."

"Hush, boy, not so loud! No one saw you, no one knows?"

"I think not, Monseigneur. They have all come to see the sky shoot fire."

Louis whispered to Margaret: "Do thou go up to my father, that one of us may appear to be friendly, which I cannot. I can see from his face that he is wondering what M. de Charmay had to say. Tell him that M. de Charmay talked about England in most friendly terms."

"He'll hate that, Louis."

"From anyone but you, my dear."

"If he asks where you are?"

"He will not. But if he does—tell him I've gone to bet an écu on a cockfight."

"A whole crown?" Margaret smiled.

Louis did not. "A whole crown."

She leaned against him affectionately as he escorted her a little way toward the brilliantly illuminated area under an old tree where the king and Agnès Sorel were standing. The circle of torchbearers around them were preparing to extinguish their lights. Down by the riverbank Louis saw a man with a slow match moving darkly among some strange scaffoldings of newly erected lumber. Henri LeClercq must be making a final inspection just before he set off his fireworks. As Margaret leaned against the body she had known so well, so intimately, so long, a whole lifetime it seemed, she felt under his doublet a hidden coat of plate mail.

"Come to no harm, *mon prince!*"

"I do not murder easily," he said. "When De Brézé staggers I shall be again at your side."

It was faster by far to gallop to the Rue Saint-Jacques and beyond to the Ass with the Brindled Fell than to go afoot. Glancing over his shoulder as the houses became hovels and the districts deteriorated, the dauphin saw streaks of fire climb the broad black sky and burst into a shower of stars, dimly outlining the squat towers of the cathedral. Here and there a sergeant with a lantern on a pole picked his way among the garbage of the streets. Louis's nose, if not his memory, would have led him to the alley he sought. How odd that the smell was exactly the same, but that his senses had twisted it into a fragrance the night before his mother died.

At the end of the cul-de-sac he recognized the structure that housed the tavern, a blacker black against the lesser black of the night sky. He rode up to the door, but he did not dismount. He had seen too many knights overwhelmed in battle by abandoning the advantage of their firm saddles and trying to fight on foot. He rapped softly, remembering the signal he had heard Villon use; but the door opened silently, moving away from his knuckles, and he found himself rapping on thin air.

"Welcome, Monseigneur," said a low voice. He recognized it.

"You have oiled your hinges, my beggarman-host, since I last visited your friendly establishment. Here is something I owe you, if you can find my hand." He felt the coin gripped by hard but curiously expert fingers.

"Please keep your voice down, Monseigneur. The place is watched."

Louis heard the clinking of the bridle as the host took hold of it and led the horse through the door, into the room that had once been the stable of the old building.

This time the host did not disappear, nor did he take him to the dining room. Louis felt an arm guiding his elbow, heard a voice that said, "Monseigneur was wise to wear something substantial under his doublet," and shortly found himself in a low vaulted chamber where Villon stood beside a rough table on which burned one dim candle. There was a straw pallet on the floor. There was no window.

"These are extraordinary precautions, my friend," Louis said.

The poet said, "Monseigneur, these are extraordinary times."

Louis tossed a purse onto the table. "You will want this, I suppose, before you speak. Would you care to count it also?"

"Monseigneur, Monseigneur, I beg you not to take that tone."

"It is the tone of your poem, Master Villon."

"I knew it would offend you, but I knew of no other way to entice you here for your own safety. Believe me, I thought of exacting no reward before telling you the reply of His Holiness."

Louis glanced toward the host questioningly. "Colin of Cayeulx is perfectly trustworthy," Villon said, slipping the purse into his sleeve. "But for him, whom we call Adonis for obvious reasons here in our little fraternity, the papal messenger would have been murdered."

"In God's name, by whom?"

All had gone reasonably smoothly until last night, Villon told him. He had patched up relations with his patron by taking a vow of chastity for three months, and had begged to be reinstated on his former familiar footing into the rectory of Saint Benoît-le-Bestourné. The good chaplain had believed him and sighingly agreed that monastic surroundings would be absolutely necessary to the accomplishment of such a formidable resolve.

On Saturday afternoon word had arrived that an envoy from Rome was in the city and could be expected at any hour. He did not arrive.

Saturday night the envoy was brought beaten and bleeding into Père Sermoise's church in the Rue Saint-Jacques.

"By me," said the host, "and my friends. The fraternity of beggars would not kill a priest; it is bad luck. Not if we were sober, we wouldn't."

"But someone was willing to kill them," Villon said. He explained that two bands of thugs, not one, had lain in wait for the emissary and his little suite of mule-mounted monks, who had come to France with no protection but their prayers, their privilege, and their anonymity, such was the faith and the slender purse of Eugenius IV. Villon's band beat off the other with clubs and knives and stones. The Italian monks were strange to Paris, and scattered in all directions. When they could make themselves understood they would assuredly ask the way to Saint Benoît-le-Bestourné, but that would take time, and a number of the fraternity had already directed various of them to Saint-Germain-in-the-Fields, to the Bastille, and to other distant, unlikely places.

"Who were the other gang?" Louis asked grimly.

One could only conjecture, Villon said. But one of them, a man whose head was not hard enough to stop a stone, had been heard to mutter before he died that Pierre de Brézé would avenge him. The fraternity threw him into a well after dividing his clothes.

"It is my belief, Monseigneur, that Pierre de Brézé, whether on his own account or acting for others even more powerful, wished to destroy the reply and all who had knowledge of it if it had been favorable to you."

Louis looked at him intently.

"It was favorable, Monseigneur. The Holy Father refuses to set you aside."

"A week ago that would have been good news, Master Villon. In the light of what has happened—I do not know."

"Neither do I. An enemy who will not listen to the highest voice in Christendom to set you aside legally will assuredly listen to other voices who will set you aside by death. That is why a place is waiting for you here, if you will use it. Here in the Ass with the Brindled Fell you will be safe."

Louis weighed the invitation, asking meanwhile, "How did you gain access to the letter?"

Villon smiled, "The singular appearance of Colin of Cayeulx should give you a hint. No man is cleverer with his hands; he is a great artist. Coiners caught by the king's ministers usually lose their ears; those who stubbornly refuse to name their confederates sometimes have their mouths opened. Colin is very stubborn; in the end, alas, he told everything. His arm mended badly after the rack, but he is still able to duplicate the Fisherman's Keys on a seal. The emissary was detained here only a few hours after his beating. We bound up his wounds and treated him with a restorative that often quiets obstreperous members of the clientele. By the time his senses cleared, his letter was safely back in his diplomatic pouch. Père Sermoise knows nothing of this, naturally."

"Has the king received the reply?"

"It might be in the council's hands already. It will surely be delivered by tomorrow morning. Either way there is still time."

Louis had reached his decision.

"Time for what, François Villon?"

"Monseigneur, you baffle me. When I first met you I thought you were guileless. Then I thought you were the very soul of guile. Now I do not know whether you are guileless or foolishly brave. The Ass with the Brindled Fell is at your disposal. This shabby room shall be made comfortable. No one but Colin and I know you are here. Here you are safe. Rest till the situation shapes itself. Here I can keep you better informed than the Grand Provost. Our men are everywhere, their tongues are silent, their ears are long; they have no secrets from me and I shall have none from you. It is quite conceivable that it would be prudent for you to disappear for a period."

The dauphin smiled. "Prudent, unquestionably." The prospect of hiding himself in this grim old pile of forgotten stone was seductively attractive. To have at his fingertips the combined intelligence of all the beggars and rogues of Paris was like having command of the most accurate spy system in the world, a means to discover his enemies and a weapon to use against them that appealed strongly to his whole nature.

But the thought of the dauphiness braving the night air to appear in public for him, covering his absence at this very moment, her alarmingly scarlet cheeks after cheeks so long too pale, brought a flush of shame to his own. He had promised to return before De Brézé began to stagger. This was not a time to desert her.

"You would make an eloquent privy councilor, Master Villon, but I cannot accept your hospitality."

Villon shrugged helplessly. "If Monseigneur le Dauphin were an ordinary man, I should call him a fool."

Louis smiled, "I think I was never in my life more ordinary than tonight."

The interview had taken longer than he had calculated. From a distance he could see no artificial shooting stars over the embankment, and as he approached the fringes of the crowds that still milled around the place he saw that the torches had been lighted again. He felt conspicuous on a frothing horse that had obviously been ridden hard from a considerable distance. He dismounted, pretended to be drunk, and made a present of the horse to the first beggar he saw. He shouldered his way through the throngs of the underworld, the half-world, and into the brilliant light of the great world again, where he found the dauphiness talking to Robert Poictevin, the king's physician.

Only in affection for Margaret were the dauphin and the king not divided. King Charles, when the torches were kindled again, had noted the dauphiness's color. He was too familiar with paint to suppose it was caused by that. He had bawled in a loud voice: "Where is that melon-headed, dog-legged son of mine? He's always in the way when he isn't wanted, never around when he is. My girl, when people don't look like they always look, they don't look like they ought to look." He had demanded that Père Poictevin take a look at her and straighten her out forthwith. He had ordered his apothecary to go home at once and brew her something to make her cheeks pale again. On which, having expressed great satisfaction with the fireworks and the wine, the king strode waist-high into a rosebush, where he relieved himself with right royal abandon, blinking into the torchlight, while some thousands of his subjects of high and low degree looked on.

Thus no one particularly noticed Louis when he quietly took his wife by the arm and led her away. "Everything is all right," he whispered. "Bless you for fighting my battles. Come home now, and let me take care of you."

She was weary, but her humor did not desert her. "It was nothing. Your father gives most unusual entertainments."

*   *   *

Oddities marked the dauphin's Monday. He arose early while Margaret was still sleeping. The apartment was oppressively hot; but since the tiles on the roof tops were wet with dew and the sun had not yet burned away a golden fog that hung over the city he feared that these vapors would aggravate Margaret's illness. Therefore he carefully drew the curtains around her bed and did not open the casements as he tiptoed out of the room, softly so as not to waken her.

There was a garden in the court to the rear of the palace. The thought struck him that she might be pleased by a vase of roses beside her bed before Marguerite de Salignac or Marguerite de Hacqueville brought her breakfast. It would be pleasant to gather them before he went to church.

In the garden a heavy tile slipped from the roof of a tool house, missing his head by a few inches. It would assuredly have killed him if it had struck him. There was no one in the garden, there was no one on the roof of the tool house, and, though he made a circuit of the little structure twice, there was no one hiding behind it.

Beyond the garden there were stables. If dew or the Devil had loosened the tile, then nothing, of course, could be done. If a human hand had loosened it, the assassin might be hiding in the stables.

A sleepy guard assured him that no one had entered the stables and, on peering in, Louis could see only the horses that belonged there. One horse indeed did not belong. It was the horse he had given the beggar the night before, now mysteriously returned.

"Pasque Dieu, there is honor among thieves!"

"Was Monseigneur addressing me?"

"Not you, you sluggard. Go back to sleep."

He did not return to the garden but rode the horse to the cathedral, where he heard an early Mass, which was ill attended. The great-, the half-, and the under-world were sleeping off the celebration. Louis prayed for the dauphiness.

Refreshed, as he always was by the cool immensity of the great church, the dauphin tossed a beggar an écu, looking sharply at the fellow's face, expecting he knew not what. The beggar merely clutched the coin, mumbled astonished thanks, and scuttled away, biting the metal to see if it was real when he thought he was no longer watched. Louis remembered that not every beggar was necessarily a member of the fraternity of thieves. Some people were exactly what they seemed, no more and no less. It was good to remember.

Then, when he mounted his horse, he saw written in spittle upon the leather of the saddle, the word FLY! Hastily he rubbed it out, wondering which of the fishwives and turnip vendors who might have passed his mount had learned the art of letters.

That day Margaret complained of a sore throat and could take no nourishment. Robert Poictevin visited her, leaving a bottle of medicine that Jean Boutet had spent the entire night concocting of twenty-six ingredients, adding a pinch of harmless salt to bring the total up to twenty-seven, which was divisible by three, contained the potent seven, and added up to nine, all of which were important numbers in pharmaceuticals from the astrological point of view. Astrology, though dying, was by no means dead. Especially when treating royalty one did not take foolish chances.

Père Poictevin spoke casually with professional optimism. The dauphiness was suffering from a temporary imbalance of the humors, he said, in which the hot dry humor of fire, set in fluxion perhaps by gazing too intently upon the fireworks, had gained an ascendancy over the cool moist humor of water, with the resultant high fever. Leveling his learning down to a plane that the layman could understand, he said that the function of Jean Boutet's decoction was to put out the fire, which assuredly it would, and with no aftereffects, since it contained two very rare and costly drugs: some powdered Egyptian mummy and a catapasm of salamander. Mummy protected the body, since mummies never decayed; and as for salamanders, do they not live and thrive in fire? And now, said Père Poictevin, he must wait upon the king, who had been in council all day on a highly important matter of state business.

When he was out of earshot, Margaret said—and Louis winced at the hoarseness of her voice—"A council for the Holy Father's reply?"

"Naturally," Louis said, forcing a confident smile. "They are wondering how to compose an answer that will save their collective faces and at the same time accept the papal decision. I feel almost sorry for them in their embarrassment. Rest, my dear, and do not worry. Everything is all right. I am safe." He thought of the tile, the scrawled warning on his saddle.

"I know your face, Louis. It is a mask to everyone but me, who can read it like a book much loved and read and pondered over. I am well. I can travel. I feel only a little"—she paused—"a little *fey*."

He did not know the Scottish word, and indeed it had slipped out inadvertently. It was a terrible word. It meant having a feeling like one under a spell, doomed, fated to die.

"A little eerie in the head, Louis. Small fevers do that. I can travel. Take me to cool, cool Scotland—the holiday we have never had time for."

Everyone was telling him to flee, everyone who loved him.

"When you are a little better, Margaret, when you are a little better. Let us ask Friar Jean. If Friar Jean says it is safe for you to travel, travel we shall." How willingly, he thought, and how fast!

"You know he'll say I can't."

Friar Jean, when he arrived later in the day, sniffed Jean Boutet's decoction and advised Louis with a tolerant smile that it would be all right to let her drink it. There was no harm, he knew, in taking a prescription compounded in accordance with the best science of one's age when the wing of God's dread angel had already brushed the patient's brow.

"But on no account should she travel," he said.

"Père Poictevin would let me travel."

"Not you, I think, Madame," he said, looking gravely at the dauphin. Louis wondered what he knew of the proceedings now in progress behind the locked doors of the king's council.

Friar Jean as yet knew nothing. He left them, promising to return in the morning, thinking of the strange and wonderful ways of God, who puts wise words into the mouths of fools. King Charles had said, "My girl, when people don't look like they always look, they don't look like they ought to look." Eighteen centuries ago Hippocrates had said almost the same words, as valid today as when they were spoken in Athens: *"This you should observe in acute diseases; first the countenance, whether it be like those of persons in health, and especially if it be like itself, for this is the best of all. But the opposite is the worst."* Who, mused Friar Jean, had been more pale in health than the dauphiness, now so unnaturally pink of cheek? Nay, the color was growing redder every hour.

144

All day Tuesday the council sat in secret stormy session. The king, whose throne Louis's campaigns had helped secure, was peevish and sulky in power. He demanded why, if he was really Charles the Well Served, were his ministers serving him so ill in this small personal matter? The dauphin was an unpredictable, disturbing personality, unfit to be king. Burghers and commoners loved him; that in itself was unregal and contrary to all natural order. He had made himself rich and no one could find out how; in that there must be some secret crime. Why could no one find it? If Pope Eugenius refused to set him aside, why not appeal to Pope Felix? Besides, the king grumbled under his breath, Louis had upset Agnès Sorel. How was it that a council of the best brains of France, noble, ecclesiastic, military, and commercial, could find the dauphin guilty of nothing that could be cited before the Parliament of Paris as a crime deserving instant disinheritance?

Bernard d'Armagnac, sitting in the council in the absence of Count Jean, who deemed it prudent to remain in the south, said stoutly that the reason must be that Monseigneur le Dauphin had committed no crime.

"You were his tutor," the king said, brushing aside the answer. "You favor him against me."

De Brézé said that the Provost of Paris had told him that a man answering the dauphin's description had been seen in the vicinity of the Rue Saint-Jacques last Saturday night during the fireworks at the time when the papal emissary had been so regrettably ambushed.

"Can you prove that?" the king demanded.

"With sufficient persuasion, Your Highness, witnesses will swear to anything."

"Then get a handful and persuade them."

De Brézé hesitated, wishing he had not pursued this line. His own part in the affair might come to light. "It must be admitted," he seemed to reflect, "that the evidence is slim and that the dauphiness was constantly seen by all, so the dauphin must have been seen by many also." He suggested as an alternative that little accidents might be made to happen to Louis, seemingly natural accidents, that would work on his suspicious nature and scare him out of the country.

Jean Bureau, master of the king's artillery, interposed. "Some of us here are in a position to remember that the dauphin does not scare easily."

Xaincoings and Jacques Cœur said that the matter was not a fiscal one and did not come within the competence of their departments, after which these great merchant-statesmen took no further part in the discussion.

To speak for the ecclesiastical members of the council, the Archbishop of Paris now rose, a venerable man with a shock of white hair showing under his purple *birrettum*. It resembled a crown, and he wore it with the dignity of a crown. This was no small personal matter, he said slowly, leveling his gaze upon the king. This was a matter in which the Vicar of Christ himself had voiced his decision. He spoke with contempt of the suggestion that Amadeus of Savoy, the so-called Pope Felix V, be consulted. "Yet even were you to consult the anti-pope, assuredly you would receive the answer that the Jews received from Pilate, 'I find no fault in him.' I would suggest to your lordships that the territories of Savoy and the province of the Dauphiny border upon each other, and Amadeus is not likely, in his present dearth of allies, to make an enemy of his closest neighbor. The dauphin has shown that he can be a most redoubtable foe."

Thus mingling political acumen with religious fervor, the archbishop continued: "For a thousand years, my lords, the kings of France have been anointed at their coronation like priests of old with Holy Oil sent by God's singular favor from Heaven in *La Sainte Ampoule* in the beak of a dove for the sacring of Clovis, King of the Franks. For a thousand years the person of the French king has been held sacred and inviolable, as history proves, since if this were not true many more of them would have been murdered than actually were."

King Charles looked vastly displeased, but he did not interrupt, since no one else did.

"This quasi-sacerdotal character of the king attaches also to the king's first-born son, not to a princess—indeed, there is a law against that—not to a second- or third-born son, but to him who will be king. This is an ancient and natural law, as we read in the Scriptures, 'They sat before him, the firstborn according to his birthright and the youngest according to his youth.' Such a law makes for stability in a realm, and no one here can deny that France needs stability."

No one denied it, particularly the king, looking at the faces of his great vassals, many of whom had made war against him no less than Louis. But he was not getting what he wanted.

"And yet it must be acknowledged," the archbishop said, "that Louis the Dauphin is a disturbing and unpredictable prince, in witness of which we have only to look at ourselves, so wont to work in unison, now divided and disagreeing in council."

"That's what I tried to tell you," King Charles said. "Why doesn't anybody listen to me?"

De Brézé said: "His Reverend Lordship has been at great pains to tell us things we already know. Only one thing he neglects. How would *he* deal with the dauphin?"

"It is written," the prelate said, "that foolishness is bound in the heart of a child, but the rod of correction shall drive it far from him. Has any of you gentlemen reflected recently upon the age of Louis the Dauphin? On the 3rd of July of this year of Our Lord 1445, Louis attained his twenty-second year. Twenty-two years old, Messeigneurs. What were you doing at twenty-two?"

The dauphin had so long been a ponderable factor in public life that his youth shocked them. They murmured all together:

"He looks far older—" The king.

"He schemes older—" De Brézé.

"He fights older—" Bernard d'Armagnac—"and he isn't foolish."

Jacques Cœur and Xaincoings smiled. "And he spends like a seasoned financier."

"I would suggest to the ministers," the archbishop concluded, "in order that quiet and unity be restored again to our councils, that the dauphin be escorted, forcibly if necessary, into his appanage of the Dauphiny, where, like new wine, he be permitted to mellow."

The king whispered to De Brézé, "More likely to go sour."

De Brézé screwed up his eyes. "Sire, the suggestion is magnificent. Might I be permitted to escort the dauphin into the Dauphiny?"

"Hm-m," said the king. "I do not know. The dauphiness is sick; the girl loves him; she would mourn his loss, if there should be an accident. I cannot decide."

"Sire, I shall watch over him night and day—like a father."

"Blast you, De Brézé, do not tempt me! Do not consult me. Do as you please."

"Thank you, Sire."

Across the room Bernard d'Armagnac watched the whispered colloquy, marked the expression on their faces, sensed the threat. The council nodded assent to the archbishop's solution of the vexatious problem.

Margaret spent a restless night. Louis, sleepless, watched her toss and turn and murmur as if her dreams were bad.

On Wednesday morning Margaret felt better and ate a little breakfast. Père Poictevin expressed himself delighted with his diagnosis of humoral imbalance and ordered Jean Boutet to make up more of the decoction. But as the day advanced, her fever rose and she said she thought the breakfast egg must have been bad.

"I'll get another cook," Louis said. But he knew the egg was fresh and good. He had tasted every morsel of her food, fearful of poison. No one would poison Margaret out of hatred for her, for she had no enemies. But it was entirely conceivable that through her someone might strike at him, as someone might strike at him through anything he loved, a friend—if he had a friend—a horse, even a dog.

Toward evening Margaret cried a little and said she felt pains in her stomach. "You need not another cook, Louis. You need another *poule*."

"Wife, wife," he murmured, "do not make jokes like that. I have never loved, I could never love, anyone else."

Her color was alarming tonight.

Jean Boutet brought the decoction, looked at her face, and suddenly left the room, closing the door noisily in his haste. In the hall outside he broke into a run.

A few minutes later Père Poictevin stuck his head cautiously through the door. "Good evening, Monseigneur; good evening, Madame la Dauphine. Ah-h-h! I bid you good night, Monseigneur; Madame, adieu!"

He too shut the door hurriedly and fled. Louis leaped to the door in a fury. Priest or no priest, physician or no physician, he would shake the fellow by the scruff of the neck till his teeth rattled. "Confound all noisy, impudent doctors!"

In the hallway the guard, who always stood at his door to protect him or to spy on him, he never knew which, was running away, shouting in a terrified voice, *smallpox!*

Louis quickly closed the door, lest Margaret hear, and tiptoed back to the stool at her bedside. She seemed not to have heard. Her breathing was shallow and slow. He did not know how long he watched her; he thought he was alone. Then he heard the well known voice that had counseled him in all his troubles for as long as he could remember.

"Are you afraid, Louis?"

"Aren't *you*, Friar Jean? Père Poictevin was."

"Your voice is as full of venom as a viper's mouth. Do not blame others weaker than yourself. I too might be afraid if this were smallpox. It is not."

Louis rose unsteadily to his feet. "Do not torture me with hope. I think I should kill you."

Friar Jean laid a firm hand on his shoulder, forcing him to sit again. "I can give you little hope for her. It is not smallpox but it is very bad, and unless God works a miracle—you must be prepared, Louis."

The dauphin's shoulders slumped. He said in a pinched voice, "He will not work a miracle for me."

"But I can give you hope for your own life. You are not entirely without a friend at court. I am bidden by Bernard d'Armagnac to warn you to take yourself into your appanage with all speed, for if you wait a 'guard of honor' is in preparation to escort you there."

"Tell Bernard d'Armagnac that I thank him; but I will stay here."

"He bade me tell you, when you said that, that the guard of honor is in command of Pierre de Brézé."

Louis stiffened and glanced at Friar Jean. "I suppose you know what that means."

"I can guess."

"Even so, tell Bernard that I will stay here."

Friar Jean sighed. "I have delivered his message. Now I can only deliver your answer."

But Friar Jean did not feel that he was duty bound to tell anyone that Margaret was *not* suffering from smallpox.

On Thursday Margaret sank a little lower. On Friday, a day which Louis had dreaded because it was the thirteenth, she lapsed into a coma toward evening, exhausted by her fever. Yet even as she lay helpless, the terror inspired by the word "smallpox" reached out to protect the dauphin. No one dared attempt to enter the chamber to arrest him; no guard of honor appeared to escort him into exile. King Charles and Agnès Sorel had hastily left for Beauté-sur-Marne near the Bois de Vincennes, where the air was pure. At the same time, however, with furious threats the king had commanded Père Poictevin and Jean Boutet to remain to treat the dauphiness. This they did, inquiring thrice daily through a crack in the door how she fared. Louis or Friar Jean would inform them.

On Saturday Friar Jean told them that he proposed to administer the last rites of the Church. He asked if Père Poictevin would care to assist. Père Poictevin replied that it would be a waste of priests for two to do what one could do, especially since he had a previous call. Friar Jean then asked that such members of the council as still remained in Paris be advised that the end was probably not far off.

Louis said: "It is not like you to play the statesman, Friar Jean. How can you think of such things?"

"Because such things touch you, Monseigneur. Soon, I fear, you will have only yourself to think about. That, of course, you cannot do now, so I must try. My public message to the council was actually intended for Bernard d'Armagnac. He will act upon it. He has always been your friend, and so has Captain LeClercq, whose actions in the past have proved that he does not wish to see you die."

"I have scarcely seen Henri LeClercq since Lectoure."

"He has been seen very little by anyone. Captain LeClercq is not in favor since Lectoure."

Louis nodded absently. He could not feel the matter deeply. But a little segment of his mind that could not stop working, no matter how heavy his heart, informed him that Henri LeClercq's career might have been blasted since the affair of the cracked cannon. It was a great step down from a trusted position of designing multi-barreled guns to the frivolous business of shooting off fireworks.

"My message will also help Madame la Dauphine, who needs our prayers and the prayers of everyone."

On Sunday solemn prayers were offered in every cathedral of France from Rouen to Montpellier; but in the palace no one came to her chamber.

On Monday during the morning she seemed better and spoke gaily with Louis and Friar Jean. "I will live, I will *live*, you two gloomy darlings! *Fi de ma vie! Ne m'en parlez plus.*" But her giddy eyes and the strangled quality in the hoarseness that had characterized her illness since its inception betrayed her gaiety for delirium. A scullery lad, leaving food at the door and racing away from the danger of infected air, heard the remark; and the story spread through the kitchens, swiftly working up to the king, that Margaret was quarreling with her husband and wanted to die, for she had said: "Fie upon my life! Don't mention it to me again." King Charles believed the story, nursing it wrathfully against the dauphin.

"I hesitated in a moment of softness, De Brézé," he said. "Get rid of that monster for me before he escapes into the Dauphiny!"

The words which the scullery had overheard and which so eased the conscience of the king were the last Margaret ever uttered. During the afternoon she went into the coma again. As night came on, her breathing became shallower and shallower, less and less frequent. Friar Jean found himself holding his own breath, waiting for her next. At length the next breath did not come. She died shortly before midnight. The end came so gently that Louis was not aware of the exact moment. Friar Jean said finally, "Margaret has left us for a space, my son."

Louis coverd his face and said, "Oh, God, oh, God, oh, God!" several times before he wept.

After the prayers that Friar Jean the priest recited when Friar Jean the physician could do nothing more, he said: "Now you must think of yourself, Louis. It is not safe for you in France any more. Only in the Dauphiny or Burgundy are you safe, and I know which one you will choose. Henri LeClercq is in the hall; he will be a better guard of honor than De Brézé. There are horses saddled and fresh in your stables. With good luck I can keep Margaret's death secret for several hours."

"You expect me to desert her when she lies there dead? For shame, Jean Majoris!"

"You would not be permitted at the funeral even if you lived to attend it, which I doubt. The king will stop at nothing now. Your prayers, not your presence, are all that Margaret needs of you now."

Thus, oddly, he echoed the sentiment that the dauphiness had expressed when she asked, looking at the mourning Louis wore for his mother, "What good does it do the dead?"

He begged, "If I go, come with me, Friar Jean!"

"Later perhaps. Tonight I can serve you better here."

That night, at the nadir of his fortunes, with Death now among the grim forces that had shaped him, Louis rode out of Paris. Henri LeClercq had put off his artillery captain's tabard for less conspicuous garb. The dress of the dauphin was always mean and undistinguished, and for several days his barber, terrified of the contagion, had not appeared to remind him that his face was covered with a stubble of beard like a peasant's.

When Henri could find it in his heart to intrude upon the pent-up, inarticulate suffering of the dauphin as they galloped toward the south, he said, "Monseigneur was prudent to remove the saints from his cap, which would have identified him."

"Prudent? Removed them? *Removed* them! Before God, I ripped them off and stamped upon them!"

Then he wept in a way that was dreadful to hear.

Book Three

Chapter Twenty-two

In the Dauphiny, much of which, like High Armagnac, is a rugged and elevated country, the peasant mountaineers will tell you that sometimes in winter, when it is very cold, when the air is dustless, cloudless, crystal-clear, and absolutely without motion, when silence hangs so heavy that the foot clicks of mountain goats can be heard for half a mile, the quiet water that lies in little mountain pools does not freeze. Swift streams may be frozen solid; waterfalls may hang in curtains of stone-hard ice; but undisturbed the little pools remain liquid, as if their water were different from all other water.

But if a man should toss a pebble into one of those pools, nay, were he but to touch with the tip of his finger its silent surface, that tiny disturbance would cause a strange and sudden phenomenon: before his eyes, before the ripples set up by his fingertip had subsided, almost in an instant a sheet of ice will form and cover the surface of the water; it will grow rapidly in thickness, and in a few moments from top to bottom the pool is changed into a solid block of ice.

Some such phenomenon, mused Friar Jean Majoris, must have occurred in the Dauphiny on the coming of Louis into his appanage. Europe had watched the disgraced French prince and supposed that his banishment meant ruin, the end of his career. If he should try to govern the lawless nobility of the Dauphiny, he would be murdered; if he should fail to try he would be scorned and sink into oblivion, a nonentity, contemptible as his father, without his father's council to support and save him.

But nothing like that had happened. Since the advent of the dauphin into the Dauphiny, the province had solidified like the mysterious mountain pools; it had become the most rigid, most autocratic, and yet for most people at the expense of the very few, the best governed principality of Europe. How Louis had managed to establish authority puzzled the statesmen of his father's council, who had attempted in France for many years to do exactly what he had so quickly done in the Dauphiny. It was known and it was marveled at that three days after he reached Grenoble, his provincial capital, the people were cheering him in the streets.

His very first official act, suddenly executed before the nobility knew what to expect, had been to dismiss their leader, the governor. The governor had departed, Louis solemnly assured his subjects, on a pilgrimage in atonement for dipping too freely into the revenues of the state. It was unlikely that he would return for some time. Louis announced that henceforth he would act as his own governor and that the peculations of the late disgraced public official would be made good, without raising taxes, from the confiscation of the governor's estates. He was asked when that would happen. He answered that it had already happened.

"He attacked the giant," mused Friar Jean. "That is something I did not teach him when he was a boy. I taught him to think first of the little people, the humble people. Or I tried." And yet, Friar Jean remembered, David too had attacked a giant, alone in front of the multitudes; and when Goliath fell the Philistines fled and the battle was won.

Friar Jean was not a military man; his study had been theology and the humanities; he had never had to learn that it is classic military strategy to attack the strongest enemy first, and that when the strongest is beaten the weaker enemies will lose heart and surrender without fighting. But Friar Jean knew the dauphin's mind, and remembered that Henri LeClercq had accompanied him into exile; this great initial success was probably explainable as a desperate gamble on Louis's part at a time when he had not cared whether he won or lost, coupled with shrewd advice from the trained and realistic Henri. Friar Jean hoped that the dauphin's heart had not frozen as rigid as his province. That could easily have happened.

It was one of those fine clear nights for which the Dauphiny is famous, when the mountains of the Grande Chartreuse, into a path of which the little party now turned, look startlingly like some northern country, with snow-bent firs and sparkling drifts on every side. It was difficult to remember that olives bloomed a day's ride to the south, and beyond that, another day's ride, lay the county of Provence and the warm blue Mediterranean Sea.

The black shadow of a bird of prey slid across the face of a full white moon. The peasant guide stopped short and cocked an ear as if he were listening for something. Friar Jean thought the man's face looked frightened. Presently it relaxed and he began to smile.

"She didn't scream," the guide said brightly. "Everything is all right. Nobody in this party is going to die."

The figure of the person who had been riding beside Friar Jean, muffled in a heavy cape with a monkish cowl drawn close around the face for protection against the cold, now raised its head and spoke with a woman's voice, "Who didn't scream?"

"Melusine, mademoiselle. This is Saturday night."

"All the world knows," Friar Jean said gravely, but smiling behind his hand, "that Melusine, a tutelary witch of these parts, changes into a serpent ever Saturday night."

154

"From the hips down, Reverend Father," the peasant corrected. "Only from the hips down. And when she screams, death hovers near."

"What happens to the rest of her?" the woman asked gaily.

"Do not laugh at them, mademoiselle," Friar Jean whispered. "They take their superstitions terribly seriously here," and he added, half to himself, "as ignorant people do everywhere, I fear." The thought struck him that Louis, whose great leaps of intuition and inexplicable skill at guessing the secrets of others had sometimes been taken for witchcraft even in the more sophisticated north, might be considered the very prince of witches here in the south where people were less educated. Here, behind their mountains, cut off from the main stream of history, sufficient unto themselves, ancient legends died hard among the people, old ways continued, speech retained the softness of the Provençal of the troubadours, laughter came easily, tears came with equal ease, literacy was nonexistent, and the level of the physicians' skill was appallingly low. Friar Jean wondered how Louis's health had fared. No breath of gossip had reached the outside world. It was, of course, quite possible that Louis had suffered no attack during the entire five years that had elapsed since he entered into his exile. Perhaps Margaret's death, tragic as it had been, had relieved some hidden tension that had precipitated the seizures.

The guide was speaking again as the party wound single file up a narrow path that approached the cross-topped buildings of La Grande Chartreuse, mother house of the order of Carthusian monks.

The peasant said, "It is easy to see that Mademoiselle de Salignac is a stranger to the Dauphiny." The tone was guileless, respectful; the accent was full of the honey of the south; in the honey was a sting: "Above the hips Melusine is as beautiful as mademoiselle herself, as everybody knows."

Mademoiselle de Salignac blushed and drew the fur of her cowl closer around her cheeks. It was annoying that her reputation had traveled so far, but it was flattering too. She had not wished to be hidden away in this barbarous province; but when one reached the age of twenty-eight, when one had never been married, when one had trespassed, not without success, upon the private preserve of a woman like Agnès Sorel and been exiled for her pains, one did not mind being told that above the hips one was beautiful as a witch or who knew it.

Friar Jean deemed it tactful to change the subject, though Mademoiselle de Salignac would willingly have chatted with the guide and asked why Melusine changed into a serpent from the hips down every Saturday night and what they were like the rest of the week.

"I observe," Friar Jean remarked, "that the path has been well cleared. That speaks well for the industry of the monks of La Grande Chartreuse and the governance of their reverend prior."

"The brothers work," the guide said, "but they do not shovel snow. We do that, as is fitting for peasants. Monseigneur the Dauphin has doubled the *corvée*; three days a week we devote to the roads. We smooth them in summer, clear them in winter, build bridges and remove the rocks that are always falling down from the cliffs." His voice was matter of fact, cheerful, even proud, as if he liked the results of the heavy and exorbitant labor.

"Three days a week?" Mademoiselle de Salignac exclaimed. "Why, in the north—"

"Hush, mademoiselle," Friar Jean said.

"Oh, we don't mind. Everybody is treated alike; we know where we stand. In the old days, before Monseigneur came to us, some of us worked seven days a week and some never worked at all. It depended on the whim of the local lord. Everything was confusion. Now even the great lords themselves must obey the laws, and if they don't—well, nothing like Monseigneur le Dauphin ever happened in the Dauphiny before. Probably nothing like him ever happened anywhere in the world."

"What happens if they don't obey the laws?"

"If they don't obey the laws, mademoiselle, as God is my witness, Monseigneur's sergeant comes to the gate of a castle, the gate opens, the lord is arrested, the lord is judged—and the lord pays fines, just like a peasant!" It would be difficult to convey the tone of awe that sounded in the guide's voice when he spoke the words.

Clearly Louis had wrought a revolution in the little world of his appanage, and now Friar Jean had an inkling of how he had accomplished it: in his own way he had not forgotten the little humble people after all. He made them work, but he made them safe.

As they entered the courtyard of the monastery enclosure through an unguarded gate in the palisade that surrounded the central buildings, the guide remarked: "As I say, we don't mind the *corvée*, but there's one queer thing we don't understand. Whenever we repair a road around a cliff where the drop is sheer, we have to build a parapet. You would think Monseigneur was afraid somebody would fall off. Of course they do look very neat, those parapets at the edge like a fence, but . . ." His voice trailed off; it was a lot of work and it was quite unnecessary, but one didn't complain, since every great lord had his little whimsicalities, most of them a lot worse than Monseigneur's, and if *he* wasn't entitled to a queer notion once in a while, who was?

"He has always been very neat and orderly," Friar Jean said, but he smiled a little sadly. Louis was still Louis, his fear was still his fear. What seizures he might have suffered and how he had hidden them, in shame and all alone, Friar Jean supposed the world would never know.

The whinnying of the horses, which smelled the good smell of fodder in the stables and sensed that the long day's march was at an end, aroused a sleepy lay brother, custodian of the gate, who approached and welcomed them in the stately words, at once humble and proud, with which the mother house of La Grande Chartreuse had extended for centuries its hospitality and shelter to anyone of high or low degree as long as he came in God's peace.

Mistaking the peaked cowl of Mademoiselle de Salignac for the fur tippit of a bishop, he addressed her first, calling her Your Grace, supposing the other ecclesiastical person to be his attendant. Marguerite de Salignac laughed. "I have been called many things, but never Your Grace before." She threw back the cowl of her cape, the custodian held up his lantern, and in its yellow light her yellow hair, much disarranged by travel, cascaded in a golden mass upon her shoulders; the effect was unexpected and somewhat abandoned-looking.

"I beg your pardon, madame," he said grinning. Lay brothers were officially attached to the monastery, and performed many of the humbler tasks around the buildings, but they were not monks. The custodian had several husky children by a strapping peasant wife, and he could appreciate Mademoiselle de Salignac.

"Mademoiselle is cold and fatigued from our long ride today," Friar Jean said. "Would it be possible to light a fire in the women's quarters?" There was always a building set aside for women travelers near the main gate, as far as possible from the lodgings of the professed members of the Order. As a rule, however, little provision was made for heating these shelters.

The custodian answered with alacrity that it would be a pleasure to attend personally to the fire; mademoiselle would be made comfortable; it was hazardous to the health of ladies to fare abroad in the cold night air. It was a pleasure, it was a privilege—

"Do not, in your enthusiasm for mademoiselle's health, burn the house down," Friar Jean smiled.

Before the custodian left the women's quarters, he had made up the bed with a double coverlet of eiderdown, plumped the pillows invitingly, and demonstrated at length how to open and close the grilled work of the shutters that protected the closet-like bed against draughts. He showed her how to bolt the door. He explained that though the place was private, she need not be afraid, since he would be on duty till morning, ready to serve her. He brought her a crystal glass of a green liqueur, the hospitality of the house, and assured her that it would keep her warm if the fire should go out, which he doubted, since the gnarled hard logs of Dauphiny pine burned like oak. And was there anything else, mademoiselle?

Mademoiselle de Salignac looked at him, thanked him, and murmured that No, there was nothing else he could do for her.

In the prior's cottage, which was a little larger than the cottages of the monks since provision had to be made for distinguished guests, the prior ordered a fire laid on a hearth that looked as if it had been cold for weeks.

"Few people turn aside in winter," the prior said, drawing a stool close to the unaccustomed warmth. "Grenoble is so close; they prefer to fare on. It is, of course, much warmer in the valley than it is here." "I had a special reason for stopping, Reverend Father."

"Reverend Father, I am glad you did," smiled the prior. To Friar Jean's clinical eye the prior's cassock looked thin and chill, wrong to be worn by such a venerable man. But it was not to be expected that an ascetic who refused himself the luxury of a fire in the middle of a forest where firewood rotted for want of burning would permit himself the luxury of an adequate cassock. As the room grew warm Friar Jean could hear the vellum of ancient manuscripts, row upon row of which lined the walls, crackling and expanding in the heat.

The lay brother custodian now placed a single glass of the green liqueur on the table before Friar Jean, who looked inquiringly at the prior.

The prior shook his head. "You, not I, Brother Jean, have traveled many a cold, weary league today; you, and not I, are entitled to the restorative."

"It is very beautiful, Reverend Father. I have never before drunk a liqueur the color of flawless emerald. I am also a physician, however, and it is not, perhaps, presumptuous of me to suggest that a restorative is indicated for health's sake in a host sometimes no less than in a guest."

The prior said vaguely, "I am sure that is sometimes true," but he made no move to ask for a glass for himself; the lay brother withdrew, leaving them alone, and Friar Jean did not pursue the subject.

He sipped the cool green liquid, which was suave and sweet on his tongue but which, the moment swallowed, infused a progressive warmth throughout all his body and limbs, as if a summer sun were shining gently within him. The chill in his toes and the tip of his nose disappeared; the soreness where the saddle had chafed him vanished.

The prior chuckled. "The Bishop of Maillezais sang me a roundelay by your François Villon, a saucy bit, on first tasting the liqueur of La Grande Chartreuse; the lay brother says he danced a *balladine* before he went to bed, but that, of course, cannot be true."

"I know the Bishop of Maillezais," Friar Jean said. "It is quite likely that he danced a *balladine*." Friar Jean knew the bishop as one of King Charles's most able and worldly diplomats, a follower of the fashionable new learning so popular in Italy. But Friar Jean did not care to gossip about a brother priest, particularly a bishop who was involved in the same delicate mission that had brought him into the Dauphiny. "This beverage would make anyone want to dance, Reverend Prior. I feel as if I had just awakened from a refreshing sleep. What is it?"

"Since you are a physician I am sure you recognize the mint, which gives it its color, the rare white sugar imported from the East, which gives it its sweetness, and the base of fine old brandy, which of itself is an excellent liqueur. What more the brother apothecary adds, certain mountain herbs, I do not know and have never inquired, though I suppose the recipe is in one of the old manuscripts here." His tone implied that he did not expect his guest to inquire either, but, lest he give offense, he added: "There is a good deal of nonsense about it really. The peasants who gather the herbs protest that they will pluck only those which grow in areas fertilized by a scale dropped from a flying serpent who is supposed to haunt these mountains."

"The witch Melusine?"

"I see you are acquainted with our local legends, Brother Jean."

"Do they gather the herbs only on Saturday nights?"

"Alas, I am afraid they do."

The prior's inborn southern reluctance to inquire into the business of others, who might not care to disclose it, had so far restrained him from asking the reason for Friar Jean's visit, why he traveled in the company of a young lady who was obviously of the court, and why he had turned aside to make the difficult ascent to the monastery when the main road lay level and inviting before him to Grenoble only an hour away.

Friar Jean now enlightened him with a sober earnestness that the prior recognized as in no way connected with the green liqueur.

"You will have heard of Agnès Sorel," Friar Jean began tentatively.

The prior frowned. "Oh, yes. At some length. The roundelay of the Bishop of Maillezais dealt with her exclusively. Most of the terms were incomprehensible to me, who am neither a physician nor an anatomist; but I gathered that they were supposed to be complimentary."

"Agnès Sorel is dead, Reverend Prior."

"Nay, that I did not know; and I am heartily sorry that I thought evil of her just now."

"Her death was holy, no matter what her life may have been. She retired from her palace at Beauté-sur-Marne and converted it into a hospital for victims of the war, which has regrettably flared up again. She retired from the king, and despite all his pleas refused to allow him near her. Everyone in Paris knows of her munificent charities, her public protestations of repentance, which were so vehement and came so shortly before her death that many skeptics accused her of hypocrisy; but I believe she was sincere. God touched her heart, but left her the same person. The woman who never troubled to hide her sins could not consistently be expected to hide her virtues. Agnès Sorel lived, sinned, repented, and died forthrightly and honestly. All France mourns her."

"I am sorry, sorry, sorry, Friar Jean; sorry that I thought evil of the dead and sorry that my limited understanding cannot fathom how a woman can sin 'forthrightly and honestly.' I think of the shame she caused Monseigneur le Dauphin, when he saw his beloved mother and that woman each, and at the same time, gravid with the children of his father. I think of the infants, poor little girls, four of them, that Agnès Sorel bore to the king both before and after the good queen died. Where was the repentance of Agnès Sorel then?"

Friar Jean could have asked him, Where was the repentance of the woman taken in adultery whom Jesus forgave? What did the prior think were those holy, mysterious words, so regrettably unrecorded and lost to the world, that Jesus wrote with His fingertip in the dust while her accusers, ashamed and unwilling to cast the first stone, left the temple one by one, leaving the sinner alone face to face with her Lord and her God, as Agnès Sorel was now.

"And I think," continued the prior, "of how she blunted the conscience of the king. She is to blame for the misery and chaos in France. Here in the south we are thankful we are part of the Empire, no part of the kingdom of France. Here there is no chaos; here everything is regularized, like a well conducted conventual house under the firm hand of Monseigneur le Dauphin. The nobles obey his laws. The peasants are prosperous and content. Brigandage is suppressed. There is no guard at my gate. But it was not always so. Five years ago there was anarchy here. There was no authority anywhere. But Louis came and the people flocked to him. He chastens them, but he loves them. You will find no Agnès Sorels here."

The world was changing, the prior said, and not for the better. Here on the mountain he could sense it, as he could sense the onset of a storm, sighting the distant clouds, spying from afar the flashes of lightning before their thunder could be heard by inhabitants of the valleys. On the other side of the Alps, in Italy and Savoy, shameless statues of pagan gods were being dug out of the debris of centuries; naked youths and naked maidens, dancing, singing, laughing, were now being set up to adorn the palaces of princes, nay, even the palaces of prelates. All this in the name of art. The prior shook his head; it was called "humanism" he said, as if humanity, not godliness, were the proper object of man's striving. Some people called it "The Renaissance." But a renaissance of what? The prior answered his own question: a renaissance, a rebirth of old evil, old error, a cult of the carnal, a worship of all that beautiful women like Mademoiselle de Salignac and Agnès Sorel typified.

Friar Jean did not care to debate the controversial subject of Agnès Sorel with the puritanical old man who had lived so long on his mountain where nothing ever changed, so long away from the world of half-achieved goals, in a little world composed exclusively of men set apart and dedicated, that a sterner set of rules had clamped itself upon his heart, uncompromising and absolute.

"It was about King Charles that I wished to speak," Friar Jean said softly. "Shortly before Agnès Sorel died, wishing to remove temptation from the king's path, she made him promise to send Marguerite de Salignac away."

"That, at least, was commendable."

"The king promised, of course, but Mademoiselle de Salignac had found some favor in his eyes and the king was reluctant to send her away. She is a remarkably beautiful young woman."

160

"I did not look at her," the prior said stiffly. "But I saw the lay brother's face, and I believe you."

"When Agnès Sorel died, the king, or his council, remembered the promise. I was about to depart on a mission to the dauphin. She was ordered to come with me. The considerable guard, which your monks have so hospitably housed in their cottages, were sent, I suspect, not so much to protect me, though I bear certain valuables, as to make sure that she was safely delivered to Louis at Grenoble. I shall deliver her, of course. But I have not seen him in a long time. Mademoiselle de Salignac was a member of his household. My message to him contains news that may distress him. I should hate to distress him further by appearing unexpectedly with a woman who was closely attached to the wife he so dearly loved and who might remind him too sharply of his old life."

"Neither do I wish to distress my sovereign lord," the prior said. "Nor would anyone in the Dauphiny."

"It struck me, when I remembered the hospitality for which La Grande Chartreuse is famed, that Mademoiselle de Salignac might stay here for a day or two till I have seen my old friend and pupil again and told him that which I am ordered to tell him. Louis must be approached with caution, shocked gently. Bad news must come to him little by little, one thing at a time. It—it is better that way," Friar Jean said.

The prior said slowly: "I do not wish to distress him; neither do I wish to distress my community. This Mademoiselle de Salignac would inspire thoughts of the life they have left for a better life, just as in springtime, when the snow melts, such thoughts arise and a certain look comes into the eyes of some of the weaker younger brothers. The rules of my house are most generous: to house the wayfarer, to succor the sick, to feed the starving, to afford sanctuary even to criminals. But there is nothing in the rules about lady pensioners, especially young ones with voices like warm honey, all smelling of jasmine. No."

Friar Jean repressed a smile. The prior had read much in the lay brother's face if he could read the identity of Mademoiselle de Salignac's perfume.

"If it will help you in your mission, Friar Jean, and if you truly believe it will spare Monseigneur pain, I might be able to stretch a point and keep her here. You would have to present evidence that she is entitled to criminal sanctuary, however."

Friar Jean sighed, "No, Reverend Father, the girl is no criminal."

"Then, Reverend Father, my duty is clear and the woman must go. First thing in the morning. And I shall remember the dauphin in my prayers."

So, thought Friar Jean, would he. But that would be nothing new. He had prayed for the dauphin for twenty-eight years.

During the night, while Friar Jean and the reverend prior were at their prayers, while Marguerite de Salignac snuggled into her eider-down coverlets trying in vain to keep warm, another cavalcade, of regal splendor, displaying the banners of Savoy and bearing the purple litter of a cardinal, slowly approached the gates of Grenoble.

Chapter Twenty-three

Members of the cardinal's suite who were familiar with the fortifi-cations of Grenoble before Louis came were startled at the increased height of the walls. If it had been daylight, and if their eyes had been sharp, they might also have noted certain low masonry structures that had been built on the flanks of Mount Rachais above the town; and, if theirs had been a military cast of mind, they might have recognized the structures as gun emplacements behind which lurked newly wrought cannon of tested strength.

Even the cardinal, nodding in his purple litter under a blanket of fox furs with a hot brick wrapped in velvet to warm his toes, awakened long enough to glance up and wonder at the thickness of the city gates, which were armored with heavy bronze plates shining like gold in the light of a score of torches.

The illumination was in the cardinal's honor, and the gates of Greno-ble stood open in welcome.

The cardinal had made his progress in leisurely state, allowing two days to travel the short distance from Chambéry to Grenoble, taking easy roads through the valleys of the Guiers Mort, the Morge, and the Isère. But a misunderstanding at the border between Savoy and the Dauphiny —while a spy spurred back to report to Louis at Grenoble—delayed him. Apologies were profuse; the captain of the border guard, when he could be found, assured His Eminence that the stupid peasant who had demanded credentials would be soundly whipped. His Eminence, molli-fied, asked that the man be pardoned, reflecting that he too had made mistakes, terrible mistakes, in his time, and the cavalcade had resumed its march. But it was long past nightfall when they arrived at Grenoble.

By that time Louis knew exactly how many men-at-arms and how many knights comprised the cardinal's guard and what arms they car-ried, down to the very length of the spears and whether the crossbows were strung, as if for an attack, or unstrung, as if for peace. They were, of course, unstrung, for the cardinal sought an alliance, not a battle.

Louis too sought the alliance.

162

On four sides of the five-sided dauphiny Louis felt secure and protected: to the north and west by the broad river Rhone; to the southeast by a chain of impassable Alps.

To the south an even happier situation existed. There, in Provence, in another principality of the Holy Roman Empire, reigned old King René the Good of the House of Anjou. He was Louis's blood uncle, his mother's own brother; and he loved Louis like a son. Even if René had not loved him, the dauphin need not have feared him, for the old man dwelt in the past, cherishing the ancient honors of his House, glorying in the title "King of Jerusalem," though Jerusalem had been in Turkish hands for generations. He painted very competent pictures, patronized poets and minstrels, and encouraged the performance of mystery plays, all of which Louis considered frivolous. But it was when King René, on witnessing a particularly inspirational representation of the Passion at Arles, broke into tears and *remitted all taxes on that city for two years* that Louis knew he had nothing to fear from his uncle René.

But Louis could not feel entirely safe in a five-sided state where only four sides were secure. The fifth was the northeast. There the Alps were lower, and a series of valleys ran through them like breaches in a wall. Beyond the valleys sprawled the ancient and powerful Duchy of Savoy. Through those valleys a cardinal might ride with ease to seek an alliance. But through them with equal ease an army of Savoyards might descend into the Dauphiny and destroy him. Many men in France would have welcomed that.

When the cavalcade reached the dauphin's palace, a fanfare of trumpets greeted it and Louis advanced into the street to welcome the cardinal and kiss the episcopal ring that was extended, rather wearily, from the furs of the litter.

Most cardinals wore amethyst rings. This was a magnificent emerald, big as a plover's egg. Louis instantly coveted it, not for its intrinsic value, though that of course was great, but for the healing properties that he believed, as did most people, resided in the gem. Emeralds preserved the chastity of the wearer, a property that could no longer be of any possible interest to old Amadeus, Duke, Cardinal, and Apostolic Vicar-General of Savoy. Emeralds drove away evil spirits, but the cardinal, Louis reasoned, had no cause to fear them, since the newly elected pope in Rome had forgiven Amadeus of Savoy all his past errors when Amadeus, having lost what little support he had had in the Church, had publicly renounced his claim to the papal throne. Perhaps, along with the sonorous ecclesiastical titles, all honorary, this gem stone was also a gift from the legitimate Holy Father, given in gratitude that the scandal of the Little Schism was finally healed and Christendom was united again. When jealous priests, and there were many, complained to their superiors that they hated to kiss the ring of Amadeus Cardinal Savoy, they were told to reread the parable of the prodigal son and exercise the same charity. Emeralds also cured dysentery, but it was far likelier, Louis rea-

163

soned, judging from the venerable age of the cardinal, that he suffered, if he suffered at all, from the opposite complaint and hence the loss of the ring should actually benefit him. But the principal reason that Louis coveted the ring was that emeralds preserved the wearer against attacks of the falling sickness. As in all such talismans, however, there was a condition difficult to meet: the gem could be neither bought nor stolen. It had to be freely given. No one had ever given Louis an emerald.

Louis's hands had always been exceedingly strong. He had had to school himself to use them gently even when patting his dogs. Sometimes, when his mind was far away, wrestling with one of the anxieties that constantly harassed him, a favorite hound would rise from the hearthstones, jealous of his master's abstraction, and come over and put his head into his lap demanding attention. Louis would run the hound's long silky ears through his hand. Presently the animal would whimper, and Louis would realize how hard he was squeezing.

He realized he was squeezing like that now. The emerald must have bewitched him. Cardinal Savoy was sitting bolt upright in the litter.

"*Perbacco!*" he swore, a lusty, unclerical oath breathing the very spirit of the new Italian liberalism. "Take the ring, but leave me the hand uncrushed to sign the treaty with! It was safer when I was pope. Then they kissed my foot."

The cardinal, now wide awake, was willing to discuss the treaty at once. He was well aware that France was against it, as France was against any alliance of anyone with the dauphin; but he was a little afraid of Louis, who was so close and who was not involved, as France again was, in the English war. He was also aware of the two-way character of the valleys that lay between him and his young neighbor. It was far more likely that Louis would invade Savoy than that Savoy would invade the Dauphiny. The cardinal was old; he had fought and lost a battle for Christendom's most exalted office; he was tired of fighting; he wanted friends; he wanted to die in peace.

Some of this Louis sharply surmised from the cardinal's jocular reference to the hand-crushing and the emerald and the fact that the cardinal made no reference to the inconvenient wait at the border. But he had just learned—he had, in fact, just dismissed Friar Jean's guide, who had run to him with the report—that Friar Jean had entered the Dauphiny and lodged at La Grande Chartreuse. It was a singular turning aside. Why had his former tutor not pressed on to the welcome awaiting him under the dauphin's own roof? Was the news from France so bad? Was his father threatening war? If so, Louis's terms to the cardinal would be reasonable. Did his father consent to the alliance? Then Louis's terms would be severe. He reflected that it was fortunate that he slept less than most men, not because he did not grow normally fatigued, but simply because an amount of sleep that was usual for most men made his head ache.

Instead of suggesting that he too might like to confer that night, he told the cardinal how sorry he was about the contretemps at the border; he said that the fires were already being lighted in His Eminence's suite to keep His Eminence warm when he should retire; he said he had ordered a supper and wine for the entire Savoy troop and would lodge them in a comfortable billet in a château at the foot of Mount Rachais. He did not say that it was directly under the muzzles of his guns.

Then he inquired after the health of his sister, Yolande de France.

Yolande de France had been sent by King Charles's ambidextrous council to be brought up and educated at the elegant ducal court of Savoy during the years when it appeared possible that old Amadeus, as the antipope Felix V, might actually win the triple crown. Amadeus failed, the name Felix V became anathema, and Amadeus became merely Cardinal Savoy, on which Yolande lost her diplomatic value and the council ordered her home to Paris at once.

To Louis she wrote that she did not wish to go home, and asked what he, as a brother, thought she ought to do. As a brother, strict in his own morals and stricter than ever where a seventeen-year-old sister was concerned, Louis replied that she ought to stay in Savoy, away from the corrupting atmosphere of the French court. He was at pains to remind her that however unusual it might be for a cardinal to be a father and sixteen times a grandfather, old Amadeus, the titular head of the house, had begotten no bastards, dallied with no mistresses, and, far from breaking priestly vows of chastity, had never been a priest and never taken such a vow. Savoy, Louis told her, now had the respect of the world; France had not. Yolande stayed.

"She is well," the cardinal said, "and prettier every year. I have grown to love her like a daughter. So has my grandson here, haven't you, Amadeo?"

The young man known as the Prince of Piedmont, who would one day be Duke of Savoy, bore the Italian version of his grandfather's name. He wore a coat of parade mail beautifully decorated with costly niello work. "To love her, yes, Grandfather," he answered. "Not like a daughter, however." He had a pleasant face, and he spoke as if he meant what he said. It seemed to Louis that the voice was a little soft, fitter to chant a prayer than to rally men in the melee of battle or even to sing a ballade into a lady's ear. But he admired Amadeo's forthright, slightly self-conscious avowal of affection for Yolande.

"He has a letter from her for you," the cardinal said. "Give it to him, Amadeo."

An equerry instantly gave it to Amadeo, and Amadeo obediently proffered it to Louis, politely removing his glove as he did so. The House of Savoy knew its manners.

"Read it," the cardinal said. "Read it and see what she thinks of him and why I braved the wrath of your father and kept her in Savoy against his wishes."

"I already know what my dear sister thinks of Monseigneur le Prince de Piémont," Louis smiled. Yolande would certainly be happier with Amadeo, whom she had known since childhood, than with some strange unknown prince the council might choose for her out of purely diplomatic considerations, and their marriage would go far toward cementing the Dauphiny-Savoy alliance. But there was one serious drawback: Even if King Charles and the council did not actually forbid the marriage, they would assuredly provide no dowry for Yolande. Louis would have to provide one. This required thought.

"These matters are too weighty for me to cope with tonight, Your Eminence. I know how fatigued you must be." He thrust the letter into his doublet. "Tonight we shall rest and refresh ourselves."

At midnight the lay brother custodian of La Grande Chartreuse was again disturbed by a stranger at the gate. It was the hour of Matins. Nothing stirred in the enclosure. The conventual church was dimly alight and full of the crowded drowsy hum of the brothers at their devotions.

Rather sharply the lay brother said that Friar Jean was asleep and so were all the other travel-weary French guests, and that on no account would he disturb anyone.

Then the smoky light of his lantern caught the glitter of the circle of saints on the dauphin's cap, a cap so voluminous and pulled so low that it muffled the features.

The man's face changed. "Monseigneur! I had no idea—I never expected—and all alone—"

"I think perhaps Friar Jean will forgive me for waking him," Louis said.

Chapter Twenty-four

Louis's first words were, "Are we alone?"

"Quite alone," Friar Jean replied. "Nothing short of a whirlwind could dislodge the reverend prior or any of his congregation from the church before Matins is over."

Then Louis said: "It is good to see you again. How are you, Friar Jean?"

The remark was so characteristic that Friar Jean smiled broadly. Under other circumstances he might have laughed and asked whether Louis had to assure himself of absolute privacy before asking a former confessor merely how he fared. Louis had not changed.

But in appearance Louis had changed. His face had lost some of its youth, his mouth had a firmer set. He looked more robust and his complexion was ruddier, though that, of course, might have been the effect of the cold.

In the saints on the dauphin's cap Friar Jean could read more significance than any casual layman. There was St. Denis, patron of France; St. Geneviève, protector of Paris—Louis was still a Frenchman at heart. There was St. Andrew of Scotland—Louis still revered the memory of Margaret. There were the pastoral saints, St. Fiacre, patron of gardeners and cheesemakers—the Dauphiny was famous for its fine cheeses; St. Balise, the patron of woolcombers—the Dauphiny highlands raised excellent sheep. Louis was attentive to the industry and commerce of his provinces. There was St. Yves, the patron of lawyers, of whom it was said in his lifetime, *advocatus et non latro, res miranda populo* (a lawyer yet not a thief, a thing everyone marveled at). Louis ruled strictly, but always within the law.

There were the warlike saints, St. Adrian, patron of soldiers; St. Barbara, patron of artillerymen. Friar Jean remembered the cracked cannon; he still had the scar. The cannon of the Dauphiny were not cracked.

Friar Jean looked in vain for St. Jude, saint of forlorn hope and lost causes. Cautious and patient Louis might be, but he would never admit that a cause was lost.

One little medal was saddening. There was in the Dauphiny a city called Embrun to which sick persons made pilgrimages. In its cathedral church above the side door was a beautiful fresco of the Blessed Virgin, to which many miraculous cures were attributed. Louis wore the Madonna of Embrun on the front of his cap. Seeing the medal, Friar Jean hesitated to ask Louis how *he* was, but Louis seemed to sense the question.

"I am well, Friar Jean. Nothing particularly alarming has happened since I came to the Dauphiny. My head often aches; that is why I wear Notre Dame d'Embrun on my cap." Friar Jean hoped he was being quite candid. But after five years it would not be strange if utter frankness could not be expected at the very first meeting.

Suddenly Louis poured out a torrent of questions. "Tell me, I must know at once: What did King Charles say? What is the attitude of the council on my rapprochement with Savoy? Why was my help so contemptuously rejected when I offered my excellent artillery to help drive the English out of Guienne? Why were you sent instead of the Bishop of Maillezais? Why did you bring Mademoiselle de Salignac with you? I never approved of that woman. Is Margaret's tomb decently kept? I sent you money for Masses. Did you say them?"

"Softly, Monseigneur! I needed no money for Margaret's Masses; I said them, I say them always. But I spent the money on a certain veterans' hospital. My news of the alliance is that the king cannot make up his mind—"

"That is no news."

"And the council is divided."

"Nay, that *is* news! Who is against and who is for it?"

"Roughly, the great nobles disapprove."

"They always do when unity is at stake. Who approves?"

"Jacques Cœur and Xaincoings approve."

"The merchants show more sense." Louis smiled happily. He had already learned what he most wanted to know. France could not stop the alliance so long as the council divided in such radical fashion; French policy was impotent without the massive financial strength of Jacques Cœur and Xaincoings, the greatest merchant princes Christendom had ever produced. Louis's terms to Cardinal Savoy would be steep, say 200,000 gold crowns.

Friar Jean said rather helplessly: "I am a sorry diplomat, Monseigneur; you came upon me so unexpectedly, before I had my wits about me; you asked so many questions. They should have sent the Bishop of Maillezais."

If they had sent the bishop, Louis now realized, they would have sent him with a flat refusal of the alliance and an army to implement the refusal. But the French armies, though winning everywhere in the final spasm of the ancient conflict with England, were apparently too occupied with their victories to oppose the dauphin in his distant province. What Charles and the great nobles could not do by force they had counted on Friar Jean to accomplish by friendship. It was a sly move, Louis thought, and a foul one.

"Were you not asked to wheedle and cajole me out of my design? Were you not enjoined to threaten, if necessary?"

"Nay, not to threaten; no man dares ask me to threaten you." Friar Jean drew from the sleeve of his clerical robe a purse of green velvet with a silver draw cord such as jewelers used to wrap their valuables. "But I was bidden by the council to give you this in all friendship, as a token of their esteem, and I was bidden to remain with you—your attitude puts such a different light on my instructions!—to try to make you see that an alliance between Savoy and the Dauphiny places a concentration of power on the flank of the southern provinces of France, actually threatening the kingdom you are destined to inherit."

Good man, thought Louis, trying to serve France and love me! "The alliance will protect, not threaten, France," he said. He opened the purse. It was a handsome gold chain of office with a pectoral cross set with a large diamond, such as the dauphin was entitled to wear as prince regnant of the Dauphiny. One of Louis's titles was Imperial Vicar of the Holy Roman Empire, of which the Dauphiny was nominally a part. In the absence of an emperor, of course, he was as independent as his daring, wit, and skill in diplomacy could make him.

168

He was impressed with the costliness of the gift and the evident anxiety of the council to treat with him; he was less impressed when he considered how much cheaper the gift was than the cost of equipping an army against him. A bauble to bribe him, an old friend to work on his sympathies. What more?

"Is Mademoiselle de Salignac as sweetly scented as she used to be?" he asked slyly.

"I am amazed that you know she is here. Yes, even the reverend prior noticed her perfume. I had not planned to present her for a few days, fearful that her presence might distress you."

Louis had a notion the council did not think her presence would distress him.

"To tell the truth," said Friar Jean, "I am convinced that the reason Mademoiselle de Salignac was exiled from court is that the council feared she might distract the king's mind from more serious matters."

"My innocent clerical friend," Louis said, "cannot you see that they generously sent her here to sweeten *my* exile and distract *my* mind? That was De Brézé's doing, or something that sprang from the fevered brain of Jean d'Armagnac. Nevertheless, Marguerite de Salignac was one of the dauphiness's ladies, and she shall be courteously received."

Louis returned the cross and chain to the purse and gave it back to Friar Jean, who asked in some alarm: "Don't you want it? I shall be disgraced if you refuse it. I should never dare report your refusal to the council."

"Do they expect you to return at once?"

"It was—indicated that my mission might take some time."

Louis laughed. "Your mission will take as long as I can keep you here, Friar Jean. For five years I have longed for you. In fact, I suspect they may have exiled you too without your knowing it. Let me make your exile happy and prosperous. Stay in the Dauphiny; serve me again; be my confessor, physician, friend."

"I should like to, Monseigneur. Some little influence remains to me in France, however, and I have always served you well there. Here you have many friends, there you have few."

Louis hesitated for a long and painful moment. "But here I have no physician." Looking away in shame, he removed his cap and lifted his hair until the scalp above the right ear was exposed. There Friar Jean saw a jagged scar, still swollen and red, obviously new. Louis dropped the hair, put on his cap, and the scar was mercifully hidden again. "I treated it myself with brandy and salt," he said simply. "I didn't want anyone to know. It happened at night. But it might have happened in open court. I should have been accounted a madman, especially here in the south."

Friar Jean had already made up his mind. "Have you fallen often, Louis?"

"Never violently before. But how do I know I shall not fall tomorrow? There was no warning this time."

"Maybe there was and you failed to recognize it. The warning is sometimes subtle and faint, missed when one's mind is occupied, restless like yours, full of great thoughts and plans."

"Will you stay, Friar Jean? I implore you to stay. I have felt helpless without your skill."

"Of course I will stay! I should have come with you from the beginning."

"I thank God."

Then, as he turned to go, Louis indicated the purse. "I wish you would wait to give me this. Could you present it officially tomorrow? I have a special reason."

"Certainly, if you wish. But where are you going? You must not go down that mountain alone."

"Friar Jean—no, not Friar Jean; that is not a fitting title for the dauphin's physician; I think I shall make you a bishop. As Imperial Vicar of the Holy Roman Empire I enjoy a certain ecclesiastical patronage. My lord bishop, I remind you that I am not even officially here. I am in my dauphinal palace at Grenoble twelve miles away, fast asleep. Officially I shall see you tomorrow for the first time in five years." He was laughing. "You stare, my lord bishop? You think I was too solemn a moment ago and now I am too gay? It means nothing. I know *that* danger; but it happens after a seizure, not before. It shall never trap me again. I am gay because I am dreaming of an alliance, an emerald, and a marriage for little Yolande. I am gay because I have found you again. You, my lord bishop, are my health; there is no treasure to compare with it. Do not look about the room and think to put on your shoes and accompany me. I am already back in Grenoble. *Au revoir, à demain, Monseigneur l'evêque de Grenoble.* Nay, it had better be De Valence; the see of Grenoble is already occupied. St. Apollinaris shall be your cathedral church, a beautiful pagan name that will delight Cardinal Savoy when he meets you tomorrow. Good night, good friend, or good morning, whichever it is. I am halfway down the mountain." The door opened, the door closed, and Louis was gone.

Friar Jean was left quite breathless, smothered with unsought honors and the dauphin's effusive gratitude. Few honors came to Louis's friends in France. He wondered if he were dreaming. But Louis's scar had been no dream. Hideously real, it effectively explained the dauphin's gaiety and gratitude. To have treated himself in secret with brandy and salt must have been excruciatingly painful. The weeks that had passed while the wound slowly healed and opened and healed again—it should have been lanced and drained—must have been torture. Many days he must have had to face his court in an agony of hidden pain. Nor could Louis, like other men, relieve the pain even at night by drinking himself into insensibility for fear of a seizure. No wonder the lines were sterner around his mouth.

But with all his admiration for Louis's courage, Friar Jean—or was he now the Lord Bishop of Valence?—had a feeling, like many whom Louis bent to his will, that somehow the dauphin had trapped him.

He rather recoiled at the thought of meeting the formidable personage of Amadeus Cardinal Savoy, so lately the notorious anti-pope, though all that was forgotten now and forgiven. Nevertheless, it would be difficult to kiss Cardinal Savoy's ring.

But say—if he were really the Lord Bishop of Valence he would not be required to kiss the cardinal's ring! It was wholly possible that Louis, so intuitive, so thorough, so sensitive of trivia which other men never saw, had elevated him purposely to spare him that scruple of conscience. But Louis usually contrived to inject some element of personal advantage into even his most generous acts.

Friar Jean's weary sigh merged into a deep yawn, and he fell asleep.

Chapter Twenty-five

Friar Jean slept; Marguerite de Salignac slept; Cardinal Savoy slept; sleep rested upon the mountain of La Grande Chartreuse; sleep descended into the valley of Grenoble. But Louis the Dauphin dared not allow himself the luxury of sleep.

The rapid ascent and descent of the mountain had caused a ringing in his ears. To have lain prone in a bed would have aggravated the ringing into a throbbing ache that would pulse with the beating of his heart. No physician, not even Friar Jean, could have explained why, since all physicians knew that the blood does not circulate, and Erasistratus had taught seventeen hundred years before that human arteries are full not of blood but of wind. No one in seventeen centuries had ever dissected a human body to discover otherwise; Friar Jean would have been the last to do so.

So, propped in his chair before a roaring fire, his head protected by a flannel cap against draughts, envying his hound Pégase, that slept on the warm hearthstones and snored as healthy dogs do, its lithe limbs twitching from time to time as it chased, perhaps, some hapless hare in a canine dream, Louis sat and, perforce, thought.

The attitude of France was clear: it was one of reluctant concession.

France did not approve, but could not prevent, the alliance. Louis had nothing to fear from that quarter.

The attitude of Savoy was favorable. Just how favorable Louis was not yet sure. Until he knew whether Cardinal Savoy was moderately favorable, strongly favorable, zealously favorable, or desperately favorable Louis could not be certain whether the 200,000 gold crowns he had tentatively set as the price of his friendship was too little or too much. Since he, not his father, would have to provide Yolande's dowry, he now thought it might be too little. Before tomorrow's meeting he determined to find out exactly how much he could demand and be certain to get.

If the dauphin had been a more typical feudal prince, if the blood of his ancestors that coursed through his body, despite Erasistratus's teachings, had been less complex, nay, if the simple boon of adequate sleep had not been denied him, he would have settled the matter in the clear light of day, not in the dark and lonely hours of self-imposed insomnia. He would have held a tournament in honor of the two opposing emissaries. He would have arranged a great feast, with wine and minstrels and mummers and dancing bears—there were many alert and agile bears in the neighboring Alps as well as wolves and other wild beasts. And after the entertainment, when everyone was in lusty good humor, he would have thrown open a council chamber and let them wrangle and shout it out till some sort of agreement was arrived at. That was the feudal way; it was colorful, honorable, traditional. It was the sturdy English way. To an even greater degree it was the splendid Burgundian way.

But it was not Louis's way. He feared the unexpected; he disliked loud voices; he had a passion for order. And there was another, a greater, reason. Long reflection had brought him to the discovery of a new element in the art of government that had never occurred to less harassed, more traditional sovereigns. It was not enough that one's rule should be orderly; it must be presented to the people as orderly in all its phases, from the promulgation of an ordinance down to the minutest details of its execution.

The alliance would be concluded. But it was important that it be concluded without confusion or public debate. Many local nobles of the Dauphiny would be present when the treaty was signed. They must not go back to their castles with a feeling that Louis had had difficulty or had had to make concessions to Cardinal Savoy. They must be presented with an accomplished fact and told why it was good for them, as they had been when, in his first week as their sovereign, Louis had dismissed their governor. Thorough and secret preparation, planned in the sleepless hours that both cursed and blessed him, gave all Louis's acts an awesome aspect of something inevitable, against which it was useless to protest.

Toward morning he dozed in his chair.

At sunrise his barber appeared to shave him. Louis addressed a little prayer to St. Luke the Physician, patron of barbers, leeches, and bloodletters, asking for the preservation of his chin from the razor nicks that the barber usually inflicted. He was not a good barber but he was the best to be had in the Dauphiny; he was cheerful, loyal and—since Louis had dignified the craft of barbery by permitting them to organize into a guild—he had tried to repay his master by keeping his ears open for bits of palace gossip, which always interested Louis no matter how seemingly trivial. He was able to report this morning, for example, that His Eminence Cardinal Savoy was already stirring.

"His Eminence is somewhat elderly," Louis said, "and it is usual for him to rise early. By no means rush the shaving."

At the door of the cardinal's room Louis saw a servant with a silver platter on which, steaming under a damask napkin, the breakfast of His Eminence was about to be served: a pheasant, a smoked fish, and fresh hot bread, if Louis's nose did not deceive him. It would be pleasant, the dauphin thought, to be blessed with such robust digestion at the age of seventy-two. He himself had had only a bland chicken broth and one coddled egg, without the seasoning either of pepper or salt, though he loved those tastes, especially the tingling aromatic sensation of pepper, that marvel of the East first introduced by the Crusaders and still so rare and costly that its price was very simple—weight for weight it was worth exactly the same as gold. Louis sniffed the prohibited aroma, sighed, smiled, and shrugged. At least he was not seventy-two.

"Let me carry the platter to my reverend guest," he told the servant abruptly. "And do thou, my good Savoyard, stand close and watch that I put no poison into your master's food."

"Monseigneur, such a thought never crossed my mind."

"Didn't it? Then why are you staring so?"

The courtesy was unexpected, to say the least, and the servant could see no good reason for it.

But the cardinal beamed at the sight of a sovereign prince entering his presence with his breakfast tray. He was shaved, dressed, and resting upon the cushions of his chair after the lengthy business of getting up. "Monseigneur, this is a most thoughtful attention. I doubt if Nicholas himself is more nobly served in the Vatican—God bless him, of course. You need not have bothered so about me."

Men have pliant minds when they first arise and have not yet determined with exactitude their actions for the day. The first writing upon a blank slate is always the most prominent. Louis wanted to write the first words.

"I thought it only fair to warn Your Eminence," Louis said amiably, "that news has reached me that a mission from France has arrived in the Dauphiny. It would be well for you and me to confer in advance, that we may present a united front to them."

"Perbacco!" the cardinal growled. "They'll protest, of course."

"I should consider that most likely, Your Eminence."

"I am not alarmed," said Cardinal Savoy, his emerald flashing as he tore off a pheasant's leg and chewed it with vigor. "I refuse to be alarmed." But it seemed to Louis that the green rays that leapt from the gem sparkled in a way that betrayed a certain agitation of the finger. "Do you think King Charles can stop us?"

"Not just now. And later it will be too late. What irks my father most, I feel sure, is Yolande's marriage. I am afraid there will be no dowry for her. But happiness is above mere monetary considerations. I will gladly supply her dowry myself."

"Now that," said Cardinal Savoy, "is what I call a truly magnificent gesture."

"I had thought you might deduct it from the cash settlement you will make to the Dauphiny on the signing of the treaty."

"Oh," said the cardinal thoughtful. Then, after a moment: "Of course, of course. A convenient way of handling the matter. Happiness is, as you say, above mere monetary consideration. We have not, I believe, finally fixed the amount of that settlement, have we." It was not a question. The cardinal, no novice at bargaining either, was about to spring a surprise. Not for nothing had he sixteen grandchildren, each one a valuable pawn in the game of diplomacy. The marriage of Amadeo with Yolande, even if accomplished by stealth, would soften the threat of France against Savoy. What was there to prevent his strengthening the treaty with the Dauphiny by the marriage of another grandchild to Louis himself, who was so providentially a widower?

"I had thought a fair amount for the settlement would be—" Louis began.

But the cardinal held up his hand. "Let us not think entirely of money, Monseigneur. I know how, some years ago, the inscrutable will of Divine Providence deprived you of your dauphiness. But in time that wound will heal and you shall have to think of another consort, a queen to perpetuate your House when you come into your kingdom."

Louis looked at him fixedly, taken entirely aback.

"I have a granddaughter," the cardinal resumed, "a pious healthy girl of a sober turn of mind of whom no king need ever be ashamed. She and the Prince of Piedmont are brother and sister. Yolande's marriage to the prince, *your* marriage to this girl, would cement and sanctify for all time the alliance between the Dauphiny and Savoy."

Louis's mind was racing. Cardinal Savoy must desire the alliance even more than he had imagined. "I had not thought of marrying again," he said quite honestly. "In fact, in my heart I had resolved never to consider it. The thought of another woman taking Margaret's place—"

"It is fortunate," the cardinal said dryly, "that she is quite young and could not take Margaret's place for some time."

"How old is she?"

"Well—" The cardinal hesitated. "She is seven. But big for her age, and promises an early maturity."

174

"I see," said Louis. The difference in age was only twenty-one years, by no means unusual in royal marriages. Actually, the youth of the little Princess of Savoy put a rather different light on the entire matter, freeing it from painful emotion; she became just another bargaining factor in a highly desirable diplomatic move.

"I am, of course, prepared to deal handsomely in the matter of her dowry," the cardinal said.

Louis's price soared into the empyrean. "Considering the wealth of Savoy," he said, "and the substantial ecclesiastical revenues enjoyed by Your Eminence, and my own willingness, poor as I am, to furnish a suitable dowry for Yolande (which is not my duty), I should imagine something in the neighborhood of five hundred thousand gold crowns would be an equitable settlement."

The cardinal dropped the pheasant. "*What!*" he roared. "A half a million gold crowns?"

Louis said smoothly, "In settlement of everything, Your Eminence: your granddaughter's dowry and, of course, my provision for my little sister Yolande."

"And how do you value your little sister Yolande?" The cardinal's voice was sharp. He knew, and Louis knew, that fifty thousand would have been adequate.

"A hundred thousand," Louis said.

The cardinal's brow furrowed. "You deal in large amounts, Monseigneur. It is a good sign, of course, firm family feeling, devotion to one's loved ones—hm, hm, hm, I do not know. I have ever so many other grandchildren for whom I must provide." Still, Louis had shaken him. He had placed the rich old sovereign of Savoy in a position where it would shame him to be less generous than the relatively poor sovereign of the Dauphiny. "It will require some thought, Monseigneur."

"There is plenty of time," Louis said rising. "I shall not receive the mission from France until noon. Meanwhile, let me congratulate Your Eminence upon the beauty of that ring. I suppose I shall never be able to own one half so superb unless someone gives one to me."

"Confound it, man! I thought brigandage was suppressed in the Dauphiny!"

"Most exquisitely beautiful," Louis murmured, softly closing the door.

After some moments the cardinal began to smile. "*Perbacco!* If I had that lad's gall I should be the pope of Rome today!" But one day that lad's gall, if his instinct did not fail him, would rule Europe. His granddaughter would be in safe, strong hands. He found himself chuckling at the thought that the dauphin had not asked, and he had neglected to mention, that the name of the little princess of Savoy was Charlotte.

Chapter Twenty-six

At noon, in a private audience, Louis formally received the French mission. To Cardinal Savoy he presented Friar Jean as his bishop designate of Valence. Since confirmation would follow as a matter of course, Cardinal Savoy congratulated the new bishop, but he felt a little uneasy that Louis had been at such pains to honor the man sent from France to oppose the alliance.

To Cardinal Savoy, Louis also presented the Chevalier Henri LeClercq, Captain-General of the Dauphiny Artillery and a member of his privy council. The cardinal had heard of the dauphin's deadly guns, and felt more uneasy than ever faced with the engineer who was responsible for them. General LeClercq had a rigid, competent look about him, and a something else, an intensity that the cardinal had rarely seen except among certain zealots within the Church. This man's devotion was gunpowder and iron.

But Cardinal Savoy felt most uneasy of all when Louis presented Marguerite de Salignac as a former lady in waiting to the late dauphiness. She had been a cherished member of his household, Louis said, and was now exiled from France; he did not say why, but he left the impression that her offense had been of a minor political nature. Now he had given her asylum, he said, a dear friend who might always rely on any service he could afford her. She would remain in the dauphinal palace.

He personally took her hand to escort her to the cardinal's chair, for Amadeus was seated, out of respect for his age. It seemed quite unnecessary, the cardinal thought, for Louis to hold her hand while she knelt and kissed the emerald. He shot a covert glance at young Amadeo, the Prince of Piedmont, whose eyes seemed unable to leave her, lingering on the radiance of her golden hair, scarcely covered by a wisp of silver net in deference to His Eminence, on her cheeks flushed with pleasure at the dauphin's attention, on the litheness of her limbs when she made her superbly graceful reverence. He felt her young hand under his aged one, singularly soft and warm—or perhaps his own had suddenly recovered some long forgotten acuity of feeling. Her voice had a drowsy quality. She wore a perfume unlike the respectable incense in a cathedral; there was a summer garden in it, blooming in the hot sun, full of flowers ready to be plucked. It would be a long time, thought the cardinal, if ever, before Charlotte of Savoy managed to achieve anything like this.

176

These factors were sufficiently disturbing in themselves. But it was Friar Jean who evoked a sudden and unexpected action from the cardinal.

Friar Jean had scarcely noticed Louis's extreme attention to Marguerite de Salignac; he had been more intent on the furnishings of the audience chamber. It was an intimate room, obviously a part of Louis's private apartments, very probably his study, to judge from the writing table, the shelves of books, and the comfortable cushioned chair in which the cardinal now sat. But there was a curious luxury about the room that was very unlike Louis, so penurious and severe in his tastes. A deeppile Turkey carpet covered the floor from wall to wall. Even on the hearthstones there was a great fur rug. Thick tapestries hung against all the walls. Rich, heavy fabrics everywhere. Strangely, they were all new.

Then, with a shock, remembering the scar, Friar Jean realized that all this soft new luxury was not vanity; it was sadly, secretly functional. Here not even a child just learning to walk could fall and hurt himself. Everything was padded. He looked to the table to confirm his suspicion. Yes, that too. Some rather superfluous-looking green felt, on which writing must have been difficult, entirely covered it and hung down on all sides. It hid the beauty of the table, but it softened the edges and corners. Friar Jean felt justified in accepting the honors that had come as a result of his decision to remain and serve the dauphin.

But it would have been quite impossible for him, even now, not to perform as faithfully as lay in his power the duty that had been entrusted to him by the overwhelming majority of the French king's council. Simply and earnestly, without sparing Cardinal Savoy's feelings, he delivered his message. His directness, and a certain logic in the French position, lent his words eloquence.

With warmer enthusiasm than the council could have possibly felt, he expressed their esteem for Louis. In his mouth their protestations of friendship acquired sincerity. Then he presented their gift, the costly chain of office. Louis put it on.

At this Cardinal Savoy complained that he felt faint, and begged their indulgence for a short time until he should recover himself. Louis expressed concern, and accompanied the old man to his chamber.

There the cardinal instantly recovered. "France chose a clear-souled man to bear her message. I have known a few such men; there is an aureole round their heads."

"The bishop is getting a trifle gray," Louis said.

"He does not lie; you are highly regarded in France, Monseigneur le Dauphin." He indicated the chain, which now shone with startling brilliance against Louis's sober attire. "But you are highly regarded in Savoy, too." He slipped off the great emerald ring. "You were good enough to admire this. Emeralds are said to give clear vision. Take it. Let it open your eyes to the greater friendship of Savoy—it is no part of Charlotte's dowry."

"Charlotte?"

"My granddaughter."

"Ah, yes. Your granddaughter. My future dauphiness."

Then the cardinal agreed to everything.

"One stipulation, however, I must make and insist on," the cardinal said sternly. "It concerns Mademoiselle de Salignac. You are an upright man, Monseigneur; no breath of scandal has ever touched you. But you are still young, and Mademoiselle de Salignac, quite without knowing it, perhaps, looks and behaves in a way that is insidiously seductive."

"I confess I have noticed that."

"Even Amadeo, who is furiously in love with your sister, could not tear his gaze from her. I think it was the way her gown happened to arrange itself when she knelt to me. She must go, Monseigneur! She must not remain under your roof. One day you will thank me for this."

"Where can she go, Your Eminence? Can I refuse hospitality to one who was formerly a member of my household, refuse food to the starving, raiment to the naked?"

"The nakedness of the lady seems already to have occurred to you, exactly as I feared. Let her go into a nunnery."

"I do not think she would be happy in a nunnery."

"Then she should marry at once."

"Alas, no one has made her an offer of marriage for love alone, which she unquestionably inspires. And though she is of noble birth, her family have no estate and Mademoiselle de Salignac has no dowry."

The cardinal smiled wryly. "I know you better than I did this morning, Monseigneur. Ah, well, what is one more? Would you agree to send her away if I provide a dowry for her? But do not squeeze the orange dry, my lad. The rind is sour."

"She has very expensive tastes," Louis said, smiling too. "But no doubt she should learn to curb them. Would it satisfy Your Eminence if I sent her to my uncle, King René? He appreciates the exquisite. He would love to paint her, probably as Aphrodite rising from the sea. In no time he will manage to marry her to some amiable Provençal chevalier, just to keep her about as a decorative touch to his court. I should think a thousand crowns quite adequate."

"Done!" said the cardinal.

That night, in full court, before the applauding assembly of the three estates of the Dauphiny, clergy, nobles, and representatives of the bourgeoisie, Louis the Dauphin and Amadeus Cardinal Savoy put their hands and seals to a beautifully engrossed scroll of parchment, a treaty of perpetual friendship, union, and mutual good will. Next day the heralds proclaimed it in the market places of cities and villages everywhere in the dauphiny, places with odd un-French-sounding names with an ancient southern beauty about them: Gap, Die, Froges; Allos, Rémuzat, Paladru; and all the rest. Lords and commons alike were delighted at the added security the alliance would give them. It amused the country people specially, with their sly, dry sense of humor, that Amadeus of Savoy would perform the marriage ceremony himself in his capacity as a cardinal between his granddaughter and their dauphin. What would Louis call him, Grandpa Cardinal? Some even whispered he might have to say Grandfather Pope. They rolled it laughingly on their tongues in their dialect: Grandpa Papa, Grandpa-pa-pa-pa.

Very soon the news reached Paris. The council were not amused. King Charles flew into a rage.

Chapter Twenty-seven

Friar Jean Majoris was an adequate horseman but by no means an enthusiastic one. He had scant patience with prelates who went hunting like lords and capered like paladins on their high horses. He much preferred the sober gait of a mule, the patient beast the Lord Himself had honored. Caesars rode horses, the mount of warriors. Riding on a mule was associated in his mind with happy memories of his youth as the humble brother apothecary of the Monastery of St. Michael of Peril.

"Yet here I am on a horse again. And here I am on a hunt, like the Bishop of Maillezais. Who knows? Next I may be required to dance a *balladine!*".

"I think you could do even that, my lord bishop."

"Nay, do not call me bishop, or I will call you the Chevalier Captain-General of the Artillery of the Imperial Province of the Dauphiny, Lord Privy Counselor to His Highness the Dauphin, which would tax my memory. Such sonorous titles for the babe I held in my arms and into whose mouth I popped sops of goat's milk!" As they rode along side by side, Friar Jean seemed disposed to talk of former days. It was the first opportunity he and Henri had had to speak personally to each other in the busy events of the last twenty-four hours. It was perhaps inevitable that his sudden elevation to a bishopric would cause him to cast a backward glance over a long life. "Now that babe's hair is beginning to show gray at the temples; my own is long since white. You are a general now and I am a bishop. God works in strange and wonderful ways, Henri LeClercq. I do not know why He made me a bishop, but in making you a general I like to think that my prayers have had some small part. There is a wonderful aspect of prayer, Henri, that few people remember. When God grants what we pray for He blesses us, and our faith is strengthened to pray for more good things. When He withholds what we pray for He

179

blesses us by reminding us that, somehow, we have prayed for the wrong things, and humbles us, as He humbled Job, to help us grow. Thus He blesses us always." Friar Jean smiled a little self-consciously. "As a bishop I shall have to make sermons. Do you know that in all my life I have never preached a sermon? I am a little afraid to start. The congregation might walk out."

"I'll plant a brace of cannon in front of the church and chase them back in again," Henri laughed.

"That might be one good use for cannon," Frair Jean said; and, after a few moments: "I do have one regret, Henri. I hoped to live to christen children of yours. I had hoped you might marry again some day."

"But I did, Friar Jean!" Henri suddenly realized how long it had been since he had seen his old tutor, foster-father, mentor. "A gentle lady of the House of Comminges. After our marriage her father confessed that Louis had furnished her dowry, but warned me I must never admit that I knew."

The ways of the dauphin too were strange and wonderful, Friar Jean thought. To have made no secret of how he had pried three thumping dowries out of Cardinal Savoy; to have quietly furnished one for Henri LeClercq's bride without telling a soul.

"And as for christening, it would be late to christen a boy already four years old."

Friar Jean sighed. "How thankful I am that I am relieved of my diplomatic duties. Even sermons will be easier. To think that I was scheming to shield you from Marguerite de Salignac!"

"The dauphin has already done that rather effectively. Early this morning she left for Provence with a letter of recommendation to King René and a thousand crowns in her saddlebag. She was very pleased."

"What did you christen your boy, Henri? Henri? More likely Louis."

"Louis did not pop sops of goat's milk into the foundling's mouth or explain the mechanics of distillery apparatus."

"I didn't really understand all that, you know."

"Then I do not either, and the new Dauphiny distilleries do not work. But assuredly they do, and many peasants who were thin before are fat and prosperous now. The taxes are burdensome but the business booms. No, there was only one name for my boy. Jean LeClercq will kneel and ask your blessing whenever you honor my house."

"He has it, he has it already. You named him for me! That is a thrill a celibate always secretly covets. I shall come to your house this very night—unless Louis needs me, which is unlikely. I have never seen him looking so well. My appointment as his physician will be a sinecure." Friar Jean wondered how true that statement was; but he had no doubts about a physician's duty to a patient. Always encourage; get others to do the same.

As a matter of fact, Louis did look extremely well. He was brimful of energy and happy at the prospect of the hunt, which was in Cardinal

Savoy's honor and in celebration of the signing of the treaty. The cardinal, of course, did not hunt any more. So Louis had promised to bring back some ermine for his cape from the marshes along the Isère. Knowing the elusive nature of the little beasts, the cardinal had smiled and said he would be satisfied with only one, and that he would probably have to wait for it in the next world.

But Louis never bothered to hunt what he could trap; there were hundreds of ermine traps in the valley; he knew he could make good his promise.

Nor was this a hunt for boars, though there were those too in abundance. Let the English hunt boars, Louis always said, as they had for centuries, to prove they were better than even the biggest pigs. When they did not eat the heads, which they considered a delicacy, they hung the hideous things in their baronial halls above their supper boards and pointed boastingly to the length of the tusks. Louis dug pitfalls with spikes at the bottom to impale the pests and let peasants eat the pork. If there had been any way of shooting them with guns, Louis would have had them shot. But firearms were used only against human beings, not against animals, because the smoke of the slow match frightened them away. Even Henri LeClercq said there was no way of exploding gunpowder without lighting it with fire.

Wolves were good hunting; stags were good hunting; fox hunting, though lowly esteemed as a second-rate sport, afforded a wonderful chance for a long fast ride and kept you fit and firm in the saddle, good for legs that might forget their skill when you had too many sedentary duties of state. Louis had hunted bears too, but they sometimes retreated into the mountains, and then he would have to return, making some specious excuse to explain why he did not wish to follow them. He was glad they hibernated in winter. Hawking was magnificent sport too, and gave you equally exhilarating rides. It could hardly be called hunting, but to set a bird to catch a bird had a certain ironical fascination about it. One could learn from that: remove the hood, open their eyes, make your prey their prey. And a faithful dog to retrieve it. But the only skill necessary in the sport was to train the falcon, an extremely tedious business. He would do it some day. But so far in the Dauphiny he had had no time to train others to fight his battles.

This was a hunt for the chamois, an exceedingly wary and agile species of antelope. In summer it fed in the high Alps, but in winter it came down from the mountains in small herds to search for fresh young pine shoots of last summer's growth in the valleys. Its ears were keen, its eyes were sharp, and the sureness of its footing was proverbial. It was very difficult to approach. At the slightest sound it would startle and flee. It could outrun a horse where the ground was rough, and it seemed instinctively to choose the roughest, stoniest avenues of escape, where horses and men would stumble and fall. In winter it grew a protective coat of gray fur, and it would hide, motionless and almost invisible, in the

181

mottled snow-patched shadows of the forest. Such habits alone would have furnished an irresistible challenge to Louis's skill as a hunter.

But there was another aspect of the chamois that interested him even more. Chamois skin was the softest known to man. It made the finest gloves, the most luxurious doublets and hose in Europe. A beautiful pale yellow in its natural state, it could be dyed scores of brilliant colors. All this meant trade, industry, and prosperity for the Dauphiny. Louis envisioned whole villages devoted to the fabrication of luxury products of chamois skin. He not only permitted, he encouraged the hunting of this valuable animal, which unfortunately could not be domesticated and did not breed in captivity. Incidentally, its flesh was a most tender and tasty venison, which he could eat without fear.

Friar Jean knew nothing about the chamois. He had heard in France that it lived perpetually on a mountaintop among eagles and everlasting snows. If Louis was venturing so high, he should certainly have his physician with him. Therefore he had asked, with a convincing attempt at jocularity, if it would be fitting for him to accompany the huntsmen.

The dauphin, somewhat surprised but greatly delighted, said: "You will bring us luck! Everyone will say the French emissary is already one of us. Pégase, you may kiss the bishop's ring."

Friar Jean had no ring, but the intelligent hound, seeing him in favor with his master, came over and licked his hand. The huntsmen laughed and applauded, Henri grinned, the eyes of Amadeo of Savoy bulged out in astonishment, for it looked as if even the dogs of the Dauphiny were trained to do complicated tricks at a word from the dauphin. It was a gay and auspicious start for the hunt.

Opposite Grenoble, on the other side of the Isère, lay a dense area of forest in a flat tongue of land formed by a great southern bend of the river. Here grew the Dauphiny maple, which made the country a blaze of color in autumn; the larch, which the dauphin protected because of its great value as building material; graceful willows on the long riverbanks where the ermine traps were set; and beyond them the pines, as the land rose first gently, then sharply into the rugged mountains of La Grande Chartreuse a dozen miles to the north.

Formerly the area had been occupied by foresters and hunters living on what they could shoot and what wood they could sell in Grenoble, a carefree, shiftless lot scarcely distinguishable from the outlaws who fled from the oppression of local lords and the criminals who fled from justice. Now the forest was occupied by a law-abiding, industrious population.

They were industrious because Louis hated idleness and made industry pay. Some hunted the chamois, on which there was a liberal bounty; some burned charcoal for Henri's gunpowder; all now farmed neat little clearings of their own that the dauphin's laws protected. An ordinance dating back to his second year as sovereign of the Dauphiny prohibited hunting without their permission on their land under penalty of ten francs fine, an ordinance that applied even to the nobility, though not, of course, to Louis himself. This was unheard of in Europe.

They were law-abiding because they were afraid not to be. Harboring a criminal made them liable to the same punishment as the criminal they harbored; if his ears were clipped, their ears were clipped; if he was hanged, they were hanged. All alike spent three days on the roads, which were the envy of every surrounding province, and yet, as the guide had told Friar Jean, they did not complain because they were all treated alike and everyone knew where he stood.

Moreover, Louis tempered his harsh rule with frequent unexpected holidays, like today, the celebration of the signing of the treaty. And he rewarded individuals for work well done. The guide who had guided Friar Jean had been given a gold écu and hired to guide this hunt, a signal preferment, though Louis knew the area well and needed no guide.

The bridge across the Isère was gay with the standards of Savoy, France, the Dauphiny, and the Empire, as well as with the arms of the nobles and dignitaries who participated in the hunt—lilies, eagles, fabulous heraldic beasts of Asiatic origin that dated from the Crusades; helms, towers, crescents, bends, and crosses of every color and shape blazoned on square standards, long streaming pennons, and stately gonfalons bellying like sails of a ship from their poles. All this color and honor fluttered and snapped from the bridge with a sound you could hear in the good stiff breeze that swept down from the mountains and promised a fine clear day.

From the window of his chamber Cardinal Savoy, with his nightcap still on, waved a brave scarlet handkerchief and bade them godspeed and good hunting. The towers on either side of the river had their portcullises raised high, their gates open wide, and their drawbridges lowered. Nets, ropes, spears, daggers, and bows were the hunting weapons. No one wore a sword, and of course no one carried firearms. A trumpet from the palace sounded a shrill fanfare, and the cavalcade crossed over into the forest; but there was no shouting after that, for this was a hunt for the chamois and even the horses' hoofs were muffled in leather boots to the fetlocks.

Some dozens of ermine traps, many of them near rabbit burrows, were emptied and the luckless little rodents were tied into special sacks, made for the purpose, weighted with a stone and drowned in the Isère. It always reminded Louis of the execution of Alexander of Bourbon, and he preferred not to watch.

"But it serves them right for trespassing on the estates of the rabbits; they're too lazy to dig burrows of their own. And there's no other way of getting the most out of the pelts, which is now at its whitest."

"Drowning is not the most painful death, though it looks so because they struggle. Sometimes I have to have animals killed for organs that go into healing medicines. I always have them drowned." Friar Jean was telling the truth, for sometimes he had been called to minister to a person apparently about to die of drowning, only to have the person recover and tell him later that, after the first terror and shortness of breath, there was a feeling of great peace. Presumably animals, without man's imagination, were spared some of the terror. However, he was comforting the dauphin, whom he had seen glance away when the ermine were killed.

Louis looked thoughtful.

"But I do not suppose that I know very much about animals," Friar Jean admitted. "I do not even know if hunting dogs are brave or cowardly. They sniff the ground, approach the traps with caution, freeze motionless, tails stiff, fur erect, and one paw off the ground as if they were ready to wheel about and retreat at a moment's notice. It is very bewildering."

Louis laughed heartily. "They are trained to do that, my clerical friend." He whistled for Pégase, who came bounding up. "Pégase, my beautiful, the bishop here says you are a coward. Are you going to stand for that?"

Amadeo of Savoy looked on as if he expected another startling trick, but Pégase merely yapped and waggled his tail vigorously and looked up into his master's face.

"You see?" said Louis. "He doesn't even know the word."

Toward noon one of the servants rode back to Grenoble with a sackful of ermine for the cardinal's cape.

*   *   *

Though the snow had been heavy in the mountains that year, the chamois had not come down as far as usual. Louis supposed it was owing to the greater human population of the forest. Late in the day, however, in the foothills of Les Grandes Chartreuses, they came across a herd of perhaps a dozen. Louis had grown uneasy at the heightening altitude and determined in his mind that the instant he should shoot even one chamois he would call off the hunt, pleading the age and fatigue of Friar Jean or the necessity of returning to the cardinal or the approach of the dusk—anything. Probably the best excuse would be Friar Jean, whose face was unmistakably weary and who shifted often in his saddle as if he were chafed from his long ride down from Paris.

Then they sighted the herd. The luck that had been against them now turned in their favor, for on lower ground the game might have been downwind of the men, horses, and dogs. Here, a little higher, in the direction from which the wind of the mountain was coming, they neither scented nor heard the hunting party before it was within bowshot.

A dozen arrows leapt simultaneously from the huntsmen's bows, and several of the chamois stumbled dead in their tracks. Others staggered, struck but not killed, and the servants dispatched them with daggers.

Louis's, a big old buck, got away. It leapt into motion when Louis's arrow, aimed a little too high while his horse was running, just nicked its horns. The direction of the danger turned all the survivors of the herd toward the mountains. Instinct directed Louis's shrewd old buck

184

to a narrow path that ran upward along the stony edge of a gully. In an instant it was out of sight.

Louis knew the gully; it was not deep, at least not at first, though later it got bad. He thought he could get in a killing shot before that. Pégase sprang ahead; Louis dug spurs into his horse and raced after him, fitting another arrow to his bow. "After him, Pégase! Point him, thou beautiful! He shall never get away!"

Friar Jean heard the shout, saw the dauphin spurring his horse up a slippery trail that looked dangerous, and dug his own soft heels into the flanks of his horse and followed the dauphin, though the gentle mare that had been allotted to him was not a hunter and would not gallop. The dauphin, the dog, and the quarry were soon far ahead.

But the mare, with patient steady steps, picked her way up the trail as if she knew the value of what she carried and had no other purpose than to get him safely where he wanted to go. Observing that the gully, though steep was not sheer, Friar Jean let her take her own pace; but he did not turn back.

Then in the distance suddenly he heard a cry like that of an animal in agony. He prayed it was an animal, and beat his heels frantically against the mare, trying vainly to speed her forward. "Louis, Louis, why did you give your doctor a plowhorse to ride when you ride a whirlwind! Sweet Mary, sweet Jesus, make that sound be an animal, not the dauphin!"

As the mare plodded upward the yelping came closer. The trail made a sharp turn and ended in a steep slope of rubble, where an antelope but no horse could go. The chamois Louis had been chasing was nowhere to be seen. But two other animals were fighting on the ledge. The cries came from Pégase, who was hurt. The bloody-jawed thing that had hurt him was like no animal Friar Jean had ever seen apart from those in a manuscript bestiary which he believed to be unreliable. He jumped awkwardly off his horse and ran forward to help. He was unarmed, but he could throw stones.

Louis had never seen a snow leopard either, though he had heard that some of them still survived in the high Alps. They were a relic of the Crusades, brought from the East as curiosities by the returning warriors. Some had escaped and bred in the mountains of Switzerland and Savoy. The heavy snows had driven this one down from the heights; it was ravenously hungry. It was seven feet long from its snarling snout to the tip of its lashing tail. Like all cats it was cunning, cruel, and bloodthirsty. Like all leopards it had an inbred hatred for dogs, and an especial fondness for their flesh, though it would eat any animal it could overtake, even ponies. This one had deserted the chamois and sprung upon Pégase.

Louis had dismounted, for to have attempted to trample the leopard under the hoofs of his horse would also have crushed Pégase. He heard a shouting behind him but supposed it was one of the huntsmen, cursed him for failing to shoot, and crept up on the fighting animals, his dagger raised for a slash, his face contorted with fury. "I am coming, Pégase! Fang him, thou faithful! The throat, the throat! Tear out the throat!" But the dog's hind quarters were paralyzed; the leopard's claws had severed some vital nerve. The animals rolled over and over, a tangle of blood and fur, the hound howling piteously, a deep snarling hiss issuing from the leopard's throat as its jaws rent and its claws tore. It was already feasting on dog flesh, though Pégase was not yet dead. It did not see the man. The dagger flashed down and slit the throat. The bloody jaws opened, gasping for breath; scarlet froth foamed out. But Louis struck and slashed and cut again and again, for Pégase lay still, with his eyes open and glazing. The guide, when he arrived and saw the dismembered beast, could not recognize it as a snow leopard; and Louis, he thought, had gone raving mad. He was weeping, yelling frightful curses, kicking at parts of the snow leopard, throwing them about with his hands which were sticky with blood and covered with tufts of fur. His face was maniacal.

Then he approached Pégase, but he could not bring himself to pat him or even to close his eyes, for all the beauty of life was gone and the mangled animal was alien and ugly in death. "Thou poor beast, you died for me. Friar Jean called you a coward. Wait, wait, you shall be avenged. Back he goes to France today! With my own hands I will rip off his miter!"

The guide approached, quaking with fright. "My lord Dauphin—"

"You!" screamed Louis. "Craven! Varlet! Strumpetson! Where were you? Why were you not here! I'll hang you! I'll crack your leg bones in the screws! Out of my sight! Give me back my écu!"

"My lord Daughin, look yonder." The guide pointed to Friar Jean's horse, riderless, placidly pulling at a tuft of dry grass at the edge of the gully. Then he pointed into the gully.

Some distance down, at an unnatural angle against the boulder that had broken his fall, lay Friar Jean.

Without hesitation Louis leaped over the edge and made his way rapidly down the steep slope. The rubble loosened and gave away at every step, starting small avalanches of pebbles and stones. The guide followed him.

"Have a care!" shouted the dauphin. "Don't go straight down to him. Circle out so that the stones don't hit him, or he'll be killed."

The two men scrambled down in a wide arc, the detritus dislodged by their feet bounding and thumping into the valley below, missing the body of Friar Jean, who lay motionless. It is nothing to see a man bent double in a forward direction; it is dreadful to see a man's body bent backward a nearly equal amount.

The dauphin knelt and gently raised his head. "What happened, mon père? Are you badly hurt?"

With some difficulty Friar Jean managed to smile. "I thought I would hurl a stone at that devil of a beast. There was quite an adequate stone

186

just at the edge. But I'm afraid my legs are not quite what they used to be; I missed my footing." It was a clear, thoughtful description of the accident, exactly like Friar Jean. But his forehead was a glaze of sweat and his lips were pressed white and thin; it was obvious that he was in great pain.

"Help me with him," Louis ordered. "If you manage gently I'll give you a hundred écus. If you do not, before God, I will hang you in an hour."

"Softly, softly, Louis," Friar Jean murmured. "Do not move me for a few minutes. In a few minutes there will be no pain. I have something to say to this good man who guided me so skillfully through the mountains to La Grande Chartreuse."

"Thank you, my lord bishop," the fellow said, glancing from one to the other apprehensively.

"Do you remember the witch that flew across the face of the moon?"

"Yes, my lord bishop."

"The witch Melusine?"

"Yes, my lord."

"Did she scream?"

"She did not scream, no, my lord."

"And therefore no member of the party was going to die. Is that not what you said?"

The guide slowly nodded his head. "So it has always been believed in the Dauphiny."

Friar Jean said gravely: "Take note, good guide, that someone from the party *is* going to die. Thus your Melusine is folly, superstition. Always remember that; and tell others. Fear God, do not fear witches. Promise me."

"I have taken note, my lord bishop. I promise."

"This isn't important," Louis whispered to the guide, thinking Friar Jean's mind was wandering. "We are wasting time. Help me up to the ledge with him, and run for a litter as fast as you can."

Friar Jean heard the whisper. "On the contrary, Louis, it was most important. But he has promised, I am content; I have snared one last soul for God. But do not move me yet." Then he said, as casually as if he were rising to pass from one room to another, which may have been how he thought of it, "My back is broken, and I am dying."

Louis, who had seen many men die from violent battle wounds, saw the quick onset of certain signs and tearfully motioned the guide not to move him.

"How fitting it is," said Friar Jean in a weaker, smaller voice, "that I should fall and you should climb down to save me! There is infinite mercy in that, Louis. Do you not see that God wants you to know there is no danger in heights? You will never be afraid of them again."

Friar Jean said nothing thereafter. If he prayed at all for himself, he must have prayed inwardly, for his last spoken words were for others. Presently his face altered and his breathing ceased.

Louis, who could not touch his dead dog, pressed the white old head against his breast and wept and kissed the cold forehead, for the dead body of a friend, like a ruined temple, is not ugly. Some of the grandeur remains.

The guide muttered under his breath: "It must have been a bird. Melusine always screams."

Chapter Twenty-eight

Death struck again less than two months later. On Thursday, January 7, 1451, in his capital at Chambéry, old Amadeus, Cardinal-Duke of Savoy, suddenly died, and the governance of the province fell into the hands of Lodovico, his son.

Blandly the new duke Lodovico wrote to the dauphin: "His Eminence had arisen early and admired the salubrity of the weather. He tried on the cape in which he had hoped to officiate at the nuptials of the grandchildren who were so close to his heart. He expressed great satisfaction at the number and quality of the ermine pelts. Then he halted, pressed his hand to his breast and, murmuring *Domine, in manus tuas,* fell down dead."

There would, of necessity, be some delay, Duke Lodovico said, in fixing a new date for the wedding of his daughter Charlotte to Louis and of his son Amadeo to Yolande.

To Louis a decent period of mourning seemed proper and unavoidable; but when he inquired how long the period might last Lodovico answered in vague and evasive generalities. It began to look as if Lodovico might reverse the cardinal's policy of good will.

In February the cause of the delay came to light. Duke Lodovico was afraid. France had sent a deputation to Savoy with protests and thinly veiled threats. King Charles did not wish Yolande to marry Amadeo. King Charles did not wish Louis to marry Charlotte, a child of seven. It was hinted that there would be something dishonorable in becoming both the father-in-law and the brother-in-law to the dauphin, which Lodovico would be if the marriages were solemnized. Lodovico, pious to scrupulosity, inexperienced in government, and far less resolute than the old cardinal, had wavered and put off the decision.

A French deputation descended upon Louis too. The Bishop of Maillezais arrived in the Dauphiny with a guard of honor nearly as big as an army.

Louis did not care for the deputation to penetrate to Grenoble. He advanced rapidly to welcome them with a guard of honor twice as big as the bishop's, appearing on the crest of a hill, while the bishop's party, strung out in a long straight line, a perfect target, slowly advanced up the slope. Not only did the dauphin have a superior guard of honor; he had artillery, for saluting purposes. And since the protocol of honor for the new weapon was not strictly fixed, there was nothing improper in the astonishing volley with which he saluted them, though it was usual, for the sake of economy, to use blank charges.

The brow of the hill burst into fire and smoke as the thunder of sixteen cannon set off in unison roared over the Frenchmen's heads. All around them, aimed as close as Henri dared, cannon balls thumped into the earth. Here and there, by some magic that was new to Europe, some cannon balls exploded with a second burst of flame after they had buried themselves. The bishop's party halted, confused. Some looked to their arms, some looked to the bishop for an order, but His Reverend Lordship was too bewildered to give any.

Louis, who dressed so meanly for himself, understood how to dress impressively when an occasion required it of him. Through the cannon smoke, which the wind had not yet dispersed, the bishop now saw galloping toward him a figure of a man with the aspect of a king. Over the saints on his cap of state Louis wore the gold coronet of a sovereign Prince of the Empire. Over his cuirass of Milanese steel he wore, out of respect for Cardinal Savoy, the purple mourning cloak of a royal de France. The cardinal's emerald glittered on his hand. The cross and chain of office flashed on his breast. He was flanked by a party of knights and Henri LeClercq in the crimson tabard of a general of the army.

Drawing rein at the bishop's horse, Louis said, "Welcome to the Dauphiny." His pleasant, low-pitched voice was in startling contrast to the fury of the welcome; and, to the bishop's dizzy senses, it seemed that an odor of brimstone hung about his cloak. His Reverence fumbled in his mind for the prayer to exorcise a demon, but could not remember it.

The bishop was not the only one, nor was he intended to be the only one, impressed with Louis's welcome. A Savoyard diplomat attached to the Dauphinal court spurred off to Chambéry with a report to Lodovico that whatever forces France might send against Louis, it was certain that Louis would foresee and outwit them. Lodovico was especially impressed with the menace of the exploding cannon balls.

Later, in Grenoble, when the bishop had recovered his aplomb, he delivered his message to Louis.

Louis was not surprised that the king objected to everything. Only on one subject, Margaret, had he and his father ever agreed. He was interested more in the manner of the bishop's delivery than in the message.

189

The manner was unexpectedly conciliatory, betraying a weakness. King Charles reproached him for espousing a child.

"There is no question of living as man and wife for years," Louis said tartly. "The rest is perfectly respectable, as Your Lordship very well knows."

"And your father deplores the marriage of Yolande with the Prince of Piedmont. It is not, frankly, a desirable marriage for France."

"She loves him, my lord bishop. That is enough for me. Ask the king where *he* found love, and count his bastards if you can."

The bishop swallowed and did not pursue the subject.

At one point Louis nearly burst out laughing. "If you *must* marry again, your father will understand and approve. But he grieves that you throw yourself away on the infant princess of Savoy. He suggests a more mature lady of high and ancient lineage, one of the royal house of Hungary; in fact, the aunt of the Hungarian king himself. It would be an extremely valuable union, to say nothing of the Hungarian princess's exotic Eastern beauty."

Louis liked the moderate tone that the interview had taken and did not wish to antagonize the bishop needlessly. "It is true that Charlotte is somewhat young," he conceded. "I shall give every thought to my father's suggestion. There is, as you say, nothing to compare with exotic Eastern beauty."

But from every point of view the notion was preposterous. Hungary was far away and useless to the Dauphiny. The Hungarian king Ladislaus, Louis happened to know, was in prison in fear of his life, tasting his food with dread lest it be poisoned. A military dictator ruled the land. And as for the lady herself, Louis had seen many royal aunts. Exotic Eastern beauty forsooth! If the bishop admitted she was mature, she must be ancient indeed. He had no intention of allowing an elderly Hungarian woman to intrude upon his privacy, which he needed more than most men.

Only at the end did the bishop threaten. "As you know, France is now happily cleared of the English. How shocking it would be, after a hundred years of victorious war against a foreign enemy, for a French king to be forced to chasten his own beloved son with his mighty, and unemployed, armies! Yet he chasteneth whom he loveth."

Louis knew that the English indeed were officially expelled from France. But they held out in isolated pockets and continually fomented local revolts and insurrections. The French armies still had much to occupy them. Order would come slowly, if ever.

He dismissed the bishop with friendly words and a promise to consider the whole matter most carefully, which he would have had to do in any case. His determination to conclude the Savoy alliance was more firm than before, for now the Dauphiny was threatened on two sides instead of one. But Duke Lodovico's indecision continued all summer and into the fall. Louis reduced the cash settlement from 400,000 gold crowns gradually to 200,000. Not even that succeeded in shaking Lodovico out of his apathy.

Time was growing short. From France came the ominous news that the only two members of the council who had approved the alliance had been disgraced and imprisoned. Both good men had suffered confiscation of their entire fortunes. The king's power was growing; there was little doubt where Charles would strike as soon as he felt himself sufficiently strong. Louis prepared for war.

Long since his matériel had been in excellent condition. But he needed men, and he knew he might jeopardize the esteem in which he was held by asking for them in his own name as if this were just another selfish, personal feudal dispute. He would have to convince the people to summon themselves.

There had never been a representative body of legislators in the Dauphiny. Louis summoned the first that the province had ever had. He told them of their danger and their duty. When the Estates learned that they were to be a permanent parliament and henceforth would have a voice in their own government, they cheerfully voted to conscript a standing army, and imposed a special tax to pay the soldiers their wages; and from the *solde*, their pay, came the name of soldiers in every European language. The peasants joined the state service in droves, since it was just as easy to fight perhaps once a year, perhaps never, as to work three days a week on the roads; their pay was secure, they still knew where they stood, and they wished neither France nor Savoy to overrun the Dauphiny.

Duke Lodovico eyed this burst of warlike activity and made up his mind that Louis was a greater menace than France, which the cardinal could have told him from the beginning. Yolande wrote an affectionate letter to her brother saying that at last she and Amadeo were to be married. The same day a herald from Chambéry confirmed November as the month, Thursday, the 11th, as the day.

On Sunday, the 7th, the dauphin, at the head of his suite, arrived in Chambéry, where Duke Lodovico had piously commanded prayers in the cathedral to Louis the Saint, the dauphin's not too remote ancestor, beseeching him to bless and intercede in heaven for the ultimate fructification of the union between his namesake and the little princess of Savoy. It was a delicate, graceful courtesy, which Louis reciprocated by hearing two Masses that day, saying the prayers in a clear voice, though he had always thought sorrowfully of St. Louis, who had typified an ideal feudalism, now so woefully decayed.

The dauphin also wanted to familiarize himself with the details of the cathedral, so he would know where to stand and what to do. The wedding would cause comment in Europe. He did not wish to appear gauche or ridiculous. He thought he might arrange for a little dais for Charlotte to stand upon when they stood up to be married, in case she proved to be conspicuously short, as was very likely. The platform could easily be hidden by a bank of flowers. King René had sent a profusion of them from Provence. And of course he must meet Charlotte, whom he had never seen, so that he would recognize her, and she must not be frightened of him. It would be a bad omen as well as a scandal if she should cry during the ceremony. He had brought her some presents. He had learned from her nurses Raoulette and Loyse de Bethléem that she liked dolls. He had also brought her some orange preserves.

He wished time also to acquaint her father with the loyal expressions of joy that the wedding had evoked in the Dauphiny and to school the duke in its deep political significance. In spite of the crushing taxes imposed by the Estates, his good cities everywhere had spontaneously sent gifts of money to Charlotte: Vienne, 600 crowns; Romans, 600; Grenoble, 900; and a score of hamlets and villages had pooled their small resources and contributed 300 florins. He had brought the money with him, and letters of authentication from the mayors of each municipality, lest Lodovico think he had made the gesture himself. He had planned to speak often with Lodovico during the days before the ceremony so that the duke might absorb, little by little, all the favorable aspects of the alliance.

Time did not allow this slow, sound bit of diplomacy.

On Monday Yolande came to him with an anxious face and said: "Good brother, there was a stranger in the cathedral this morning. His air was proud and contemptuous. No one knew him. You always ask me to be on the lookout for spies. We did not like him. Did we, Amadeo?"

"Not at all," said the Prince of Piedmont.

Louis smiled. He had a notion that if she had said, "He looked like an angel," Amadeo would have equally agreed.

"How was he dressed, Yolande?"

"Why, nobly; richly, I should say."

"Good doublet, good hose, new shoes?"

"I think so."

"But sober, quiet of color, Yolande?"

"Probably, since I did not particularly notice."

"Was his face wind-burnt? Had he been riding far?"

"Oh, I noticed that most especially," Amadeo said, proud to be able to contribute something definite.

Louis frowned. "He is a spy; he is disguised; he is noble; he is formidable. I feared this, but not so soon."

"We know where he lodges," Amadeo volunteered brightly. "A somewhat shabby inn."

"Naturally," Louis snapped. "Take me to him."

"I think I ought to tell Father first," Amadeo said.

"No," said Louis.

The Prince of Piedmont hesitated, looking from brother to sister, at their remarkably similar expressions, their strong family resemblance. "That is exactly what Yolande said. Just, no."

"Please, dear Amadeo," she said softly. "Louis is right."

"Very well, my dear. If *you* command me."

The dauphin smiled.

At the inn the stranger readily identified himself. He was the herald *par excellence* of all King Charles's heralds, the Normandy King of Arms. All heralds were privileged, since they were essential couriers, but the person of a King of Arms was sacrosanct. He could ride inviolate through the bitterest wars. To insult him, though he himself was usually some scion of a petty noble House, would have been to insult the coat he wore and the monarch he served, an act of war. The tradition was older than feudalism, dating back to the fetiales of the Romans. Only once, at Lectoure, had Louis ever seen a herald's person violated, and he had always considered that an act of insanity.

Normandy King of Arms was handsome, young, and overbearing. He had letters for the Duke of Savoy, he said. Louis demanded the letters. The courier quite properly refused. Louis demanded his credentials. These the King of Arms produced, flushing. Louis scanned them. They were genuine.

"Where is my father?" Louis suddenly barked at him.

Normandy King of Arms was nettled and somewhat rattled by the brusque manner, as Louis meant him to be. "You will soon find out!" he said stoutly. But he said too much.

Louis now knew what he wanted to know. His father was on the march, and these days King Charles did not march without his army.

"And now, if you please," said the herald, "I shall be about my mission. It seems that here one cannot even pray without being spied upon. I arrived only this morning." He seemed to want to make excuses for not going to Duke Lodovico at once. Actually, as Louis could see, he had ridden all night and was very fatigued. "Or do you dare try to stop me!"

"Nay, quite to the contrary," Louis said in a quick turnabout of manner. "We intend to accompany you, since you came without an escort. A King of Arms is worthy of more consideration than has been shown you. Put on your pretty tabard, which I noticed in the closet, and let us approach the duke in a dignity befitting your high office."

Again the herald flushed. "Sir, I need no dignity other than that which attaches to the documents I bear."

"Very well," smiled Louis.

Thus, when the duke received them, Normandy King of Arms appeared in simple doublet and hose, without the awesome garment blazoned with the redoubtable arms of France, shorn of half his strength.

His mission was only to deliver the letters and return with an answer, not to parley. He delivered them, while Louis spoke quietly to an aide, and was courteously escorted to a suite of rooms reserved for distinguished visitors.

As soon as he was out of earshot, Lodovico said in dismay: "This is appalling. Your father positively forbids both marriages. He threatens war. He is already on your borders with an army."

"Softly," said Louis, "not on *my* borders, or I should know. Have you given a thought to your own?"

"My agents are not so swift as yours, Monseigneur."

"Not only through agents do I know what I know, good future father-in-law. Normandy King of Arms has been riding hard and far. Armies do not march with the speed of heralds. There is still time."

"No, no; I could never think of permitting the marriages now."

"In that case," said Louis gravely, "our provinces will fall one by one, beginning with Savoy, since you are my ally and I am better prepared than you. I have already sent the alert. By morning my army and cannon will guard every inch of my borders. I cannot guard yours also, and the weaker of us will be attacked first."

The menace of the situation loosed all the persuasive eloquence that great emotion could generate in Louis. He painted a gory picture of beautiful Savoy ravaged and burned by the brutal veterans of the Hundred Years' War, the duke shorn of his coronet, his dynasty destroyed, his heirs destitute, his son forlorn, without a bride, without a sou, for Charles, who had not scrupled to rob his friends, would scarcely scruple to annihilate an enemy.

Amadeo said: "He is right, Father. We have gone too far to go back now." Yolande squeezed his hand.

Louis dwelt on the fidelity of the Dauphinois, their spirit, their pride in their new free institutions, their touching gifts to Charlotte, their readiness to fight, the excellence of his new military roads, and the strength of his fortifications. All this Lodovico knew to be true.

Finally he said he would never give up. He would fight alone if he had to till the Dauphiny was overrun town by town. And even if the Dauphiny should fall, he would still fight on in the mountains of Savoy, even beyond the Alps.

Willy-nilly the duke envisioned Savoy a battleground. His face showed his fear.

But all this need not happen, Louis said. Confronted by a firm alliance King Charles would retire. The French armies had never been as strong as they seemed. Their victories had come through English weakness and disunity at home. He reminded Lodovico of Jack Cade's rebellion: an unknown Irishman, able to raise an army of forty thousand disgruntled commoners, to capture London, to execute great English nobles! Weakness and anarchy, the nemesis of princes, *they* were the conquerors of the English armies, not the French king.

And, lest he neglect a single argument, he recalled to pious Lodovico the sanctity of pledges, the sin of breaking an oath. The marriage banns had been proclaimed in the cathedral of Chambéry. To repudiate them now would be to stand forsworn before God and man.

Lodovico said heavily, "I see that I have no choice but to do as you say and pray God you are right in all this."

Louis quickly added: "Normandy King of Arms is probably sleeping. Would it not be prudent, my lord duke, to solemnize the marriages before he wakes?"

"What? Tonight?"

"I am ready," Yolande said shyly, and Amadeo echoed stoutly, "I have been ready for a long time."

"But the preparations, the cathedral! It will not be decorated till Thursday, the indignity of all this haste—"

By Thursday there would be war, Louis said, a war that would inevitably reduce Savoy to a shambles. "And as for the cathedral, sir, I have no doubt that God is in your private chapel also."

"Nay, Louis, that is true, and piously said. It was sinful of me to be vain. But not tonight. Tomorrow, at the soonest."

"Dawn, then," said Louis.

"And I suppose Charlotte ought to be told to be ready."

"By all means." Louis had nearly forgotten Charlotte.

Next morning, when Normandy King of Arms awoke after a refreshing sleep and presented himself for an answer, he was informed, with every expression of esteem, that he had arrived too late and that the marriages had already been performed.

Chapter Twenty-nine

Four days later the French army arrived at the Rhône and stared across the river. There stood the combined forces of the Dauphiny and Savoy. Dauphinois and Savoyards paraded menacingly side by side up and down the riverbank, though Louis ordered no shouting, no insults, and above all no firing of cannon.

Neutral ambassadors on both sides watched to see who would attack first, the father or the son, in Europe's most notorious feud. The Burgundian ambassador to the Dauphinal court reported to Duke Philip, his master: "At one point Monseigneur le Dauphin could make out the figure of his father the king across the river, on which, with a most melancholy look, he ordered the cannon turned away from that spot, though I doubt if it would have made any difference, Monseigneur's new grenades being most fearsome."

King Charles's ambassador from Burgundy also reported: "His Highness the king, on witnessing the forces massed against him, took council with his advisers, who deemed an assault hazardous without reinforcements, for they had not expected a coalition. Nor were the council disposed to attack two provinces of the Holy Roman Empire at once. Nor did they see how the marriages could be annulled, the damage being already done. Nevertheless, an assault might have been attempted, such was the rage of the king against Monseigneur le Dauphin. But suddenly there appeared at the council tent a herald with a report of an uprising in Bordeaux. Thereupon, over the king's protests, the council decided to withdraw."

There was a *post scriptum*: "On reaching Bordeaux King Charles found the city peaceful. Search is being made for the herald. The dauphin is greatly suspected of sending a false message."

Duke Philip, with tongue in cheek, congratulated King Charles on his restraint and on what he termed his philoprogenitiveness, a word suggested by a cynical man of letters, Philippe de Comines, who prepared the Burgundian dispatches. It perplexed the king, then infuriated him when he was told it meant "love of offspring."

To Louis the duke wrote in a cordial, almost wistful vein: "Often I bethink me of how in the old days Christendom won honor against the Infidel in the Holy Land. Now in the East I see rising once more the menace of the Turks. They say the Crusades are over; they say I am old-fashioned in my views. But honor is still to be won on a Crusade. Think what great deeds my sword and your cannon, wedded together in one holy mighty resolve, might not accomplish even now in this degenerate modern age! Come and see me, bring your bride, and let us talk together." It was signed with the affectionate name he always used when addressing Louis, "Your Uncle Burgundy."

Louis promised to come, answering in his own hand. Usually he wrote small, to get as many words as possible on the sheet; but now he wrote a big round script so that the duke could read it without difficulty. Louis had seen a new Italian device of polished Venetian glass that elderly men could perch on their noses to make everything look twice as big as it really was; but he could not imagine the duke, dreaming of a Crusade, still vigorous in a tourney at fifty-five, submitting to the indignity of the instrument. A shining knight in spectacles? Not Uncle Burgundy!

Moreover, as yet he had scarcely seen his bride. Little Charlotte remained in Chambéry, where her nurses now addressed her as Madame la Dauphine, learning her catechism, learning to sew, learning to eat like a lady with the Italian forks, learning the names and countries of the reigning kings of Europe, which was very difficult since three of them were named Henri. The heads of the great seignorial Houses were even more confusing, for everybody seemed to be named Jean. Yet this was all part

196

of the education of a princess, Charlotte was related to dozens of them, and one day, if she was to be a good wife, mother, and queen, she would have to know all about them. She applied herself dutifully, but sometimes she thought growing up and getting married was not much fun.

There was little leisure for the dauphin either. The days were never long enough to accomplish all the projects he dreamed of in his study at night: more and better roads, more and stronger castles, a regular system of posts, faster-shooting guns. These works progressed, but never as fast as the dauphin's impatient imagination. He drove himself; he drove everyone else. He knew he was safe only temporarily from the vengeance of his father, who would assuredly return with a punitive expedition as soon as the council would let him.

Often at night he missed Pégase, though another hound now stretched itself on the hearthstones apparently dreaming the same canine dreams, since his limbs twitched too when he slept. Always he missed Friar Jean, whom no one could replace, and in consequence saw much of Henri LeClercq and his family, watching the boy as he grew, speaking often of Friar Jean, though he learned little that he did not already know. Searching in his memory Henri said: "Once Friar Jean did tell me that he knew a great lord who knew the secret of my birth. I was always ashamed to press him for details, not caring who I was. Now that I have a son, I should like to know, but of course it is too late."

"If your blood isn't noble, I'll make it noble," Louis said. But, remembering Lectoure, he thought it already was. One day he would make inquiries of Bernard d'Armagnac.

Another, rather eerie memory of Friar Jean struck the dauphin quite suddenly one day in summer when, inspecting a new mountain road, he looked over a sheer drop and realized that in all the months that had passed never once had his former fear of heights troubled him. From that time forward the Dauphiny roads were built without parapets, and Louis rode up to inspect them even in winter when they were slippery; the works progressed faster now. Whether his release from the old terror was caused by Friar Jean's earnest prediction, almost like an absolution, or by some virtue in the cardinal's emerald Louis did not know. He treasured both, but he put the ring in a little velvet bag and wore it around his neck. He suspected that Friar Jean, looking down from beyond the clouds, might label it superstition and disapprove. He hoped Friar Jean would not spot it under his doublet.

During this period an emperor was crowned; for the first time in fifteen years the Holy Roman Empire had a head and the Dauphiny had an overlord. At first Louis hoped for great things. It seemed for a time that Philip of Burgundy might be right, for the pope preached a Crusade against the Turk, calling on the new emperor for help as titular head of all Christendom. But the Emperor, Frederick III, was a disappointment, and the only help he ever gave against the Turks was to distribute some letters of indulgence to any prince who might care to encourage the venture. A package of these arrived at Grenoble with an imperial letter of instruction to distribute them to such knights, nobles, and foot soldiers as might decide to go to the East on their own initiative and at their own expense. No one went. The cheap-looking little letters distressed the Holy Father, but they interested Louis because they were all absolutely identical in appearance down to the smallest details and could not be manuscript. He showed them to a man who might know how to explain them. Henri LeClercq agreed that they were not manuscript. "This is something mechanical, perhaps some kind of printing. I have seen printed pictures, but never printed words."

"Could whole books be printed? It would be a wonderful thing."

"Monseigneur, I do not know. Shall I pursue the inquiry? I have a foundryman who might contrive to cast the characters."

"What is he casting now?"

"Hollow grenades."

"I think that is more practical," Louis said.

During these few years, peaceful but anxious ones for Louis, Charlotte grew into her adolescence, young Jean LeClercq grew to show more interest in swordplay than engineering, and bloody history was made both in Europe and the East but swept past the little Dauphiny. King Ladislaus of Hungary died, poisoned in his prison. Constantinople fell to the Turks after a weary war. The internal disunity of England flared into the full-fledged War of the Roses. It was extremely bitter and gave every indication of lasting many years.

Louis was as thankful as any other good Frenchman that the hereditary enemies of his homeland were at last reduced to a state where they could no longer harm France. France could bind up her ancient wounds, cultivate the blessings of peace, and, please God, look across the Channel and learn a lesson of unity from a hideous example of civil war. But Louis did not think France would learn by example. It was far more likely that King Charles, his armies unemployed, his hands now free, would march south upon the Dauphiny in overwhelming force with the full approval of his council. It had always been their policy to give the veterans a campaign to fight. Louis remembered the Butchers he had led into Switzerland and the Rhineland. This time there would be more of them. And this time *he* would be the victim.

All his years of work in the Dauphiny would be undone, his reforms abolished, his policies reversed. He saw in his mind's eye his roads ruined, his castles torn down, his forests burned, his loyal peasants slaughtered. They did not deserve that. No ruse, no false report of an uprising would work this time. Nor did he think he could bully or cajole Lodovico into helping him. Three years ago chances of success had been slim enough. Now resistance would be virtually hopeless, and Lodovico knew it. Nor would an appeal to the weak new emperor have been of any use even if Louis had been willing to involve France in another great war.

France was already scheming to drive a diplomatic wedge between the

Dauphiny and Savoy. Louis knew that pressure had already been applied to Lodovico, for the installments on Charlotte's dowry had suddenly stopped.

Next came a report from the northern border that the bridge across the Rhône was heavily patrolled on the French side; then that a French army was gathering in Lyons; then that the king himself had joined them.

Henri said to the dauphin, "We shall not worry till the artillery comes."

Louis said grimly, "I'm afraid it will come."

Next day a herald reported that Jean Bureau had joined the king with a train of mobile cannon. Henri said, "Mine are as good as his, and my grenades are better."

"Do you want civil war for France, General LeClercq?"

"If you do, Monseigneur."

"Like the war in England?"

"If you do."

"I do not think I do. Moreover, we couldn't win this time."

"What will you do?"

"I do not know."

At length there came a rumor, which Louis quickly substantiated, that a second French army was marching through the Armagnacs, edging eastward. "They're taking no chances," he said bitterly. But he had to admire the strategy. The armies that had fought the English for a hundred years were slowly converging in a mighty crescent, flanking the Dauphiny.

In great agitation the dauphin looked south for help, but King René replied that neither he nor Louis, as sovereign princes of the Empire, ought to involve themselves without express command of their overlord Frederick, "who does not fight, as you know. Nor would I willingly take up arms against Charles, who was husband, though a bad one, to my dead sister. Nor could we win." In return he offered Louis asylum in Provence, "though I doubt how long I dare harbor you." Clearly old King René's fighting days were over and he viewed the approaching French armies with terror.

In the latter days of August a Burgundian herald arrived at Grenoble. Duke Philip, having realistically appraised the movements of the French armies, wrote just one line: "Louis, my boy, don't make a fool of yourself."

"Those are harsh words from my good uncle," the dauphin remarked.

"I suggested a poem," the young herald volunteered rather impudently, "but, as you see, the duke wrote this himself."

"And who might you be, young fellow?"

"I am Philippe de Comines, Sieur d'Argenton, secretary in chief to his lordship, your Uncle Burgundy."

He was impudent, he was impish, but he was also, as Louis knew, able and highly trusted by Duke Philip. "I pictured you a much older man. What was your poem?"

"Not mine, Monseigneur. I had in mind the words of good advice that were spoken to the paladin Roland in the fatal ambush at Roncevals. He did not heed them, and he died." Then he spoke a couplet from an epic in the old tongue that few men nowadays could pronounce:

> "Kar vasselages par sens nen est folie,
> Mielz valt mesure que ne fait estultie."
> (Valor with common sense is not unmixed;
> Bravery is bravest when not overbrave.)

"I should have expected my good uncle to bid me stand and fight it out no matter what the odds."

"Your Uncle Burgundy has a keen sense of the possible, Monseigneur, quite distinct from his dreams of glory."

"What does he counsel me to do?"

"I am forbidden to return to Burgundy unless I bring you with me. Burgundy is rich and fair, Monseigneur, and I should regret my homeland."

"So is France and so do I, Philippe de Comines. I shall think about it."

Then from Chambéry Duke Lodovico rode into Grenoble with crushing news. "I would stand by you if there were a chance of success," he said. "But read this from the emperor. It came from Vienna today. The gold double-headed eagles on the imperial herald's tabard were dusty, his horse was all covered with foam. I'm afraid it's no use."

In a beautifully engrossed Gothic parchment Frederick deplored the threat of war with France, positively forbade Savoy to engage in it, and bade Lodovico detach himself at once from the alliance with the dauphin. There were some pious generalties deprecating a feud between a father and a son. "But I am not unmindful," the emperor said, "of my duty to my vassals," and he offered Louis asylum in Vienna.

Philippe de Comines remarked dryly, "He offered King Ladislaus asylum in Vienna too. If it please you, Monseigneur, I think you will find the food in Burgundy far more digestible."

In the final week of August the combined French armies stood poised along the Rhône from Lyons to Avignon, ready to strike. Now came the ultimatum. King Charles sent a demand to his son to appear before him to answer a heavy list of charges. Everything Louis had done in the Dauphiny was represented as a crime. He had treasonably armed a foreign state against France. He had forsworn his allegiance by marrying without permission. He had overworked his peasants and abused the corvée. He had instituted, without royal sanction, an illegal parliament of representatives of the people of his appanage. It was hinted that he might be a murderer, since Friar Jean, a French emissary, had mysteriously died while on a mission to the Dauphinal court. The dauphin was even, read this remarkable document, a horsethief. Louis supposed this last item, bearing the stamp of his father's mind and probably inserted over the protests of the council, must refer to the fact that, on the night of his flight into exile, the night Margaret died, he and Henri had ridden horses from the royal stables.

Duke Lodovico received a copy of the charges together with a letter threatening reprisals against Savoy if Louis should seek shelter there. "Clearly," said Lodovico, "you must go—speedily—tonight." His face was drawn; the hand that held the threatening documents shook.

Louis hesitated. Against the forces that beat upon him from every side, the vast armies, the attitude of the emperor, the attitude of King René, the apathy of Duke Lodovico, his own inner scruples, he was helpless. But he was reluctant to desert the province on which he had spent such labors, which he had molded into a neat and orderly little state, which indeed, as he now discovered, he had learned to love. But to remain would mean war, a war of unpredictable extent and duration, certain only of failure and misery to the Dauphiny. He felt sick at heart and uneasy in body.

"I shall go," he said heavily. "But I cannot go tonight."

"Since you agree to go," Lodovico quickly said, "why cannot you go tonight?"

Philippe de Comines also wondered why, but said nothing. He thought Monseigneur le Dauphin looked extremely tired. He too was struck, as Frair Jean had been, by the great profusion and richness of the tapestries, but he could not explain them. Both he and Lodovico found the room oppressively warm.

"It is already evening," Louis said, knowing the excuse would sound lame and foolish. "Horses are fresher in the morning—it is Sunday— no, no, I cannot go tonight."

How could he tell them on this hot August evening that he had felt chilly all day and was now actually shaking with cold? How could he tell them that a winter wind was blowing through the room when the candles burned so steadily and the tapestries hung so still against the walls? How could he ask them to feel what was not there, what he himself knew was not there? But, hideously real to him, it nipped him to the marrow. He clenched his teeth lest they chatter. They did, however, just a little, in spite of all he could do. The warning was very strong this time.

"Now—leave me—till dawn. Then I promise to go."

His set teeth, his faraway stare, the tautness of the muscles about his jaw made his face unfamiliar and unpleasantly menacing. The two men hurriedly left the room. Louis, usually so punctilious of the courtesy due his father-in-law, sat motionless at the felt-covered writing desk.

The instant he was alone he flung himself across the room and bolted the door. Then he stuffed his sleeve into his mouth lest he swallow his tongue.

He began to run. He felt consciousness slipping away, but he knew he was running in the direction of the bedchamber. He hoped to reach the bed and lie down before he fell. When he did fall, the surface felt

soft and for an instant he thought he had won the race. Then the spasm
twisted him over onto his back and he found himself looking up through
the casement window at the night sky.

A giant comet hung like a scimitar against the firmament. Through it
shone the stars. But Louis had experienced disturbances of vision before
during seizures. The comet was merely a new manifestation. It was not
so terrifying as the colors he sometimes saw.

Later in the night, when consciousness returned, he rose from the floor.
The thick carpet had saved him; he had broken no bones, suffered no cuts
apparently, for he could see no blood. About an inch of the candles still
burned, steadily as ever, in the candlesticks on the writing table. The attack, then, had lasted five hours. It had been severe. He washed himself
and burned his clothes in the fireplace. As the flames consumed the velvet and fur, he found himself regretting their loss, probably twenty
francs, less, of course, three years' wear, say twelve livres, six sols; seven
livres, fourteen sols, net loss. Then he smiled to find himself capable of
normal and characteristic worry about his personal economies. At least he
was himself. There would be no aftereffects like that weird time when
he had given his purse to François Villon.

The smile hurt him. He glanced into his mirror. He had bitten his
lower lip rather nastily. Never mind. He could easily blame that on his
barber.

Then, without hesitation, he looked out of the casement window at
the sky. There was, of course, no comet. In earlier years he had feared
to examine the dark corners and blank walls where his tortured vision
had pictured frightening things during a seizure. Now he had learned
that the surest way of forgetting the hallucination was to examine carefully the background against which it had appeared. Nothing so thoroughly proved its unreality, and hence its harmlessness, as to find it no
longer there.

At dawn the barber came to shave him. Always clumsy, the poor fellow seemed clumsier than usual today. Louis took the razor from him and
shaved himself with a steady hand while the barber held the mirror
and chattered like a nervous magpie trying to sit on nine eggs at
once and unable to do justice to all of them. He excused himself in ver-
bose and grandiloquent phrases; he found himself desolated that Monseigneur was reduced to the indignity of serving as his own barber. Louis muttered that it was better than being flayed alive, pointing to his lip. The
rattled barber believed him. Privately Louis was glad of an opportunity to
test his hand, pleased to find it steady. The barber pleaded in extenua-
tion of his awkwardness that he had been unnerved by a celestial apparition during the night. Had His Highness deigned to take notice of the
fiery star? Did he think it presaged war with the Turks? It was shaped
like a scimitar. Did Monseigneur le Dauphin think it had caused the
birth of a two-headed calf in the village of Domène and the plague of

the pip in the hens of Sassenage? Did it mean, as many said, the end of the world?

Louis let him chatter. The comet, then, was real. "I did not see it when I awoke," he remarked casually.

"Oh, no, Monseigneur; it set with the other stars among which it found itself."

"Pray that it does not rise again tonight," Louis said.

The barber said: "Indeed I will, and so will everybody else. The cathedral is already packed to the portals."

Louis would willingly have joined them, for a comet, particularly one of the size he had seen, was a baleful thing full of evil portent. But there was much to do.

He dictated an order dissolving the Estates of the Dauphiny. They would hate him for that, but at least King Charles, when he came, could not punish them for existing.

He disbanded the army and ordered the soldiers back to their homes, but let them keep their weapons to defend their homes against the veterans.

He ordered Henri LeClercq to destroy his grenades and prepare such few technicians as knew the secret of the fuses for instant flight with him. Their families could come later, he said, for modern as the age might be, the wives and children of soldiers never had been and never would be held hostage for their men or tortured to reveal secrets which they probably did not know anyhow. In this the dauphin acted in good faith with no thought that an age might degenerate to a point where everyone, regardless of sex or age, would be treated with equal barbarity in war.

Lastly he wrote a letter to his father. It was couched in submissive terms, and it galled him to write it, but the Dauphiny was worth any amount of personal self-abasement if that might save it from destruction. He himself, he wrote, was the sole cause of the present tense situation; therefore he would remove himself. If it pleased God he would go to Duke Philip of Burgundy, who had already asked him to join the Crusade which heaven itself now seemed to demand. Meanwhile he left a tranquil province of orderly subjects. He besought his father to spare them.

The comet rose again when night came on. It rose every night for six weeks before it faded, and the chroniclers called it the most terrifying ever seen by man. It frightened everyone in Louis's party, though most of them were practical engineers, freer from superstition than most men. It frightened everyone but Louis, who had seen it first under circumstances that most men are mercifully spared.

Book Four

Chapter Thirty

Burgundians of high and low degree called Duke Philip "The Good." If they had not called him good they would assuredly have called him "The Magnificent" from the pride they felt in a sovereign who seemed to unite in his person all that was rich and splendid in Europe's richest and most splendid principality. Burgundian wool was the warmest, Burgundian lace was the finest, Burgundian cloth of gold was the most glittering in the world. Burgundian burghers were the wealthiest, Burgundian nobles were the haughtiest. Burgundian geese were the fattest, Burgundian cream was the creamiest, Burgundian wine was the sweetest, Burgundian beer was the foamiest. Burgundian feasts were the longest, most lavish, and Burgundian appetites matched them. All this abundance his grateful subjects attributed to Philip the Good, who had held profitably aloof for many years from the wars that devastated states all around him.

There was much to be learned from the statecraft of Philip the Good. He was friendly to everyone, and his court swarmed with ambassadors from the whole civilized world, seeking help against their enemies, which he never gave, and seeking trade, which he pretended not to understand: but he turned them over to his Dutch and Flemish merchants, who understood the matter exceedingly well. Money poured into his treasury. It poured out just as fast. But gold, like water and wind, cannot flow without exerting a force, and the movement produced the most brilliant court in Christendom. "The talent that is buried in the earth?" Duke Philip would smile. "No, not in Burgundy!"

Louis remembered Duke Philip from the days of his earliest childhood: an imposing figure of a man, vastly tall, with a thunderous voice and a great chain blazing with gems from which hung the curiously limp little Lamb of the Golden Fleece. He remembered playing with it as he sat on his good uncle's knees. It was soft as silk, but the duke said it was made of metal threads such as only Burgundians knew how to spin.

The duke's hair was white now, his color high with years of good living, his voice less fearsome, and of course he did not seem nearly so tall. Louis supposed the memory of childhood, when everyone had looked alarmingly tall, had magnified the duke's stature. The duke had also put on some inches of girth, and each spring his new suit of parade armor was a little more elaborate, a little bigger about the middle. He would laugh and say that he was providing employment for his ironworkers, his armorers, the engravers and artisans who decorated the plate with niello work. Then he would wear it into a friendly joust with one of his great vassals, who would take care to give it a diplomatic dent with some deft and harmless spear thrust so that the duke could point to the spot to show he was as good as ever.

The only man who had dared fight him seriously in the lists in recent years was his own son Charles, Count of Charolais. Duke Philip called him bold; his mother called him rash. During one vicious passage of arms she swooned and refused to eat for two days till both her men, husband and son, swore on a relic of the True Cross in the pommel of the duke's sword never to fight each other again in the lists. In the lists they never did, and that was all the oath covered.

Duke Philip was inordinately proud of this holy relic, which the Grand Turk had sent him from the church of Santa Sophia when Constantinople fell. The sultan had accompanied it with a letter of authentication written in Turkish script, which no one in Burgundy could read, countersigned in Greek by Cardinal Bessarion and the Patriarch Gennadius, which no one could read either, till Greek scholars, refugees from the faraway catastrophe, began to make their slow way into Europe. Then Duke Philip discovered that he had a treasure, and that the sultan had addressed him as "The Grand Duke of the West."

"They have heard of us in Turkey," he said with satisfaction. "When we march with our swords—and your artillery, Louis my boy—they will hear more of us."

Louis did not remind him that he had left the Dauphiny artillery in the Dauphiny or that Henri LeClercq had been given no employment in the Burgundian arsenal, which Henri characterized as primitive in the extreme. "They don't seem to take guns seriously here," he said privately to the dauphin.

Exile in Burgundy was honorable, safe, rich, and annoyingly inactive. Only young Charles saw anything good in artillery. On several occasions he had questioned Henri searchingly about the new bursting grenades. Henri had overwhelmed him with a flood of incomprehensible technicalities, which Charles of Charolais listened to with impatience.

"Don't tell that restless hothead too much," Louis warned. "He didn't once mention a Crusade. I don't trust him. He wants guns for something else."

"Did you understand what I told him, Monseigneur?"

"Frankly, Henri, it didn't make sense to me."

"Monseigneur, it wouldn't make sense to anyone." They both laughed. As usual they understood each other. Envy and fear of Burgundy died hard in Frenchmen even when they were guests in noble and hospitable exile. And there was an intemperance in Charles of Charolais that Louis, perpetually schooling himself against dangerous extremes in all his own appetites, instinctively mistrusted.

To welcome the dauphin and initiate the Crusade with appropriate solemnity, the duke of Burgundy gave a great feast. In earlier days, when the Turk threatened, Christian chivalry fasted and prayed. In these latter days, when the Turk not only threatened but conquered and, from the plenitude of power made presents of relics of the True Cross, the greatest chevalier of Christendom commanded an entertainment.

Louis, astonished at the prodigality of the meats and the fantastic forms into which food of all sorts could be coaxed, calculated that this one feat of culinary extravagance must have cost as much as an entire year's revenue for the Dauphiny.

The great hall of the Hôtel de Ville of Louvain, a magnificent new structure with ten glass windows facing the city square, was brilliantly illuminated with scores of torches that burned with a steady clear yellow flame. They imparted a pleasant scent to the air, for they had been impregnated with beeswax, a substance reserved in France for only the finest of candles.

On tables spread with exquisitely figured Flemish linen stood a treasure in silver plate, silver forks, silver candlesticks; pastry castles three feet high; churches of cake with golden bells ringing from the steeples; a unicorn with a candy-stick horn, cunningly sculptured from the meat of a noble stag; cranes stuffed with pheasants which were stuffed with quails which in turn were stuffed with humming birds; swans covered with white sugar feathers swimming in a lake of their own succulent juices, in which bobbed oranges, plovers' eggs, and plums; and in one corner a Holland windmill with sails of cake frosting pumping a miniature river of wine into a silver ewer which constantly ran dry as the knights dipped their goblets into it, toasting the health of Duke Philip the Good.

The dauphin counted forty-eight different kinds of meat, fish, ragouts, pasties, and game, some of it so super-refined that he wished that he was back in Grenoble—he politely refused the pink dormouse pie, for example, and a snail *salade* made more interesting by the addition of pickled snake fillets, which Duke Philip found very tasty. While the mighty meal was in progress, there was continuous music of minstrels, not in the old manner, when musicians paraded and declaimed in front of the diners, but with the orchestra hidden behind a screen of roses so that the harping could supply accompaniment to lustier entertainment. The great age of the minstrels, like the great age of chivalry, was passing, though no one was aware of it.

Cocks fought, bears were baited, there was a wrestling match. All this was noisy and bloody, since the birds squawked and died, the bears roared when the dogs' fangs ripped them, and the wrestlers not only grappled and threw each other but boxed bare-knuckled and kicked, with no holds barred, no blows foul. Passing also was the stiff old sense of honor.

Ladies were present all through the feast: the Countess of Charolais, who was pregnant, the Duchess of Burgundy, Duke Philip's wife, who was a Portuguese princess of stately manners and not quite accustomed after all these years to the lusty freedom that characterized Burgundian customs. "But the Duke," she said fondly to Louis, leaning toward him and smiling, "always says that a feast without ladies is like a year without spring and a spring without a rose. Isn't that knightly? Do you agree? Is it different in France?"

"It was different in the Dauphiny, Madame la Duchesse. As for France, I cannot say. It has been many years."

For the ladies, who might not care to drink the heavy wines and brandies that came near the end of the banquet, there was juice of oranges and melons sweetened with sugar in the Oriental fashion and iced with snow. The dauphin, of course, had drunk orangeade in the south and he had even heard of icing it with snow from the Alps. But there were no mountains in Flanders, and he wondered by what mechanical means Duke Philip had contrived to save the winter snow. He could not ask Henri because Henri did not sit at the same table with the Duke and Duchess of Burgundy and the Count and Countess of Charolais.

Charles made some sly reference to the countess's condition; the countess smiled and looked demurely into her crystal goblet. Charles then said, "I have not heard that you, Monseigneur, ever had an heir." He was full of pride and reckless with wine.

"It is one of the blessings that God has seen fit so far to withhold from me," Louis said coloring.

The duke said, "Charles, you forget yourself."

The countess said: "We did so hope that Charlotte would accompany you, Monseigneur. We hear she is quite a woman grown and most ravishingly beautiful."

Louis answered guardedly, "Charlotte is a woman indeed, most charming, most educated, most pious like all the Savoys."

Charles snickered, "The piousness of old Amadeus went almost too far, if my memory serves me."

"Charles!" reproved the duke. And to Louis: "We hope to receive her soon. Only her absence mars the pleasure we take in your visit."

"I constantly ask her to come," Louis said, "but Duke Lodovico deems her safer in Savoy."

"Does he indeed!" Count Charles sputtered. "Father, since when is a miserable province of the Empire safer than Burgundy? Will you permit such impudence?"

The duke looked helplessly at Philippe de Comines. That wily diplomat, never far from his master's elbow, remarked casually: "Monseigneur le Dauphin perhaps hesitates to admit that so long as his father-in-law keeps Madame la Dauphine in Savoy he feels under no pressure to pay her dowry, which is long overdue."

"Louis, my boy, do you need money?"

"No, good uncle."

"Philippe de Comines, does he?"

"He arrived with his skin and precious little else. The Dauphiny treasury he left intact, not a sol subtracted for his personal use."

"Incredible!" muttered Charles.

"Sir, what do you mean!" There was a sharp note in the dauphin's voice.

"I meant only that it is incredible that one should leave so much behind," Charles said smoothly.

The duke said something in a low voice to Philippe de Comines, who nodded. "Yes, Your Grace; yes, my lord duke—the castle of Genappe, two thousand livres a month. It shall be arranged. He is quite economical."

"Then make it twenty-five hundred," the duke said promptly. "It shall never be said to my shame that the heir to the throne of France must practice economy when he honors Burgundy with a visit. Will twenty-five hundred keep him? I am not good at budgets."

"Royally, my lord duke."

"Royally is how it should be."

Count Charles looked unhappy. It was indeed a royal pension. Louis pretended not to hear. The ladies had not listened. At this point a handsome young wrestler was gnawing the ear of a spectacularly ugly opponent who howled for mercy while men cheered and ladies waved wispy lace handkerchiefs in excitement and delight. As the level of noise and shouting rose, the harpers played more lustily lest Duke Philip fail to hear them.

Suddenly the din fell silent. Duke Philip rose to his feet. In his hand he held the naked shining blade of the sword in whose pommel, visible through the crystal, could be seen the splinters of the True Cross, dark with age, awesome with history. Many of the assembly fell on their knees, uncovering, bowing their heads, crossing themselves.

Then in a voice shaken with emotion Duke Philip swore the oath for which all the pageantry of the evening was but a prelude. If it should please God, he solemnly pronounced, he would lead a Crusade to the liberation of the Holy Sepulcher, to the restoration of Constantinople and the rehabilitation of the East. He called on all the splendid company there present to join him.

The dauphin swore first, with a full heart, removing his cap, touching all the saints.

One by one the duke's great vassals all swore, each more vehemently than the one before lest his enthusiasm seem to suffer by contrast. One vowed to wear no armor on his right arm, another to eat nothing from sunrise to sunset on Tuesdays, another to live apart from his wife until they should return victorious from the East with the Grand Turk in chains.

Then Golden Fleece King of Arms approached with the glittering chain and the lamb of the Order of Toisson d'Or, and placed it around Louis's neck, making him a member of that most select and highly privileged order of knights.

And then, in a moment of silence, broken only by heavy breathing and fiercely muttered prayers of the kneeling assembly, Philippe de Comines whispered something into Duke Philip's ear.

"Quite so," murmured the duke. "I forgot."

He raised his voice again to the company and added certain qualifications to his oath. Not only must it please God that the Crusade take place. It must also, to preserve its legality, please the seldom-thought-of overlord of Burgundy, King Charles of France. That, Louis knew, could be taken for granted. King Charles and his council would like nothing better than for all the dangerous chivalry of Burgundy to perish miserably in the deserts of Palestine. As a Frenchman Louis could understand something of that feeling. And there was another qualification: Burgundy, the land that God had given Duke Philip to rule, must be securely at peace, unthreatened at the time when the Crusade should depart.

Thereupon all the nobles who had taken the oath renewed their allegiance to him, making his will their will, his vow their vow. Some of them smiled wryly. It would be some time, if ever, before they would have to set out on the dreary journey to the dim and faraway East.

Studying their faces Louis wondered whether the qualifications had not, after all, been wise. Quite obviously no one wanted to go. Philippe de Comines might have saved his master from the terrible sin of forswearing an oath on the Holy Cross. A subtle, cynical, valuable man.

But it was outrageous that a whispered word from the counselor should have strangled the Crusade at its birth. Unquestionably that was what had happened, whether Duke Philip knew it or not. In that moment Louis made a resolve that no counselor should ever gain such power over him when he should be king.

How long would that be? It had been so long already! Would he be like the Black Prince of England, who should have ruled, who could have ruled nobly except that his father outlived him for one year? Death, one little twelvemonth between a crown prince and a crown!

Philippe de Comines smiled into a pink peppered wine that he drank with great delicacy and deliberation from a deep goblet of paper-thin Venetian crystal.

Louvain, Duke Philip's favorite capital of his favorite province of Brabant, was situated in a soft and gentle country of winding rivers, pleasant seasons, great fertility, busy industries, and immense wealth. In addition to the beautiful new Hôtel de Ville, with its amazing glass windows, something new in secular architecture, there were ancient churches, a famous university, and a hundred-year-old guildhall owned by the Honorable Company of Clothworkers. Clothworkers' Hall had a series of long arcades on the street level where heavy-wheeled wagons of commerce had worn deep ruts into the cobblestone. Above the street were the workshops of the members, and in a gracefully pillared assembly room on the upper story was the meeting hall where the Grand Master received candidates for membership who had finished their years as apprentices. In Flanders the merchant guilds were proud and strong, a ponderable factor in government. This too Louis noted with care. The people; that new force; a sovereign was wise nowadays not to forget them.

It was dark when the dauphin walked into the Street of the Clothworkers. Of the forty-eight-course banquet he had eaten as little as he dared; but politeness, and the sharp eyes of Charles of Charolais, had demanded that he eat more than he knew was good for him. A brisk walk, he thought, would loosen his legs after sitting so long at table and allay the apprehension he always felt after eating more than usual. Not always had he fallen after eating a hearty meal; but never had he fallen without eating a hearty meal first. He walked rapidly, alone. It was a gamble to walk alone, but whom could he trust to walk with him? Who knew his secret? Not even Henri LeClercq.

There was some chance, of course, that he might be set upon and robbed, but he thought he could give a good account of himself; the notion of fighting was actually rather attractive. It had been a long time since he had swung a sword or plunged a dagger in anger. He had both with him, and he loosened them in their scabbards as he strode down the unlighted streets and alleyways of Louvain, picking his way sure-footedly over the cobbles that were slippery, like all cobbles, with the nightsoil that good citizens always heaved from their windows, not wishing it in the house. In addition to his weapons he also had the cardinal's emerald. He also had his saints.

He did not feel the queer overconfidence that once had led him into danger, nor had there been a warning chill. He did think he would be sick. But since the possibility was always with him, every hour of every day and night, he constantly had to plan ahead what he would say if suddenly he should wake up from a period of unconsciousness and find himself lying on a street, staring up into the faces of strangers. This time he decided that his story would be that he had drunk too much at the banquet, a most plausible excuse since many of the Crusaders who had taken the oath so cautiously and celebrated so enthusiastically had been helped home by their squires in varying stages of intoxication.

Louis was used to scheming, like a cripple used to his limp, and he seldom thought any more how pleasant it would be to be completely normal. Normal men took walks; he too took walks. They did not think twice about it; he merely had to scheme a little, and the scheming was long since habitual.

As he approached Clothworkers' Hall he saw torches waving and bobbing among the arches and heard laughter, cursing in Latin, and shouting in half a dozen European languages. In a university town like Louvain, the good-natured babble, the healthy young timbre of male voices, and especially the Latin could only mean that this was a band of students, probably celebrating in their own way the oaths that their elders had taken in the Hôtel de Ville. Louis smiled and would have liked to join them, but he supposed they would think him a little old to accept on an equal footing, and his golden chain would embarrass them if indeed it did not tempt some needy young rascal to try to snatch it and make off with it in the depths of his academic sleeve. That would have involved a street brawl, foolish and unnecessary. Nevertheless he would have liked to buy them a hogshead of wine—nay, for students a few bottles would suffice—and he was a little sorry that he could not help out with the revel without revealing himself. It was unlikely that *these* young men had just dined on forty-eight different kinds of meat. He shrugged slightly and, like the Levite, would have passed by on the other side.

Then he saw what amused them so.

If they had been fighting a brace of cocks Louis would not have flickered an eyebrow, since cockfighting was good sport and the birds could be eaten afterward.

If they had been beating a dog Louis would not have interfered, since few men felt the way he did about dogs and many of the beasts were dangerous, especially the lank and hungry mongrels that scavenged in the offal of the streeets.

But they were beating a man, and the man was a cripple.

Fury seized the dauphin. His first impulse was to charge with drawn dagger and sword, to kill. He would happily have slit the throat of the leader, a tall blond youth who, as he kicked, was yelling in English, "Luck from thy dungy rump!" and "Luck from thy hairy hump!" as he rubbed the deformity between the shoulders of the man who now groveled on the cobblestones, shielding his face and screaming for mercy.

Louis, however, did not act on his first impulse. It was extremely impolitic to kill students. They enjoyed a privileged status, the universities always backed them up, and you never knew when you might be killing the younger son or some favorite bastard of a powerful foreign prince. Therefore he ran swiftly and silently to the shadowy edge of the laughing circle. He dealt an unexpected blow with the flat of his sword on the head of one of the students, seized the torch that the fellow dropped as he fell senseless, and whirled it around him like a mace. He was shouting, as he shouted in battle, thrusting the torch into startled faces that drew back from the flame: "That, for a coward! That, for a craven! That, for a strumpet dropt!" He burned some fingers and singed some

214

hair, but it was not difficult for his battle-trained arm to menace without murdering. He found himself laughing aloud at the way they fell back in disorder, tripping over their gowns. "Shorten your skirts, lads, shorten your skirts, and next time take on a man!"

When he reached the leader he did not feint. He thrust the torch into the breast of the academic gown, which took fire. As the leader's companions clustered around him, beating at the flames to extinguish them, finally ripping off the gown and stamping on it, Louis had time to raise the cripple and drag him into the shadows of the arcade.

"Now run for it!" he hissed.

"My lord, my master, my savior, I cannot run."

"Did they hurt you greatly, thou poor creature?"

"I always hurt. That is nothing. It is my legs. They are wrenched, useless. I cannot walk."

"Then I shall have to carry you," Louis said grudgingly. He did not wish to remain in the vicinity. Lights were appearing in windows. Burghers, alarmed at the shouting and perpetually afraid of fire, were looking out of doors at the torches that lay flaming in the street. In the distance a watchman's whistle sounded. The students faded away, up alleys, around corners, into the shadows, a couple of them supporting their stunned companion.

Louis hoisted the hunchback onto his shoulders. "Where do you lodge?"

"I have no home. I am a stranger in Louvain. I arrived from Thielt this morning to practice my profession."

The dauphin felt something wet and warm against his hand as he steadied his living burden. He knew the slippery feel.

"You are bleeding, my professional friend," he said. He supposed the fellow was one of that wretched class of vagrant clowns who did tricks on street corners for pennies. "Now I suppose I shall have to get you to a doctor."

"I am a doctor," the cripple replied with such dignity as he was able to muster. "The wound is nothing—a tooth or two that the Englishman kicked out. But I shall fashion new ones, beautiful ones, white ones. Does Your Excellency require any beautiful new white teeth?"

Louis laughed. "No, thank you, not yet."

Shortly he felt the man's body relax and go limp. He had probably fainted.

Late that night, to the bewilderment of Duke Philip's kitchen staff, the dauphin appeared at the back door of the palace carrying a soiled and beaten cripple.

Louis bade them attend the man, and forgot the incident.

Chapter Thirty-one

Duke Philip made much of the incident, to the dauphin's surprise and to the intense annoyance of Count Charles of Charolais. Half in spite, half in grudging admiration, he said to Louis: "They told me to be on my guard against you. They said you would worm your way into the duke's affection. You knew exactly how to tickle his romantic fancy, didn't you? He calls it the very spirit of Christian charity. Next Sunday the bishop is going to take his text from the parable of the Good Samaritan. Father gave the hunchback a new suit of clothes and actually let him shave him. What I cannot fathom is, how did you manage the student riot?"

"I didn't," Louis said. "I just happened to be there."

"What a remarkable coincidence."

"Is the fellow really a doctor?"

"Father says he never was shaved so smoothly."

"Oh, then he's only a barber-surgeon."

"Does that disappoint you, Monseigneur?"

"Why should it? I don't need a doctor."

"Of course not."

"I must say, I could use a competent barber, however."

"My dear cousin, he will make you look very handsome," Count Charles said pleasantly, and walked away, all strutting six feet of him, with his curly bronze hair and his bristly little mustache and those calves that were the envy and despair of half the dandies of Duke Philip's court.

Louis thought grimly, "He need only have added *by contrast.*"

Louis did not willingly trust his neck to razors wielded by strangers. But the fellow pestered him so, plucking at the hem of his cloak when he came out of church, running after him like a dog in the street, and one day blocking his path to point to a brilliant ivory restoration that he had made to fill the gap caused by the Englishman's kick, that Louis finally said, "All right, all right, I'll let you try." After all, Duke Philip had not hesitated.

The shaving was a revelation. The lather did not dribble and the barber actually warmed it. The razor edge was keen, feather-light under a sure hand in which Louis sensed immense strength. The dauphin's stubborn beard simply disappeared.

"If you nicked me I didn't feel it," Louis said, pleased, rubbing his chin appraisingly.

"Oh, Monseigneur!" The heavy Flemish voice was doleful with reproach and injured pride. "Rather would I slash myself to ribbons."

"How are you called, barber?"

"In Thielt they called me Olivier the Bearded, from my custom of wearing a small beard."

"A beard isn't a very good advertisement for your profession. Why do you wear it?"

"I would not tell anyone but Monseigneur, who may perhaps understand better than most men." The barber was deftly combing the dauphin's hair and had noticed the scar. "My beard hides—a small wart."

Louis, on closer inspection, could see the small wart. It was almost as big as another chin. In addition to his bandy legs, the hump on his back, and his long apelike arms, Olivier the barber was cursed with a grotesque excrescence on his chin. Louis did not pursue the subject, allowing the poor fellow his privacy. But the full force of Count Charles's insult struck him: Olivier the barber had all his own physical characteristics, caricatured, exaggerated to repulsiveness.

"What do they call you in Louvain, Master Olivier?"

"Ah, Monseigneur, in Louvain I have changed my name and got rid of that ludicrous term 'the bearded one,' which in Flemish means also 'the Devil,' since the devil is bearded, as those who have seen him know. Now that I have learned French," he said proudly, "I am Monsieur le Malvays."

Louis laughed. "Someone has played a trick on you, Olivier. When you really learn French you will find out that 'le malvays' means 'The Evil One,' so you are no better off than before."

Olivier le Malvays muttered something in Flemish that Louis did not understand, but he caught the name "Karl."

"Did Count Charles play the trick on you?"

"Monseigneur, Count Charles is a noble lord and the duke his father is my sovereign. But my razor will scrape and pull if ever I have the honor to shave Count Charles."

Louis wondered if Charles also kicked dogs.

When Louis left for the residence in Genappe that Duke Philip had given him, he took Olivier le Malvays with him, and shortly it developed that the barber had other talents.

He had spent his whole life in city gutters and crowded slums, among the poor and sick, the maimed and misbegotten, among fugitives, outcasts, criminals, where shame was unknown and love, when it existed at all, existed in a peculiar form which no noble chevalier would have understood. It was intensely personal and, like a dog's, applicable only to a living human being, never to an abstraction. Olivier le Malvays was incapable of loyalty to an ideal; but the same animal instinct

217

rendered him incapable of anything but loyalty to his master, a loyalty selfless, cunning, and absolute.

Louis now found himself possessed of a creature who, like François Villon of the Fraternity of Beggars in Paris, had his hand on the pulse of the people. Through Olivier le Malvays he could tap that great ocean of information that always filtered down from the heights to the depths and remained hidden to all but the few who knew their way into the dark underground places where it collected. Olivier had been born on such a level; on such a level he would always be welcome.

One day he casually told Louis that the Englishman who had led the students had died after gorging himself on a highly seasoned fish. "The university doctors diagnosed his illness as cholera, since he had been talking to a Greek refugee. The refugees are supposed to carry the Eastern infection in their long hair."

Louis crossed himself at the mention of the dread disease.

"Further, his body grew hot after death and the limbs contracted into queer positions, as if he still felt pain. Naturally the learned doctors threw him into a lime pit, along with the fish and the Greek's hair." The barber was shaking with silent laughter, but his hand was steady as he shaved.

"What are you laughing at, you ghoul?"

"Nothing, Monseigneur. I am laughing to think what a frail thing the body is to those of us who know it. One day the big Englishman is alive, kicking my teeth out; next day it is I who am alive, all stunted and humped, and the Englishman lies dying, agony in all his extremities."

"How do you know he was in agony?"

"I hear it was not the cholera, Monseigneur. There is a white powder which produces symptoms exactly like cholera, if you are a university doctor. It smells like garlic. Some people eat it to increase their weight, strength, and appetites. Students who contract the burning sickness from tavern wenches use it to cure themselves, which it does for a time. In small quantities it is most valuable in the treatment of rheumatism, weak stomachs, thin blood, aching backs, creaky joints, twitchy nerves, quartan fevers, warts, and the common cold."

"It would seem a veritable elixir."

"But in larger doses, if someone, say, should inadvertently season a fish with the concentrated powder, thinking it the ordinary mixture, anyone who ate the fish would almost certainly die of what looked like the cholera to a university doctor."

"Olivier, you are justly called 'the Devil.' What did you have to do with this wicked murder?"

"Nay, my lord, I was in Genappe and the unfortunate Englishman was in Louvain. No doubt he had many enemies."

"No doubt. And you have many friends."

"I have heard that Your Highness has enemies. If ever Your Highness—"

218

"I do not need your white teeth and I do not need your white powder, Olivier the Devil."

"Nay, Monseigneur, I was only suggesting that you have friends too if I have, for mine are yours."

"God will dispose of my enemies."

"Yes, Monseigneur."

"When it pleases Him, not me."

"Yes, Monseigneur."

"Never, never make such a suggestion again."

"No, Monseigneur."

"This white powder—it seems to have many uses—if one should unhappily suffer from, say, the falling sickness—would it be of any value?"

"No, Monseigneur."

"I was merely curious."

"For that one would drink a decoction of ferret gall. I could make such a decoction."

"I was merely curious. I do not know anyone who suffers from the falling sickness."

"Neither do I, Monseigneur."

But Olivier le Malvays, who had noticed the scar, stole some ferrets from Count Charles's huntmaster, who used them to scare rabbits out of their burrows. He pickled the galls in brandy and kept them among his barber-surgical supplies, which were varied, unorthodox, and not all respectable.

On another day he told Louis, a week before the French ambassador told Duke Philip, that King Charles had suffered a severe attack of the gout.

"I am not at all surprised," the dauphin said.

"And he beat Bernard d'Armagnac with a riding crop in front of Pierre de Brézé and the entire council."

"Why?"

"D'Armagnac was defending Monseigneur's great wisdom in accepting the hospitality of Burgundy, as my information has it."

"Good old Bernard!"

That incident was not reported to Duke Philip. Every effort was made in the king's latter years to present him to the world as a benign father of his people. Olivier le Malvays seemed to be better informed.

"He grows more splenetic, more irascible every day."

On another occasion, through some connection with an apothecary who had sold a packet of squill to the midwife of the Countess of Charolais, he told Louis that the pregnancy of Madame la Comtesse had passed its term and that drastic measures were to be taken. Next day it was announced from the pulpits of Louvain that the countess was brought to bed, and prayers were offered and asked for her in her labor. Duke

Philip sent Louis a message that the Crusade would have to wait a while longer now, since it would be his grandfatherly duty, as soon as the child was born, to see that the little heir to the ducal throne was brought safely through the first months—at least six months said the duke—of his infancy. He referred to the child as a prince as a matter of foregone conclusion. But in a few hours Olivier reported that it was a princess; shortly Duke Philip confirmed the report. In a week all Europe knew that Marie of Burgundy had been born. Louis sent a little silver cross and a letter of congratulation to Count Charles, who did not answer.

The dauphin had been at particular pains to be friendly with the son of his noble and liberal host. He could not understand Count Charles's antipathy.

Olivier le Malvays said, "If I were Monseigneur's privy counselor—"

"I have no privy council."

"But Your Highness will have."

"What would you say?"

"I should say that Count Charles resents the twist of fortune that one day will reverse the present situation: the guest will be the overlord and the patron will be the vassal. Count Charles will have to bend those fine long legs of his and swear homage to Louis, King of France. He will hate that."

"And as much as he hates it, Olivier, exactly that much will I relish it. I do not envy him, save perhaps that I envy his having a child." The castle of Genappe, though well staffed through the liberality of Duke Philip, was lonesome. The ducal court in Louvain was perpetually occupied with tournaments, feasts, theatrical presentations, and musical entertainments. Louis did not care for tournaments, which only played at war and accomplished nothing. Like many strict churchmen, he considered the theater sinful, since every year it dealt with increasingly secular themes; nay, companies of actors were even building special buildings with raised stages on which to caper and cavort in scandalous comedies, deserting the cathedrals where miracle plays had always been presented for the edification of the people. What possible good could come out of entertainment for its own sake? What good could come out of anything without a purpose! Music, indeed, could be useful, since it calmed the nerves and aided digestion; but Burgundian musicians played too loudly. As for feasting, he had had to avoid it all his life; and though Duke Philip complained that his guest was morose and unsocial, Louis went only occasionally to the spectacular dinners at Louvain. And when he did, the dreadful expense of them made him wince. The political activities of the ducal court, which he would have enjoyed and where his voice would have been of value, were denied him through the jealousy of Count Charles.

Thus in Genappe, with nothing to mark the passing of time but the slow march of the seasons, Louis's lonesomeness increased. By day he hunted, but the Flemish game was spiritless. By night he ruled phantom empires, fought phantom wars, and forced Henri LeClercq to take up chess, while Mahomet his hound grew fat, sleeping on the hearth.

At length he wrote a sharp note to Duke Lodovico. If he did not forthwith send Charlotte to Genappe, Louis would personally come and get her with a Burgundian army. The threat was largely pretense. Count Charles would never have permitted it, and the count's influence on the aging duke was stronger every year. But no one knew the duke was growing senile; his renown as a romantic knight still flourished. To send an army to rescue a princess was exactly what Duke Philip would have done with gusto in his younger days.

Duke Lodovico instantly complied.

As soon as Charlotte was reported en route, Louis dispatched a courier with an accurately drawn accounting of the back payments due on her dowry.

When Charlotte arrived, Louis looked at her in amazement. He would not have recognized her. The child was a child no longer.

She curtsied with supple Italian grace and smiled at him, presenting her warm young cheek to be kissed. "Good morning, my husband," she said. "Why did you tarry so long?"

Chapter Thirty-two

There was no room for lonesomeness in the grim old castle of Genappe after that. Charlotte brought with her a bustling suite of ladies, an Italian cook, and a happy little long-haired bitch that Louis's hound instantly took a fancy to.

"I do not know, my dear," Louis said, rubbing his chin reflectively. "This presents something of a problem. Don't you think we ought to keep them apart?"

"Certainly not, my lord husband."

"I mean to say, Mahomet is such a huge beast and Bianca is such a delicate little thing."

"I think we can trust Bianca not to make a mistake."

"I mean to say, the result of such a union might be a monster."

"Nay, for that we must trust God. I learned from Grandfather Cardinal that the good Lord watches over us all, even little sparrows."

"Then," said Louis, "assuredly we can trust Him to watch over little spaniels also."

"You worry too much, my dear lord."

Louis feared God, for the fear of the Lord was the beginning of wisdom. But perhaps it was only the beginning. It was also written that man should work out his own salvation. He consulted his barber-surgeon, whom he had lately advanced to the post of Groom of the Chamber.

"By no means, Monseigneur! The hound would grow in the spaniel so big that she could never whelp it, and both would die."

"Charlotte loves Bianca."

"I could alter the hound," Olivier suggested.

"Try that, Pasque Dieu, and I'll alter you!"

"Nay, my lord, rather roast me alive."

"That too, since you ask for it."

"I could spay the bitch. I am deft with my instruments."

"I know you are."

"There would be no evidence of my handiwork."

"Like the poisoned fish?"

"Madame la Dauphine would never know."

Louis weighed the suggestion but shook his head. "It isn't bad, Olivier, it isn't bad. But Mahomet would know. In the months since Charlotte came to me I have observed that her placid exterior cloaks a keenly observant nature. She would notice Mahomet's lack of interest, and the secret would be out. No, I shall have to trust God, as Madame la Dauphine says."

Olivier le Malvays sanctimoniously cast his eyes heavenward and crossed himself with his razor. "Assuredly, assuredly, Monseigneur. But while He isn't looking suppose I take the entire matter off His hands. I know of a spaniel, larger than Bianca—what dog is not?—but not so dangerously large as Mahomet. It is one of the hunting dogs belonging to Madame the Countess of Charolais. Next time Bianca comes in heat, if Your Highness could arrange to take Madame la Dauphine for a ride in the country, I could arrange a meeting—"

Louis began to laugh. "Olivier, one day you shall be a privy counselor!"

And so it was in the fullness of time, with no untoward accidents, that Bianca whelped a litter of perfect little spaniel pups. "I knew Bianca could not make a mistake," Charlotte said happily. "Don't you see how foolish it is always to worry?"

"Clearly, my dear."

"They don't look a bit like Mahomet. That is the influence of the mother, I suppose."

"It was hardly to be expected that a sire with a pagan name like Mahomet could gain the ascendancy over a highly Christian dam from Savoy."

"Nay, Louis, you are teasing me. But he acknowledges them, see?"

Mahomet was nuzzling at the little balls of squirming fur, licking them. Whether it was curiosity, affection, or dumb instinct Louis did not know, but it did look like acknowledgment.

Louis smiled. How fortunate that animals could not talk. But his

222

mind leapt ahead, as it always did: how imperative the necessity for silence after a crime! How many princes were supposititious, the witnesses dead? How many great lords with guilty consciences had acknowledged bastards who were really legitimate, sons to their mothers' own wedded and cuckold husbands! How many foundlings were unacknowledged bastards of princes? Who, for example, was Henri LeClercq, with the House of Armagnac in his features? Nay worse, how many men and women, apparently human, were in actuality changelings, spawn of the devil begotten on brides while they and their husbands lay senseless in a hell-conjured stupor? The stream of ugly thoughts spiraled down into a dark and bitter mood.

"You are eating so little tonight," Charlotte said to him at supper. "Does my cook displease you? He shall go back to Chambéry if he does."

"He is quite competent. No one goes back to Savoy. I am—not hungry."

"It is wrong to starve yourself."

"Now it is you who are worrying needlessly."

"My own appetite has seemed so gross of late. I wanted company." But Louis attached no significance to the remark. It was summer again, the summer of 1459, and Charlotte was sixteen, an age when many princesses were mothers of growing children, widowed, and married again. He was waiting for a chill in spite of the lowland heat. He thanked God when it did not come, and touched his emerald.

Some weeks thereafter, before the shortening days marked the advent of another winter of exile, an unnerving incident occurred. Pain is a selfish thing; the dauphin's infirmity was intensely his own; he had lived with it in secret so long that the thought of another person suffering from it had never seriously crossed his mind. That frightening possibility now struck home.

The dauphiness had been pale and listless all day. She had kept to her bed during the private Mass that they always attended before breakfast. The absence of his princess, pious to scrupulosity, was notable. Louis asked one of her maids what was amiss. Raoulette replied that Madame la Dauphine was indisposed.

"Indisposed? Indisposed! One is indisposed to tradesmen, not to one's husband. Do not be vague with me when I inquire after Madame's health. Never be vague. Quick, girl, what is the nature of her indisposition? Well, well, well?"

Charlotte had entered the room, perfectly disposed; the unfortunate Raoulette had fled in a panic.

"Louis, how black you look! Poor Raoulette is so thoughtless. You scare the life out of her."

"I am sorry. No, I am not sorry. She had no right to scare the life out of me."

"Were you scared for me, Louis?"

"Of course I was. 'Indisposed' could have meant anything. Indisposed forsooth!"

"I feel better now."

She certainly did look well.

But that evening as they were entering the castle hall for supper, Charlotte's arm tightened in his. She had never learned to walk like a high-born French lady, resting her fingertips lightly on the back of his extended hand. She always passed her arm through his in the warmer Italian fashion, a gesture that had somewhat embarrassed Louis at first since it looked like a public embrace; but he was used to it now and he liked it.

Her arm tightened, then it went limp. Without warning she stumbled slightly and slumped to the floor. The swoon was so sudden that Louis could not prevent her from falling, though instinctively his arm cramped hard on hers and broke the force of the fall. She collapsed at his feet, her full skirts in a colorful circle around her, her tall headdress of fine Genoese lace toppling off and rolling a little distance away, her delicate slippers exposed with their high red heels sparkling with gems, an extravagance troubling to Louis, since no one saw them, but they were Savoy gems. There were no emeralds among the brilliants.

In his mind's eye Louis saw her limbs twitching, her eyes rolling white under half closed lids; in terrified imagination he heard the gasping, saw the colors, tasted the foam.

"Dear God," he prayed, "not Charlotte too! Sweet Jesus, sweet child, sweet wife. Oh, no, oh, no, oh, no!"

He shouted aloud, "Ho, guards! A moi! A l'aide! Raoulette, Loyse, your mistress! Henri! Madame LeClercq! Master Jean! Attend the dauphiness!" He was calling on his entire household, even young Jean LeClercq for help. Then his voice rose to a hysterical scream. "Olivier! Fetch ferret gall!"

He ripped open the neck of his doublet. With trembling fingers he fumbled at the little velvet bag. He slipped the cardinal's emerald onto Charlotte's finger. The ring was too big. It fell off. He pressed it into the palm of her limp hand and closed her fingers tightly around it, gripping her like iron. "Hold it close, Charlotte. Never lose it. Wear it always. On you always, always, do you hear?"

No one had ever seen the severe and reserved man so completely forget himself. Everyone came running at once, mailed feet of guards clanking down the stone-flagged halls, watchmen with torches, young Jean with a small drawn sword, Charlotte's ladies in a whirlwind of muslin and flying lace, the kitchen staff peeking through cracks in the doors. Outside in the gathering twilight an alarm sounded and the portcullis thundered down, while slowly, creaking on long unused chains, the drawbridge over the moat began to rise.

Loyse de Bethléem, who had been the dauphiness's nurse and was now her dowager matron in waiting, elbowed her large motherly form through the tightly packed circle around Charlotte. She took one look, smiled, and disdainfully shouldered the dauphin aside.

"Men!" she sniffed. "They always make such a fuss. A body would think *they* were going to have the babies! Now Charlotte, up with your pretty head; there you are, *there* you are. Everything is going to be all right." She cradled the dauphiness against her ample bosom, crooning softly, rocking her gently to and fro.

"Congratulations, Monseigneur," she said smiling up at Louis, whose face was a battleground of conflicting emotions, on which joy was rapidly winning a radiant victory. "The important thing now is to keep her happy and calm, a moderate amount of exercise, of course, but no hunting, no riding. A bland regimen, yet hearty too; sweet thoughts above all, that the prince may be strong and wise—"

"I think you had better take charge, Madame Loyse," Louis said. "All this is a little foreign to me."

"Naturally," said Loyse de Bethléem with monumental complacency.

Detaching himself from the circle, Olivier le Malvays slunk off to his closet, hiding a flask of ferret galls under the skirt of his doublet.

Charlotte bore the infant proudly, effortlessly, joyfully.

"He should be named Charles," she said. "He is a beautiful prince."

"I agree in part," Louis said, rocking back and forth from toe to heel, from heel to toe, his thumbs hooked under his chain of the Golden Fleece, his face glowing with pride. "Beautiful, yes; but Charles, no. Anything but Charles."

"Charlemagne is his ancestor. I am Charlotte. Charles is a good name, in spite of what you think."

"Charles is an unlucky name: my fatuous father, my mad grandfather, my weakling brother, my enemy the Count of Charolais—a Charles, every one. No, no, I cannot abide the name."

"It shall be as you please," Charlotte smiled. "If you promise to let me name the girls when they come."

"Agreed."

"And the little prince?"

"He shall be named Joachim, from the great theologian who foretells in his writings the coming of an age of strict justice and peace, when nations shall live under law, without war. That is my hope for France, some day perhaps for all the world. When I come to reign I shall teach him all I know and all I learn, and he shall learn from me, and when I die he shall go on, and after him his son, and his son's sons for generations, till the golden age is won and a resting season comes upon the world, the sabbath of weary humanity, in accordance with the great vision of Joachim of Floris."

"All that for this little head?" she smiled, touching it gently. "All that burden of responsibility for these little shoulders?"

"You ought to thank God for them," said Loyse de Bethléem, who had

225

no interest in the visions of Joachim of Floris. "Big heads and big shoulders, *oi me lassa!* How they torture the poor mothers!"

"His shoulders will broaden," Louis said, squaring his own with a fatherly strut. "Never had France such a dauphin!" In his mind he was already king.

But he was not yet king. Nor in the long annals of France was there ever to be a dauphin by the name of Joachim. That same year he died, drowned in his tub.

"It was an accident," Charlotte sobbed. "Raoulette loved the child. She left him alone only for a moment."

"Before God," shouted Louis, "she ought to be sewn in a sack and thrown into the Dyle!"

Olivier le Malvays overheard the remark.

Chapter Thirty-three

The death of the infant, who never lived to speak a word or even to care for his most elementary needs, wrought a major change in the position of the dauphin. Sly gossip in King Charles's court now abruptly ceased; clearly the heir to the throne of France was able to beget princes; the dynasty was secure; Louis's succession was only a matter of time. Bernard d'Armagnac dared write him freely now. Other great lords wrote also. Most of them were cautious after so long a period of neglect, confining their messages to formal expressions of condolence. These men Louis marked in his memory as proud and strong, dangerous. Others wrote at greater length, hinting that they had always been faithful to him. These men Louis forgot, since they were weaklings whom he need not fear.

To Olivier le Malvays he said: "I am suddenly smothered with attention. My father must be sick indeed. Bernard d'Armagnac hints as much, but he does not know the nature of the complaint."

If Olivier had had a tail he would have wagged it. "It is the royal stomach, Monseigneur. I have it on unimpeachable authority."

"That is a failing which runs in the family. God's will be done."

"I venture to suggest that God's will may take a year or two to complete its course, Monseigneur. Friends of mine are friends of the king's doctors. Perhaps some special medicines—"

"God's will, Olivier, not mine. I have trusted you too far with the secrets of my heart. I yearn to rule, but I will not have murder on my soul."

226

"If Monseigneur could only think of it as an execution."

"You are very bad and not very subtle, Olivier. You would rather be privy counselor to a king than barber to an exile, would you not?"

"Yes, Monseigneur."

Louis smiled, "At least you don't mince words."

Burgundy officially mourned the death of Joachim. Duke Philip appeared in church in the violet mourning cloak of a *royal de France* to honor the dauphin. Count Charles, who was equally entitled to wear one, pointedly refused, muttering within hearing of the Count of Saint-Pol, his equerry, which shortly came to Louis's ears, that France was a foreign country to which Burgundy owed not even nominal homage. Philippe de Comines prepared a manifesto to the effect that the Crusade would have to be put off yet another year, since Burgundy would be in mourning all that while. Louis and all the chivalry who had taken the oath smiled; no one took the old duke's idea of a Crusade seriously any more.

During this period, when the minds of the great were occupied with great affairs, the nurse Raoulette, who had been in blooming health, sickened and died.

"Her heart was broken," Charlotte said. "She blamed herself, and indeed she was careless, and she thought God was punishing her, for sometimes at night she would feel hellfire burning in her body. I shall pray for her."

"Who tended her, Charlotte?"

"Why, your own physician."

"Olivier?"

"After her illness became serious I thought it wise to consult him."

"It was," said Louis grimly. He did not question Olivier le Malvays, and he did not pray for Raoulette. The line between murder and execution could sometimes be thin indeed.

During the winter and summer that followed, indications stronger than hints continued to reach the dauphin. Henri LeClercq received a letter from Jean Bureau, his old master at the French arsenal. It addressed him respectfully as the Chevalier Captain-General of Artillery, the title Henri had borne in the Dauphiny. Ostensibly it dealt only with grenade fuses, congratulating Henri on having invented them and stating that France too was working on them, particularly the knotty problem of the timing control so that the missiles would wait to explode till they were over the heads of the enemy, not incontinently burst immediately after leaving the muzzle of one's own cannon. But interspersed among the technicalities were friendly references to Henri's services of former days and how welcome they might be again.

"They are weaving his shroud, even the engineers," Louis growled. "I do not enjoy how subjects wait upon the death of kings."

Olivier thought: That is what he says, but that is not how he looks. He is thriving on this. I wish he would let me help speed things up.

Louis had never been in more radiant health. He had even forgotten to ask Charlotte to give him back the cardinal's emerald. He ate sparingly as ever, but his food seemed to digest better.

"If, as you once said, a certain weakness of the stomach lamentably runs in the royal House of France," Olivier told him one morning, "it has providentially missed your own; for either the fabric has shrunk or the girth of this doublet was skimped in the making. Monseigneur certainly should buy a somewhat ampler one."

"Have it let out."

"There is nothing to let out. No material was wasted when this garment was cut."

"Then have a patch put in," Louis grinned. "I cannot buy a new doublet just because I've put on a pound or two."

"Your Highness was far too thin, almost like a boy. Now Your Highness looks like the king he soon will be. What the father loses, the son gains."

"Olivier, you are exasperating. What are you hinting at? What have you learned from your bat-winged companions?"

"I am afraid to tell you. You would blame me."

"Not if you had nothing to do with it."

"On my mother's soul, poor woman, the only human being I ever loved but you, my master who saved me from death, I swear I have nothing to do with your father's present state; though it would have been easy for me to bring about his death long since. You told me not to, and I did not—"

"Well, well, well?"

"Briefly, he is wasted away to a skeleton."

"No word of this has reached Duke Philip."

"Nor any other sovereign. But it is God's own truth, Monseigneur."

"How do you know?"

Olivier was vague.

"Friends of friends of friends?"

"Yes, Monseigneur. They say he refuses to eat."

"My—father—refuses—to—*eat!*" Louis roared with laughter. "That is a mad report."

"Some degree of madness is hinted at, Monseigneur; but even my informants cannot guess the truth of that, God's greatest enigma."

The barber seemed at great pains to bring God into the scheme of things. "You are never reverent unless you are afraid, Olivier. What are you afraid of?"

"It is whispered, sir, that you are poisoning him. King Charles himself believes you are."

"Through you, of course."

"Through someone, Monseigneur, and I would be the likely instrument."

228

Finally Louis said, measuring his words, "If I were convinced that, through any means whatsoever, you were hastening my father's death, I should quietly collect the evidence and turn it, *and you*, over to the French ambassador. If, as is likely, there should be no evidence and I were still convinced, I would poignard you. I do not like killers of kings. But since I am not convinced, you may continue your shaving. And be sure to get that patch put in my doublet, and don't let Burgundian tailors cheat you."

Olivier sewed in the patch himself. The tailor with whom he bargained asked too much to suit the exalted mood that uplifted him after his master's expression of trust. When he left the tailor's shop a small length of material was missing. Lest Louis accuse him of stealing it, Olivier said that the patch had cost ten sols, which Louis counted into his hand and Olivier put into his pocket.

"A very good tailor, Olivier."

"Monseigneur, the best."

"And not a cheat."

"He is to be trusted, Monseigneur."

"Give him all my work."

Olivier's face changed slightly. Now the barber-surgeon-groom must also become a tailor. "Yes, Monseigneur. He will be honored."

And honored he felt, in a curious twisted way.

By the middle of July the condition of King Charles was so serious that it could no longer be hidden. Neighboring states were informed that His Grace's recovery might be a matter of many weeks, perhaps months.

"The way diplomats talk nowadays," sighed Duke Philip, "that means your poor father is doomed. I shall be sorry to see him go, though I shall be glad to see you king. I am afraid my Crusade will have to wait a little longer. Louis, lad, I am beginning to feel a trifle old."

"You are in the prime of life, dear uncle, and assuredly you and I shall make the Crusade together when I am king." But Louis knew that the duke was not in the prime of life, and he himself was a lad no longer.

Charles of Charolais said darkly, "It is a stipulation of the oath that the Crusade cannot take place if the security of Burgundy is threatened." Count Charles looked balefully at Louis. "We should have friendly kings on our borders, my father."

"Now why can't you two boys ever get along together!" the old man said petulantly. "Upon my faith, what is there to fight about?"

"Burgundy," said Charles.

France! thought Louis, but he said: "My good uncle, Charles and I shall always get along together if I have my way. I do not know how I have managed to displease him."

"Charles," said the duke, "let's try not to have any wars. Look at England; don't let it happen here. In the end you're always right back where

229

you started, a lot of good men get killed and, as I understand it, taxes become very burdensome to the poor people."

"In any case, my dear father still lives," Louis said.

"Dear father forsooth!" muttered the count. The old duke, whose musicians played louder every year to break through the barrier of his deafness, did not hear the remark. In spite of his failing hearing, however, he had lived a sober life, and his body, though heavy, was still strong in contrast to that of the dissipated Charles.

"What really ails the king?" the dauphin later asked Olivier. "I shall be able to bear up under the details."

"His illness is not pretty, Monseigneur. There is an abscess in his mouth the size of a goose egg; his tongue is swollen and he cannot close his jaws or even swallow, so that a surgeon must stand by night and day with a napkin—"

"Nay, that is enough."

"It is doubtful if he could eat now even if he dared."

"If this is true I am sorry. I do not like even a dog to suffer."

"I do not think he suffers, Monseigneur. When the mind goes, pain goes with it."

"Perhaps that is a blessing." But Louis was frightened that the old madness of the House of Valois was showing itself in his father in his last days. What would his own be like?

He was frightened for another reason also.

His sojourn in Burgundy had been placid. The dauphiness loved him, without Margaret's fire, but dutifully and calmly; she was young, she made him feel young. She retired at sundown, and she did not write poetry. And she had given him a prince. There would be another. God had blessed him in Charlotte of Savoy. Moreover, there was a reasonableness about her: she had given him back his emerald when he observed that it looked too big for her little hand, and she had been happy with a small diamond that he gave her in exchange. Yes, in Burgundy many old doubts and fears had resolved themselves into nothingness while he had remained the guest of Duke Philip the Good.

His sojourn had been protected also. Burgundy's great power and prestige had stood like a wall between him and his enemies. It had been a long time since he had fretted the sleepless nights away, scheming to ring himself with a rampart of strong natural frontiers. He had come to think like a Burgundian.

But now the situation was changing, and Louis's thinking was changing with it. Now the power of Burgundy, no longer a protection, loomed as a threat. The death of his father was upon him. True, Duke Philip was peaceful, but Duke Philip was old. Count Charles was young and unfriendly, rash, proud, and unpredictable.

Louis began to think of the frontiers of France. Between France and Burgundy there was only one natural barrier, the Somme, the historic line of defense north of Paris. And at this moment the Somme was in Burgundian hands. France needed the Somme.

To Duke Philip, at intervals when they met, which Louis took pains to make more frequent now, the dauphin began to talk in a pleasant general way about some little towns along the Somme: Roye, Montdidier, Péronne. He dwelt on their quaint old charm, their peaceful, bucolic aspect, the flavor of ancient days that hung over them, and their present uselessness. "Ah, yes," said the duke, "very splendid they must have been when the Frankish kings built their villas and used to joust in that neighborhood. No kings there now, just sheep. Personally, I prefer the activity in my big cities."

Only Count Charles guessed that Louis was interested in the river and a certain strategic line of hills along its banks.

On Thursday, July 23, 1461, Olivier le Malvays nicked the dauphin slightly on the chin with his razor.

"You devil, you never did that before! Why is your hand shaking? What are you laughing at? Why are you grinning?"

The grin disappeared the moment Olivier saw his master's blood. "What have I done!" he wailed. "I have wounded my king! I have shed his blood! Ten thousand devils drain out mine and drink it before my eyes! Nay, I will not wait to go to hell—" He slashed his palm with his razor and would have bathed the dauphin's chin with his blood. "My own will wash yours away, and with it my sin!"

Louis sprang away from him.

"You pitiful, poor, dim-witted creature, bind up your hurt and behave yourself. What did you say about a king?"

"Am I forgiven?"

"Pasque Dieu, answer my question!"

"Not until I am forgiven!"

The barber was groveling at Louis's feet, beating the floor, sobbing, shaking, leaving red hand prints on the carpet.

"Do you dare bargain with me, you monster?"

"Kick me, beat me, hang me, I deserve it. But I will not answer till I am forgiven."

Louis softened. He sensed that something in the barber's mind, twisted perhaps like his body, made it terribly important for him to hear his master pronounce words of forgiveness. "Yes, Olivier," he said gently, "I forgive you."

Olivier instantly jumped to his feet, smiling again. "Why, then, everything is all right," he said, "and now if Your Grace will just lean back I will repair the damage to your chin. Dear God, I'd rather have died than hurt you."

"It would appear that you have somewhat effectively hurt yourself," Louis muttered as Olivier applied a dab of astringent. He was unnerved by the barber's violence, and he did not immediately press for an answer to his question, but the royal form of address, "Your Grace," instead of the princely "Monseigneur" had not escaped him.

"I scarcely feel my hand," Olivier said. "It is nothing compared with the hurt that is always in my back. Some people believe devils live in a cripple's hump and claw at him, but I know better. The trouble is in the spine. Oh, how beautiful is a strong, straight spine, how delicate the hinges that articulate it! I know. I have seen them. But mine is crooked and gross, and the hinges grate and I cannot oil them. That is why I am accustomed to pain."

Louis did not say anything to that. There was only one way his barber could have gained such knowledge, which was not taught in the surgical schools. That was by robbing a grave and dissecting a human body, a double crime in all Christian countries. Yet Olivier spoke with authority and perhaps such knowledge, if it was accurate, might prove useful. Some day someone might learn how to oil the hinges.

When the little nick on Louis's chin was expertly cauterized, Olivier casually bound up his own injured hand and resumed.

"Today a French herald arrived in Louvain on a horse caparisoned in mourning, purple harness, purple saddle pouch, the lilies on his tabard all edged in black."

"It could be my brother Charles, the Duc de Berri. It could be my sister Yolande. I hope it is not Yolande."

"Nay, it is the king. It happened yesterday. I have it from a street sweeper who sells fertilizer which he enriches with nightsoil from an inn in Louvain where nobility lodge, his product thereby commanding a higher price. Tomorrow, when his tabard is washed and starched, which is already in train, the herald will present himself to Duke Philip and officially notify him of the news that King Charles VII is dead. Your Grace is now king of France."

Olivier had been at pains to identify each link in the chain of his information. The news sounded authentic.

That night Louis slept soundly. This was the moment for which he had lived long weary years of exile. This was the moment for which he had been born.

Book Five

Chapter Thirty-four

"How does it feel to be a queen, Madame la Reine?"

"Very much as always, Louis; except that now I shall have to open fairs—"

"Help me encourage trade, by all means."

"Dedicate bridges—you will be forever building bridges and roads—"

"Yes, but not over the Somme."

"Erect churches—"

"Assuredly, my dear. The best way to do that will be to visit the bishops and encourage them to exhort their flocks to pay for the buildings themselves, lest anyone get the notion that heaven is cheaply come by."

"Visit the sick in hospitals—"

"That, indeed. Together we shall found many hospitals. There are never enough hospitals and, unlike churches, those who need them most cannot pay for them: the blind, the crippled, the mad."

"I shall always carry a purse to give charity to beggars."

"Give money away? Charlotte!"

"What else is there to do for them?"

"From what I have seen of beggars, my dear, half of them are frauds and the other half thieves. Still, for such as are genuinely helpless, a sol could be spared. But the real remedy is work, something light that they can do with idle hands that now get into mischief: spinning, weaving, sewing. It is a pity France has no silk industry. That would keep them busy without fatiguing them throughout the entire working day, from sunrise to sunset like every other worker, and it would be very profitable for France. I shall have your father send me some silk workers from Savoy. There shall be a Queen's Guild of Silkworkers. Each year you shall give a prize—a lead medal of St. Louis would be appropriate—to the weaver who weaves the most—"

"The best, Louis."

"Very well, a prize for the most *and* a prize for the best. We can afford two prizes."

"And our dauphin, when he comes," Charlotte added excitedly, "will have a christening gown of French silk, to set a style!"

"That proves you are a statesman. But two sons would be preferable, Madame la Reine. One is always a dolt—witness the Duc de Berri—and it would be well to have one in reserve."

"Very well, Your Grace," she smiled. They were playing with their magnificent new titles. "But you must grant me a moment's leisure also to say my prayers from time to time. I shall be a busy queen."

They both laughed gaily; the king said, "God bless you, Charlotte," and leaned over and squeezed her hand. She squeezed back without dropping the reins. Charlotte was a superb horsewoman.

They were riding slowly in the midst of a great Burgundian escort from Louvain to Reims, where the king would be crowned and anointed. In order that accommodations along the route might be as good as possible for the long cavalcade, Louis had suggested that they should not go directly through Champagne, which was a heavily wooded and sparsely settled province, but that they swing in a leisurely westward arc that would take them through the well farmed valley of the Somme. That suited Duke Philip because inns were more frequent there and he no longer enjoyed sleeping in a tent as most of the escort, a hundred thousand Burgundian knights, nobles, and soldiers, would have to do.

Olivier le Malvays, noting that the king and queen were deep in some pleasant private conversation, rode up to him and whispered, "Yonder is Péronne!"

Louis whispered angrily in return: "Ride on to the head of the company as if you had business there! Tell a Burgundian flagbearer to hold his banner more smartly, as befits the honor of Burgundy. Tell him I noticed it drooping. Inquire after the spirits of a Burgundian foot soldier. Suggest that I am concerned lest he have a blister. Offer to cure it. You must never approach me and then go back to your place as if you had told me something important. Never be obvious."

The barber's face fell. "Forgive me, Your Grace."

"I do."

Charlotte said, "You must have given him a tongue lashing. He looked like Mahomet when you whipped him for growling at Count Charles."

"May God forgive me for whipping Mahomet. I counted every blow—they were less severe than I made them look, my dear—and for every one I will some day deal a dozen to that miserable count, who is spoiling everything."

"Hush, Louis, he will hear you."

"No, he has dropped back to speak to the duke. Do not turn to look. I know where he is."

"How do you know? You did not look either."

"He could be nowhere else. We are approaching Péronne. In a few moments I too shall drop back and speak to the duke."

Charlotte sighed, "I do not understand."

After a little time, when Louis was certain that the momentary pause of Olivier le Malvays would not be connected with what he did next, he said: "I am going back now, Charlotte. Go join the countess, who is riding alone. It is not fitting for a highborn lady to ride alone, though they do it in Burgundy all the time."

"They do it in Savoy, too."

"This is not Savoy. This is France and you are France's queen."

But Louis was far ahead of reality as usual. The valley of the Somme was not France. Nor was the line of hills that could make an attack from Burgundy so hazardous for an invading army. Nor did Count Charles wish them to be. For Burgundy to lose them would be like draining the moat of a castle and surrendering the outer wall.

Louis dropped back to Duke Philip, who was vastly enjoying this royal progress toward the solemn pageantry of a coronation and the splendid feasting that would follow. He was dressed in a richly embroidered doublet sewn with French lilies and Burgundian lions, and the ducal circlet of gold that he wore like a coronet on his cap was of greater value, gem for gem, Louis calculated, than the crown of Charlemagne which shortly would be placed on his own head. Ignorant peasants in this borderland valley, observing Duke Philip's regal mien, would gather along the roadside and cheer him, taking him for the king of France, shouting, "*Vive le roy!*" Count Charles would glower, the old duke would chuckle, and Louis would murmur, "Wait, wait, I'll show them who's king!"

"As you see," Louis said, "this is a backward region, where your fame and your person are scarcely known."

"I don't mind," Duke Philip said. "I rather enjoy being taken for a king. It isn't their fault that they don't know me. I haven't been here since—goodness, Charles, how long is it?"

"Apparently far too long."

"When was it, Comines? You always know these things."

"Your last significant visit to these parts was in '35, my lord, when, in return for breaking off the alliance with England, the late King Charles gave you the French cities of Roye, Montdidier, Péronne, Amiens, Pont Remy—"

"It was the whole river from here to Abbeville," Count Charles said impatiently.

"Oh, yes, I remember now; the Treaty of Arras, the year the English general Bedford died—no use holding with England after that. Besides, those English burned Joan of Arc, poor pretty little thing. So I joined your father and made him king. Yes, Louis, I made Charles VII king of France, I, your old Uncle Burgundy. I went to *his* sacring, too."

"As I remember," Louis said quietly, "Father didn't actually give you the region. I believe that the Treaty of Arras states that repurchase is possible."

"Does it?" the duke asked Philippe de Comines in amazement.

"It does, my lord—for four hundred thousand gold crowns."

"Oh, well, then," the duke laughed. "No wonder I forgot. Such a sum was never possible for your father, Louis, and I don't see how you'll manage it either. Don't worry, Charles, we'll keep the Somme."

"It had merely occurred to me," Louis continued, "that repurchase of this area might give me an opportunity to repay you for all the honor and hospitality that I have enjoyed at your hands. Now it is my turn to be generous, good uncle. I have seen something of the splendor of Burgundy, but splendor costs money, and 400,000 gold crowns would go far to ensure that the royal state in which you live and which you so richly deserve shall never fade."

"Philippe de Comines, do I need money? He talks as if I did."

It was on the tip of the counselor's tongue to retort, "My lord, you always need money!" but Philippe de Comines said, "The treasury could unquestionably use 400,000 gold crowns."

"Think how long it would take for this area to produce that much in taxes," Louis said. "Years!"

"I suppose it would, I suppose it would," the duke said, looking around him. "I'm sure I don't know."

"Father," the count said angrily, "Louis is leading you into a trap. You are forgetful. He never forgets anything. If you must forget things, forget the Treaty of Arras."

"Why, you young whelp, are you suggesting that I would repudiate my given word? Is chivalry so dead in the hearts of young men nowadays? If the treaty says the Somme towns are repurchasable, Louis can repurchase them—any time he has four hundred thousand gold crowns! I swear it on the True Cross!" He slapped the crystal reliquary in the pommel of his sword.

"Oh, God!" muttered the count, "he means it!" This time there was no qualification to the oath, and Philippe de Comines, eyeing Louis with respect, did not suggest any. He sensed where power lay.

So did the Count of Saint-Pol. This courtier, a boyhood friend of Count Charles and his equerry, was a supple lord with fiefs both in France and Flanders. In France he was Count Louis of Saint-Pol; in Flanders he was Graf Ludwig of Luxemburg. Just as his domains straddled two countries, so also his nature could straddle the sophistry that a man could serve two masters. "No doubt the king, who admires this area so much, though truly it does appear to be a financial liability, would willingly add something to the price of its redemption," he said.

Louis glared at him, but he did not want to make enemies, and he did not want Duke Philip and Count Charles to quarrel. "I have already stated that I wish to be generous," he said. He promised free transit of all Burgundian goods through France, an enormous tax boon for Burgundy. He promised that Philip could name at his pleasure two dozen deputies to the Parliament of Paris, reminding the duke only, as a detail of no consequence, that parliament was required by law to signify their acceptance of such concessions by enregistering them. The duke nodded vaguely. He

238

was a little tired of statesmanlike activities and somewhat weary from riding.

Lest Philip forget his oath, Louis remarked: "That is a beautiful sword, my good uncle. One is privileged to own such a relic. One must be greatly loved by God to possess the True Cross on which His Son suffered death."

No creature sewn into a sack and tossed into a river was ever more firmly bound than Duke Philip was now by his unequivocal oath.

Philippe de Comines was alarmed by Louis's casual boldness. "The Grand Turk owned it too," he said softly.

"You double-tongued scribbler!" Duke Philip sputtered. "You—you —you *diplomat!* Do you class me with the Grand Turk?"

Louis rode up to where Charlotte and the countess were riding together, their tall lace headdresses nodding, the summer breeze gently fluttering the wispy veils that hung from the church-steeple peaks. Assuredly the hennin was the silliest and prettiest fashion ever to spring from the mind of some foolish, style-conscious woman. But much silk, much lace went into the things; that meant work and wages for many good people; that meant taxes.

"We were talking about your barber," Charlotte said. She could tell from Louis's face that he was in rare good humor and would not resent what she said.

Louis laughed. "He's my surgeon now. Very proud of himself, is my Olivier the Devil. He thinks I am going to make him a privy counselor, but of course I'm not."

"I do not seem to recognize the hood on his surgeon's robe," said the countess. "What university is it?"

"Pasque Dieu, it may be the university of the moon for all I know. One day he tells me he graduated from Heidelberg, another from Cologne, another from Louvain."

"It isn't any of those," the countess said. "I know them."

"Probably he guessed you would. This one, I think, is supposed to come from Crakow in Poland. It's the longest one yet. None of the others was quite so cape-like. I humor him. It hides the poor fellow's hump."

"I do not like him," the countess said. "Neither does Charlotte."

Louis looked at her inquiringly. "Don't you, my dear?"

"I didn't say I didn't like him," she answered. "That is not what I said, Louis. I just said I did not quite trust him. He is always so close to you —and those dreadful razors of his!"

"Oh, Olivier's trustworthy enough. I know he may not be attractive to a lady, but he's a great comfort to a man. If you ever grow beards, which all the saints forbid, you will know what I mean."

"His Grace says the most atrocious things in the nicest way." The countess smiled icily.

Charlotte laughed, "I *never* know what he means."

From Péronne the spectacular cavalcade progressed to Reims.

Louis's accession to the throne of his ancestors was orderly. It could hardly have been otherwise with the massed might of Burgundy behind him. But even if he had not arrived in Reims with an escort the size of a conquering army, there were no factions, no dissident elements to oppose him.

Caesar had said, "Gaul is divided into three parts." There were still three parts, *mutatis mutandis*, the three estates of the realm: nobles, clergy, people.

The nobles favored the prince who, in his youth, had upheld their feudal privileges and led them in civil war against King Charles VII. Now, they said, their ancient rights were secure.

The clergy, knowing the strong religious strain in his nature and the strictness of his morals, exemplified by his whole life in startling contrast to that of his libertine father, acclaimed him with protestations of loyalty in hundreds of eloquent sermons, calling him fondly "the pious prince."

He had always been a favorite with the people: his simple dress, his bourgeois manners, his easy approachability. Soldiers knew him for a courageous fighter—one of themselves; merchants knew him for a canny bargainer—one of them too; peasants (though they did not count) knew him for a powerful man with hulking shoulders that toil might have formed as it had theirs—in Louis they saw themselves glorified. He was married to a bland and proper young wife, who could bear and would bear him children, just as they wished for themselves and their sons.

Everyone knew him for a devoted Frenchman. That, if nothing else, would have endeared him to a nation so recently released from a hundred years of foreign occupation.

And everyone, as always at the end of an era, was hopeful and excited at the change simply because it was a change. What had been bad he would reform; what had been good he would make better.

"It is heavy responsibility," he said to Duke Philip on the morning of coronation. "I must get to work at once."

"Rein in your ambitions, Louis, lad, and take things soberly. Especially at first."

"How can I? *There is so much to do.*"

Chapter Thirty-five

The beautiful city of Reims was close to the heart of the king. Here was crowned Louis the Saint, whose namesake he was. Before that, for time out of mind, French kings had sought to receive their crowns and other symbols of their authority on this spot where a thousand years before, King Clovis of the Salian Franks had renounced his heathenism and been baptized. Ten centuries, one thousand years! One single man might hope to live—how long was it? No one had ever calculated. Louis guessed it might be forty years, before battle or murder or sudden death made an end to him. The calculation made it twenty-five generations. For twenty-five generations France had remained loyal to the ideal of kingship. Some kings had been weak, many bad, some mad. But for a thousand years, since the Holy Dove flew down from heaven with a vial of sacred oil for the anointing of King Clovis, the monarchy, if not each individual monarch, had remained the unquestioned constitution of French government, venerable, awesome, the fountainhead of honor, the last resort of the oppressed.

Two thrones stood raised in the sanctuary of the cathedral, the king's elevated a little above the queen's. Neither Louis nor Charlotte yet sat in them. It was high noon, Saturday, August 15th. The year was the year of Our Lord 1461. Casting his eyes over the multitude that thronged the great cathedral, Louis beheld the sternfaced chivalry of France, his premier vassal lords with their ladies beside them, dressed in their robes of state, their breasts ablaze with jeweled orders, their brows circled with ancient coronets. These were strong men and proud women bound together by a thousand interlinking ties of kinship and a tradition of independence. It was a formidable society, threatening in its massed members, the living fortress of feudal privilege. At the moment it was friendly.

Ranked behind them were the leaders of the rich bourgeoisie, self-made men with their plump middle-class wives in costly but more sober dress. Here too was power, great power, and here too was friendliness.

Beyond the burghers, shunted behind pillars, standing against the walls, crowded against the doors, stood the awkward, silent, petty bourgeoisie. Yet they were the friendliest of all, for never before had a king permitted them inside the cathedral during a coronation. Louis had been adamant in his determination that no Frenchman should be denied the privilege of witnessing the solemn event that affected all Frenchmen.

On the high altar, shining in the light of tall candles, rested the crown of Charlemagne. It was a heavy thing, Louis thought, rather crudely wrought, the jewels cut in a long abandoned style that any modern lapidary could have improved upon, especially the cabochons in the cross that stood on the foremost of eight gold plaques which, hinged together, formed the body of the crown. But over it seemed to glow a halo of ancient authority, passed down in an unbroken succession of thirty-three kings since the time when, centuries ago, Charlemagne had worn it. That authority was now his.

"Dear God," he prayed, "make me like Charlemagne, who united an empire." And, lest the good Lord consider his prayer presumptuous, Louis bargained a bit with the Deity: "I do not ask for an empire; all I wish is France, and if you deliver it to me I will honor the Blessed Virgin in a way such as no king has ever honored Her before." He had a plan, but he did not divulge it to God just then. He was particularly anxious to steal a march on the prayers of the great nobles, which must be now rising above the cathedral in one mighty clamor for enlargement of their feudal privileges. Louis had no intenton of enlarging them.

The Archbishop of Reims, who held primacy over all the clergy of France, now entered the sanctuary and made his obeisance to the Presence on the altar, for if the king about to be anointed was the fountainhead of honor for the realm, God was the fountainhead of honor for kings.

Then as he turned to the people a hush fell over them: the great, the middle, and the little estates fell to their knees. On the archbishop's breast, over his episcopal robes, hung a brilliant golden circular plaque. Round it were set in a border twelve magnificent jewels, signifying the twelve tribes; twelve crosses, signifying the twelve apostles; twelve fleurs-de-lis, signifying the twelve original peers of France, though their number was greater now. In the center of the plaque was the holy relic, the *Sainte Ampoule*, the tiny tear-drop crystal vial that a dove might easily carry and, as venerable tradition held, a dove did carry from heaven to earth.

The archbishop let fall one drop of the miraculous chrism into a chalice where it mixed with precious ointment. Then, as the organ softly played the anthem "Zadok the Just Priest," Louis advanced and knelt before the archbishop, who dipped his finger into the chalice and signed the cross on the top of Louis's head, at the same time murmuring the prayer of consecration. Louis then bared his breast, which the archbishop anointed also, and dropped the light cloak prescribed for the ceremony, so that the spot between his shoulders could be anointed. Even at this most solemn moment of his life he was thankful that his shoulders, not his breast, were exposed to the view of the public behind him. Then at the bending of both arms the forefinger of the archbishop traced a little cross of holy oil, while the choir chanted the *Veni Creator*,

Come Holy Spirit. At the anointing of each member the archbishop would murmur an ancient prayer of consecration: the head, that it might rule wisely; the heart, that it might love greatly; the shoulders, that they might sturdily bear the heavy burdens of kingship; the arms, that they might be strong against the enemies of God and the king.

Thus blessed and anointed Louis rose from his knees. Now the archbishop invested him with the dalmatic and tunic, since his person henceforth partook of a priestly character like an Old Testament king; and over the sacerdotal garments the archbishop placed the long scarlet cloak of state, bordered with ermine and sprinkled with golden fleurs-de-lis.

This Louis knelt again, while the archbishop anointed the palms of his hands and drew over them the gloves of state, ancient symbols of kingship, and placed on his wedding finger, over his glove, another regal symbol, the ring that bound him to his people. It was a costly jewel, but it was not an emerald; it was only a sapphire engraved with the image of St. Louis. Then the archbishop delivered into his right hand the mightiest secular symbol of them all, the royal scepter of France. The scepter was originally a battle mace; now it was shaped like a marshal's baton, topped with a cross and orb to soften its brutal character; but it still signified the king's right to smite his enemies. Louis gazed at it fixedly, and scarcely noticed when the archbishop placed in his left hand a slender ivory wand surmounted by the figure of a white dove, which signified how a king's justice ought to be tempered with mercy.

Then slowly and reverently the archbishop approached the altar and took into his hands the crown of Charlemagne. He turned toward the people, elevating it for them to behold, pausing. At this point the great vassals left their places and formed a circle around Louis, for now ancient custom demanded that they assist in the ceremony: it was the moment when their pagan forebears had signified their choice of a leader by raising him on a shield and bearing him with shouts and acclamations to an elevated chair, usually on some bloody battlefield among heaps of the slain. Christianity had softened the barbaric old custom, but something of its rude character remained; they were gathering to escort Louis to the throne, the higher of the two that stood on the raised platform within the sanctuary. In the quiet confusion of movement as the great seigneurs formed the circle, Louis did not notice a significant absence. Count Charles had left the cathedral.

The circle parted; the archbishop walked through it; the circle closed. Now as the organ and choir burst into a mighty *Te Deum*, Louis felt the crown of Charlemagne come to rest upon his head. From that moment he was *rex regnans*, king regnant of France.

Anointed, vested, robed, and crowned, he walked to his throne in the midst of the smiling escort and sat down. The archbishop held his ivory staff, Louis transferred the scepter to his left hand; briefly the great lords knelt and kissed the right hand he extended to them.

He called them all by their names as they made their homage: his sullen brother Charles, the Duc de Berri; venerable Bernard d'Armagnac, with rheumy old eyes alight with pride; Pierre de Brézé, who did not guess what was behind the king's smile; Antoine de Chabannes, the late king's chamberlain; the Duc d'Alençon, whom Louis had just pardoned from a death sentence inflicted by his father; Gaston de Foix—what an odd resemblance to someone very familiar in that face; Count Charles of Melun, the Grand Master of France—a singularly weak chin for an army man; Pierre de Beaujeu, lord of the House of Bourbon; Louis, lord of the House of Orléans; the other lords of the princely Houses, Anjou, Artois, Montmorency, Laval, La Tour, Rohan, Penthièvre, LaTrémoille, Clermont-Tonnerre. As one by one the Princes of the Lilies knelt, kissed hand, and retired to their places, Louis noticed the absence. Where was the House of Burgundy? The Burgundian Ludwig of Luxemburg had just made his homage in his character as the Count of Saint-Pol. Where was Count Charles?

Old Uncle Burgundy, of course, had not bent the knee, and that was as it should be, since the Treaty of Arras specifically exempted him from doing personal homage to the King of France. But the treaty did not exempt his son. Louis shot an angry look at Philippe de Comines, who seemed deep in prayer. Pasque Dieu, what a sophist! Had that hair-splitting, logic-chopping counselor confused personal with territorial exemption in the mind of the old duke? It would be a trick eminently suited to his talents. Had he convinced Philip that since he need not do homage his son need not either?

Apparently he had, for Duke Philip was smiling and nodding in the frankest, friendliest manner imaginable, as if nothing were wrong. Louis smiled back, glad that Uncle Burgundy could not look into his heart.

Now it was Charlotte's turn. The ceremony was shorter and prettier, for her crown was new, a delicate, costly thing sent to her from her father in Savoy. Louis stepped down from the throne and escorted her into the sanctuary where the archbishop, taking the crown from a cushion held by the Savoy ambassador, placed it upon her head. She was not anointed, nor did she receive the other regalia, for in France the wives of kings were queen consorts, not sovereigns. They could never reign, although, on the death of a king, they could legally act as regents during the minority of his son. Louis had always considered this strictly masculine old French law eminently sensible; it was unthinkable to him that the entire Kingdom of France should ever constitute a woman's dowry. But in England that would always remain a possibility, for English queens not only could reign but were publicly anointed, an exposure shocking to Louis. True, the Archbishop of Canterbury was always a doddering old man and would doubtless look the other way, but the idea of a woman baring her breast before even the oldest man struck Louis as distinctly immodest.

Charlotte bore her crown with dignity and simple pride, smiling at

Louis as, for once, she placed her fingertips on the back of his hand like a high-born lady of France and let him escort her to the throne on the dais beside his, while the organ and choir, in which women's voices now joined, burst forth into another *Te Deum* of praise and joy.

Count Charles had not sworn allegiance. With a hundred thousand Burgundians in Reims during the three-day festivities following the coronation, the king deemed it vastly impolitic to make an issue of the omission. In fact, he hoped it had passed unnoticed.

It had not; and much hinged on it.

Chapter Thirty-six

On the third day Louis touched for the King's Evil. He somewhat doubted his power to heal scrofula, but since there *might* be some efficacy in his touch he resolved to go patiently through the revolting duty that tradition, dating back to Louis the Saint, imposed upon him. He took the precaution beforehand, however, to consult his surgeon. "Do thou stand by me, Olivier, and separate the sheep from the goats. Wash any sore that looks as if it might be painted on."

"Yes, Your Grace."

"If it washes off, the malingerer shall taste one of my prisons."

A swarm of scrofulous beggars assailed the cathedral steps to receive the king's touch and the king's penny that always accompanied it, men, women and, pitifully, children.

"Nay," Louis relented, "I will touch them all."

But he ordered his guard to herd all the children into a separate group, and he commanded the Provost of Reims to find out if they had any parents, and why the children were begging on the street if they had, and why the parents were not working at some honest trade. Many scared little urchins were washed fresh and clean that day for the first time in their lives; many lazy parents decided it would be unprofitable to send their children out to beg during the reign of King Louis XI. Many of the waifs, however, were genuine orphans, and these he commanded the provost to turn over to the archbishop, who was resting after the fatigues of the coronation ceremonies. The provost and the archbishop were the first to learn that Louis never gave anybody any rest.

"I think when I do this again next year," Louis said, "I shall have to give a somewhat smaller coin. Scrofula is altogether too popular among my good people."

Meanwhile the Burgundian hosts remained in Reims, uncomfortably close. Louis sent for Count Charles's equerry.

"Shall I call you Ludwig, Graf von Luxemburg, or by your French name and estate, Louis, Count of Saint-Pol?" the king asked pleasantly.

"By the name and estate I love most, since both are yours," the courtier answered.

A snake tongue, thought the king; but he said, "Thank you, Monsieur de Saint-Pol. Can you tell me how long I shall have the pleasure of entertaining my good uncle and his hundred thousand Burgundians? I hesitate to ask him, lest he mistake my meaning, and Count Charles, I understand, is suffering from a very bad cold."

Saint-Pol said he would probe the subject. Louis gave him a diamond ring. "Probe delicately," he cautioned, "and not as if the inquiry came from me."

Later a deputation from the Reims Guild of Butchers asked for an audience at the king's pleasure and were astounded to be admitted that very night. The Burgundians were eating and drinking up everything in the neighborhood, they said, and not one sol had been offered in payment, neither for meat nor fowl nor cake nor wine nor salt—

"Why do you give them credit?" Louis asked.

"How can we refuse, Your Grace?"

How could they, indeed?

"Trust me," he said, "the Burgundians will be back across the Somme —in a very few days."

They thanked him humbly and wondered how he would accomplish it. So did Louis.

The Count of Saint-Pol resolved some of the difficulty. "There is a certain shortage in the Burgundian treasury, Your Grace. The old duke doesn't know and Count Charles doesn't care."

"What does Philippe de Comines say?"

"He says it will be a great day for Burgundy's treasury, but a sad day for Burgundy, when you buy back the Somme."

"Present him my compliments. You can say that I wish he were a Frenchman. Even half a Frenchman, like you."

The Count of Saint-Pol smiled. "Have I not served Your Grace faithfully in this matter?"

"Yes, Monsieur de Saint-Pol."

Saint-Pol looked at him expectantly.

"Well, man, what do you want? Didn't I give you a diamond ring worth a hundred crowns?"

"It is so difficult for a seigneur with estates on both sides of the Somme to be trusted, but if Your Grace could see your way clear to making me a Constable of France, who knows what useful information

246

I might not pick up from my master, whose equerry I have the honor to be?"

"Pasque Dieu! Pick up something useful and a Constable of France you shall be."

It would be enormously valuable to have a spy in the enemy's camp. But let the snake tongue waggle first, then give him his bribe.

Now Louis knew what to do. He offered to pay the expenses of the entire Burgundian escort. But since he would not know the exact amount until the cavalcade returned to Burgundy, payment could only be made when they reached home. Meanwhile, he regretted to say, some of his guilds were impatient and some of his peasants had ceased making deliveries to the markets of Reims, and if his good uncle tarried much longer he was afraid he would soon be subsisting on roots.

The Burgundians left at once.

Louis lived up to his bargain, but the salt tax doubled in Reims. Soon the people forgot why.

Shortly the king too left Reims and took up residence in Paris. It was good to feel the strong old walls of his capital around him. He convoked the parliament and, with the same impetuosity that in his youth he had thrown himself into war, he now threw himself into the business of government.

In the first flush of their loyalty he had only to suggest and parliament would act. Count Jean d'Armagnac for the second time in his life found himself sentenced to death; but he shut himself up in Lectoure, defying both king and parliament. Louis did not immediately march against him; for the present there was too much else to do. But he confiscated all of High Armagnac up to the gates of the count's provincial capital, leaving the count prisoner in that fragment of his former great estates, to let time and diminished revenues sap his strength.

Both Pierre de Brézé and Antoine de Chabannes he imprisoned, though they protested that they had never been personally disloyal to him, merely loyal to the late king, and now were ready to serve the new king with the same devotion. Parliament duly enregistered and ratified the decree of imprisonment.

The merchants of Reims, whom the Burgundians had despoiled, were paid in full out of the national treasury. But the salt tax was proving so productive, it would go so far toward redeeming the Somme towns, that Louis did not lift it.

The salt tax, like the hearth tax and the tax on wine, was extremely unpopular. They were drawn from the very base of the economy; everyone must eat salt in his bread, heat his home with fire, and drink wine. One morning Louis was awakened by a breathless herald from the Provost of Reims with an ominous report that the people were rioting in the streets and that one of the royal tax collectors had been stoned.

"The people?" he gasped. "But the people are my friends! Or I thought they were." He had saved them from a host of Burgundian

247

leeches that might have gone on sucking their blood indefinitely, and they were the first to revolt. "Do they think I can pay for a hundred thousand ten-course suppers every night?" He determined to check this rebellious movement before it gathered momentum and set a bad example.

He sent the herald back with a stern letter to the Provost. "My good people are thoughtless children. This is not a time to spare the rod, lest worse happen in the future. The instigators are traitors; lesser leaders are malefactors. Deal with them strictly according to the law. But do not touch the followers."

The law was horrible, and the Provost enforced it to the limit. These were the first clipped ears of Louis's reign, the first executions of traitors by drowning. Sewn on to the sacks were patches that read, "Let Pass the Justice of the King!" Some twenty of the sad objects floated down the Vesle, so small upon the broad expanse of the river, so mighty in their implications. The people watched them in silence. They were orderly after that, and the salt tax was paid regularly. Louis viewed his act as impersonal justice, which legally it was. But it destroyed some of his faith in the vision of the masses. Since they could not think for themselves, he would have to do their thinking for them. Perhaps this was why a king's shoulders were anointed. His conscience was at ease. It was better for twenty rabble rousers to be executed than for a thousand peaceful merchants to be mulcted, to say nothing of the threat to the national security that a hundred thousand Burgundians had constituted.

Emboldened by the success of his prompt measures in Reims, thinking always of the Somme, Louis extended the salt tax to all of France. But the monies could not immediately be applied against the strategic river. Count Charles of Melun, the weak-chinned Grand Master of France, approached him with troubling news. In the last years of his father's reign, when King Charles had acted without the sober financial counsel of Xaincoings and Jacques Coeur, payment of the French armies had fallen into arrears. They would have to be paid immediately, Louis knew, or they might desert, nay, worse, they might revolt like the citizens of Reims. Their back wages drained out of the treasury vast sums that the new taxes had supplied, and the Somme could not be redeemed that year.

Indirectly the riot in Reims brought about the release of De Brézé and De Chabannes, for Louis did not wish to quarrel with nobility and commons at the same time. De Chabannes, though Louis did not like him, was a capable general, and he was reinstated.

For De Brézé, however Louis devised a sly punishment. "The Isle of Jersey, a pleasant place in the English Channel, deserves a governor with talents like yours," he said. "True, it is English territory, but the English have other things on their minds just now. Take Jersey for France, and know that my good wishes are always with you."

De Brézé, poised between two disinterested worlds, mustered a small company of his own vassals, and captured a few square miles of the island, neither France nor England paying any attention, and settled down there to govern in the fog among the cows till the king's anger should cool and put an end to his exile.

At this busy beginning of his reign, petitioners besieged his court. The King of Aragon sent word that he needed money, as did many sovereigns who heard of Louis's successful new taxes. Aragon was close, and Louis lent a more attentive ear than was usual when he heard requests for funds. He looked at the map. In the south a fragment of Aragon incongruously spilled over the strong natural frontier of the Pyrenees. It was an inconsequential bit of territory in itself. But it opened the door to invasion from the Spains. "Give me the cities of Roussillon and Cerdagne," bargained Louis, "and I will give you the two hundred thousand écus you need." Roussillon and Cerdagne were the only fortified places in the territory.

Aragon demurred, "If I can buy them back one day."

"Done!" said Louis.

Again Louis had to drain the treasury, again funds set aside to redeem the Somme had to be drawn upon, and the tax gatherers were busier than ever. But the money was paid, and the map changed.

Louis immediately garrisoned the towns and gave their government to the greatest of his southern lords, Gaston, Prince of Foix.

"You should have had the command," young Jean LeClercq said to his father. Madame LeClercq thought so too.

"From me the king needs cannon. It is enough that he has made me master of the Arsenal. Don't aim so high so soon. From Foix he needs the prestige of a great southern name."

"Isn't LeClercq a great name, and aren't we southern too? Mother is a Comminges. Where is the estate of LeClercq, Father?"

Henri sighed and turned away from a mechanical drawing of a new grenade, pushing a pair of recently acquired Venetian spectacles up onto his forehead. He could not tell his son he did not know. How quickly Jean had grown up to ask embarrassing questions.

"Go practice your swordsmanship," he said severely.

Louis had closed the threatening door through the mountains, and the rugged wall of the Pyrenees now stretched unbroken, protecting all the southern provinces of France from the Atlantic to the Mediterranean.

Parliament now began to murmur. Some of the deputies had friends in Reims who had lost their ears. Why, parliament asked, must the taxes go on, now that the brilliant expansion in the south was completed and the treasury fuller than ever it had been under his late father? Louis said: "Roussillon and Cerdagne are nothing compared with the Somme. I *will* have the Somme!"

Taxes were growing harder to collect, they said, especially in some of the more distant provinces.

"If parliament cannot get the money," he answered, "I can; and if your jurisdiction suffers by what I do, do not blame me." He reestablished the parliament of Grenoble in the Dauphiny, and the elated representatives of his former appanage immediately expressed their gratitude by a levy that surpassed in severity anything the Paris parliament had ever dared to impose. Now again the Dauphinois could govern themselves without interference from Parisians who did not understand their local problems.

The Dauphiny response was so encouraging that Louis convoked another provincial assembly. Nobles and the Paris parliament alike suffered another loss of prestige, but more taxes flowed in with less effort. Originating in necessity, these moves had an incidental result which Louis quickly recognized as a powerful weapon against enemies, then smiled when he remembered that the Romans had thought of it ages ago. *Divide et impera:* he was dividing, and by dividing he was establishing his rule.

In the south also he accomplished one of the ambitions he had spoken of to Charlotte. He set up a silk factory at Lyons, staffing it with workers from Savoy. Since it was not to be expected that Duke Lodovico would part with his best craftsmen without payment, Louis wrote: "They need not have two eyes, so long as one is sharp, nor two hands, so long as one is quick. And as for legs, those are scarcely necessary at all. But let them be healthy, if possible, not given to swooning or drowsing at their work." Wondering what his crazy son-in-law would do with them, the duke gladly sent a mule train of raggedy cripples culled from all the silkworks of Savoy, where they had been the butt of much ill natured sport from normal workers. They worked themselves almost to death for the king who housed them adequately in a quarter of their own and punished anyone who dared laugh at their infirmities. A physical ailment was never a joke to Louis, though it was high sport for everyone else. In this, and in his compassion for dogs, he felt himself at odds with his age.

Spurred by his need of money for the Somme, his mind leapt ahead from the silk factory to the uses of silk; and now the king with so notable a lack of interest in dress found himself pondering the intricacies of ladies' garments. Why was it that one lady's hennin was a yard high and another lady's only half a yard? Why shouldn't they all be alike? Then they could be produced in enormous quantities by unskilled laborers in central establishments. One pattern would serve for all. The same thing could be done with gowns. Not only would they be cheaper, so that everyone could afford them, but a manufacturing tax could be levied at the source. It would probably run into millions. As it was now, the industry was so decentralized that no manufacturing tax could be collected, since it was obviously impossible to send a collector to every sempstress in the kingdom.

"I do not think you will progress very far along that road of endeavor," Charlotte smiled.

"It would be a great boon to the poor."

"Dear Louis! How little you know about women. If every petty bourgeois woman could have a hennin, no lady would wear one."

"That is very uncharitable in you, Charlotte."

"I don't even like it when one of my ladies in waiting happens to wear a gown like mine, and you know how they are always copying me."

"That's just what I mean! You shall set the style, costume shall be strictly regularized on that pattern, the treasury will have an enormous new source of revenue, and everyone will be happy."

Charlotte laughed. "My busy, busy king, no woman in France would be happy, I least of all."

"Then I suppose I shan't try it," he said.

But he did, in a small way, on the sly in one of Count Jean d'Armagnac's towns in Gascony which he had recently confiscated. It was one of the strangest places in the world, unique even in Jean d'Armagnac's territories, where almost anything might be expected.

The town had a large population of congenital morons, from whom normal people of the vicinity lived apart, shunning even their touch. Though none of these strangely afflicted persons owned shoes, they were forbidden by law to walk barefoot on the roads, and hence kept to the bypaths or wrapped rags around their feet. They had no social or political rights. Trades were denied them, and most of them worked as woodcutters in the forests. Their condition resembled leprosy, yet they were not lepers, for lepers had heads of normal size. Theirs were small to the point of conspicuous deformity. No one knew their ancestry or of what race they were. They were fair-haired and blue-eyed, and officially they were known as Cagots. Surely here, Louis reasoned, he could get acceptance of his regularization of dress, and the experiment could be conducted without publicity.

But even the simple-minded Cagot women were feminine enough to refuse to dress alike. The experiment was a failure, Louis dropped it as impracticable, and decided that the sex was incorrigible, which he had suspected all along.

In foreign affairs, where he dealt with men, he was more successful. He busied himself in the problems of Savoy, knowing from times past that Duke Lodovico was incapable of vigorous action. Savoy was hard to protect on the Italian side. No rivers, no mountains provided a strong natural frontier between Savoy and Milan. There were only two ways of protecting yourself: an alliance or an appeal to arms. There was always hazard in battle where the conflict took place in the open. Louis preferred the secret maneuvers of diplomacy, that no one ever knew about till the project was successful. By an alliance Louis arranged to protect his father-in-law in Savoy and, as a result, France and himself.

France held an ancient claim to Genoa. Louis could not enforce the claim and did not particularly want the little republic, which was far away. But it was close to Milan, and the Duke of Milan did want it. Louis relinquished all rights to the place, but in return he arranged for the marriage of one of his many sisters-in-law, Bona of Savoy, to the heir of the duchy of Milan. Duke Lodovico was delighted to marry off another of his daughters; the Milanese prince was eager to take her. Thus Louis locked and double-locked the gate of those valleys that ran the wrong way through the Alps to the Dauphiny, which now was France. He had relinquished only a right he did not want, and he had spent not one sol, fired not one shot, lost not one man, and involved only one woman, who was happy to be involved.

From Italy there came to the new king's court another ambassador, the legate of Pope Pius II. He approached Louis on the thorny old subject of King Charles's Pragmatic Sanction of Bourges, a royal decree that rendered the French clergy virtually independent of the pope. Louis, who did not want his own great nobles independent of him, could understand how the Holy Father too wished discipline among his sworn subordinates.

He agreed to abolish the Pragmatic, but he wanted something in return. What, he asked, was there to prevent the pope's granting Naples to his Uncle René of Provence, who held the title of King but not the kingdom of Naples? Louis had nothing to fear from René, but Provence bordered on France and it would cost nothing to bind his uncle closer to him.

Louis was working fast. He had not yet negotiated with an organization that dealt in terms of eternity. He got much, but not what he expected. Word came from Rome that the arrangement he suggested for King René might be worked out as soon as it could be done without prejudice to present conflicting interests, which the Holy Father, deploring all conflicts, hoped would not be long. Louis deemed the report favorable.

But there was more. The legate was further permitted to state that if Louis abolished the Pragmatic immediately the Holy Father, in recognition of the king's known piety and in gratitude for the abolition, would confer upon him an impressive title, a title never before borne by a mere king. It was "Majesty" prefixed by the honorific "Most Christian."

No territorial French interests were involved. Louis abolished the Pragmatic. But time went on, René did not press his claim and, though he wrote Louis thanking him for the gesture, he said it might take a fight to make him king regnant of Naples and he much preferred to paint pictures in the twilight of his life. Louis was afraid that he had given something for nothing.

But he found he had not. There was a new awe in the voices of foreign ambassadors, a new deepness to their bows when he received them. "Pasque Dieu!" he said to Olivier, "Am I not the same man? Is my

252

beard any different now that I am a Most Christian Majesty than it was when I was simply Your Grace like every other king?"

"Your Majesty is not like any king that ever was or ever will be," Olivier replied soberly. His manner too had undergone a subtle transformation. It was as if the king had put on more stature and everyone around him had shrunk to a like degree.

"Three little words instead of two," Louis snapped. "Words, wind, puffs of nothingness. I am glad the negotiation was not vital like the Somme. But maybe I got something out of it. The queen loves her new title. Did I tell you Her Majesty is going to have a baby?"

"No, Your Majesty."

Louis screwed up his face. "But you knew, you devil. I can see it in your face."

"Everyone knows."

"How can they? She only just told *me*."

"Your Majesty has been very occupied with great affairs."

Chapter Thirty-seven

As the queen's time approached she said to Louis, "Remember, you promised that I should name the princesses."

"Pasque Dieu, Charlotte, I want a dauphin."

"God will decide," she said quietly.

He consulted Olivier. "What have you got in that closet of yours to ensure that Her Majesty will have a son? I must have a dauphin; the good of France demands a dauphin. And in addition, I should not know how to teach a princess her duties. Clearly, after the Cagot women, I do not know the female mind."

The barber-surgeon shifted his glance to the tips of his shoes, which curled up in long points and were secured by yellow garters just below the knees. The hunchback happened to have well formed feet, and was extravagant in his purchase of footwear. "Her Majesty herself and her maids and matrons would doubtless be capable of instructing a princess—"

"Answer my question, Olivier."

"If Your Majesty were anyone else, or if I did not care what happened to Madame, or if I could be happy away from you, I should immediately brew a potion and leave Paris the moment I administered it—"

"Answer my question, Olivier."

"There are many drugs; I know them all. They cost thousands of crowns—"

"In this I care nothing for cost."

"But all are frauds, and some are dangerous."

"Nay, I want no danger for the queen."

"The odds are fifty-fifty, Your Majesty, that it will be a dauphin."

"I do not care for fifty-fifty odds."

"Then I am helpless, though for anyone else I would gamble on fifty-fifty odds and make a fortune if I was lucky."

"I do not care for gambling at any odds. It is far better to be sure beforehand."

"Only God can be sure, Your Majesty."

"Perhaps so, perhaps so; it is a pity."

He would have ordered public prayers for a dauphin, but that would have indicated a lack of confidence in his own ability to rule; so he simply prayed, long, secretly, and with all his heart.

But the child was a princess, and Charlotte named her Anne. "She is beautiful," the mother whispered fondly. "Do you know, Louis, I think she looks exactly like you."

Mentally Louis sputtered a great guffaw. Almost he said, "My dear, to be beautiful and to look like me is an impossibility. She is very sweet," he said, "but a girl ought to look like her mother."

"The long noble nose, the high Valois forehead; she will be subtle and strong and wise, like you."

Louis hoped so, for Anne of France gave no promise of beauty. "Next time perhaps it will be a dauphin," he said.

But even if it were only a princess, a royal birth was an occasion for national celebration. A three-day holiday was declared and, though Louis remitted no taxes, he made a long royal progress through the heart of his kingdom, showing himself to his subjects, touching for the evil, speaking to them personally regardless of their station in life, setting an example of economy by the simplicity of his escort, who all slept in cheap tents, and pardoning and releasing prisoners from jail if their offenses were not serious. Thus, in a measure, he won back some of the personal popularity he had lost by the severity of his levies. Everywhere he made speeches, telling why the taxes were necessary. That he condescended to explain endeared him to thousands of little men and women who, even if they did not know what he was talking about, knew that he, their king, was talking to them.

At Meung-sur-Loire he viewed some shabby creatures hustled out of their prison cells by the local provost to receive the royal pardon if, on inspecting them, the king decided to extend it. As the provost called their names and read their crimes, Louis was nodding yes, yes, yes, and the pardoned felons were kissing his hand and skulking off, when suddenly he saw a familiar face. But it was woefully changed. The prisoner's complexion was sallow, his eyes had lost their poetic fire, and his hair was white, snow-white, though Louis knew that the man was still young.

"Stop your reading, Provost," he said. "This one I know." The man advanced and knelt before him in a spiritless way like the others.

"Well, François Villon, how is it I find you in this predicament?"

"It was alleged, Most Christian Majesty, that I spent a night with the alleged mistress of His Reverence the Lord Bishop of Meung. I got a flogging and permanent lodgings, both bad, both free."

"Were you tried?"

"No, Your Majesty."

"Was he?" Louis asked the provost.

"I find no record of a trial, Your Majesty, but my orders——"

"Judges should give orders to provosts. Were the orders to retain this man given you by a judge? What is the name of the judge?"

"The records are somewhat faulty, Your Majesty," the provost said, fumbling through this papers.

Louis sighed. Probably everyone was guilty. It was not a subject he wished reviewed in the full glare of publicity. The clergy would surely accuse him of maligning one of their members.

"There are too many allegations in this case," Louis said affably. "Alleged mistresses, alleged spending of nights—Pasque Dieu! there must have been a mistake. I cannot pardon you, for that would imply that I believe all the allegations"—this brought laughter from everyone—"but I can free you, and free you I do." This brought applause.

Later the king said, "And now, François, what can I do for you?"

"Nothing, Your Majesty."

He had changed in spirit as well as in appearance. "But you used to want so much! You used to dream and scheme and write——"

"I want nothing now, and I have written my last poem."

Perhaps the man was sick. "Surely not your last, François. What is it called?" he said encouragingly.

"What a poet's last poem should always be called. I call it *The Great Testament* of François Villon, and in it, having nothing of worldly value, I leave all my hopes for my friends, and what I hope for my enemies. Especially for my enemies."

He looked and he sounded sick. "You must send me a copy," Louis said, knowing that poets feel better when people ask for copies of their poems. "And since you find yourself short of funds, as indeed who does not, even kings, I shall ask your good patron of Bestourné to give you back your old place in his cloisters. Are you friendly with him?" It was not likely.

"I do not know. I doubt it; I doubt most things."

"He will give you your place if I tell him to," Louis said. "Soon you will be your old self again. Will you go to him?"

"As readily as anywhere," Villon said apathetically.

He went, as Louis knew, for shortly the prelate of Bestourné sent a bill for his wine, and Louis paid it. Later the king received a copy of *The Great Testament*.

Louis did not consider himself a judge of poetry, since poetry was seldom factual, but he could find a use even for a poem. Always thinking of the Somme, wishing to flatter by his attention the able Burgundian who unfortunately was not a Frenchman, he sent a copy to Philippe de Comines.

Comines laughed heartily. "It is good poetry, even great poetry. But the Bishop of Meung will wish it had never been written," he wrote in a friendly letter. The king at once tried to suppress *The Great Testament*, but it was too late. Everyone was already laughing at the bishop, whose only defense against the ridicule heaped upon him was proud and sullen silence. Louis did not enjoy the incident, and he would have liked to hear the other side of the story. But from it he drew a lesson, as he did from everything: even a sick pauper of a scribbling poet could be a formidable enemy if the people were on his side.

The king protracted his tour through his realm, for he had a feeling, and Olivier le Malvays confirmed it, that the people were getting used to the heavy taxes. Why should they not? The barber had got used to his hump. He himself had got used to a certain infirmity. He sensed that some of his original popularity was trickling back, just as gold was flowing into the treasury. Not too long hence he would be able to buy back the Somme! Then, *then*, behind that river, behind those castled hills, he and his people would be secure. He wanted no treasure for himself. He spent nothing on pageants and feasts like Uncle Burgundy, nothing on vain theatrical entertainments like Uncle René. Charlotte pleaded with him constantly to dress at least as well as his barber. He wanted money only for France, one mighty cohesive battlemented state; and to that great end he was willing, if need be, to choke whole rivers with bodies of traitors who stood in his way.

Meanwhile, throughout that year and the next, despite heavy expenses for cannon, swords, and the soldiers' pay, the treasure slowly accumulated and the people were loyal. Nothing marred this period, no seizures, no ominous chills, save only perhaps that the king was constantly overworked and complained to Charlotte one day in the nursery that he felt weary and middle-aged. She smiled and looked at him in a quizzical way that at first he did not understand.

François Villon, after a lengthy rehabilitation in the cloisters of Bestourné, got into trouble again. He stole the silver altar fixtures from a church and was thrown into the prison of the Châtelet. Louis pardoned him again and made good the theft. No sooner was the poet released than he became involved in a drunken street brawl in which Père Sermoise was killed. Arrested, imprisoned, and racked, Villon confessed that he had killed him. He was sentenced to be hanged. Again Louis pardoned him, but this time he banished him for ten years, lest the laws that were inflexible for everyone else be made a mockery of by a poet.

"France has probably seen the last of him," he said regretfully to Charlotte. "I have a feeling the world will never hear of him again. It is a pity. He was a good friend to me when I was dauphin; and Philippe de Comines says he writes great poetry. My dear, I am getting old."

The queen whispered shyly in his ear, for her ladies were within hearing. Then Louis understood the quizzical look. "Now does Your Majesty feel old?"

"Neither old nor depressed. I think I feel majestic! Who wants to make poems when one can make princes? God has blessed me in you, Charlotte."

"I did not say it would be a prince, Louis. I only said it would be a baby."

"Nay, this time surely it will be a dauphin!"

Chapter Thirty-eight

But it was another princess. Louis was not with the queen when the royal infant was born, and the news reached him at secondhand; the herald with the dispatch had fallen sick en route; the courier he delegated to ride to the king had lost the letter, and the account that finally reached Louis was garbled. He lost his temper and boxed the courier's ears. "Well, which was it, Jean or Jeanne? Answer me, fellow! Dauphin or princess, boy or girl? Well, well, well? Pasque Dieu, don't you know the difference?"

The courier said he was certain it was Jeanne, nay, he would stake his honor it was Jeanne, a princess. Louis did not want to believe it.

"Be hanged with your honor! How dared you lose a royal letter, you strumpetson?"

The courier, panic-stricken as he was, protested stoutly that his blood, though bourgeois, was legitimate and honorable, and that the letter had been lost to a highwayman who saw the crest on the pouch and probably thought it contained money. He had a bandaged arm to prove he had tried to protect it.

Louis relented. "Nay, then, it was not your fault." But he resolved to do something to improve the system of intelligence. Heralds still enjoyed the immunity of their feudal tabards. But what happened when a herald fell sick? Confusion like this! The king resolved to institute a system of posts throughout the kingdom. Fast-riding couriers with armed escorts would gallop on schedule all over the length and breadth of France.

Relays of fresh horses would be kept at regular intervals, calculatedly spaced, not so close as to let the couriers dawdle, not so far apart as to injure the horses. He would allow others to use the royal mails too, nobles, merchants, bailiffs, mayors, anyone who could pay. For there was in the scheme a possibility of postal revenues, a new source of income, in addition to absolute certainty of an end to all such accidents as this.

News that the child was a princess was shortly confirmed in a placid letter from the queen, who said: "If God had given us a dauphin I should never have named him without your leave, remembering our covenant; so there was no need to box the poor courier's ears. She is a pretty child, prettier even than Anne in the face"—Louis hoped so—"very dark of skin, and Madame Loyse assures me that the slight curvature in her poor little back will straighten out as she grows older." Louis shuddered. He did not trust Charlotte's prejudiced estimate of the child's beauty. Swarthy skin, twisted spine, beauty forsooth! Did he have a hunchback like Olivier for a princess? It was not easy to see how a beneficial alliance might ever be gained by marrying off such a girl. Why could it not have been a dauphin? Was God punishing him for hating the name of Charles? Had he broken the Fifth Commandment? He admitted he had, though he had honored his mother. Perhaps there was resentment in heaven. If God Himself was not punishing him, perhaps he had offended some St. Charles. Charlemagne? Charlemagne's place in the hagiarchy was not firmly established, and presumably the great emperor wielded less authority there than he had on earth. There was a St. Charles the Good, also called the Dane. Probably he was the source of the bad luck. Hastily Louis bought a lead medal of him, a good saint to honor in any case since, in his lifetime, he had opened the granaries to the poor during a famine in Denmark and broken the monopoly of a powerful gang of grain merchants. Louis put the medal on his cap, assuring St. Charles in his prayers that he had intended no offense and asked in return only that he be given strength to break monopolies in France, especially the monopoly of feudal power so zealously prized by the Princes of the Lilies. To God he promised that in return for a dauphin he would henceforth obey the Fifth Commandment and honor his father by naming his first son Charles. Louis did not divulge these prayers to anyone, lest they betray a weakness; they were intensely sincere and he kept them secret. Meanwhile he kept in reserve his scheme for honoring the Virgin.

Having, he hoped, appeased heaven, he turned to the equally practical business of the Somme, anxious to consummate it so that he could hurry back to Paris and see for himself what ailed the infant princess.

Only a matter of paramount interest to France would have kept him in the north during the queen's critical time. His mission now was nothing less than the final redemption of the Somme.

On September 12th he had made a down payment of 200,000 écus on the vast area. It was now October 8th. "I charge you," he said to Olivier, "each year remind me that October 8th is my lucky day. Some saint, some star, some numerological combination blesses October 8th for me. Let me never forget it!"

"Never, Your Majesty," Olivier replied, though he lumped stars, saints, and numerology all together into one vast sink of cynical doubt except when he was talking to Louis. If faith made his master happy, he was for faith. "I will never forget."

To secure the other 200,000 gold crowns Louis had drained the royal treasury and exhausted the municipal coffers of every city and hamlet in France. When the sum still lacked a little of the required total he had even reimposed old royal *aides* against his nobles—if they wanted their feudal rights let them remember that a king also had feudal rights, no matter how long forgotten or fallen into abeyance. The great lords grumbled; Louis explained his grand strategy, which benefited them all, pleaded, begged, and finally threatened when two seigneurs proved obdurate. When the Sieur of Neuchâtel refused, the king suddenly sent a column of soldiers against his city of Epinal and confiscated it to the crown. When the Sieur of Châteauneuf refused, the king imprisoned him, not in elegant confinement but in an iron cage like a wild animal, where there was room to lie down and little more. These object lessons proved effective, nay, he considered they served a double purpose: death would have been final, tied his hands, prevented a reversal of the punishments. Louis always preferred imprisonment, which did not trammel the future, and which also broke no commandment, especially at a time when, it would seem, one's negotiations with heaven were not wholly prospering.

The treasure was gathered now, every sol of it, securely packed in iron chests on wagons protected by the best of Henri LeClercq's quick-firing guns; a marksman corps of engineers manned them; an army of soldiers surrounded them. Louis was at Péronne to make final payment and take instant possession, in accordance with Duke Philip's sworn oath.

"Péronne, October 8th," he said. "Let me never forget Péronne either."

"Péronne, October 8th," echoed Olivier le Malvays. "Your Majesty must never forget." But he wished he could look into the future to spare his master disappointment if the date or the town might some day fail him.

Count Charles and Duke Philip arrived in Péronne. "I should hazard a guess," Louis whispered to Olivier, "that Cousin Charles would like to steal my treasure and keep the Somme. His retinue is big enough."

"That would be my idea too if I were the heir to Burgundy, for then I should not love Your Majesty."

"The best thing about you," the king laughed, "is that I need only listen to your honest tongue to divine the workings of a black heart."

Henri LeClercq ran his critical eye over the Burgundian host. The armor glittered on horses and men; the spear points glared needle sharp; the flaunting Burgundian lions on the banners looked freshly painted, a gaudier red. "He couldn't do it," he said. "It is an army; but as usual there is no artillery."

"What are your grenades charged with this time, Henri?"

"A handful of crossbow quarrels in each, but steel, not iron, and sharply pointed to increase their armor-piercing qualities, Monseigneur." Henri was having trouble getting used to the king's majestic title, and Louis always smiled, but Olivier always looked angry.

"Since there is no artillery the old duke is still in command," Louis commented with satisfaction. "Gunpowder and my good uncle have no more in common than—" *My nobles and I* was on his tongue, but as usual he thought twice before he spoke. "—than this century and the last."

"If the old duke still commands, I do not think he will do so much longer," Olivier said. "From the purely medical point of view, Your Majesty, prognosis is bad when old soldiers travel in litters like women."

Louis nodded. There was another bad sign too, that only he had noticed. There were no women in the Burgundian cavalcade. Duke Philip liked to have them around; he must be failing fast. But that he was here at all in Péronne meant that the chivalrous old man meant to keep his word.

The Burgundians advanced, Count Charles riding beside the litter, full-armed, his face red with anger and shame, his eyes blazing, their fire curiously enhanced by the shadows that the helmet, in which his head was encased, threw over his features.

"He need only lower his visor and he'd be ready for battle," Oliver said.

Louis answered: "He's ready now. I would to God his father were astride that splendid horse and he were in the litter."

"Would you, sire? You need not wait for God. Olivier le Malvays could manage the matter. Will you dine with Count Charles? I have no grenades, but I do have a small quantity of the white powder—"

"None of your poisoned fish, Olivier."

They met in a tent, since the king had not yet taken formal possession of the town and Count Charles did not invite him into the château.

"Says he won't let you under the same roof with him," said the old duke from his litter. There was a senile cackle in his voice.

"Father, please don't talk," Count Charles said sharply.

"Oh, very well, very well. I only said what *you* said."

"Please don't say anything. The spider has trapped his fly, isn't that enough?"

Philippe de Comines was busy at the table, appending to the Treaty of Arras a sheaf of accounts which listed the treasure contained in each iron chest.

"Would you care to count it?" Louis asked.

Count Charles said Yes. Philippe de Comines looked uncertain.

"No, by God!" shouted the duke, rising shakily to his elbow.

Charles stepped over to soothe him. Olivier muttered, "Too red, too red that face." He saw apoplexy, paralysis, death, hovering over the angry old man.

"Louis, lad, it is all there, isn't it?" Duke Philip inquired plaintively.

"Every penny, dear uncle."

"Pity you two boys can't be friends. Seal the treaty, Charles. I have kept my word."

The count sealed with the duke's seal.

Louis smiled to himself, "A sinful waste of candle. His glare alone would have melted the wax." But he did not permit his face to betray the satisfaction he felt.

With the pressing of the seal into the soft hot substance of the wax, the map changed again and the border of France leapt north to rest upon the Somme.

The king looked significantly at Henri; Henri spoke softly to his son, who withdrew from the council tent. Outside, the young man jumped onto a waiting horse.

Philippe de Comines raised his eyebrows.

"Young Jean has probably gone out to obey some call of nature," Louis shrugged.

"Someone should teach the sons of your *haute noblesse* their manners," Count Charles sneered.

But Jean LeClercq was too elated and too far away to hear or resent the remark. He had begged his father, and Henri had obtained permission from the king, to be given the honor of setting off the signal that would announce the transfer of sovereignty of the Somme. It was a new use for fireworks. Jean spurred his mount into a thicket; he touched a slow match to the fuse of a rocket; it arched into the air with a whoosh and a fiery tail like a comet. From hill to hill to the westward till their fire was lost in the distance the signals were repeated, and in an hour the French forces, poised and waiting, from Péronne to Abbéville were on the march; by nightfall the Somme towns were occupied.

In the tent Louis said: "Good Uncle, it would honor me if you were to rest in Péronne till the fatigue of your journey passes; and since I seem to upset Count Charles, I and my men will withdraw from the city."

"That is very chivalrous in you, Louis, lad. I am not fatigued, of course, but as you say, a little rest, a little refreshment—"

"No," said the count.

"But he just offered to withdraw, Charles. That is a knightly gesture, since it's his town now."

"We will retire, Father."

"He shouldn't sleep in a tent," Olivier whispered.

The count's sharp ears picked up the remark. "You will sleep better in a tent, Father, than in Péronne, where barbers and bastards counsel a spider."

"Gentlemen," the duke said, "I beg your pardon for my son. He is a good boy, but he cannot bridle his temper. Even his mother calls him Charles the Rash."

"I am not offended," Louis said. Looking at him, both Henri and Olivier realized that, amazingly, he was not, though they were. Olivier remembered the king's remark that words were wind, puffs of nothingness. Henri sighed, remembering only that he was in truth a bastard.

"I hope that the duchess and countess are well," Louis said pleasantly. The business was done, and Philippe de Comines was rolling up the sealed papers; it would cost nothing to be polite.

"My lady is well, thank you," Duke Philip said.

"The Countess of Charolais enjoys the best of health," Charles said stiffly.

But that evening, as the Burgundians were leaving Péronne, the Count of Saint-Pol made a stealthy visit to Louis's tent under cover of the confusion and the early autumn dusk.

"The Countess of Charolais is dying," he said.

"You promised to pick up something of value," Louis retorted. "It is not good news when a lady dies, nor is it very significant." It was proof that Saint-Pol was a watchful spy, however.

"Nay, Your Majesty, think what possibilities her death will open up! What opportunities the count will now have for contracting favorable alliances for Burgundy. Whom will he marry next?"

"That would indeed be information worth a constable's baton," Louis conceded.

"When I know, you shall know!" Saint-Pol promised eagerly.

The king returned to Paris and saw his daughter. He ordered bells rung and proclaimed the three-day holiday, and he made a long speech to the parliament, who loudly cheered the strong new northern border and asked for instant tax relief. He promised relief as soon as the terrible costs had been made good, in part at least, since obviously the army could not be paid out of an empty treasury. He released the Sieur de Châteauneuf from the iron cage, extending pardon. Châteauneuf at once fled to Burgundy, whither the Sieur de Neuchâtel had already taken refuge in sullen, impotent wrath.

But the king made no royal progress and did not touch for the evil. Louis was sick at heart, and felt himself under a curse. The new princess was not quite a hunchback, but her little spine was pitifully arched and she would always have a pronounced stoop to her carriage. Anne was no beauty; Jeanne would be ugly.

"Is it the hinges in her back, like yours, Olivier?"

"Yes, Your Majesty, but not nearly so bad."

"Will she hurt too, always?"

"I—do not think so. She does not cry much in her crib."

Neither had lumpish, big-headed Charles, the Duc de Berri, the king's brother.

"Tell the queen that Princess Jeanne will grow out of her trouble."

"I will, I will, Your Majesty. But she won't."

"Tell the queen anyhow."

Some day, though he knew he would raise a storm of protest, he would do something to improve the state of medical knowledge in France. Why should doctors be forced to rob graves in order to study the human body? Why?

The year 1464, which had achieved so much, closed on this note of private sorrow.

The year 1465 opened with a secret message from the Count of Saint-Pol; Louis deemed it worth a constable's baton.

It threatened disaster for France, but the king was forewarned.

Chapter Thirty-nine

In quick succession the Countess of Charolais died and Duke Philip sank into a state of senility that affected his mind and rendered him incapable of governing. His heart still beat, but he dwelt in a twilight world of his own, far from reality, waging phantom crusades that were always victorious. Saint-Pol kept Louis apprised of the situation, which ended as, logically, it had to end.

On April 12th, which was a Friday, a day Louis had always superstitiously dreaded, an instrument of regency was drawn up. The Burgundian nobles signed it, Count Charles signed it, Duke Philip signed it, thinking it proclaimed the capture of Jerusalem; and from that moment Count Charles the Rash became Duke Charles, sovereign of Burgundy.

"He said in my hearing," Saint-Pol reported, " 'My father made Louis king. I will make not one but *six* kings of France.' Excitement here is high among the great lords."

Louis replied: "Come to me at once. Your constable's baton is waiting," and he added, "Bring your vassals, fully armed, and cannon, if there is time and you have any."

Quickly the news spread to France. Charles the Rash made no secret of his determination to make six French kings. The great French lords heard of it, pondered its implications: for them it would turn back the centuries to the golden days of the beginning of feudalism when every petty prince could aspire to kingship, strike his own coinage, dispense his own justice without appeal, hang, hunt, make war upon his neighbors at his pleasure without hindrance from any central authority. And, to them most pleasing of all, the burghers and peasants, to whom Louis was always at such pains to explain his acts, would be stripped of the authority he was constantly giving them in even larger measure. Only recently this tradition-shattering monarch had sold to the bourgeoisie of many cities the right to run their own police forces and choose their own nightwatchmen, a right that had been vested since time immemorial in the local lord of the city. Where would it end? Would Louis XI make nobles of peasants and peasants of nobles? He had done another thing that irked their pride and pinched their purses. They had always had the privilege of appointing municipal magistrates, who were always willing to pay dearly for the positions and hence were constantly removed, that new ones might pay to replace them. The king had decreed that henceforth the magistrates were to form a single cohesive civil service and, once appointed, could not be removed short of gross incompetence, of which royal courts would be the judge. He had authorized free assemblies; he had ensured free elections. And he had taxed them, the hitherto exempt nobility, like everyone else in France.

In Charles the Rash they saw the exact opposite of King Louis XI; they saw not a reserved, meanly dressed, calculating man who looked like one of his own tradesmen, but a tall, imperious prince, flashing with orders, contemptuous of money, ignorant of trade, heedless of the people, the living symbol of a chivalry already hoary with legend. In him they saw the good old days of their privilege.

They had never forgotten how Charles had proudly refused to do homage to Louis in the cathedral of Reims at his coronation, the incident Louis had hoped would go unnoticed and on which so much now hinged. In Charles they saw a leader who would save them from extinction at the hands of their bourgeois king.

Louis knew it was unlikely that Charles alone was capable of organizing the great revolt that now suddenly burst all around him. But Philippe de Comines was capable, that cynical, resourceful man! The revolt even had a high-sounding name, The League of the Public Weal.

"I wish that man were mine!" Louis muttered. Even in his anger he had to admire Comine's subtlety. "If it were called *The League of Traitors Against Their Rightful King* no one would join it. But everyone gives lip service to the public welfare. Pasque Dieu, I would give my emerald to win him over! Olivier! Can you manage to poison Duke Charles? In a week? Ten days at most?"

"I—I shall try desperately, Your Majesty, though it would be difficult to accomplish within ten days. Philippe de Comines would be easier."

"No, not Comines. He is my enemy now, but one day he shall serve me. If you cannot eliminate the Duke of Burgundy immediately, there is no use eliminating him at all. I suspect war is already inevitable. Fortunately I have Foix, Chabannes, Alençon, Nemours, LeClercq, old Bernard d'Armagnac, and," he added slyly, "a little surprise for Cousin Charles. I have the Count of Saint-Pol."

Olivier avoided the king's glance.

"Well, man, what is it? There is always something amiss when you stare at your feet."

"Your Majesty has always asked me not to blurt out little unpleasant-nesses, and indeed, as Your Majesty's surgeon, I deem it most unwise to reveal bad news too suddenly, for the mechanism of digestion, though ill understood by even the best of us, is often, through fluxions of the humors, set a-bubbling and a-burbling—"

"Pasque Dieu, Olivier, answer my question! What is amiss? Well? Well? Well?"

"Your Majesty, I have learned from a gravedigger who buried a fishwife trampled to death by the horses on which some of Saint-Pol's vassals were riding north, that the Count of Saint-Pol has called all his Frenchmen to Burgundy."

Shortly, in addition to Saint-Pol, there were other desertions: the Duc de Nemours, whose fortune he had made; the Duc d'Alençon, whose life he had saved; Antoine de Chabannes, whom he had pardoned and reinstated in command of an army. Then it was announced from Burgundy that the king's own brother, the Duc de Berri, had joined the rebels as commander in chief. In this Louis again saw the subtle hand of Philippe de Comines, for, since there was no dauphin, the king's brother stood next in succession to the throne. With him as titular head, the League now had a specious appearance of legality.

At the news the king sent the queen and the princesses into the Dauphiny.

"If God wills that I die," she said, "then die I must, and there is no reason for me to desert you too."

"You silly goose, you'll be deserting the princesses if you don't. I can trust no one. There are enemies everywhere, overt and covert, more overt every day. One fine morning we shall wake up to find the nurses strangled, the nursery empty, and a letter will come from Burgundy: 'Madame the Queen, My Lord the King, I have your children in my care. No harm will come to them if you grant me forthwith . . .'"

"Nay, Louis, what a fearful imagination you have! Who would steal my innocent little girls and hold them to ransom?"

"The same rash Charles that refused to let his poor old father rest in Péronne after a weary journey, and hustled him out into the cold and made him sleep in a tent. The same tall shining knight who is stealing my vassals, promising fine things that no longer exist. Oh, damn him! Damn his ermine and vermin and beautiful nonsense! Go, Charlotte, go, go, go!"

The queen was alarmed. "I had not thought the children could be threatened. But if it is as bad as you say, then surely I must go. Is even the Dauphiny safe?"

"I think so. Nay, I am sure so. There is a territorial situation there that works in my favor: the great estates of Foix lie close, the Dauphiny could not revolt without endangering them—and Gaston's wife is a princess of Aragon. The King of Aragon would not want the infection to spread into the Spains. Foix will stand by me."

Charlotte said proudly, "Your wife is a princess of Savoy. I will take the children to Chambéry, and Savoy will stand by you too."

"God bless you, Charlotte, for thinking of that. I ought to make you my prime minister."

"It is difficult to imagine myself in such a position," she smiled, "to say nothing of the anomaly of a prime minister's bearing children. But if I were, I should say, 'Your Majesty, you have done too many new things too soon.' "

Oddly, old Philip and young Charlotte, with nothing in common, neither age nor sex nor experience, had given Louis the same counsel. He had attempted too much, too fast. The implication did not escape him. When the war that was surely coming was won—he had utter faith that somehow, anyhow, he would win it—he would walk more warily, step by step, one at a time.

By July every great noble in France except Gaston de Foix and Bernard d'Armagnac had joined the League of the Public Weal. Englishmen paused in their War of the Roses to look across the Channel, and sniff the wind from France. They smelled another try at a continental conquest now that there was civil war there too. European sovereigns believed that the ill fated French prince, who had so narrowly escaped destruction as dauphin, was hopelessly doomed as king. Their ambassadors reported that no suppliants now came to Louis's court; they were crowding into the ducal court of Burgundy. But Louis was not quite deserted. His urgent appeals for help, backed by money and promises of further payment, sped over his system of new roads. The couriers had to ride unattended, since an armed escort would have slowed them down; disguised, since Louis had reason to believe that his heralds' tabards would merely serve as an invitation to assassination. But thanks to the speed now possible over his superb new highways they got through.

From Savoy, Charlotte sent him a capable regiment of crossbowmen.

From Milan her sister sent a wild company of astonishing Italians, full of strange new ideas, who could wench all night, drink delicate wines, compose sonnets, swear classical oaths by pagan gods, and in the morning run, actually run, into battle brandishing poisoned swords and daggers. Bona of Savoy, pious like Charlotte, hoped her good brother-in-law would not be shocked by them. They were "new men" she said, produced by a cultural ferment in Italy which they called the Renaissance. Louis would not have been shocked if they had been produced by a cultural ferment in Hell. He needed men willing to run into battle.

266

From Switzerland, where once he had admired their stamina, came the best allies of all: the Swiss longpikemen. They tramped into France by the thousands, and his only regret was that he could not afford more of them, for they insisted on payment in advance. *Pas d'argent, pas de Suisses* was their motto. But once they were paid they stubbornly refused to live if they could not win. There was a splendid functional simplicity about them, like Henri's machines of war.

Machines he had too, and he thanked God for them, the mighty artillery of France. With the forces at his disposal, outnumbered as he was, he did not consider himself outclassed.

In the second week of July, Duke Charles crossed the Somme. Louis had thought of the Somme as a wall, a buckler of defense; but Charles and his Burgundian host crossed it as one might step over a puddle in the highroad, and advanced unhindered to the very outskirts of Paris. Louis lost some of his faith in walls. With chaos and treachery behind them, they were useless. Alliances and mercenaries were proving more substantial.

Simultaneously the king's brother, the Duc de Berri, that other Charles—two Charleses! two mortal enemies! It would be difficult to remember his promise to God about that name—advanced at the head of an army of Bretons from the west. It was a flanking movement like the one that had crushed the Dauphiny.

But word came from the king's well knit corps of spies that the Breton army was moving slowly. One intelligent agent, whom Louis rewarded for observing so well, reported that the Duc de Berri was wearing a suit of armor that seemed to wrinkle when he rode. The king sighed and shook his head; he knew what the report signified. His unfortunate brother had never been robust. Weak in body, torpid in mind, the weight of the steel exhausted him. To simulate armor, which he could not wear, the Duc de Berri was wearing a cloth-of-silver doublet.

"Poor dupe, poor silly brother! May God forgive you, for I doubt if you know what you are doing. But you are killing France, and me."

The king threw himself between the armies before they could unite, and attacked the stronger of the two. At Montlhéry, outside Paris, he met the Burgundian host.

The king took command of the battle from an overlooking height, a small hill from which he could observe and direct the engagement as a whole. Beside him stood Gaston, Prince of Foix, and Bernard d'Armagnac, the only chivalry who remained loyal, and General Henri LeClercq, who was in charge of the artillery. Runners stood by, waiting to carry the king's orders.

The prince of Foix was ashamed of Louis's new method of command. With no attempt to disguise the sarcasm in his voice he said: "What a pleasant arrangement Your Majesty has provided here for us four. Here we stand, safe as in a church, our swords sheathed. It is not in the tradition of my House, Your Majesty, for Foix to stand idle while Foix's vassals bleed and sweat and die."

"Then the tradition of your House must change, my good friend. They will bleed and sweat no doubt; but not so many of them will die if you fight my way. Do not do the expected. Burgundy counts on our rushing headlong into the melee—you with your white hair, Bernard with his limp and his eighty years, Henri there with his spectacles, me with the weight of my crown and the fate of France! Burgundy counts on killing the leaders first, eliminating the command; then to dispose of the headless rabble at leisure."

That the king was right was soon borne out by taunting shouts from thousands of knightly Burgundian throats.

"Hear them?" he said. "Let them howl, let them scream! Let them call us cowards. Words do not make us so. Stand firm and do not be trapped to your death by mere words. If we die, our army is lost and the fault will be ours. The big thing is to win. Rome won an empire by management; management will win now for us, and all the battles of the future from now on." Louis had also heard the taunt of "Spider," first hurled at him by Charles of Burgundy in the treaty tent at Péronne.

"I do not think I should relish the battles of the future," Foix said, but he loyally obeyed his king.

"Neither should I," said old Bernard.

Henri LeClercq said nothing. He was suffering more than either of the old-fashioned chevaliers, for young Jean LeClercq was serving as one of the runners. Louis had forbidden him to wear armor, the weight of which would only slow him down. Let the runners dodge the javelins and arrows, he said; let speed be their defense and make them difficult targets. And as for the cannon shot and crossbow bolts, armor had never protected anyone against such fast-moving missiles anyhow.

In his good sound mathematical mind Henri could understand the king's reasoning, and even agree with it; but his heart rebelled at the sight of his son spurring through the melee armed only with a sword.

Viewed from the hill, the battle lost some of its detail and loathsomeness. The two grappling armies, seen in the mass, took on the character of their commanders: Burgundy all color and individual bravery, flying standards, shining mail; France grim and sober efficiency, foul-smelling cannon, and disciplined ranks of foot soldiers with only a few mounted leaders. Distance softened the agony in death cries of men as they fell on both sides.

Louis watched the Burgundian horses; they furnished a sure indication of how the battle was going. At every charge more and more of them left the field riderless, no longer feeling the spurs in their flanks or the weight of their masters upon their backs. They would drop back from the fighting line and crop the grass at the edge of the field, patiently waiting for human voices and human hands to direct their next move. It was beyond the scope of their animal minds to imagine what had happened when the vicious hook of a Swiss longpike had grappled their master to the ground or some stray fragment of cannon shot had blasted a window through their master's body in the place where a human heart had beat a fraction of a second before.

On the French side too, after every charge men were dying impaled on Burgundian lances, struck through the skulls by Burgundian swords. And yet, counting the riderless horses through the ugly pall of smoke that hung over the field, Louis deemed victory still possible. Henri's artillery and the Swiss longpikemen were working a terrible havoc on the Burgundian chivalry, and behind the hill, held in mobile reserve, the Italians had not yet come into battle.

"It is not chivalrous to conceal a reserve," the king said slyly to Foix, "but Pasque Dieu! concede that my methods are effective. We will win."

The prince said distastefully, "War doesn't smell right since you and your General LeClercq futurized it. Sulphur, faugh! That man would bleed brimstone. What a devil must have spawned him!"

"Who knows?" Louis shrugged. "Who cares? It was a lucky devil for France."

Henri was far too busy to hear this exchange, nor, very likely, would he have listened. He had long since given up hope of ever solving the mystery of his bastardy.

But Bernard d'Armagnac heard it. The king saw him looking from the prince to the general and from the general back to the prince, and on his fine old face there was a battle of emotions as fierce and indecisive as the battle that raged around them on the plain.

"Pasque Dieu, D'Armagnac, what is amiss?"

The old man looked away. "Nothing, Your Majesty."

"Nothing, nothing! I know you better than that. Tell me."

"Not now."

Yet he might have told, for his face was still undecided. But just then, in the center of the French line, which was hard-pressed but holding, something unexpected happened. Charles of Melun, the Grand Master of France, lived up to his weak chin. He suddenly reined in his horse, wheeled about and, trampling down his own men, turned tail to the enemy and fled the field.

Witnessing the desertion, Louis proved to be not quite the prince of the future he sometimes thought he was. "Pasque Dieu!" he screamed. "Another Charles! O coward! O craven! Unknightly! Forsworn! For shame!" The old-fashioned feudal curses burst from him as readily as from any Burgundian chevalier. He took his horse from his squire, mounted, drew, and pricked into the thick of the fighting from which the Grand Master had fled, shouting: "Round me! Round *me!* Round your king! For France!" He felt the old strength in his legs, the old long reach of his sword arm.

"So?" said the prince, spitting on his hands, grinning. "So he can still strike like a man after all? And so can I! You there, squire! My horse! Now this battle will smell better."

Through his spectacles Henri LeClercq watched the king and the prince charging shouting down the hill. "Fools, fools!" he muttered, "both of them." There would be more work now for the engineers if the great ones were to be protected. "My lord D'Armagnac, witness the folly of noble blood. Never was I more sure that my own is simple."

Never was Bernard d'Armagnac more sure that nothing was simple, Henri's blood least of all. In fact, blood was curiously unpredictable. He knew—the only man in France who did—that here at Montlhéry three generations of Foix-Armagnac had stood and rubbed elbows, grandsire, sire, grandson—the Prince of Foix, Henri LeClercq, young Jean. How differently they were proving themselves! Yet how splendidly alike in their loyalty to the king and to France. That, at least, was something to be proud of in the sorry, hidden old shame.

The king held his own in the battle, though many men of forty-two, especially among the high-living chivalry of Burgundy, found their breath short. Inside their heavy suits of steel the temperature of their bodies rose, sweat streamed into their gauntlets and sollerets and could find no egress, so tightly riveted was their armor, and their limbs grew weak like meat simmering to tenderness in a pot. The heat in their helmets acted on them like a fever, affecting their judgment and vision. Panting, by reason of the violent exertion that hand-to-hand combat entailed, they were forced to breathe their own breath over and over, since the little slits in their visors that kept out deadly weapons also kept out fresh air. Louis, by contrast, forced by his infirmity, had lived his whole life like one long Lent of abstinence, and his vigor was proportionately greater than theirs. He was unencumbered by heavy armor. He had more to lose than they, who were fighting only for their individual lives. And he was in a fierce rage, which lent him strength beyond his own great normal strength. Watching the king rally the sagging center of the line, Henri LeClercq, who was now in sole command of the battle, feared only some accidental arrow or crossbow bolt; against all ordinary hazards of battle Louis seemed able to fend for himself, and to spare.

It was far otherwise with Gaston, Prince of Foix. The years had taken their toll of him; his wind was short, his sword felt suddenly heavy as lead, his slashes had lost their power to cut, and glanced impotently off the steel helms and shoulder pieces of his opponents. He was soon in trouble.

He had beaten off some lesser assailants, among them a knight with red leopards on his shield, whom he recognized as Jacques de Nemours, one of the great lords whom Louis had specially favored only to have him desert like all the rest. But after Nemours came Duke Charles of Burgundy himself, thirty-two years old, at the height of his vigor and young manhood. Foix knew him at once by the black armor he always wore: shield, horse, and armor, from the plume on his helm to the tips of his sollerets, all black, dead black. Only the ducal coronet that circled the helm, gold on black steel, relieved the funereal aspect of his theatrical, but frightening, accouterment. And even the coronet was effective for battle in a curious way: it was burnished so brightly that it played tricks on the eyes, especially old eyes. Foix struck at it, thinking it close, and missed; his sword glanced off the black breastplate.

Duke Charles had sought out the Prince of Foix, since King Louis had paid no attention to his loud shouts of defiance and offers of individual combat. Since he could not get at the king, the prince was the next best opponent. In addition, Duke Charles deemed that no glory could be won by riding through the curtain of artillery fire that Henri LeClercq at that moment threw up around the king. The Burgundians drew back to let him through, and paused to watch him gain what glory there was to be gained by butchering the weary, white-haired chevalier.

Foix, of course, had accepted the offer to fight single style in the old manner, and ordered his men too to fall back. From the hill Henri LeClercq watched the traditional circle form, and cursed. It was chivalrous; it was honorable. But it was murder.

He called for Jean with the intention of ordering a brace of cannon turned away from the area around the king to this newly critical area around the Prince of Foix. But Jean LeClercq was not there. For a moment he was tempted to carry the orders himself, even lay the cannon, plunge into the fighting like Foix and the king. But that would have meant losing touch with the battle as a whole to engage in one small segment of it. He put the temptation from him and stood his ground.

But he resolved that if he lived to direct a future battle, he would do something to improve the system of command that Louis had inaugurated. The king's innovations, like his mind, dealt with human beings; Henri's dealt with mechanics. Runners were good, but they could be killed. Where in God's name was Jean? Missiles were beginning to fall on the command hill now that the Burgundians had grasped the importance of the king's couriers. Ambition for his son to gain distinction and fear that he might have been slain divided his heart. He thought briefly of the possibility of a mighty trumpet that would amplify the voice of a commander and carry orders with the speed of sound to every corner of a battlefield, but no practical means of accomplishing so unheard-of a thing ever seemed likely to be discovered. Or perhaps something could be done with fireworks, which had already been used for signaling. It had been noticed that gunpowders sometimes unaccountably burned with different colors. If he lived and the king lived, he would find out why and suggest colors as signals. Louis, always interested in speed and new things, would listen.

Shortly a runner, not Jean, came up for orders. But Henri did not give the command he had previously decided upon. Something unprecedented was happening down in the circle where the Duke of Burgundy and the Prince of Foix were fighting single style: the prince suddenly had an ally; he was no longer fighting alone. Young Jean LeClercq had broken all the rules and rushed in to aid the old paladin.

"Thank God he can use a sword," Henri prayed. But he knew Jean's action would have instant and violent consequences, and so the order he gave the runner now brought the Italian reserves into battle on the run.

The weary prince had just commended his soul to his Maker; he could hardly lift his arm; the duke was already glancing out of the corner of his eye for his next victim.

"Get away from my funeral!" Foix gasped. "Begone, boy, whoever you are!"

Jean saved his breath and did not answer.

Duke Charles, yelling "Unfair! French puppy, French brat! Unknightly like your king!" saw the blue haze of Jean's blade form a protective wall around his prey and could not get through it. But neither could Jean get through the duke's black armor, which was extraordinarily well tempered and thick, its weight being no burden for a man of the duke's strength.

Since Jean had first broken the rules, everyone now broke them. The circle collapsed and filled; French and Burgundians alike joined the fight. For some minutes all was confusion; and Henri, heartsick, could not see what was happening.

He did two well considered things. He ordered a volley of grenades that broke over the heads of the main body of Burgundians, causing terror, confusion, and death. He ordered another at extreme elevation: these burst beyond the battlefield. Their target was not human. It was the area just beyond lethal distance of the hundreds of riderless horses. The animals, heavily shod and armed with spiked steel plates, reared up and stampeded into the rear of the Burgundian host, inflicting many casualties and adding immeasurably to the confusion in their dumb panic.

Then the Italians, shouting and slashing with poisoned weapons, raced into the melee, and over the yelling of human beings, the screaming of stampeding horses and the roar of artillery no one could hear the steady, methodical whistling of Savoyard crossbow bolts save those whose bodies stopped their flight, and the hundreds who heard them thud into their flesh never heard another sound.

Viewed from the hill, certain inescapable tactical facts impressed themselves on Henri's mind. His son, having lost contact with Duke Charles, was slowly helping the Prince of Foix, who seemed to be wounded, back through the melee to the safety of the rear. One leader was out of action. The king, having restored order where the line was weakest, seemed content to hold. And, ominously, the Burgundians, though badly disorganized, still outnumbered the royal army two to one.

These facts fused into a decision. Montlhéry was not yet a disaster, but the mathematics of the situation were against him. To prolong the battle would lose it, and to lose it would lose Louis his crown. Henri, like the king, had been tutored by Friar Jean, whose spirit seemed very close at that moment, as it always did when gunpowder began to burn, a smell Friar Jean had hated. Through his mind flashed a fragment of the Scriptures. It had been beautiful as Friar Jean had recited it; Henri now remembered only what was applicable to the battle: There is a time to kill and a time to heal.

This was the time to stop the killing, to heal the king's cause and to salvage what could be salvaged. It was time to break off the battle, if that most difficult of all military maneuvers could be managed. It was always easier to start a battle than to stop one. To extricate one's fighting men from hand-to-hand conflict was like trying to separate a tangled mass of string from another tangled mass of string. But it could be done if one kept one's head, especially with well disciplined troops like the king's. Every runner who dashed out from the hill now carried an order, first to one section of the field, then to another, to break off the engagement and fall back. Only the stubborn Swiss required a second order: they had to be assured that their pay would not be stopped. That assurance was given and presently, grinning, they too fell back. Wonders would never cease in the service of the unpredictable French king. This time they would be paid for *not* dying.

Between the milling Burgundian mass and the better ordered ranks of the royal forces, a belt of neutral ground took shape and slowly widened. The Burgundians set up a mighty shout of victory; hundreds of steel gloves were hurled contemptuously after the unperturbed French, thousands of curses and taunting cries. A few Burgundian hotheads charged across the widening neutral area in pursuit, and were shot dead in their saddles by Louis's crossbowmen, who could aim very well in a measured retreat. After that, the Burgundians contented themselves with beating their victory drums, yelling their victory yells, and rounding up their horses and their dead. They made no further attempt to follow the French. Henri, who had feared he might have to spike his guns, was able to salvage them too.

"It might have been worse," he said to Bernard d'Armagnac. "We mangled them. There will be another time."

In the noise and shouting he had not heard the fleshy thud of a crossbow bolt close beside him. Bernard d'Armagnac answered him from the ground. "Will there? Will there be another time? For you. For Louis. For Jean. But not for me. Take me to the king. Quickly."

"Great God!"

"Quickly, Henri, quickly. I will live till you get me to Louis. I must."

The bolt had buried itself deep, and Henri could see from the blood in the wound, spending itself in time with the beating of the heart, that an artery had been cut. There was nothing to be done in such cases when men were as old as Armagnac. They died of shock at once if a surgeon applied the iron remedy, the red-hot cautery, the only recourse in arterial bleeding. He gathered him up like a child and, mounting, rode down the hill. The wing of the royal army that had been anchored on the hill now fell back, leaving the field of Montlhéry to the Burgundians and the pen of Philippe de Comines; but not even that master of the double-faced word could chronicle the battle as an unqualified victory for Duke Charles. Altogether too many Burgundians had been killed.

In a tent in the rear that night, when a battle surgeon had done his futile best, when the armies had separated, and while Burgundian bugles still trumpeted their victory over the field of Montlhéry, Bernard d'Armagnac called the king to his side and asked that the others be sent beyond earshot. "Only for a moment," he said feebly. "I shall not trouble you long. There is something a king should know," and then, with the unconnected leap from subject to subject such as infants, the very old, and the dying are prone to make, he said, "To purge myself of the ancient dishonor is like lifting a yoke, healing a pain. I have lived too long with shame."

Louis sent away the Prince of Foix, Henri LeClercq, and Jean. "We are alone now," he said, for Armagnac's eyes were closed. "Good tutor, good friend, good vassal, what have you to tell me?"

"Will you right an old wrong for me, Louis?"

Too readily the king answered Yes.

"Do you swear it?"

Too readily the king swore.

Often thereafter he mused in fancy how the pen of Philippe de Comines might have set the stamp of genius on Bernard d'Armagnac's last words: some long inspired speech, some peaceful farewell, perhaps a gentle benediction on the king. But the old man, like most men, expired as he had been born, in blood and sweat and pain and incoherent gasps.

And yet, closing the rheumy eyes, wiping the wound-black blood from the lips that had croaked their last feeble message, disposing the death-twisted limbs into an attitude of repose, Louis felt the monumental dignity of a long life nobly lived and bravely ended.

Before he died Bernard d'Armagnac had rid himself of the burden of silence he had borne so long alone. From the labored words, interspersed with periods of speechlessness, the king had been able to grasp the essential: The prince, General LeClercq, and young Jean were grandfather, father and son. "Tell Foix who saved him, Louis!"

The dynastic implications were enormous, threatening. The king at once regretted his promise.

Chapter Forty

Louis never willingly broke an oath, particularly an oath sworn to a dying man, when angels cluster thickly around, sharp-eared and ready to fly back to heaven and record forever the breach of faith. He was fully aware of what Bernard d'Armagnac had asked him to do and why he had asked it. Pround of Henri LeClercq's career, proud of young Jean's battle courage, the old man in his last moments was asking recognition for the best representatives of the House of Armagnac. One word from the Prince of Foix, who would certainly remember Isabelle of Armagnac, and Henri would be legitimate, recognized and honored because he united in his person two of the most famous bloodstreams of Europe; and Jean, already legitimate, could bear on his coat the arms of Foix, Armagnac, and those of his mother, Comminges. A not inconsiderable lord. Perhaps too considerable.

Probably the grateful, aging prince would be in a mood to acknowledge the Armagnac union, now so old as to have lost much of its adulterous sting in the eyes of the princess his wife, since wives grew statesman-like and learned a great deal about their husbands over the years. If Her Highness, at this late date, should object, the prince would only have to say: "My dear, who is the mother of your good brother Ferdinand, whom your father the king (so aptly called The Magnanimous) has recently legitimized? Not *your* mother." And his wife would have had to concede that her brother was her father's bastard.

Far too considerable a lord, Louis decided, for there was more. The Prince of Foix was heir-designate to the double crown of Aragon and Navarre. He might never live to inherit it, nor might his single legitimate son. But Henri LeClercq was alive, and Jean had demonstrated an ability to survive battles and act nobly. No one with a decent respect for the permanence of his House would throw away bastards who showed such promising qualities. It would require no great twist of fate to elevate General LeClercq to a throne, and after him Jean. King Jean of Aragon and Navarre! Even the name was traditional and right.

And King Jean would possess legitimate claim to the vast territories of Foix, Armagnac, and Comminges, all on the French side of the Pyrenees. In his mind's eye Louis saw the map of France fall to pieces. There was trouble aplenty in the north: the Somme gone, a humiliating peace now necessary with Burgundy. Must he also make trouble for himself in the south, strip France of the Pyrenees, and call into being a rival king? Was that not the very policy of his greatest enemy, a multiplicity of French kings? All for an idle oath made to a dead man, when to avoid it all he need do was keep silent? No, no, there was only one king, there must be but one king, King Louis XI. They called him a spider. So be it. No spider was ever yet caught in his own web.

He would keep his word to Bernard to the letter. To the letter, but no more. He would make a point of saying the words, "My lord of Foix, Jean LeClercq saved you." Let the big-eared spying angels carry *that* up to heaven and inquire of Bernard d'Armagnac if the King of France had forsworn himself.

Louis smiled. There was little to smile at these days, but Louis always smiled when he outwitted men. When he felt he had outwitted the angels, the smile was a little broader.

With the passion that first had driven him to seek glory in war, when he was very young, then snared him into too many reforms, too fast, on his first accession to the throne, he now threw himself into a fascinating art that was new to a world in which national states were forming: diplomacy. "National honor will be different from personal honor," he said. "Nothing but success is true honor for a state." By all his saints he swore an irrevocable oath: to win back by guile everything the hazard of battle and overwhelming odds had cost him at Montlhéry, regardless of how long it might take, regardless of peril to his own soul. "For I do not think," he would say to himself, "that I am composed of the stuff that saints are made of." Louis of Valois, the King of France, might burn, one lonely individual soul; but the bargain seemed not too bad if sixteen million Frenchmen should prosper as a result.

He never displayed such outward affability as during the first few weeks that followed Montlhéry, nor put down so firmly the natural impulses of his heart: Charlotte was ordered, not very gently, to stay in Savoy till the air of France should clear. It was now full of storms.

Duke Charles, having raged but having reflected, counted his dead and proposed a peace, though a stern one. Above all he remained furious at the Burgundian loss of the Somme, taken as it were like a sweetmeat from a child in his father's great age and decrepitude. He demanded return of the Somme. On October 5th, in a quick turnabout, Louis pleasantly agreed to return it. Philippe de Comines, sealing the treaty, eyed with suspicion the smiling king.

On October 29th Louis signed another treaty, this one with the rebel French princes who had fought against him, some in the Burgundian army, some in the Breton army, which had finally arrived, only to discover, much to the amazement of the king's brother, that the war was over and peace was being arranged. "If Burgundy has made peace," said the Duc de Berri, causing even his mistress, a plumpish woman, to smile, "then I suppose I too am victorious and ought to make peace. Is that not so, Louis? You always know what to do in these technical matters. As for me," he said, smoothing the wrinkles out of his cloth-of-silver doublet, "I do not understand them, being at my best on the battlefield, like my cousin Burgundy."

"Dear brother," the king replied, "Duke Charles wants peace and so do I. In that at least we agree. If you too agree, why then we are all agreed and the war is over and everything is all right."

"That is an interesting simplification," Philippe de Comines commented.

"What do I get out of this?" the Duc de Berri asked. "How I have ridden and sweated in my armor for the League!" He looked at Duke Charles. "Cousin Charles, what do I get?"

Duke Charles bit his lip in contempt and looked to Philippe de Comines, who answered smoothly: "My master is sovereign of a far-flung state, composed of many tongues and many peoples, some of whom would be restive under a purely French lord like yourself. There can be no transfer of Burgundian lands. Moreover, my master, though he richly deserves a regal crown, regrettably does not technically possess the title of king. Therefore, my lord duke, since your brother is an anointed king, fountainhead of unquestioned titles and lord of many rich fiefs, it would seem that *he* is the one to reward you—for your incalculable services to the League." With an unmistakable flutter of an eyebrow, Comines added the last phrase, glancing slyly at Louis.

The Duc de Berri was a little confused and looked instinctively to his elder brother for an explanation.

"He means," Louis said, "that I have more to give than he. Even now."

"And will you give me something?"

"My dear Charles! To a brother? What brother would not?"

"Good," said the duke. "Oh, good."

Louis gave him Normandy, calling him a doughty warrior, reminding him how another duke of Normandy had conquered England. "Who knows what the future may hold for you!"

Philippe de Comines also wondered, but Charles, Duc de Berri and now Duke of Normandy, was content. Content also was Charles, Duke of Burgundy, for the moment at least.

Louis now set out to appease and win back the other princes of the Lilies who had formed the coalition of the League. One and all, seeing no reward likely to come from Burgundy, they followed the lead of the Duc de Berri and approached the king with outstretched palms like a swarm of beggars, but formidable in their noble birth and present unity. One and all he satisfied their demands, a province to one, a county to another, titles, money, privileges to even the most brazen of the renegades, Nemours, Alençon, Saint-Pol, Châteauneuf, Neuchâtel. And to everyone smiles, smiles, smiles. The sophisticated citizenry of Paris, sneering, called it the Piteous Peace. Thereupon Louis included them too: he lifted the salt tax and the wine tax. Then the citizenry cheered him.

"Now," said Louis grimly to his barber, before whom he did not have to smile, "everyone is satisfied. The ulcerous face of France is scabbing over. What does that mean, Doctor? Well, fellow?"

Olivier le Malvays sighed, "If Your Majesty would only be as patient with the dog who loves you as you are to the dogs who hate you."

"Answer my question."

"Scabbing is usually taken as a sign of healing."

"Only an outward sign. I know from experience. How do wounds really heal?"

"I am not orthodox in my medical views, Your Majesty. I have treated many wounds, especially in backs, and it has been my observation that they heal slowly from the bottom up, more learned doctors to the contrary notwithstanding."

"That is how I will heal France. I am not orthodox either. I want your help."

"A confidential mission? If you would only permit me to serve you! Not even blood royal is proof against my white powder!"

The king snorted contemptuously. "I was thinking more of your friends in Flanders, Olivier, and of how some thousands of écus, properly invested—I am by no means a pauper even now—might set rebellious tongues to wagging against Duke Charles."

"Sire, the ragged rascals among whom I grew up would sell their own mothers for a thousand écus."

"Devil take their poor mothers! I want them to whine about Charles's taxes, grumble about his extravagances, complain of the poverty in their filthy garrets, riot in the streets, break windows, set fires."

"That should not be difficult to arrange," Olivier said, "since the provocation is already in existence. They need only a little money to buy wine, to loosen their tongues and make them feel big and brave and rebellious. I also have friends in France, should Your Majesty desire to institute the same healing measures in the territories of some of your newly reconciled great lords."

The king shook his head. "Burgundy, not France."

Though the scheme was to be slow, and there seemed in it no place for the murderous white powder, Olivier cunningly noticed that the king had not definitely, or at least not angrily, forbidden its use against the Duc de Berri. In Olivier's mind, faithful and dark as a dog's, a fitful gleam began to grow and take shape, then steadily to shine. What more glorious mission could there be than to rid his beloved master of the commander in chief of the League of the Public Weal! He imagined himself no longer a hunchback whom no armor could fit, but a shining knight, tall, straight of spine, a paladin on a self-imposed and secret quest for his king, over and above the call of duty. But he would not speak of it again, lest Louis forbid him and snatch away the dream.

The king settled back to let time and the quarrelsome tempers of his great nobles work out the inevitable decay that in peace always separates allies. Quietly, on the sly, from the bottom up, he would spread disunity It was a time-consuming, covert thing that would come to fruition only after long months of management.

Meanwhile one deed of retribution was grim and swift. Count Charles of Melun found a rope around his neck, and his chin, weak as it was, proved big enough to keep a noose from slipping. The execution was immensely popular, especially among the soldiers he had deserted. Crippled footmen his horse had trodden down hobbled to the gibbet, shaking their fists at him while he dangled, pointing to their crooked limbs and disfigured faces. With difficulty they were prevented from spitting on the corpse when the hangman cut it down.

As always when a great lord was executed for treason, his titles and estates reverted to the crown. In the case of Charles of Melun, these comprised the City of Melun and the surrounding County of Montfort. In accordance with ancient, unquestioned feudal law, Louis confiscated them. But he did not keep them long. He never hoarded anything for the mere joy of possession, which would have struck him as miserly. Pasque Dieu, let things be put to use! He put the dead lord's patrimony to use at once.

Henri LeClercq was suddenly summoned to court shortly after the king's return to Paris. The herald found him in the powder room of the arsenal, dressed in a leather apron, grimy, smoke-smudged. Gingerly he was mixing a measure of powder with a smaller measure of what looked like green dust. An assistant stood by with a smoldering, shielded slow match. The air was sharp with the irritating smell of brimstone.

"Have I the honor of addressing the Chevalier de LeClercq, General of the Artillery of His Most Christian Majesty of France?"

"You have," Henri smiled. He could understand the herald's hesitation. "You'd better stand back, young man."

"He's going to set off some new explosives," the assistant whispered with a malicious air of mystery that technical initiates always employ to scare innocent laymen. "It'll be *green*, and you know what *that* means!" He glanced upward and signed himself with his slow match, which traced in the air a smoky momentary cross.

It sounded ominous, perhaps fatal. "Saints preserve us!" the herald muttered.

"Quiet, you two!"

"I was commanded to deliver my summons at once," the herald said nervously. "The matter is urgent."

"So is this," Henri said. He poured the mixture in a long thin line on the stone workbench, taking great pains that there should be no gaps in the train, sweeping up with his hand some stray grains and wiping his hand in his hair. This habit of his was largely responsible for the odor of gunpowder that the Prince of Foix had noticed always hung over him. "Now give me the match," he ordered.

The assistant, who had thought he might be asked to light the untried

279

mixture, was glad to give up the fire, and retired instantly to the door. Henri touched the match to the train of powder; a blinding, sputtering flame shot up and raced from one end to the other, consuming it all.

There was too much smoke and it burned too fast. But it did not explode and it was green, pure brilliant green! "Beautiful, beautiful!" Henri murmured. *That* would be a signal soldiers could see and be trained to obey. It was the first step in what he promised himself would be a new means of command in battle. He wished he had thought of it before Montlhéry.

The room was small and he had to leave it for fear the dense fumes would be poison. The secret of the green was a rust that one scraped from weathered copper such as was constantly being removed from leaking church roofs. The king would be glad it could be salvaged.

The herald and the assistant were already outside. "Well now, young man?"

The herald spoke his summons more rapidly and less officiously than usual, glancing apprehensively around the frightening, smoky arsenal. General LeClercq was commanded, he said, to present himself before the king's majesty that very night. "In full court dress," he added emphatically.

Henri, full of the triumph of his successful experiment, grinned. "Don't worry, lad, I know how to wear a tabard too," and waved him away with his leather apron. "Off with you, before I call my imps and throw you into a pot of tempering oil!"

Tempering oil meant nothing to the herald, but boiling to death was a common method of execution, and General LeClercq, in charge of this dark, infernal region where green fires could be conjured out of dust, was probably quite capable of tossing a young herald into one of his big caldrons just for the fun of it.

Scampering away, the herald flung after him, "No hat, no sword, no belt, no spurs!"

"No?" Henri said. What had he done? Why was he to be punished? Louis had long permitted him to wear a hat at court, though only old friends and great lords might appear uncovered in the presence of the king. Henri was not a great lord, but he was the king's oldest friend. A sword was a common article of dress, and as for spurs, Henri had been entitled to wear them even since Louis had made him a chevalier in the Dauphiny.

Disappearing, the herald shouted something else. Henri, whose mind had been busy with his thoughts, had to ask the assistant, "What was that last he said?"

"He said to bring Her Ladyship and Sir Jean!" There was a note of awe in the assistant's voice.

"Her Ladyship? *Sir* Jean?"

"That's what he said."

"Louis always bewilders me," Henri sighed. But there was a broad smile now on his grimy face, and he no longer feared that he was going to be punished. "Whatever he does is bound to be a surprise, because he always stuns you before he reveals his intentions." If Olivier le Malvays had been Henri's adviser instead of the king's, he might have observed that that too is a characteristic of spiders.

Louis's court was never as spectacular as Burgundy's. By the same token it was never as extravagant, especially now when secret royal funds were seeping into enemy territories, fomenting discontent, fanning hidden sparks of rebellion that ultimately, he knew, would flame up into civil war. Like Saint-Pol's ring and Saint-Pol's pardon, he viewed these funds as investments, not bribes. So were all his pardons and recent grants—investments that one day would repay themselves. But his court was not shabby either, for he knew the publicity value of the trappings of power.

Thus, when Henri advanced to the throne that night, he found himself in a brilliant assembly of lords and ladies in orders and ermine, chains of office and coronets, and Louis on the throne. The Duc de Berri held the king's scepter for him, a signal honor which the Prince of Foix considered ill bestowed on one who so recently captained the League of the Public Weal; but the king's methods were always his own. It seemed to Foix that the Duc de Berri looked hungrily at the scepter, "like a gawky peasant at a soup bone!" he muttered to himself.

Jean and Madame LeClercq stood close to the prince, whose arm was out of its sling, though Olivier, who tended him, had warned that it was too soon. "I've use for my sword arm tonight," the tough old gallant retorted.

It was not yet time for him to use it, however. Everyone was looking toward the throne, and at General LeClercq, spurless, hatless, swordless, who was walking down the narrow red carpet that led to the dais on which it stood.

"Kneel," Louis said to him.

Henri knelt.

"*Mon général,* you forgot your hat. Not many privileged to wear one would have forgotten."

"But Monseigneur—" The old dauphinal title had slipped out again.

"Henri, Henri," the king laughed in a low tone, "you cannot get used to my Most Christian Majesty, can you! Confidentially, I cannot either. How did the green fire go?"

"Not perfect, but green."

"So I hear."

Henri was not surprised that Louis already knew the result of his experiment. "The herald specifically commanded me not to wear a hat, Your Majesty."

"Your lack of headgear we shall remedy at once." Raising his voice so that the others could hear, the king spoke in bitter tones of the cowardice of Charles of Melun, and referred sharply to the justice of the execution that had followed. He knew his words would be repeated everywhere; he chose them for the effect they would have on all Frenchmen, great and small. Swift death for the man who had all but lost the battle of Montlhéry; honor and recompense equally swift for the man who had salvaged it. Such was and would always be the king's justice.

It was a short speech with the virtue of simplicity. No one could misinterpret it; all could take heart from its promise and warning from its threat.

Then the king made a motion with his finger to a herald who stood a little to the side of the throne—not directly behind it. Olivier le Malvays always stood there, protecting the king's back. The herald advanced and knelt, lifting a pillow on which rested the coronet of a count. The king took it in his hands and placed it on Henri's head.

Without removing his fingers from the coronet, as if some mysterious power were flowing from his touch, and indeed tradition held that it did, Louis solemnly pronounced, "The blood of him who last wore this has been judged and declared corrupt and attaint, and on such corruption and attainder the County and Countship of Montfort have escheated, returned, and do now lie in the Crown, as is lawful and in accordance with custom." How odd the stately feudal phrases sounded on Louis's modern tongue, Henri thought; yet no more odd than his mad charge down the hill at Montlhéry. What a mixture of the past and the future King Louis XI was!

While he spoke these words the king let his eye linger on Nemours, Alençon, Saint-Pol, and some of the other recent rebel lords. Then he proceeded, just as gravely but more amiably, "Now of our right and desire and free good will we do grant the County of Montfort, together with all its revenues and privileges, with this coronet, symbol of its sovereignty, to Henri LeClercq and the heirs of his body, to have and to hold in fief of the Crown of France, forever." The Duc de Berri handed Louis his scepter; Louis touched Henri's forehead with it.

Henri had been prepared for something for Jean, but not a gold coronet to circle his own temples. It seemed to burn like one of his fires in the arsenal. He found himself wondering, as one does in moments of great, unexpected events, about something entirely remote from his immediate surroundings: he wondered if a gold fire could be invented. Nonsense. Gold was yellow, and so was most fire, the commonest color of all.

The king had to nudge him. "Get up, Henri. Don't just kneel there. You forgot your sword and spurs too. How absent-minded of you, my lord count. It would seem that I shall have to repair that lack also. Fortunately, I am prepared."

Rather dizzily Henri rose to his feet. A herald buckled on them a pair of gold court spurs. The king then girt him with one of the most spectacular bejeweled swords he had ever seen. "You can keep the spurs, but you'll have to give this right back after the ceremony," Louis whispered.

"It's state property, and I may have to raise a little money on it for a special purpose."

The spurs and the sword of state were the insignia of the Grand Master of France; they signified the Grand Master's duty to protect the kingdom. "This time I've got a Grand Master with a chin, and his name isn't Charles, thank God!"

Henri heard his name, his new honors, and titles, and also his new responsibilities being proclaimed by a herald who stood beside the throne. He saw tears in the eyes of Madame LeClercq—nay, in the eyes of Madame la Comtesse!—and glowing pride on the face of his son.

"Kneel again and renew your oaths to me," Louis sighed wearily. "Pasque Dieu! Oaths of the faithful I do not need, and oaths of the false are useless wind, puffs of nothingness." Henri knelt, placed his hands in the king's, and swore.

"Now go and glitter among your peers. I promised to make your blood noble, didn't I?"

"I am speechless, Your Majesty, but grateful, believe me. Is this what the herald meant when 'Sir Jean' slipped out of him?" For now, of course, Henri LeClercq, the Count of Montfort, could knight anyone he pleased.

"My faithful friend, it will require no nepotism to knight your son, though I like it in you that you thought of him first. No, the Prince of Foix is ahead of you there. I said to him only this afternoon, 'Jean LeClercq saved you,' and he said to me, 'By God, Sire, what do you think I threw away my sling for?' "

"Jean deserves it," Henri said.

"He certainly does," said the king. "He certainly does. Henri, so far this has been pleasant. My heart is not in what I shall do next."

Nor was it. But his mind was. He bestowed another coronet and touched another forehead. The circlet of sovereignty was that of a duke, heavier and more ornate than a count's. The brow his scepter touched was the low, dull-witted brow of his brother Charles.

It was the king's pleasure, the herald proclaimed, to give his good brother, for the love he bore him and for his brother's loyalty to the Crown, the Duchy of Guienne.

There was a good deal of astonished smiling and whispering as the herald read the long list of titles, cities, and revenues which now fell to Duke Charles. Guienne was ten times as big and rich as Normandy. One of the great lords said audibly, "He's beggaring himself!" All of them felt elated that they had won back their privileges, but some of them experienced unwonted twinges in their consciences for their forsworn oaths. Others remembered that Charles of Burgundy had given them nothing. Most of them, as the herald droned on through the long, long list, felt heavy in their hearts: if the king, the fountainhead of honor, beggared himself, the fountainhead went dry; then what would become of their own honor, traditionally inseparable from his? Would they soon be fighting one another to preserve the integrity of their own lands? Perhaps there was something to be said for a strong central authority after all. Only that foreign Burgundian had said he wanted six French kings.

Louis, whose mind but not whose heart was involved, smiled down at them slyly from the throne. In the shuffling and murmuring while the herald was reading the scroll, few had heard and even fewer had attached any importance to a momentous detail: in exchange for Guienne, Charles had agreed to return Normandy to the crown.

Normandy had a common frontier with Burgundy; Guienne lay far to the south. By recapturing Normandy, Louis had successfully driven a wedge between the territories of his two greatest enemies. He had lopped off the western horn of the crescent that threatened to flank the northern provinces of France. The map looked a little better now.

Later that night, in the royal chapel, before the misty eyes of his mother and the stern proud face of his father, Jean LeClercq knelt before the Prince of Foix, who smote him on the shoulder with the flat of his sword, a rougher blow than future generations would see, and bade him rise Sir Jean, a belted knight. It was not a bad start in the world for the son of a bastard, Henri thought, not bad at all.

"I mean to make this lad my equerry," the prince pronounced as if it were a matter already settled, and looked around to receive the thanks that should come from an offer of such honorable employment. "He's got an arm like my own of years ago, a great comfort to discover these days. He shall be my alter ego—by God, he even looks like me! Your pardon, Madame la Comtesse." She was blushing angrily, and Henri's face was positively purple.

Louis said smoothly, "It would be a great wonder if courage did not put a stamp of purely fortuitous similarity on the features of all who possess it," and quickly changed the subject. The family resemblance was far too strong to let conversation dwell upon. He had divided his enemies; now he must divide his friends. "I have plans for both you and Sir Jean, my lord of Foix, and for the time being at least your duties lie in different directions. Someone must escort the queen and the princesses back from Savoy." He looked significantly at Jean.

"Nay," grumbled the prince, "that is more than I can offer. I am happy for you, lad."

"And someone trustworthy must represent me in the Languedoc. Who but the great prince who already holds the hearts of those distant provinces? You should start south at once, I think, if your arm permits."

"The king's representative?"

"Plenipotentiary. Watch for restiveness in Cerdagne and Roussillon. Do not worry about Lectoure; I am starving an old traitor there. Where you touch on Guienne, do not bother about my brother; let him run wild. He will show less interest in Burgundy. Be good to my crippled silkworkers, and do not treat my French Jews like your Aragonese Jews. England has not prospered since she drove them out."

"Your Majesty, I thank you, and I will know how to handle the south."

"Henri will want to go to Melun for a few days and let them see their new count and swear him homage. It's a good plan to wash your hands afterward, Henri—lice, the itch. Pasque Dieu, you never know what they've got! Then I shall want you back in the arsenal."

It had been an exhausting day. He nodded to them one by one. He had smiled so much his cheeks ached. "Madame la Comtesse, Messire le Comte, Your Highness of Foix, Sir Jean—good friends, good night." He turned on his heel while they made their several reverences and left them abruptly.

His head ached from the heavy air and the smoky illumination of the throne room. He was dead tired; but he looked forward to a night of insomnia more acute than was usual even for him. In spite of the blazing torches and candles and the animal heat of the bodies of scores of men and women who had crowded the hall, Louis had felt cold.

He found Olivier le Malvays industriously plying a large warming pan between the sheets of his bed.

"Why are you doing that, Olivier?"

"Your Majesty, I consider it a healthful measure. It smooths the sheets where the laundresses leave wrinkles. It kills bugs. The fumes of the charcoal purify the air."

"It does everything but warm the bed, eh?"

"Nay, it does that too. I thought it was a little chilly there in the hall."

"You know very well it was sweaty hot."

The barber, who had seen him shiver slightly, did not answer but carefully tucked in the coverlet to keep in the warmth and put the warming pan under the bed. The king discovered that his nightclothes and nightcap had also been warmed. He did not dimiss the barber immediately after he retired.

"Build up the fire, Olivier, and sit and talk to me."

"Yes, yes, Your Majesty!" It was unusual for him to be invited to sit. In a moment the fire was roaring. It seemed to Louis that the logs had been specially chosen for their extra dryness and richness in pitch.

"Olivier, sometimes you frighten me. I think you read my mind. I confess I did feel a sort of chill in the throne room in spite of the fact that I know it was uncomfortably warm. Probably I am about to come down with a cold."

The barber opened his mouth to answer, but Louis did not give him the opportunity. "Olivier, what is the best way to make a sword invisible?"

"If Your Majesty is posing a philosophic riddle, I should answer, Let a coward wear it."

"I am never philosophic. This is an intensely practical matter."

285

"Then let the man who habitually wears it continue to wear it. It is part of him. Some people no longer stare at my hump."

"Nobody really wears this sword. It is all jewels and ornate uselessness. Probably it wouldn't even slice butter."

"The sword of the Grand Master?"

The king nodded. "My revenues will shrink woefully by what I did tonight, but I cannot entirely eliminate all my expenses, especially my little investments in Burgundy. I shall have to pledge the sword and many other state jewels."

"It should not be necessary to render the sword invisible for that. Cannot a paste replica be made? I know several successful jewelers who deal in nothing else—"

"Pasque Dieu, so did my father. Every king does. Excellent imitations of all the state jewels exist. That is not the problem. They must actually be concealed. I am not going to pledge them in France. That would be known and cause comment. I am sending them out of the country to the Bank of San Giorgio in Genoa. Thank God my Italian relations are cordial. I shall also get better terms there."

Olivier suggested: "A crutch! The sword would fit admirably into a crutch. How swiftly I should hobble to Genoa if Your Majesty would trust me with this mission! How convincing I should look with a crutch!"

The king hesitated. "No, not you, Olivier. I want to keep you by me. My chill may get worse."

Olivier said very slowly, measuring every word, conscious of the danger in which he was placing himself but willing to risk it, "Is it a chill, my master, that forewarns you of—your sickness?"

Louis sat bolt upright, furious. "Sickness? Sickness? You creature! You ape! What sickness? I am never sick! I have never been sick! What sickness? Well? Well? Well? Find your tongue! Who tore it out? Who spoiled me the pleasure of tearing it out?"

Olivier fell to his knees and buried his weeping face in the bedclothes. "Tear it out, Master! I will not name the sickness. But I have treated you for it in secret for a long time now."

"Treated me? How? How have you treated me?"

Olivier raised his tortured face; his chin trembled; his tear-wet beard clung to the ugly excrescence under it, accentuating its size and repulsiveness. "The bitterness in your wine at times, when I blamed the cellarer, was ferret gall. The silver cup I gave you and you graciously deigned to accept from me, it is not silver but antimonium, an alchemist's metal—"

"That alchemist is doomed."

"Nay, he suspects nothing. I stole it. The antimonium goblet imparts purgative soothing properties even to pure water, far more to wine. Often when your face felt taut under my razor, I treated you by these means without your knowing. I could have done more if you had confided in me. I did the best I could."

"So you knew all the time!" Louis murmured. "You knew all the time."

"Yes, I knew."

"The others who knew are both dead."

"I am not afraid. I expect death."

"No, no, you do not understand. They were my confessor and—my dauphiness. I loved them." He was silent for a moment, remembering.

Olivier ventured, "I am forgiven?"

"Forgiven! Pasque Dieu, you are treasured! A doctor who can make such a diagnosis when the patient consistently, laboriously interminably conceals his symptoms? Olivier, I have not done you justice. How did you first suspect? I have not had an attack for years. The scar in my hair? It was the scar, of course."

"Yes, Your Majesty."

"Some day," Louis said gruffly, though he felt far more at ease now that he was not alone with his infirmity, "some day the craft of barbering and doctoring will have to be separated. There is altogether too much overlapping of jurisdiction. Nobody has any privacy as things are now."

"Perhaps that will happen some day, Your Majesty, though it is hard to see how a mere surgeon could make a living without the additional income that comes from pulling teeth and trimming hair."

"I suppose that's true," Louis said. "You know, Olivier, you could have poisoned me with your secret medications."

"A hundred times. But I did not."

"I think I shall have a good night's sleep after all," the king said yawning. "Olivier, you rascal, did you give me some kindly drug on the sly?"

"Nothing, I swear."

"Nay, I believe you, and also I remember that I drank nothing. Oh, but it is good, good to feel at peace again!"

Smiling, the barber watched him fall asleep, and tiptoed out of the room. But before he went he knelt down and silently pulled the warming pan from under the bed. It had continued to burn and send up its soothing heat, and also its odorless, sleep-inducing fumes. He patted it affectionately. One could do murder with a well charged warming pan. One could also give a peaceful night's rest to a beloved master who had worked very hard that day.

Chapter Forty-one

The next thirty months proved to be a period that Louis positively enjoyed. On the surface it was the period of the Piteous Peace, and European sovereigns, as so often in the past, gave up the French king for lost. He has thrown away everything, they said. But underneath, a continuing battle of wits went on more fierce than the battle of Montlhéry. This was the sort of battle that Louis preferred, because it was the kind he always won.

To understand order is also to understand disorder. The king who worked all his life to regularize everything in France knew exactly how to disrupt everything in Burgundy. He now proved himself a master of chaos.

Not for nothing had he pledged the crown jewels. They had been secreted in a special wagon of horse fodder that followed the considerable train of soldiers to Savoy to escort the queen and the princesses back to France. But the royal family did not return at once, for on reaching Chambéry Sir Jean opened sealed orders and discovered what the wagon contained and went on to Genoa with it.

The Bank of San Giorgio, in return for all the jewels, gave him merely a slip of paper to deliver to the king. Jean's knightly education had not included the fiscal niceties of letters of credit. He was ready to challenge the governor of the bank to single combat: A scrap of paper for a bushel of priceless jewelry? What did they take him for! The venerable Italian, over a period of some hours, explained that the Bank of San Giorgio had beeen issuing them since the year 1148, and during a period of three centuries had never defaulted. "It is like taking a solemn oath and remaining faithful to it, Sir Jean."

"Nay, that I can understand. Why didn't you say so at first?"

"Commercial integrity is always a bit difficult to explain to young chevaliers," the governor smiled. "But your king will understand."

"I shall set a strong guard around this," Sir Jean said, handling the paper with new respect.

"That will not be necessary. No one can cash it but the king. It is valueless to anyone else."

"This is like magic!" Jean said.

"It is magic, young man: the magic of credit."

Jean wished that his mission had been confined to protecting the queen. That was something a knight knew by instinct. The soft air of Italy was full of strange subtleties; he would welcome the simpler, more invigorating climate of France. In this, though he was a king's man, he was at one with the old-fashioned rebel lords, and in this, perhaps, the blood of his unknown grandsire was speaking. He wondered why the king had chosen him to go to Italy; he had rather welcomed the invitation to become equerry to the Prince of Foix, to whom he felt strangely drawn and whose plight at the battle of Montlhéry had made him break all the rules.

But he did not return immediately to France, nor did the royal family. When he reached Chambéry an order was waiting for him from the king, and it entailed further delay. Owing to the failing health of Duke Lodovico, the king wrote, the queen had decided to stay some months with her father. Sir Jean must remain too. Meanwhile, send back the letter of credit at once! In fact, a herald was waiting to speed it back to Paris over the king's fast royal roads. Jean felt himself managed, kept on the periphery of things, away from the heart. But there was no doubt that his employment was honorable, and though he was vaguely dissatisfied he could find no just reason to complain.

From the heart of the kingdom Louis was managing everything. Management was developing into his dominant trait; no one since the Roman emperors had managed as he did now, just as no one since them had built such roads, which made it all possible. When the roads became so good that even the Italians, the most modern people of the age, sent engineers to study them, he still was not satisfied. Now the French horses were too slow to get the best out of the roads. He sent to the Prince of Foix for better ones, and the prince sent him hundreds of Spanish stallions from the stables of his father-in-law, the King of Aragon, and Louis began breeding horses on a royal scale. These Spanish horses had Arab blood and were powerful as well as fast. Crossed with French strains, they developed a new and magnificent breed. But the king's imagination did not stop at horses; something traveled faster than horses and did not require roads.

Louis had always enjoyed the sport of hawking and knew something about birds. Now he sent to the Bibliothèque du Roy for all the books that dealt with carrier pigeons. He discovered dusty rooms and empty shelves. His father had allowed the venerable royal library to fall into decay, then sold it, actually sold it, with all its inestimable treasures and useful information, to the English in the second year of his reign. "Pasque Dieu, my father! Better to have burned them!" He immediately set out to repair the loss, founded a new library, and put a gentle, studious soul named Laurent Paulmier in charge of it—he could put even gentle, studious souls to practical use. "And get me an *enlumineur*," was his first order. "More people will read if books have pictures in them." Laurent Paulmier discovered Jean Fouquet, who, with a steady pension, developed into a painter that was an ornament to the king's reign, in addition to his work of illuminating exquisite manuscripts in the new library.

From Savoy Duke Lodovico wrote to him: "Your patronage of the arts is much talked of in Italy, and down in the Peninsula men call you a humanist, the greatest compliment they can bestow, and point to the prince who will usher the Renaissance into what they still term 'barbarian Gaul.' Congratulations!"

"Now what is he congratulating me for?" Louis asked in genuine amazement. "All I want is some carrier pigeons. I'll get them, too." Soon he did.

Duke Lodovico added that his health was better, that he had persuaded Charlotte to return to France, and that the king might expect her soon. He sent the good wishes of Amadeo and an affectionate letter from the king's sister, Yolande. "Duke Lodovico thinks he is well," she said, "but for your private ear he continues to fail. I praise you every day to my dear Amadeo and remind him often how the security of Savoy rests on friendship with France and always will when he is duke as well as now. My´ dear Amadeo always agrees with me."

"Faithful sister, faithful Yolande," the king smiled. "She is worth a regiment of soldiers to me." He still hoped for a dauphin, but princesses could be almost as valuable as princes, nay, more valuable than princes like his brother Charles, now posturing and strutting and spending vast sums on his silly mistress in Guienne. "But let him run wild for a while," the king mused. At least he was not intriguing with Burgundy. It was sad to have to separate friends like Foix, Henri, and Jean; but it was a positive pleasure to separate enemies like Charles of Guinne and Charles of Burgundy.

Breeding fast horses, founding libraries, training carrier pigeons, pawning the crown jewels, separating enemies, separating friends, hiring painters, watching for a change of ruler in a neighboring state and assuring himself that the next, like the last, would be friendly—the busy, busy king! No wonder he bewildered everyone with his multifarious activities. Yet through them all, like the red strand at the center of a rope, ran one vital thread, consistent, unchanging, unbroken: the consolidation of power. Nothing was too great or too small to attract his notice if it contributed to the ideal that dominated his life. Some men's genius was holiness, some learning, some science, some war; Louis's was statecraft.

Early in the thirty months that followed Montlhéry, statecraft began to pay. His investments began to bear fruit. On Monday, August 25, 1466, Dinant and Liége in Flanders revolted against Duke Charles. Dinant was small, but Liége was a great city. The terrible duke rode against the smaller place and sacked it like some Oriental despot, till the gutters ran red and slippery with blood. The lesson pacified Liége also.

In the quiet of his palace Louis smiled grimly when he heard the report. "Butchering women and children is hardly the way to win the hearts of your subjects."

By every publicity means at his command, including the theater, of which he disapproved, by strolling entertainers, minstrels, pamphlets, and royal letters of shocked surprise, the king made known his horror of this Burgundian tyranny. How foolish, he said, one was to look to Duke Charles for justice. How darkly such cruelty foreshadowed the future of Burgundy.

Little by little the great French lords came to agree with their master, who had given them so much, and drew further away from the Duke of Burgundy, who had given them nothing. Little by little, also, the French taxes crept back. Soon he was able to redeem the state jewels from the Bank of San Giorgio, which sent him a cordial invitation in accordance with their most up-to-date banking procedure: if ever His Most Christian Majesty should desire another loan, the Honorable Board of Directors, having due regard for the excellence of His Majesty's credit, would be only most anxious—

Who knew? He might.

On another Monday, in the next year, old Duke Philip the Good died. His mind had long been dead, while his body lingered on, but his passing offered Louis an opportunity to fire another secret shot at his enemy. Two couriers galloped out from Paris, one all silver lilies and gold brocade and violet mourning, bearing a scroll of condolence from the king to his good cousin Charles in accordance with feudal protocol. The other left by night in common dress, but he had money in his saddlebags and letters to agents in Liége. Liége rose in revolt again.

Louis began to think that Monday was one of his lucky days. To quell the revolt in Liége, Duke Charles again had to make war on his own subjects.

An unusual opportunity for capitalizing on Charles's action against Liége presented itself; Louis pounced on it; never before had he had a chance to accuse his enemy of warring against the Church. Liége was ruled by a bishop.

Soon every cardinal, bishop, and archbishop in France received a letter from the king denouncing the monstrous impiety of Duke Charles, and Louis was careful to sign it with all his own ecclesiastical titles: Vicar of the Holy Roman Empire, Gonfaloner of the Roman Catholic Church, Most Christian Majesty. Preparing all the manuscripts proved a great chore for the royal chancellery. Louis bade them look into the new invention of printing. In Germany a craftsman was said to be printing books. Why not in France? It would certainly speed up the writing of royal letters. Meanwhile, he drove the scribes, and shortly every French pulpit rang with sermons denouncing Duke Charles's crimes against the established faith of the whole civilized world. Frenchmen great and small listened and had to believe, since the facts were indisputable. Louis merely made them known and reaped the benefit they brought him. The great lords drew closer to the throne, not anxious to consort with an infidel. It was safe now to reimpose a few more taxes.

That same year Lodovico of Savoy died. Louis was genuinely sorry, sinch his death greatly saddened the queen; and even the little princesses, who had known their kindly grandfather, wore their violet mourning dresses with something more than childish unconcern. But the accession of Amadeo to the ducal sovereignty of Savoy immeasurably strengthened France, since one's influence over a brother-in-law was always greater than over a father-in-law.

Thus as the thirty busy months drew to a close, the king could congratulate himself that he had won back all that Montlhéry had cost him, together with peace of mind, for his health was in capable hands. Olivier le Malvays strutted these days, overbearing and insolent in his manner. Everyone found him insufferable except poor little Jeanne with her crooked back, who would take his hand and toddle around the palace with him, because that was how, with infinite patience, he had taught her to walk when no one else could. He also knew how to concoct sweeter candies than the best cooks in the royal kitchens. On Jeanne's account the queen hid her dislike of the barber.

Then, like a quick change of scene in one of those theaters that Louis had at first discountenanced and subsequently put to use, everything changed. The sunny, diplomatic climate went menacingly black. Duke Charles of Burgundy, finding his French lords siding again with their rightful king and mysterious rebellion erupting in his own cities, turned to England. On the 2nd of July, 1468, he married an English princess, Margaret, daughter of the English king. An English invasion fleet soon began to gather in British harbors.

Louis was aghast. His nights were again sleepless, and when, as dawn stole in at the windows, he would finally creep exhausted into his bed, nightmares and visions of another Hundred Years' War tormented him.

All through the summer he tried to dislocate the Anglo-Burgundian alliance, and failed. He requested, in terms that amounted almost to pleading, a personal meeting with Duke Charles so that they might talk together. Man to man, cousin to cousin, sovereign to sovereign, nay, even enemy to enemy, the duke had only to name the level on which he would agree to confer and Louis would meet him on that level. Nothing, nothing would be gained for either of them by calling in the hated English.

Duke Charles agreed to meet the king at Péronne on October 8th.

The king, whose mind was very full, said idly to Olivier, "That date seems to have a familiar ring."

"It is the date on which Your Majesty acquired the Somme. Every year I remind you that it is your lucky day."

"So it is," said the king, brightening. "A propitious day. An infallible day. And the same lucky place!"

All had gone so well with the king for so long that Olivier answered: "Your Majesty, I think so too. You are unconquerable now."

Chapter Forty-two

Duke Charles took keen delight in watching his enemy squirm and had purposely set the date of the meeting several weeks in advance so as not to appear in a hurry to parley. The longer he delayed, the greater Louis's concessions would be. Moreover, the weather of October was usually inclement, and Louis's journey would thereby be made as uncomfortable as possible. And he would have a little more time to convince the English that an invasion of France was feasible.

Louis made use of this period as only he could make use of time, forgetting no detail that would contribute to the success of his mission. First, of course, he called off his *agents provocateurs* in Flanders, bidding them lie low and bide their time. Instead of paying them to incite riots, he paid them to be quiet.

Next he laid down explicit orders for mustering and equipping a large army to escort him to the very outskirts of Péronne. He said to Henri, "Let Burgundy actually see with his eyes the might of France, for if I cannot reason with him I can threaten." The army that would compose his escort would be formidable—foot soldiers, cavalry, artillery, ready for instant battle at a signal from one of the new flares. He planned to dispose his forces at deceptively isolated intervals. "But let their orders be understood in advance, and let them be ready to overwhelm Péronne in a matter of minutes."

Henri smiled, "We can bottle him up in an hour!"

"Let us hope that will not be necessary."

But he was taking no chances. He paid an extra month's wages to his Swiss guards. "My person may be in some danger. I should not care to take chances with it at a moment which I consider the most critical of my life." Thirty months of conducting successful diplomacy had made him cautious. Often and often he had thought of his folly at Montlhéry, and determined never again to let an old-fashioned feudal impulse tempt him to endanger his life, for if he should be killed, in the absence of a dauphin, his weak-minded brother would succeed to the throne. It took no great exercise of the imagination to foresee how the great lords would triumph, how France would relapse into chaos. Then the English would inevitably come in, with or without the invitation of Burgundy.

In his systematic preparations for the meeting, the king did not forget ecclesiastical prestige. There was a great prelate, Cardinal Balue, a man whose rise in the hierarchy was directly attributable to the king's favor. Cardinal Balue had worked diligently to help bring about an understanding between Duke Charles and the king, and Louis planned to employ him as one of his negotiators. Balue was able, eloquent, and persuasive, and of course he carried with him the enormous dignity and authority of a prince of the Church.

Nor did he neglect to extract from Duke Charles a solemn promise of personal immunity, which the duke sent in writing to Cardinal Balue: "It could hardly be more comprehensive, Your Majesty. Listen to what he says: 'You may come, rest and sojourn in safety, and return in safety at your good pleasure, freely coming and going as often as you please with no obstacle or hindrance put in your way whatsoever; and no harm will be done you by reason of anything that has happened in the past or may happen in the future.' "

293

"I wish he had put it in the form of an oath," Louis muttered.

"Surely Your Majesty does not doubt the duke's word."

"It has always paid me to doubt everything, Your Eminence."

Nor did he forget the great French lords, who were now faithful to the crown. They too would accompany him.

Nor did he forget his doctor, to watch over his health.

He forgot nothing. The cavalcade that set out from Paris for Péronne was made up of all the elements that comprised his strength: feudal nobility, modern artillery, the enormous prestige of the Church, a faithful bodyguard, a fanatically faithful personal physician.

Louis reasoned that the English menace, so serious at the moment, would not necessarily last. Right now the English king was powerful but the War of the Roses continued; King Edward might lose his throne to King Henry in a single ill advised battle. The two rival kings had been fighting for the English crown for some years. If fate should tip the scale against Edward, then Burgundy would lose its ally and France would again be safe from its hereditary enemy. Louis had only to point to his own record of alternating power and weakness to prove to Duke Charles that blind faith should not be put in the stability of thrones. Charles was not stupid, and Philippe de Comines was astute to genius: it should not be impossible to convince them. If worst came to worst there was always the tremendous French army, in full view, to use as a threat. French guns under Péronne's walls would argue more convincingly than British guns far away across the Channel.

This sober estimate of the situation heartened the king, though he did not minimize his difficulties, for Duke Charles was certain to demand large concessions. Louis did not know what they would be but, within reason, he was willing to grant them.

Like everthing else about the meeting, the progress of the French army had been carefully planned for its maximum effect on Duke Charles. There was to be a sudden dash from Paris to the outskirts of Péronne, to demonstrate the mobility of the French forces; then a leisurely advance to the city with the king and the cardinal leading the cavalcade, the royal standard flying, the cardinal's gorgeous gonfalon draping from the crosspiece on its staff, pennons streaming from the spears of the Princes of the Lilies, who would be dressed in their embroidered coats of arms, with plumes on the horse halters, silver trumpets pealing Burgundian fanfares—all the feudal pageantry that Duke Charles loved and respected. The artillery would bring up the rear.

The dash from Paris was expertly maneuvered in warm autumnal weather under a brilliant sun. On the night of the 7th, the army pitched camp three miles from Péronne, to wait for morning and the slow ceremonial march upon the city. The king retired to his tent, soberly satisfied.

During the night a storm burst in from the distant cold Atlantic, swept thunderingly up the valley of the Somme, and precipitated a deluge of early winter rains on all the northern provinces of France. Louis heard hailstones snapping on the canvas of his tent. Cursing the accident of the weather, resolving to order the doctors of his University of Paris to investigate the causes of hailstorms, and smiling grimly at the difficulties of the demands he sometimes made on people, he threw a cloak around him and went outside to determine what damage the storm was causing. He had to see for himself that the gunpowder was put under cover. He had to make sure that the flags were sheathed in their waterproof cases—sometimes the dye ran. He could risk neither a bedraggled appearance nor cannon that might misfire. Too much was at stake.

The cannon were adequately protected; engineers were already slushing them with grease. Tarpaulins were securely lashed on the gunpowder wagons. Henri smiled, "Didn't Your Majesty trust me?"

"My lord of Montfort," the king said severely, "I never trust anybody. Not at a time like this."

He sloshed in the wet from tent to tent of the great lords. Most of them had taken in their flags. Saint-Pol and his squire were a little drunk and had neglected theirs. The king personally threw it into the tent. "Have a care for your standard, my lord of Saint-Pol, lest you lose it." But he tempered his rebuke with a smile, remembering Saint-Pol's Burgundian fiefs and Burgundian influence. One day there would be no more of these split-homaged vassals.

After an hour he returned to his tent. Everything was in fairly good order in spite of the unfortunate turn of the weather. By the suddenness and intensity of the squall, he judged that it would probably pass over by morning and that the advance to Péronne could be accomplished in sunlight.

Olivier le Malvays was waiting for him in his tent, concern on his face, a steaming goblet of liquid in his hand.

"What is that?" Louis demanded.

"Nothing but a little warm wine, Your Majesty."

"That is the antimonium goblet."

The barber pleaded, "It is very cold outside. You are drenched to the skin. Please drink it."

"It will purge me, will it not?"

The barber hesitated, "Slightly, Your Majesty."

Louis thought carefully for several minutes. Finally he said: "I am, of course, wet and somewhat chilled. But so is everyone. So was Henri. So are you; your lips are blue. Under ordinary circumstances I should drink your draught. But tomorrow is an important day. Duke Charles sets great store on elegant behavior. I cannot risk the indignity of excusing myself for a call of nature during the most critical negotiations of my reign. So I will not drink from the antimonium cup. It is normal to be chilly in an October hailstorm. That is my considered judgment."

"It will rest Your Majesty and give you a good night's sleep. You will be fresh for the parley tomorrow."

"I am normally fatigued; and I expect a good night's sleep. I am not nervous about the parley, for I have marshaled my arguments and have them well in mind. Even if I were to forget some pertinent point, Cardinal Balue will be there to recall it to me. So throw away the physic, Olivier. I cannot risk it."

The barber flushed. "Your Majesty does not trust me!" Incontinently he raised it to his lips and gulped it down. "There!"

"That was foolish," Louis smiled. "You'll be the one with a painful belly at the meeting tomorrow I fear. Go to your tent, Olivier, and have a good sleep, as I shall."

Abashed, the barber said, "Will Your Majesty permit me to be present? After what I just said?"

"Thin-skinned, faithful Olivier. Yes, you shall accompany me."

The king said his prayers, asking St. Denis to reach down his holy hand from heaven to help France in her hour of peril, hoping St. George would look the other way tomorrow and not concern himself with furthering the prospects of England, and went to sleep. He was satisfied that he had done all that could be done to ensure the success of the interview at Péronne.

During the night, with intermittent gusts of wind, the storm blew itself out. No one heard the gasping that came from the king's tent, or, if anyone did, it sounded too much like the wind or the faraway howl of some wet, unhappy dog to attach importance to. The doctor, who would have recognized the sounds, slept deeply.

The morning rose sunny and clear and cold. The king saw something white on the blanket. He thought it was hoarfrost formed by his breath. He brushed it away. The dry flakes of crusted foam fluttered to the ground. Pasque Dieu, he must have had a little attack after all.

How fortunate it had occurred during the night, while he was asleep. Now it was over and done with. No one would know, not even that faithful, prying Olivier. He had experienced a little nightmare too, he remembered now. He had dreamed he was Charles the Simple (*he* a Charles! *he* a simpleton!) an unfortunate ancestor of his who, hundreds of years ago, had died a prisoner in the château of Péronne, the old fortress that still stood. How silly dreams could be! Probably the reason for the nasty nightmare was that Charles the Simple had died on an October 7th, the same date as last night's. But this was October 8th, the lucky day of King Louis XI. How gloriously the sun was shining! How rested he felt, how light of body, how sure of himself! How sharp everything looked! How good his breakfast smelled! How fast and clear his thoughts came racing into his consciousness!

What foolish, elaborate precautions he had taken to ensure the success of this fundamentally simple mission of his, when all he had to do was to point out some little errors in the thinking of Duke Charles of Burgundy, who was an honorable man, not really a bad fellow at all. "That is the trouble with you, Louis," he said amiably to himself. "You are too damned suspicious of people." He would apologize to his good cousin of Burgundy

296

for the vast escort. Nay, he would disband it. That would be better. He would do everything differently than he had planned. He nodded and smiled to himself as Olivier, sleepy-eyed and dull, made excuses for the cold breakfast.

"My dear fellow, it is excellent, positively enchanting! It is venison, is it not?"

The doctor eyed him oddly. "I am afraid it is only veal, and I thought it a trifle tough."

"Toothsome!" the king said, smacking his lips. "Succulent as venison." He chewed it and chewed it, smiling. "Venison, a deer, a deer. What a delightful thought has just struck me! Olivier, you have been a commoner too long. I am going to ennoble you. A propitious start for my lucky day. Henceforth you are a nobleman, the Chevalier Olivier, Olivier le Daim. Now kneel and swear me your homage."

The king laid down his hunting knife, wiped his fingers on the table cloth and, still chewing, his hands clean, cupped them in the traditional gesture.

Blushing crimson, his eyes tearful, Olivier knelt. "Your Majesty is making cruel sport of me because of what I said last night. I am of all creatures the least like *le daim*, a fallow deer."

The king took his hands in his. "Reluctant vassal, swear! I was never more serious in my life."

Haltingly, Olivier swore.

"Now you are Olivier le Daim," the king said. "Call in my King of Arms. We'll have you a coat made up at once. A fallow deer on a vert field. Well, call him! Don't you want a pretty device on your shield for your sons to inherit? Have you sons, Olivier? See to it you beget sons. I will. Well, fellow, what are you staring at? Up off your knees, get me my King of Arms!"

Olivier hurriedly left the king, not knowing if he were le Malvays, le Daim, or the butt of a particularly heartless joke. But even if it should turn out to be a joke, he did not even think of disobeying. He returned with the chief of the College of Heralds and looked at the king like a dog that cringes before a whipping but does not growl.

Rapidly, but soberly, Louis ordered the name of Olivier le Daim inscribed in the roster of the nobility of France, and dictated the form of Le Daim's arms: a fallow deer on a green field. The astonished herald made the notation, congratulated the barber, and departed. It was early in the morning to be conferring honors, but it was not entirely surprising that the royal surgeon, valet, and constant companion of the king had finally achieved nobility.

"Your Majesty was not joking!" Olivier said incredulously, falling on his knees again.

"Pooh, pooh, pooh! Get up off the ground. Do you want to take a chill? Ha, ha; ha, ha!"

Olivier le Daim bit his lip for shame. "I know nothing, I understand nothing," he said. "But I will serve my master to the death."

"Nobody's going to die, *mon chevalier*. Not today of all days. Now I am going to Péronne and pound some sense into that handsome head of my cousin Charles."

"I will watch over you every second."

"Eh? *You're* not going."

"But last night I understood Your Majesty to say—"

"Now you are calling me sick again, Olivier. I do not like that in you, Olivier. I am not sick. I do not need a doctor in attendance. Pasque Dieu, will Duke Charles have a doctor? I do not need anyone. I am going alone."

A few minutes later he strode into the tent of Cardinal Balue, who was busy with last-minute preparations among his assistants. "I have reconsidered my plans for the parley today," the king said waving his hand disdainfully at the inkpots and pens and sheafs of parchment on which a record of the meeting was to be taken down. "All this paraphernalia is nonsense. Why slow up a simple proceeding with a lot of tedious details? Besides, it would look as if I did not trust my good cousin."

The assistants gasped, but the cardinal unexpectedly agreed. "Your Majesty is unquestionably right. I have thought for some time that a simpler approach would be preferable. We shall assuredly accomplish more if we do not nettle the duke with trivia."

"Who is *we*, Your Eminence?"

"Why, Your Majesty and myself. I have handled so much of the correspondence that I can easily do without notations and memoranda."

"Oh, you're not going," the king said.

The cardinal faltered. "I think he is expecting me."

"I'm going alone."

"I see," said the cardinal smiling broadly. "That is surely best of all."

Henri LeClercq resisted to the point of rudeness. "It is preposterous for Your Majesty to venture unattended into Péronne."

"My dear Henri, everyone is so thick-headed today! I cannot understand how all my good friends advise me so ill. I might have mismanaged the whole thing. It is perfectly clear to me that I must go alone."

"It isn't clear to me, and I won't permit it."

"Softly, my lord count. I am your king. You shall not take that tone with me."

Henri scowled and set his stern mouth.

"Come, come, old friend. It is too beautiful a day for us to quarrel. Ride with me a little way and let me persuade you."

The king set off at a furious gallop toward Péronne. Henri had never seen him sit so easily in his saddle or handle a horse so masterfully, or heard a man speak with such force and clarity at such a pace.

Suddenly the king noticed that the Swiss guard were following. "Send back that absurd bunch of body watchers!"

Henri did not immediately obey.

"If you do not, I shall."

Henri opened his mouth to protest. The king interrupted, "And I'll make them take *you* back with them. They would, you know."

Henri knew they would. He gave the order that sent them back. The king rode on at the same frenzied gallop, talking incessantly. He would not, he repeated, insult his good cousin. He was perfectly capable of handling the matter alone.

At the gate of Péronne there was a little delay. The king was not expected so early. But he called cheerily to a guard. An official appeared who recognized him, and the portcullis was raised, while a hastily summoned troop of trumpeters blew a welcoming peal on their bugles. "Where is Cousin Charles?" the king shouted. "Send him out and let me shake his hand!"

There was another delay. Mailed heads crowded the walls, bewildered Burgundian soldiers peering furtively through the crenelated battlements. They had expected an army. The unpredictable French king was up to his old tricks again.

In a little while Duke Charles rode through the gate. He was fully armed in his beautiful coal-black armor. Glancing up at the walls, Henri saw crossbowmen winding their crossbows, squinting suspiciously into the distance.

Advancing, the duke raised his visor and extended his hand. "Welcome, Your Majesty."

"I thank you for your welcome. Are you ready to parley, good cousin?"

"Whenever your escort and negotiators arrive."

"I intend to negotiate in person, as friends and kinsmen should."

"I see," said the duke. He also was searching the distance with his eyes, but there was nothing there. Only half convinced of the king's good faith, he said, "That is quite all right with me." He looked inquiringly at Henri. "General LeClercq will be your only attendant. Do I understand you correctly?"

"General LeClercq has smothered me with well meant but unnecessary attention," the king said amiably. "No, he is going home now."

"I am not, so help me God!"

"As I remember, the LeClercqs never did have any manners." Duke Charles grinned. Whatever the king was up to, it was gratifying to see him and his oldest friend bickering, and the notion of Louis alone in the walled city presented unexpected possibilities. "Shall I set aside some comfortable barred quarters for him while you remain my guest, or would you prefer that I detail a squad of soldiers, no, two squads for him, to escort him back so that we can parley without the disruption of this presumptuous engineer?"

"Nay, he is a good fellow. I can handle him. Henri, ride aside a pace or two with me."

Out of earshot the king said pleasantly: "You see how it is, Henri. Go back, like the reasonable man that you are. I should hate to see Burgundian soldiers taking you back forcibly."

"I will go, Your Majesty."

"And Henri, I've been thinking about my army. When you get back, disband the army."

"Do *what?*"

"I said, disband the army."

"Disband the magnificent fighting machine we have labored for years to build together? Your Majesty cannot be serious. You do not appear to be yourself at all today."

"Their lives are so barren, so lonely. Send them back to their wives and sweethearts. Pay them off."

Henry looked at him sadly.

"Yes, Your Majesty."

"Good, good, good. That matter has been on my conscience."

He wheeled his horse and returned to the duke. Together they rode into Péronne. The portcullis thundered down with the speed of a closing trap.

Henry turned and rode slowly away from the city gate.

He said to the empty air around him, "The king is mad."

Chapter Forty-three

Inside Péronne the king's personality change was so obvious and extraordinary that Duke Charles said: "I can get him to agree to anything! Draw up a treaty, tight as a thumbscrew. Let him sign, swear, quickly, at once!"

"Softly, softly," Philippe de Comines cautioned. "There is duplicity somewhere in this. Far better man the walls, double the watch on the gates, and send out scouts to find out where his army is. And try to get an agent through to Cardinal Balue. Louis is altogether too careless, happy, and debonair for no reason at all. Whistling ballades, smiling and dreamy like a lad in love! He didn't even seem to care that we shut the gates on him. Something makes him confident."

"Well, what? That is your province, Messire d'Argenton. You are the diplomat."

"I wish to God I knew. There is some secret in this mood of strength. Have I your permission to send an agent to the cardinal?"

"Oh, very well," the duke said peevishly. "Would you also send an agent to a fish when you'd hooked it?"

"If a fighting salmon suddenly acted stupid as a weakfish, I think I should."

"Nay, he is changed indeed," the duke said less enthusiastically. "He is queerly changed. People say he is a witch. Even I should not care to fight black magic."

"I say he is hiding something," Philippe de Comines replied positively. "I strongly advise a treaty embodying your absolute minimum demands. You can always stiffen them later."

"You are just like him," the duke said contemptuously. "Full of guile and deceit."

"On the international level that is now called diplomacy," Philippe de Comines smiled.

"Oh, go draw up your damned agreement. But I must have Normandy!"

"If he gives Normandy back to the Duc de Berri, that will be the same as if he gave it to you. And the French parliament would not object. There is a danger of uniting all France against you if the king agrees to cede national territory."

"Very well. I can handle the Duc de Berri. And I must also have Champagne." The French province of Champagne lay like a corridor between two Burgundian districts, separating them from each other. Louis had always exacted heavy tolls on Burgundian merchandise that had, of necessity, to traverse it.

"I shall stipulate that—or at least free transit in perpetuity for our goods."

"And make him pay me some money. A lot of money."

"Naturally," said Philippe de Comines.

"That will do for a beginning," the duke said. "I can be a diplomat too, eh?"

"Unquestionably, my lord. And in return you will agree not to call in the English, will you not? You'll have to make some sort of concession."

"Why should I? Louis is my prisoner, isn't he?"

Comines knit his brow. "I really do not know. We'll know when the cardinal answers."

"Damn that double-dealing cardinal."

"Yes, my lord. But he has been very useful to us. Actually, if you do call in the British, and if they agree to come, then in addition to the hazard of war—which I must remind you they did not win at the end of a hundred years—and the danger of unification of sentiment that a foreign invasion will arouse in France, there is another consideration: your commerce will suffer."

"I know nothing about commerce, and care less."

"Whenever there is war," Comines said patiently, "trade does not prosper. England will no longer be a good customer."

"Why not? She'll be my ally, won't she? She'll buy my wool, won't she? Which side are you on, anyhow?"

"Do you think she'd pay her bills?"

"Oh," said the duke.

"It is better to exact a ransom from an enemy than to try to collect trade debts from an ally in wartime."

"Nay, a ransom I understand. A ransom is knightly and honorable. Why didn't you put it that way in the beginning. A ransom is chivalrous."

"Whereas trade is the concern of the rabble. At last I have made myself understood. You are quite right, my lord duke."

"I feel better about the agreement now," Duke Charles said. "For I did give him safe-conduct. I am glad you made yourself clear before I thought of that. I could not go back on my word, of course."

"It would be unthinkable," Comines smiled. "I had entirely forgotten the safe-conduct."

The king spent a delightful day, walking rapidly through the twisting old alleys and streets of Péronne, complimenting the grocers on the size of the vegetables that grew in the valley of the Somme, speaking cheerily to everyone. He saw one man taking down the cabbages from a street stand and loading them into a peasant cart.

"Are you going back to your farm so early? What superb cabbages, so heavy and firm!"

The fellow muttered something in Flemish and whipped up the mule. The cart rattled away.

"I should have thought it customary to bring produce *into* a city to sell, not take it out," Louis mused.

A young man approached him from behind. "I could not help overhearing Your Majesty's remark," he said, doffing his hat. "I happened to be going in the same direction as Your Majesty. The ignorant peasant is not fortunate enough to speak French, so of course he was unable to answer. The reason is that trade is poor today, when great things occupy men's minds."

The king gave him an écu. "What a pleasant fellow you are. How kind of you to concern yourself with me. Who are you? Walk with me and keep me company."

"If Your Majesty please, I am a poor student. If Your Majesty please, may I go and buy food with your gift?"

"Run along, run along," laughed the king. The courteous, well spoken young fellow was probably hungry. Offhand, however, he could not remember there being a university at Péronne. Oh, well. It didn't matter.

The young man stopped following the king. As soon as he was out of sight, he ran indeed. Back to Philippe de Comines.

"Well, did you learn anything?"

"The king saw the cardinal's agent and stopped and spoke to him."

"What wretched luck! How in the world did he happen to be on the other side of town?"

"He walked very fast. I could hardly keep up with him. Fortunately, the agent pretended he could not understand French and got away without an argument—the king was asking him why he was taking his cabbages out of town to sell in the countryside."

"Who wouldn't! Louis of all people. Nothing escapes him. What then?"

"I approached him and told him trade was poor because of the parley; I said the peasant had given up trying to sell them."

"Did he believe that?"

"I think so. He gave me an écu and asked me to walk with him."

"If the king of France gave you an écu, he believed you," Comines said grimly. "Did you walk with him?"

"No, Messire d'Argenton. I said I was a poor student and needed food. I wanted to come and report to you at once."

"You idiot, there is no school of learning in Péronne."

"He seemed to think there might be."

"He probably knew you were shadowing him and wanted to get rid of you."

"Shall I go back and observe him again?"

"Good heavens, no! Nay, perhaps you had better. No, he knows you now; I'll send someone else." Philippe de Comines was seldom at a loss what to do. "On the other hand, he has probably learned everything he wanted to know."

"What is he looking for?"

"I have no idea. I wish I knew."

Only the cabbage vendor could tell. Noon came, the afternoon wore on, and the cabbage vendor did not return.

Shortly after noon, however, the king walked into the Hôtel de Ville by way of the kitchens, where he congratulated the cooks and tasted the soup, and presented himself at the door of the council chamber. "Isn't the duke ready to parley yet?" he asked the guard.

"We had better," Philippe de Comines said when the message was brought to him.

"He missed his dinner," Duke Charles said. "Or did he?"

"I do not know, my lord."

"I thought you were having him followed."

"I called off the spy."

"Why?"

"It—it seemed best."

Duke Charles snorted. "I think you're the one who's afraid of the witch. Well, he's back now, and it serves him right if he parleys on an empty stomach."

"I am forced to report to you, my lord, that the French army is camped

303

a scant mile away. It is large, and the artillery is to the fore. And the agent I sent to Cardinal Balue has not returned."

"You bungler! I'll crush that spider Louis under my heel! I'll dagger him with my own hand."

"Perhaps you should. But perhaps that is what he wants."

"Nonsense. Who wants to die?"

"Saints, lunatics, patriots—anyone fanatically dedicated to a cause."

"What cause would be served by his death?"

"France's, perhaps, in some deep maneuver that I cannot fathom."

"That would be bad," the duke said slowly. Moreover, he remembered, there were certain hazards encountered when trying to kill a witch. "And I must not forget that I promised no harm should come to him."

"Let us see first if he will sign the agreement."

Philippe de Comines did not believe that Louis was actually a witch, though he did not entirely discredit the universal belief that a league with the devil was possible, and the French king's behavior had been so irrational that lunacy or diabolical possession seemed almost the only explanation.

He could take precautions against witchcraft. "If he swears on your father's sword," he suggested, "there is nothing supernatural in the fearlessness he has shown and we can safely assume that the madness of his grandfather is showing itself."

"That would be most gratifying," Duke Charles said.

The king indeed had eaten nothing since breakfast, when he had mistaken the veal for venison. Nor had he felt any hunger. But little by little, as the day wore on, his rapid pace had slackened, and the galloping thoughts in his mind had slowed to a canter, his too exalted mood had fallen slightly to less dizzy a height. The conviction kept nagging at him that this had happened to him once before, but he could not remember where. He was still extraordinarily cheerful. But that other time, if there had been another time, had there not been some clouding of judgment?

He clearly remembered everything he had done, from the ennoblement of Olivier le Daim to the disbanding of the French army. One by one he reviewed the events of the day. No, they were all quite logical, a little drastic now that he came to ponder them, but well conceived. He was merely fatigued and anxious to get on with the parley with that good fellow Charles. Then he would go home.

It was warm and bright in the council chamber. Tall wax candles in silver candlesticks shed a clear glow over copies of the agreement that Philippe de Comines had prepared.

Louis listened as Comines read it, not looking at the copy in front of him. It would surely be a duplicate. Why read it as if he did not trust his cousin? He nodded agreement as he heard the provisions:

"For payment to Duke Charles of one hundred thousand écus—"

"A little high, but I can pay it, Charles."

"—to be used as a wedding gift to Her Highness the Duchess of Burgundy—"

"Charming, even if she is English."

"—and for Louis's promise to return Normandy to the Duc de Berri, his brother—"

"He shall have it again. I gave it to him once. I forget why I took it away."

"—and for free transit of Burgundian merchandise through Champagne—"

"Agreed."

"—Duke Charles of Burgundy would agree and promise not to ally himself militarily with the English or to encourage an English invasion of France."

"Nay, Charles, I knew you could not do that. That was my only concern. Now I think I shall bid you good night and go home."

"If Your Majesty would sign?" Philippe de Comines said, handing him the pen.

"Oh, yes, yes, of course. How thoughtless of me." He scribbled his signature rapidly. "Good night, good cousin; good night Messire d'Argenton; good night, gentlemen."

"One moment, Louis," the duke said.

A priest brought the sword of Duke Philip the Good. Through its crystal pommel the king could see the holy splinters of ancient wood disposed in the form of a miniature cross.

The duke said, "How do I know you will keep your word?"

"I swore to."

"Swear it on the True Cross."

The king extended his hand.

Philippe de Comines narrowed his eyes; Duke Charles expected he knew not what miraculous manifestation—a searing of the flesh, an inability to touch the sacred relic.

But the king touched the crystal reliquary without effort. "Certainly I swear, good cousin. What is it you wish me to say? *I swear I will keep my word and honor my signature on our agreement.* Will that do?"

"That will do," the duke said unpleasantly. He glared at Philippe de Comines. He could have got more.

Philippe de Comines sighed. Louis was no witch. Then he must be mad. He had always admired the king as the ablest diplomat in Europe. It was hard to look without emotion on the shipwreck of such a mind.

The king said, "I should like my horse brought, Cousin Charles."

"Are you riding back tonight?"

"Why not?"

The duke shrugged, "As you please."

Philippe de Comines interposed, "The countryside hereabouts is somewhat wild. Does Your Majesty consider it safe to venture out unattended?"

"Of course I do. I sent the army back to Paris, but probably I'll find them a league or two away."

"Let me provide you with an escort," Duke Charles said. He thought he had caught Phillippe de Comines's meaning. They both knew the French army was only a mile away. How conveniently the king could be made to disappear forever in the forest before he got back to the forces he had just lied about.

But Comines had not meant to suggest murder. "Duke Charles is remembering his solemn safe-conduct to you," he said. "His offer of an escort is only the fulfillment of his knightly word that no harm shall come to you. Surely Your Majesty should avail yourself of his offer, lest he bear the shame if some accident should befall you."

Under his breath the duke cursed. The priest and the scribes still remained in the room. They were all in the presence of the True Cross. No one could now forget that he had given the king safe-conduct.

There was a moment of silence while Louis seemed trying to make up his mind. It was broken by a noise of scuffling in the hall. A mud-covered herald burst into the room, shaking off the guards who had attempted to bar him from the parley.

"I will not be denied!" he shouted. "There is murder, my lord duke!"

"Calm yourself, man," Philippe de Comines ordered. It would be the cabbage vendor, of course. He had already suspected that the spy had been caught. Spies had to expect that sometimes; it was part of the game.

"Who is murdered?" the duke said darkly, scowling at Louis.

"The lord Bishop of Liége and Count Humbercourt! Liége is in arms again, and French agents are at the head of the revolt!"

Louis pressed his hand against his forehead, swaying slightly. His ears rang; the candle flames danced before his eyes. The process of healing that had been at work in his mind suddenly won through, to the goal for which it had been vainly striving since early afternoon. All at once he was himself again. The monstrous delusion had passed. He saw the enormity of everything he had done and understood clearly the situation in which he had placed himself. The wonder was that he was still alive.

The only thing he could not understand was the renewed revolt at Liége. He had called off his agents weeks ago. He had never given orders for the murder of the bishop or of the mayor Humbercourt, especially the bishop, who was a kinsman of Duke Charles. Their murder would have ruined his chances at Péronne.

"That is impossible!" he shouted at the herald. "Fantastic! Cousin Charles, Messire d'Argenton, I beg you to verify this man's report before you believe it!"

"What do you know of the matter?" the duke said, purple with rage. "Verify it! Verify it!"

The duke pounded the table so vigorously that inkpots overturned and

306

the candlesticks jumped. Venting his fury in one great roar, he screamed, "Lock him in the château!"

Chapter Forty-four

The château of Péronne was a grim structure of rotting stone and rusting iron. Squat, ugly, and virtually without windows it stood, like many another ruined French castle, a useless monument to the remote age from which it dated, an age which enlightened men were already beginning to stigmatize by the name of Dark. An aura of evil surrounded it in the minds of the superstitious peasants of the countryside. The death of a French king ages ago, though now almost forgotten, had started the legend. Since then the castle had served as a prison, and most recently the courtyard had been used as a sheepfold. No one had lived in it within the memory of the oldest inhabitant. A damp odor of fungi from the cellars, which some said were edible mushrooms and others poisonous toadstools but which no one was ever hungry or hardy enough to gather, added to the evil reputation of the place, as did a profusion of bats that at sunset would issue in a dark stream from a crack in the masonry of one of the dilapidated watchtowers.

The king, who had inspected and rebuilt many such ruined castles, half expected to be thrown into one of the deep and windowless chambers underground. That would be an effective way of murdering him by accident, for the foundations of these old fortresses were always rotten, and water always seeped through and flooded the lower areas, especially after a downpour such as that of the night before.

But the guards seemed to have received no orders to kill him, not yet at least, for they took him to a tower room. No one for many years, never indeed since his father had punished him as a boy, had laid hands roughly on his person or applied bodily force. The blows received in battle were less humiliating than this manhandling by common guards. Yet he realized that he was not being intentionally manhandled; they were merely holding him roughly and firmly, as if they feared he might sprout wings, probably webbed ones, and fly over the wall. It was gratifying, if not amusing, that they still feared him.

The tower room was perfectly circular and without furniture of any kind. There was, of course, no fireplace, for towers were functional structures, built for fighting, not as living quarters.

"It's a long drop," one of the guards said, motioning with his torch at a narrow window slit. "I wouldn't try anything if I were you."

"Fortunately for you you are not," the king said without rancor. "I could wish you were."

Another guard said more feelingly, "It's the best chamber in the château, Your Majesty. This one's dry."

"Thank you. It will do." It was not their fault that he was a prisoner. It was his own—or his insane grandfather's.

The second guard, who had spoken almost apologetically, whispered something which Louis could not hear, but he could see the man's breath in the cold still air of the room. The first, who seemed to be in command, shook his head. "No, no light was ordered."

They went out, and the heavy door screamed shut on rusty hinges. The king would have been glad of the torch; it would have shed a little warmth. He heard keys being tried in the lock, but either the old mechanism had rusted solid or they did not have the right key. It would not matter much; the door would be guarded. He thought for a moment they might have gone away, for he heard their hobnailed boots clanking down the stairs. But he heard them return again, grunting and muttering over some heavy labor. Then there was a thumping of stone on stone, closer and closer, till the door shook under the impact of a heavy weight: they had found a loose block of old masonry and set it against the door. Like a headstone on a grave, Louis thought.

In the torchlight, before the torch had been taken away, Louis had seen a name scratched in the stone under the window. It was common for prisoners, with nothing else to do, to scratch things on walls: prayers, rude pictures, personal calendars—but usually their names. This name was Charles. The name was so common that the king was by no means certain this was the work of his ancestor, and yet it might easily be, for it was written in the ancient Carolingian script of the time; and a later hand had added in more modern letters *Le Simple*. Genuine or no, it proved how the melancholy legend of the old king's death still hovered over the place and how harshly succeeding generations had judged him.

"How will history judge me?" It would be Louis le Simple without doubt.

He walked over to the window. The pitch-black of the room, where his eyes had nothing to rest upon, made him dizzy. It was colder there, but he could look at the stars. "I had hoped to do great things for my country."

There was a flickering ruddy glow in the clear night sky. The chill of the room nipped him to the bone. Colors, where no colors should be, were a frequent phenomenon in his seizures; perhaps he was going to have another, one perhaps that would blast his reason forever and leave him mindless as a vegetable, though it had never happened that there had been two within two days. He sighed helplessly. Neither had it ever happened that the exhilaration and warping of judgment had persisted a full day, or died out so gradually. He longed for Friar Jean, whose science had been so superior to Olivier's. The cold had been a bad sign too, though he had seen the guard's breath. But how did he know that was real? How did he know anything was real?

There was one test he could make on the weird glow in the sky. He almost feared to apply it. But he shut his eyes tight, clamped his hand firmly over them to be sure all natural light, if the glow was natural light, would be excluded. He counted slowly to a hundred. During that time the glow disappeared, as was normal. Now if he opened them again and the glow was still there, he could be sure it was not an hallucination. He removed his hand, but he could not immediately open his eyes for fear that the glow would be gone.

Praying, he forced himself to look again. Pasque Dieu, there it was, flickering. It was real!

Now, sure that he was in his right mind, he could examine the lights and reason what they were. Open fires, of course; but no peasants would be burning anything in the open. They were warming themselves around their hearths in their homes, small economical fires, and shielded moreover by the walls of their cottages.

Suddenly the truth burst upon him: only soldiers, soldiers who did not care if their position was disclosed, built such fires. Campfires! The fires of his army, drawn up in its strength before Péronne! "Thank God for Henri!" Far from disbanding the army, his Grand Master had brought it up almost within gunshot.

"If I am not released I shall at least be avenged," he muttered to himself. It was sad comfort. Henri might wipe out Péronne, and even Duke Charles might be slain. But only King Louis could keep order in France, and King Louis would also be dead.

Others had seen the fires too. The monotonous march of the guards outside the door was suddenly interrupted; the king heard a softer catlike tread of someone in velvet shoes. Then the stone was dragged away from the door, and Philippe de Comines entered the room. In the light of several attendants' torches he scrutinized the king's countenance searchingly.

"Well, Messire d'Argenton? Did you expect to find me counting my fingers?"

The king looked as he always looked, sharp-eyed and rather formidable.

"I confess I did not know what to expect. Your Majesty is cut to a different pattern from most of us. When these men do what I have ordered, I shall have something to tell you."

They set up a camp bed, covered it with blankets, brought a table, candles, a chair, a brazier full of glowing coals, wine, and a steaming pot of soup. "I am afraid my master made you somewhat meager cheer," he said.

"It was thoughtful of you to better it." He could see that Comines, or the duke, wanted something. He wondered what he was still in a position to give. The attendants, having made the chamber more comfortable, withdrew and closed the door.

Comines glanced at the door and glanced at the window with a conspiratorial air. The king repressed a smile.

"I will be very frank with you," Comines said. "I am here entirely on my own responsibility."

"You are most welcome, Messire d'Argenton. Almost you make me feel welcome too."

"We saw the campfires, of course, Your Majesty."

"My escort has no reason to hide itself."

"And we have scouted its size and position. My master feels that you have tricked him. Not once tonight did he put off his clothes. Two or three times he lay down on his bed, then rose and paced the floor, for that is his fashion when he is troubled, uttering dreadful oaths and ready, as I who know him know, for any act of violence. His choler is now greater than it was in the council chamber, if that is possible."

"I put myself in his power unattended, trusting his honor and pledged word. There is no trickery in that."

"Oh, yes, there is, Your Majesty, the neatest trickery of all, since now the whole world will condemn my master whatever he does."

"You refer to his pledge of safe-conduct; that, as you say, is known to all the world. Would he have preferred me to keep it secret?"

"He would certainly have preferred a smaller escort," Philippe de Comines said.

"The world will not condemn him if he keeps his word and sets me at liberty immediately. I could forget this temporary confinement, knowing the quick temper of my cousin."

"That is impossible now. The double death of the bishop and Humbercourt has enraged him almost to apoplexy. Only his pledged word restrains him."

Smiling grimly the king motioned toward the window beyond which flickered the lights of the French army.

"That too," Comines admitted.

"Well?"

"I had planned to tell you casually of the further demand he has resolved upon, trusting that you would agree to it with the same unthinking readiness you evinced in the council chamber," Comines said doubtfully.

"While I counted my fingers and gibbered perhaps?"

"Your mad act convinced me completely, Your Majesty."

"And now you are not so sure, eh? Try me, Philippe de Comines. I have liked you ever since the Dauphiny. In fact, I have often wished you in my service. What more does he want?"

"He insists that you accompany him in person and help put down the

310

revolt in Liége and avenge the death of the mayor and his kinsman the bishop. You are responsible for the uprising; you must ally yourself in its repression."

The king flushed scarlet and turned his face away.

"If you do not," Comines said, "I have not the slightest doubt you will never leave this room alive regardless of the consequences to my master's good name."

The tables were neatly turned. To march with a Burgundian army against an episcopal city would ruin his own good name and draw upon himself all the shame and obloquy he had so successfully heaped on Duke Charles.

"Is this the duke's own idea?"

"The duke holds inseparably to this idea, Your Majesty."

"I see. It's yours." Such a masterpiece of humiliation almost had to be.

Unless he chose to die forthwith, to bring civil war to France among the fractious lords whom only he could control, to provoke a Franco-Burgundian war, since Henri would assuredly fire on Péronne if he did not return, and worst of all, to subject the Continent to another English invasion, which the Islanders were already considering with favor—unless he was prepared to do all this, he must sacrifice his personal honor, march with his enemy, and put down an insurrection for which, in origin at least, he was responsible. Liége would never have revolted now if, months ago, he had not struck the first spark. Once kindled, such fires were hard to put out, as he knew from experience with them in his own domain. He had no alternative.

"I do not think I could persuade any of my army to join such a venture," he said heavily.

"The duke does not expect any. Just you."

"A few Swiss, perhaps," Louis said. "They'll fight anybody as long as I pay them." They would also protect his person in the midst of the Burgundians.

"The duke would probably not object."

"A servant or two. I rather treasure my barber."

"Naturally, Your Majesty."

"I'll want to tell the Grand Master to send the army home."

"Nothing would please the duke more."

"Pasque Dieu, I'll do it! Bring that confounded sword and I'll swear on it if you want me to."

"I repeat I am here on my own responsibility. This is quite an unofficial visit. In fact, I should prefer that Your Majesty did not mention my visit at all."

"Do you mean to say the duke won't hear of it?"

"My men are reliable fellows." Comines smiled, gesturing in the direction of the closed door.

"Philippe de Comines, I admire you more than ever. But when you serve the King of France, do not flatter yourself that I shall permit you a corps of 'reliable fellows.' "

"Who knows, Your Majesty?" Comines smiled. "Shall I intimate to the duke that you are probably still as *amiable*, shall we say, as you were last night?"

"Yes—yes I think you should. If you like I shall actually count my fingers."

"Nay, that would be too much for even his thick head."

"Very well. Just pleasant, gullible foolishness. Thank you, Philippe de Comines."

In his own devious way the Sire of Argenton had served Burgundy well and the best ends of international diplomacy, since war was no longer inevitable.

"And remember me!"

"Your Majesty is hard to forget."

The king stood long in thought. He must drink a bitter cup to the dregs. But somehow he would square his shame with his conscience. True Cross or no True Cross, Heaven was kind to madmen, and mad assuredly he had been. He need keep only such terms of the treaty as he chose to keep. Nay, better, he would squirm out of it legally. There must be a way. There was always a way. And as for Liége, after all, it was Burgundian. He ate his soup, which was now cold.

Toward morning he got some sleep.

He was awakened by the sound of bugles boldly blowing before the city gate. From the window he looked down on a strangely assorted trio of mounted men: Cardinal Balue, Henri LeClercq, Olivier le Daim. None of them was armed. In his mind's eye the king could see crossbows being wound behind the battlements, being pointed at their hearts through the crenels of the walls.

"Pasque Dieu, what foolish chances they take!"

But beyond them the early sun shone on the sleek bronze bodies of cannon aimed point-blank at the city, and beyond the cannon, in all their strength, with all their color and snapping flags, he saw the army and chivalry of France. It was that army and the figure he would cut in their eyes that made his decision so hard to carry through. He wanted to fly. He wanted to spread wings and sail through the air from the tower to the midst of his army. Then, *then* he would parley from strength, as he had planned before the storm. But only angels had wings. He was no angel.

Shortly Duke Charles came into the chamber. His face was red with anger and gaunt with fatigue. He spat out his ultimatum, cursing and threatening. Louis was thankful that he had been forewarned. "By God," shouted the duke, "I hope you refuse! This holy sword has tasted no blood since Charlemagne wore it. Today it shall. Then come what may."

"Softly, good cousin; how you rant! Your suggestion strikes me as eminently reasonable."

"I am sorry it does."

"Just let me go out and send home this disobedient army of mine and I shall be ready."

"Swear it!"

"Of course I swear it, Cousin. Don't shake so; you quite unnerve me."

"Swear it now!" He held out the crystal pommel. Louis touched it.

"I swear to send my army home."

"Swear to fight against Liége!"

"I swear to fight against Liége."

"Swear to keep the treaty you made last night!"

"I swear to keep the treaty I made last night. But Cousin Charles, that treaty had no time limit. Shall we swear it into perpetuity, you and I?"

A note of caution crept into the duke's voice. He did not like the concession that Philippe de Comines had insisted on inserting into the treaty. Perpetuity would tie his hands forever, and there might come a time when English help would be even more desirable than it was now.

"Swear it for a year."

"I swear it for a year."

Philippe de Comines, who was present, said, "An addendum stipulating the time limit shall be appended to the treaty."

The king had found his legal way out. Now to get those Swiss! "Are your forces sufficient to reduce Liége without assistance, Charles? You can borrow some of mine."

"There shall be no Frenchmen in my army but you."

"I was thinking of my Swiss. They are mercenaries, you know, and I like to keep them employed. Let me bring a few hundred with me. They could reduce your casualties substantially, I feel sure."

The duke saw no harm in that. "But not your precious LeClercq."

"Oh, no. He isn't Swiss. Are we finished with all the swearing, Cousin Charles?"

"You don't seem to take it very seriously."

"I defy you to point to a single instance in my whole life when I broke my pledged word!" The strain was telling, he spoke angrily, and it seemed to Comines that the king was forgetting to be pleasantly, gullibly foolish.

"Nay, that is true. But are you sure you know what you are swearing?"

"Do you imply that I have lost my reason? Then why swear?"

The duke looked uncomfortably at Philippe de Comines. It would have been more satisfying to have run him through and have done with it.

"If His Majesty were mad," Comines said, "it is quite true that the treaty and his oath would be equally void."

"Are my three friends still at the gate?" Louis asked. "I saw them through the window. I should like to go out and give them their orders to retire."

"Oh, no, you don't! You are not mad. I see what you are up to now. You'll gallop back to your army."

"Oh, I shan't require a horse. I'll walk."

The duke grinned. The King of France, unshaven, his slept-in clothes wrinkled, humbly afoot before the eyes of thousands of his subjects. It was almost worth it.

"How do I know what you'll tell them?"

"Come with me, Cousin, and listen."

"No—no I don't think I shall." He too would have to walk like a peasant, for if he rode while the king walked he would lose dignity. Duke Charles could envision the murder of a king but not feudal bad manners. Anyhow, it might be a trap, and he had no desire to change place with Louis as prisoner. "No, you may go."

The interview with the three was short and intense. Oddly, the cardinal said nothing. He was pale and his lip trembled.

Henri and Olivier made a motion to dismount.

"Stay where you are!" ordered the king.

In unison they asked, "Are you all right?"

"I am—now. Thank God you disobeyed me, Henri."

"I thought you were under a spell."

"I was, in a way."

Quickly, lest the duke grow suspicious or some nervous-fingered Burgundian crossbowman fire a bolt at them and touch off inevitable war, he traced the essentials of the treaty he had made, the way he planned to evade it, the necessitous concession of marching against Liége. "Parliament must register the treaty. See that no quorum can be got for thirty days. I'll be back by then. Let the noble members be called into the army, Henri. Olivier, send the burgher members on trade missions into the provinces. The cardinal can help by sending the clerical members on pilgrimages. I suggest Our Lady of Embrun in the Dauphiny. That should take thirty days and prove edifying as well."

"The cardinal hasn't helped a bit," Olivier said. "We brought him along so that if we got shot he would too. Burgundians aren't likely to fire on *this* cardinal."

"Oh?" said the king.

"A certain Burgundian cabbage vendor was caught sneaking into his tent—" Henri began.

"Quickly, quickly, Henri! The cabbage vendor was a spy? I understand now. You hanged him?"

"Naturally. And so is the cardinal a spy. Olivier went through his papers."

"He caught a little cold in the storm," the barber could not help boasting, though it took valuable seconds. "I gave him a draught; he slept like a babe, I went through his papers. I found treasonable correspondence with Duke Charles."

"I cannot hang a cardinal, unfortunately," Louis said, "but I can cage a rat. Put him in a cage, Henri, and keep him there till I get back. Paint it red, to honor His Eminence."

"I am innocent!" Balue protested feebly. "Listen to me—"

"I haven't time."

"I pray Your Majesty—"

"Pray God. From your cage!"

Olivier said in a low tone to Henri, "The king is himself again."

Chapter Forty-five

As a Burgundian army advanced on rebellious Liége, with the King of France ingloriously in their midst, some of the sneering Burgundian lords saw his lips move, as if in prayer. Heaven would not hear *him*, they laughed. No king had ever abased himself more profoundly.

The cup of shame he had chosen to drink to the dregs was bitter even beyond his expectation. His own army had obeyed him reluctantly and turned back from Péronne only after Henri's repeated orders; now the Burgundians laughed at him. Probably the whole world was laughing at him. To be laughed at had always been a torture. True, he had his Swiss and he had his doctor; he no longer feared assassination. But his honor was dead. Already there was shame, shortly there would be blood, on the crown of Charlemagne.

But Louis was not praying. Over and over again to himself he was murmuring the words *Qui nescit dissimulare nescit regnare*—he was knows not how to dissimulate, knows not how to rule. "That is the first lesson I shall teach my son, when God grants me a son."

As they drew up before Liége, he could see his own flag, gold fleur-de-lis on a sky-blue field, flying over the walls. The city was appealing to him for protection, yet he was marching against it in person, for history to laugh and wonder at. If the world needed an object lesson in faithlessness, unknightliness, chivalry far gone in decay, let it look at King Louis XI. "If ever I smile or laugh again, dear God, dear God strike me instantly dead!"

Since he did smile very shortly thereafter, however, and was not struck dead, he could only assume that the angels, who separate curses from prayers, not always an easy task, had taken his bitter imprecation for a curse and thrown it out. Pasque Dieu, he had fooled the angels again; perhaps even they were smiling. His concept of heaven was that it must be very like France, but better organized. Even on earth a king needed a chancellery to sift the petitions of his subjects; how much more so the King of Heaven.

Duke Charles found nothing to smile at in the incident that amused the king. A courier arrived from Liége with the news that the bishop and Humbercourt were still alive. The city indeed was disorderly, a tremendous riot was still in progress; but the bishop and the mayor, far from dead, were alive and vigorously leading a large faction of loyalists.

"I should say that this rather changes my position, Cousin. I swore to avenge their deaths."

"You swore to put down the revolt," the duke retorted, "and put it down you shall, by God!"

He racked the unfortunate herald who had brought the garbled report and finally hanged him naked in front of the whole Burgundian army. That was when Louis smiled. Observing the grotesquely elongated body as it dangled from the noose with a curious jointlessness, the king said, "It is always well to insist on accurate information. But your lesson would have lost none of its force if you had clothed him before you hanged him."

"You were always a prude," the duke said.

Some of the weaker-stomached Burgundian lords did not enjoy the spectacle. Philippe de Comines, though he viewed it without personal revulsion, since the poor creature was now beyond suffering, feared that his master might have gone to unnecessary, certainly to undiplomatic, lengths. The king, he was persuaded, would have handled the matter more tactfully.

The duke spared no pains to make known the fact that the French king was with him. Louis was forced to ride in the van of the host where he could be seen and recognized. Already disheartened and divided among themselves, the Liégois very shortly surrendered. The racks and the hangmen were busy then. All the executions were public. "Let them learn what it is to rebel against their lord!" Duke Charles said.

The king asked Philippe de Comines, "Why aren't the trials public too?"

"There haven't been any," Comines replied uncomfortably.

"Then how does he know which are the rebels?"

"Denunciations."

"I see," said the king. "The duke's justice is instructive." Many personal grudges must have been settled among the townspeople simply by virtue of one man's ability to denounce his neighbor more speedily than his neighbor could denounce him. "I once drowned some rebels in Rouen, but they had a fair trial. Perhaps he would listen if I tried to reason with him."

Comines shrugged helplessly, "Not in his present mood, Your Majesty."

"Your advice is usually worth following. But it was no part of my oath to witness all these executions as if I sanctioned them."

316

"They are nearly over."

In a few days they were over, and the king became aware, with a growing sense of wonderment, that the duke's mood had become almost jovial. "Now they know what it is to rebel against their lord, eh, Cousin Louis?"

It was not that he enjoyed the screams or the sight of his victims being stretched on the racks, though Louis knew there were such men; it was the terror in the faces of the crowds—who eagerly gathered—that gave him satisfaction. "I actually believe," Louis said to himself, "that he thinks this is proof of his power." There seemed to be a strange Oriental quirk in the character of Duke Charles, who had always been called "The Rash" and who was now coming to be called, in angry whispers, "The Terrible."

Where the quirk came from the king could not even guess; certainly not from the blood of his father, Duke Philip the Good. Where did Henri LeClercq's stern devotion and mechanical genius come from? Not from Foix or Armagnac. Where indeed did his own quirks come from? The madness of his grandfather Charles VI was in no way like his own infirmity. If blood will out, then whose?

If the problem was medical, he would found universities. If it was spiritual, he would build more churches. Nay, better do both and be on the safe side all around. He thought of Cardinal Balue, who was surely in a red cage by now, and determined to let him out, not free him entirely but to imprison him a bit more comfortably. There was no use borrowing trouble; he had already lost ecclesiastical stature by marching against an episcopal city.

His mind had raced ahead. He reflected that he was still virtually a prisoner himself. What had the duke just called him? *Cousin* Louis? Then seize upon that happy mood before it changed!

"Cousin Charles," he said affably, "admit that I have kept my word, and your city is pacified, and I have helped."

"I admit it."

"Now if you have no further use for me, I think I should like to go back to France."

"I am just getting to like you, Louis. Tarry a week or so, and we can celebrate our victory together. You have not enjoyed a good Burgundian feast since you were dauphin at my father's court."

"I am a little concerned," the king said with a wonderful air of innocence, "that I have had no word from Paris of parliament's action on our agreement. I ought to go back and stir things up."

"Still afraid I'll call in the English?" Duke Charles joked heavily. "Maybe you ought to be; the agreement's only good for a year, you know."

"And I have only a year in which to raise one hundred thousand écus."

That put a different light on the matter; the duke dropped his bantering tone. "I'll ride with you part of the way," he said. Europe watched cynically as the two great princes rode side by side at the head of their escorts, who mingled and marched together, away from the melancholy doings at Liége.

An easy league from the city they parted, the duke inviting the king to return for a feast in the summer, the king promising he would. "And Cousin Charles," he said smiling, "about my brother Charles. Suppose he doesn't *want* Normandy when I offer to return it to him?"

"Why then," laughed the duke, "if he doesn't want it, as long as you satisfy him, I'll leave the matter up to you two. But who wouldn't want Normandy, eh, Philippe de Comines?"

"You are quite right," Comines said, which was always a safe thing to say to Duke Charles. But he did not consider the king's question quite so innocent as it sounded.

The escorts drew away from one another, the smiling princes waved farewell. "Au revoir!" shouted the duke gaily.

"Au revoir, *bon cousin!*" the king shouted heartily in reply. But under his breath, "Adieu, black-armored, black-hearted, black, black, bloody man!" Yet he was smiling grimly. He had sworn on the True Cross to offer his brother Normandy. He would make the offer. But if his brother accepted he would take away Guienne.

Duke Charles gleefully and immediately published the humiliating terms of the Péronne agreement. The news spread like wildfire, and Europe had another good story to tell on King Louis, the spider who had enmeshed himself in his own web. Before he reached Paris, the citizens of his capital were publicly laughing at him. He had never been able to tolerate ridicule; he had never understood the tendency in his countrymen to poke fun at the serious. Some essential ingredient in the sly, wry Gallic type of humor seemed to be lacking in him.

The Parisian citizenry lined the streets and cheered him when he returned, as they always did. There was no doubt of their loyalty, even affection. But he had seen the word "Péronne" chalked on walls, he could hear stray shouts of "Péronne!" among the cheers, followed by smirking laughter and fingers touching foreheads when people thought he was not looking. Later he learned from Olivier le Daim that street entertainers were drawing large crowds by singing scurrilous ballades that dealt with his epic display of finesse in the negotiations at Péronne.

"I can give you their names," the barber suggested brightly. "Your Majesty may have some well deserved punishment in mind."

"Rack a few balladeers for doing what everybody is doing? No, that would be like the Duke of Burgundy, and what is like him is, by definition, bad government."

"I was only suggesting, Sire."

"Why are they laughing at me? Why?"

"They do not understand the cause, my dear master, as I do now that you have told me more of your little failing. We shall be on our guard in the future. It shall never, never happen to you again, or my spine is as straight as that of my lord count of Montfort, Grand Master Captain-General of His Majesty's Artillery, the chevalier Henri LeClercq!"

The parvenu nobleman could always coax a smile from the king when he spun out some long, magniloquent title of one of his peers.

"Keep me healthy, Olivier, and I may find a countship for you too."

"I am searching, reading, studying every day, striving to equal and surpass the sainted Friar Jean. Not only from books and learned surgeons, who now speak courteously to me since I am Le Daim—"

"You don't tell them who your patient is, you scoundrel?"

"My dear old father," Olivier laughed. "It may not even be a lie. Whoever he was he must have been extremely sick. I also have sources among the rabble that were denied to Friar Jean. They know nothing of his potable gold, but I am learning many other remedies."

"Cures?"

"I—have not run across a real cure yet."

The king sighed.

He asked Henri LeClercq, "Why do you think they are laughing at me? What was so funny about Péronne? Are they not also involved in my humiliation?"

"No more than children in a temporary reversal of their fathers' fortunes, which is common. They depend on you to get yourself, and them, out of this passing predicament. They do not know how much you have already done to nullify the agreement."

"Certainly they don't, Henri. Pasque Dieu, that would mean taking them into my confidence."

"Till you do—"

"Which I won't!"

"—they will sing their silly songs about Péronne."

Henri's blunt analyses were never very comforting. The ridicule still-rankled.

Yet it was true that the king was fast nullifying the agreement. The Duc de Berri, dull-witted as he was, was not fool enough to give up Guienne for Normandy. He remained in Bordeaux with his mistress, spending the vast revenues of that rich province on his pleasures and attracting around him a brilliant but worthless crowd of sycophants. The king, who kept himself informed, read the names of all his least faithful vassals among the hangers-on of the ducal court of Guienne: Saint-Pol Alencon, Nemours, even the monstrous Jean d'Armagnac, who had dared to venture out of Lectoure now that Péronne had blasted the king's reputation.

Louis was also collecting the taxes with scrupulous vigor. Treasure was piling up in the royal coffers, though he wrote his good cousin to the contrary; and parliament as yet had no quorum, he said, many members being out of town. From time to time, to whet the duke's appetite he would send him something on account. The rest he hoarded for a greater purpose.

But this, though progress, was secret and under cover. As yet no one knew what he was doing. The little princesses seldom saw their busy father, and when they did he was short with them. The queen, concerned at his hollow cheeks and the sleepless shadows under his eyes, overcame her dislike of Olivier and approached him one day in his study. He was reading a bestiary.

"I should have thought that you might find something better to do than amuse yourself with pictures of freakish animals, Monsieur Le Daim."

He snapped shut the book, which was opened to the page on apes. "With respect, Your Majesty, they are not necessarily freakish. To understand human anatomy one must study the anatomy of animals, which are all that science is permitted to investigate."

Anatomy was not a proper subject for the queen's ears. "I am worried about His Majesty's health."

So was Olivier le Daim, but not acutely; for in spite of his short temper the king was in vigorous health, as Olivier knew from every gossipy page and kitchen wench in the palace. Privacy for royalty was difficult; there had been much listening at doors by the guards and much speculation on the pleasure Their Majesties seemed to take in each other's company and the time they spent together.

The doctor was therefore encouraging. "His Majesty is my whole concern, Madame la Reine. He is stimulated and invigorated by his present activities, thriving on a schedule that would kill an ordinary man. True, he is somewhat thin, but so is a greyhound. Has his digestion been bad of late? No. Has he suffered a fever? No. Has there been a diminution of his vital powers? Your Majesty can best answer that herself, but it seems to me that the king's health—"

The queen gasped, flushed pink, and fled from the doctor's study. "What a frightful creature!" In the hall she dropped her voluminous skirts, which she had raised an inch or so above her ankles to permit her to run faster, and, still insulted at the personal question, swept past the guards and pushed open the door of the king's private audience chamber. He was alone with one man in a foreign cut of doublet. They were speaking English.

"Pasque Dieu! Charlotte! What is amiss? Are the princesses hurt?" She had never intruded on his privacy before.

"My lord husband," she said, still blushing, "I have been outraged!"

The Englishman sank to one knee in the abrupt British reverence, a poorly suppressed smile on his handsome face. He was about the age of the king.

"Nay, Charlotte, surely not," the king said, smiling too.

"By that dreadful barber of yours!"

"Nay, worse and worse." Then more formally, "Your Majesty, this is my lord the Earl of Warwick. In England some call him the kingmaker."

"In France that is an honor reserved to kings," the Englishman said gallantly, "and beautiful queens, like Madame."

It seemed to Charlotte that everyone was terribly flip today. She did not answer, and Warwick saw tears of anger or chagrin gathering in her eyes.

"If Your Majesty permit," he began tactfully, addressing the king, "I think I had better—"

"I think so too, my lord. I shall send for you. Do not be observed by spies, of course."

The earl bowed himself out, his face now under control but smile wrinkles crinkling the corners of his eyes.

"Warwick's French is a little lame," Louis explained, "and 'outraged' has an indelicate overtone in English. Now what is all this about Olivier?"

Tearfully she told him.

"Consider the gutter he came from, Charlotte; the rabble are very direct. And after all, he is a doctor. And after all—well, I am not actually senile yet."

"I think you're just as outrageous as he is, Louis. Maybe I won't tell you what I was going to after all!"

"Tell me what?"

"You'll know," she smiled. "Everyone will know."

"Charlotte, my dear, tell me what everyone will know."

"Never mind. And this Warwick person, whoever he is, has a grossly evil mind."

"Oh, the British don't have any manners at all, especially the great British lords. This 'Warwick person' is very important. A little French gold—nay, actually an enormous amount, but I have it—Burgundy thinks he's going to get it, but he won't—over the Channel to England flies my French gold, and voilà! King Henry will snatch the British crown right off King Edward's head. You invaded my audience chamber, my dear; now you must carry the burden of this great state secret. What else do you carry that makes you blush and turn away?"

She hid her face against his shoulder. "I do not know; you talk so fast; perhaps another secret, half mine, half yours."

"Oh, I thank God! My sweet Charlotte, sweet wife, sweet queen!"

"I didn't say it for sure."

"Nay, it's got to be true. God has heard my prayers."

"Mine too, Louis."

The queen's disclosure of her probable condition set him to strutting like a peacock and made the ridicule of the Parisian citizenry doubly intolerable. Pasque Dieu, he was not a man to be trifled with! Shortly from the steps of all the churches in the city, from the portico of the Hôtel de Ville, from all the public squares, a solemn manifesto was shouted by the heralds with all the pomp and circumstance of a declaration of national emergency. He racked no one, he hanged no one, but he was determined that never again should he hear the name of Péronne.

Most of the manifesto dealt with abusive street singing, chalking on walls, defacing public property, exhibiting defamatory placards, and the like, all of which were strictly forbidden henceforth under threat of imprisonment. It had long been expected, people wondered why he had not acted immediately after his return; the game had begun to lose its interest anyhow, like bear baiting when the bear refused to growl back at the dogs.

But the last of the manifesto—King Louis XI was nothing if not thorough—provided amusement to everyone except a few Parisian bird fanciers. Either they would now have to destroy their pets or reeducate them, which was almost impossible. Talking birds were proverbially tactless and always said the wrong thing when the wrong people were around.

In Paris many good citizens kept caged birds and taught them to mimic human speech. A cheap and delightful hobby. But embarrassing now. For "Péronne" was a word which birds could easily learn and which had been taught to scores of them.

"On this day by the authority of this summons," proclaimed the solemn manifesto, "the sergeants of the City of Paris shall bring before the king all starlings, magpies, parrots, ravens, and jays, whether in cages or leashed or tamed in any wise soever, and the said sergeants shall register the said birds, together with the names and residences of their owners. And be it further known that all the words which have been taught the aforesaid birds and which they shall speak shall be registered and written down."

Many a luckless bird found himself suddenly transformed into an inarticulate pie. A few were taken into custody and had their vocabularies gravely recorded, then were duly returned to their owners when proved innocent, as of course they were bound to be or they would have been pies too. *Péronne* was not safe to say, even for the birds.

In Burgundy, Philippe de Comines heard of the incident, which in his scholarly mind he called the Ornithological Inquisition, and contrasted King Louis's ways with the terrible ways of Duke Charles. The subtle Burgundian noted also, as summer came and went, that the king seemed to feel himself strong enough to write to his good cousin regretting that a press of business kept him in Paris and that a return visit for the feast was impracticable. Comines sniffed the political wind suspiciously. Then suddenly everything became clear. From England came news that King Edward was overthrown and that King Henry, friendly to France, had the crown again. The spider had somehow thrown his web across the Channel and influenced the course of English civil war. He could manage something bigger than revolts in Burgundian municipalities now. Duke Charles had lost both his ally and his power to threaten Louis with invasion. It was a significant omen, even if it should not last, an auspicious turn of fortune for France. He was less superstitious than most men, but he could not put out of his mind how the ancient Romans predicted the future with birds. The very word *auspicious* meant bird watcher! The letters from the Burgundian chancellery became more cordial than Duke Charles's present weakness, which might be temporary, necessitated.

Chapter Forty-six

It was soon apparent that the queen had been right when she told the king that she carried a certain secret. Louis's desire for a son was so fanatic, his jubilation at the possibility so intense, that he rushed to his barber for an explanation of every trivial symptom. It was a trying time for Olivier le Daim. One morning Louis said: "Her Majesty ate some pickles for breakfast. Four pickles; I counted them. What does that mean? Well, fellow, is it to be a prince or a princess? Quickly!"

The barber sighed. It meant, of course, that the lady craved pickles. Last year's crop was old and soft; this year's wasn't ready yet. Queen or peasant, that's how they always behaved. But you could not tell King Louis that.

Olivier put on his most serious professional face, leaning forward, which accentuated his hump, frowning in concentration, stroking his beard and nodding. In such a pose he looked immensely wise. "What did Her Majesty desire most when the princesses were born?" he inquired gravely.

"Why, as I remember, it was peaches and cream for Anne, sugar, I think, for Jeanne."

"Ah, yes," mused the barber. "I see; I see." Too much significance should not be attached to Madame's appetite, he warned, but one could hazard a certain inferential prognosis. It was widely held among the lower classes—and God forbid that His Majesty should think he applied their rules to Madame—that a craving for sweets like peaches and cream and figs and sugar meant a girl, whereas pickles and lemons and sour things meant a boy. "It is not too much to predict, Your Majesty, and I would be willing to stake my reputation on it, that France will soon have a dauphin!" Well, the chances were fifty-fifty. It was as good reasoning as that of the university doctors who solemnly taught that the world was flat because the winds were said to come from the four corners of the earth. He could always hang himself if he was wrong. Most of all, it was what the king wanted to hear.

"If the rule applies to the rabble, who are wise in some ways, assuredly it applies to royalty too. I doubt if there's any real fundamental difference anyhow."

"That is one of the reasons the people love Your Majesty."

"Do not suppose that I am ignorant of the fact that they call me 'the bourgeois king,' " he said severely. It was not flattering, but it was better than being called a spider.

Pickles and politics and pregnancy could occupy his mind at the same time. "Is it safe for the queen to ride about the town? She is pale. She keeps indoors too much."

"Not ride, Your Majesty."

"An open litter, then?"

"Nothing would be better for her than a little sunlight."

Louis took her to the Fir Cone Tavern, famous for its food, but public, where the pickles, he assured her, were the best to be found in the kingdom, having first apprised the proprietor, a Dennys Hesslin, of his intention. And Pasque Dieu, let there be such pickles as no one had ever before eaten in June! The proprietor, rich, respectable, but plebeian, almost wept for joy. "Your Majesty, you have immortalized me!" The pickles were divine.

"But Louis," the queen said demurely, "could you not have had the proprietor deliver them to the palace?"

"My dear," the king said, "the constitution of a pickle is perpetually poised in a state of most delicate balance. It slumbers in a bath of aromatics; it must not be rudely awakened. Shake up the barrel, roil up the spices and brine—Pasque Dieu! Everything is ruined. Like vintage wine, a proper pickle is always tenderly decanted."

The queen laughed. "You do not deceive me, Louis. You wanted me to get out in the sun." Yet she enjoyed the gentle ride in the litter, the warm sunlight, the fresh air, the cheering crowds.

"I confess it," he smiled.

But he did not confess it all. He had wanted the crowds to cheer. They had seen their king often in public, seldom their shy little queen. Now she too, in spite of her condition, mingled among them. They took her to their vast plebeian hearts as the king helped her descend from the beautifully caparisoned litter, young, regal in her silver-embroidered cloak, a little cautious how she stepped but graciously smiling acknowledgment to their cheers—their queen, about to become a mother like the lowliest goodwife in the kingdom!

The little excursion proved such a success that the king, always quick to follow up an advantage, actually consented to act as godfather at the christening of a son who had just been born to the proprietor of the Fir Cone Tavern. After the ceremony he called the beaming father aside and whispered, "Where did you get those pickles, Maître Hesslin?"

"Your Majesty, a servant foundered three horses running them up from Auvergne."

Louis laughed heartily. Pasque Dieu, what a shaking up those barrels must have had!

In Burgundy Duke Charles, who was vitally interested in the king's having no heir, waited impatiently for the royal child to be born. His temper was foul, and he was difficult to get along with. Moreover, there was trouble in his province of Lorraine. He could not discover the agitators, and appointed a tyrannical governor to teach the people their places. Philippe de Comines again contrasted the ways of the two princes: one racked his rebels, the other wooed his people, standing godfather to the son of a tavern keeper! In a changing world was he not, perhaps, serving the wrong master?

On Saturday, June 30, 1470, the royal boy was born. King Louis at last had a son, France had a dauphin. The bell ringing and jubilation continued for hours; royal decree extended the traditional holiday to a full week; there was feasting and merrymaking at the king's expense for everybody, and a display of colored fireworks every night. Prisoners were pardoned, Cardinal Balue was released from his cage and given a cell in the Châtelet prison with only the bars on the window painted red. The king, remembering his vow, dutifully named his son Charles.

But the birth was not easy.

Louis could not remain in the stifling apartment where the great nobles and ecclesiastics had gathered to see the child born, traditionally authenticating the blood royal. It was not his prudery in the face of so solemn and mighty a thing that kept him away; it was Charlotte's screams. He strode like a panther back and forth in his private audience chamber, thankful that the walls were soundproof, though he had made them so for other reasons. Olivier raced from the queen to the king every few minutes to bring him news. At one point the doctor was able to say, "It is a boy." The king wanted to see him at once. Inexplicably the doctor had said, "The birth is not yet complete."

"Do not trifle with me, you creature! How do you know it's a boy if he isn't born yet?"

As tactfully as possible, lest he precipitate some crisis, Olivier explained that the dauphin was being born not as is ordinary but feet first. There was no cause for alarm. The midwives were competent. But—the head was large and still involved.

"Oh, God, so it was with me. My poor mother! My poor queen! Cannot something be done to blunt her pain?"

Such things had been tried, Olivier said, but nothing known to science could alleviate birth pains without endangering the life of the mother or the child or both, particularly the child.

No one who knew the queen, Olivier said, and the king had to agree, would suggest such an expedient.

"Nay, Charlotte would spit it out like poison. Damn you doctors, discover something!"

Olivier had been helpless.

After the dauphin was finally born successfully, had breathed and cried normally and kicked vigorously in his cradle, and the queen had recovered from the ordeal, he turned his attention to the improvement of medical knowledge. No one immediately discovered how to blunt the pains of childbirth, but great universities arose in Bordeaux, Valence, Nantes, and Bourges. The medical college in Valence in the Dauphiny was soon graduating the most capable physicians in Europe. Bordeaux in Guienne, site of his brother's ducal court, was ordered to specialize in theology, though law, letters, and medicine were taught too. "But I think," said the busy king, "that theology is right for Bordeaux. An odor of sanctity in the air ought to be good for my brother. It may offset the perfume of that woman of his."

His brother did not like the erection of academic buildings in the midst of a favorite park. "I take it unkindly," he wrote to the king, "that Your Majesty has spoiled a pleasant vista and attracted a noisy crowd of lowborn students to my capital without my leave."

The king answered testily, "Neither did your great university cost you anything, my lord duke of Guienne, and I know of no law that requires a student to be noble."

The king did not forget God in all his building of secular institutions; he built churches too. The clergy forgave him the imprisonment of one cardinal when they found new bells in their steeples, new vestments on their backs, new endowments in their parishes, splendid new soaring cathedrals with empty episcopal thrones to which any learned and eloquent churchman might aspire. The people had long since forgotten Péronne now that their sons could hope to be bishops, doctors, lawyers, even great officers of state; for it was increasingly clear to every Frenchman that Louis XI set no store whatsoever on birth, but much on ability.

He could afford these heavy expenses, for not one écu had he sent to Burgundy since the dauphin was born. And sensing the double loyalty of clergy and people, two of the three estates of the realm, he increased the taxes slightly, as he always did when he felt strong enough to do so. The people grumbled, but they did not revolt. They were getting a lot for their money.

Louis never forgot anything, especially Péronne. At the end of the year, the time during which he had solemnly sworn to observe the agreement, he summoned his parliament, which now suddenly could muster a quorum. He made them a long speech in person, which passion, daring, and natural eloquence made memorably convincing. Appealing to the ancient laws of the realm as King of France and overlord of Burgundy, he cited his vassal Duke Charles of Burgundy to appear before him and answer a formidable list of complaints: he had not sworn allegiance at the king's coronation; he had seized the Somme towns; he had attacked the royal standard displayed at Liége; he had abused his vassals, which were ultimate vassals of the crown—a feudal maneuver which took parliament by surprise—he had worn in public the British Order of the Garter, all contrary to French law. If, therefore, the Duke of Burgundy should not appear within three days, it was the duty of parliament to declare him a forsworn vassal with whom no agreement was possible.

Parliament voted favorably.
Duke Charles did not appear.
The Péronne agreement was dead.
The year had been wonderful.

In Burgundy, Philippe de Comines took up his pen to write a secret personal letter: reports of the continuing good health of the dauphin had reached his ears, he planned to say; he longed to see the little prince and renew his pleasant acquaintance with the king. Did His Majesty's invitation still hold good? He could come at once.

Just then news burst out of England that Warwick the kingmaker was dead in battle, King Henry was a prisoner in the Tower, King Edward was back on the throne. Philippe de Comines laid down his pen. Patience. One must wait and see.

Chapter Forty-seven

At first Louis refused to believe the news. It was well authenticated, but he tried by an effort of will to conjure it out of existence. If he could only do that, he would gain a few more days, a few more weeks to walk with Charlotte in the gardens, where the flowers were particularly luxuriant this year, or bend over the dauphin's cradle and admire with her the right royal kicking of their son, perhaps even assure her—and himself—from time to time that that large Valois head held promise of intellect beyond the usual capacity of princes. So much room to hold virtue and knowledge and courage, all the good things he would need when he came to govern the nation that was his birthright, all the lessons the king had learned and would pass on to his son. The queen, who had adored all her babies, was thankful she had a boy, since Louis now spent less time in that gloomy audience chamber where great diplomats came in by the front door and dirty, furtive little men, smelling of the people, sneaked in by a secret entrance. And her husband was happy beyond anything she had ever known him to be.

Some men had a capacity to deny reality, Louis knew. He tried hard.

But common report and his own agents, some of them English, verified the news of the upset across the Channel. Then the king tried to reason away the reality. True, the signs were bad, but Pasque Dieu, the British crown had been tossed back and forth for years. Henry would get it again. He, Louis, would see that he did.

But the king had soon to admit reluctantly, like a thirsty man from whom a cup is snatched after only a tantalizing sip, that he was not so constituted as to deny facts. How happy the infirmity of old Duke Philip the Good must have been: he had been able to make his own world where everything he longed for came true. His own infirmity only made him more aware of his danger. The news from England continued bad and got steadily worse.

The English king Henry had had a son, a boy of eighteen. The first report said he was wounded in the battle that cost his father the crown. But the second report said the boy had been murdered after the battle by King Edward's victorious nobles. Then Olivier whispered that Edward himself had stabbed him.

For a few shadowy weeks King Henry lingered a prisoner in the Tower of London. Then, like Charles the Simple at Péronne, he died. Then it was openly admitted that King Edward had had him murdered.

Louis felt his spine creep: kings were being murdered, kings' sons were being murdered! He looked at his queen over the cradle of the dauphin. "I am afraid I shall be unable to spend much time with you here in the future, Charlotte. It has been a blessed time. Remember I said that when I seem to neglect you. I have a presentiment that if I do not do my duty now as never before, the dauphin will not live to take my place."

"Are things so bad, Louis?"

"I've always won before," he said. But she did not like the look on his face. Savagery seemed out of place in a nursery where children were sleeping.

He had not answered her directly, but things were incomparably bad. True, King Henry had been the most hapless of monarchs, well meaning and trusting to a fault. But there were similarities too, too many for comfort, between him and Louis. The English king also had founded great schools of learning, Eton and Cambridge. He also had struggled with fractious nobles. He also was deeply religious. He also was lettered, cultured, and studious. He also had had an heir—for a hideous moment Louis pictured a dagger in the breast of his son, and passed his hand over his eyes, shuddering. And King Henry, like King Louis, had had mad old Charles VI of France for a grandfather.

Shortly the news out of England assumed the shape of catastrophe. Not only was King Henry murdered along with his heir. Sixteen great nobles of Henry's party were executed in rapid succession. Edward was taking no chances; his throne smoked with blood, but he had made it firm. The Wars of the Roses were over; the wrong man had won.

From France the Burgundian chancellery now began to receive conciliatory letters. Let not his good cousin take the recent action of parliament too seriously, Louis wrote. He wished to remain on the friendliest terms. Philippe de Comines tossed them aside for what they were worth. The Spider King would never be able to cheat *this* turn of fortune's wheel. He knew what even Louis did not yet know, and found out only after a cycle of weary months.

Down in Guienne his brother's sluggish wits were stirring. Till now he had been heir to the throne if Louis should die. But now there was a dauphin, a crown prince. Charles of Guienne became merely a younger brother without prospects. Even an oyster reacts when conditions are just right for it, when the sun shines warm and bright and the summer tides flood in. At such a time a brainless instinct tells it, This is the time to feed.

Now or never Charles must bestir himself. Many voices urged him to action. He had an ambitious mistress, who saw herself elevated to mistress, perhaps even queen, of a king of France. He was surrounded by a swarm of Louis's disgruntled nobles who, alarmed at the growth of Louis's power, saw in his brother Charles not a spider but a sheep, to be fleeced at their pleasure. What King Edward had done in England to King Henry and the Prince of Wales they plotted to do to King Louis and the little dauphin. Charles had Edward on his side; he also had Louis's bitterest enemy, the Duke of Burgundy. His courtiers whispered that he had brilliant prospects if only he would assert his power. "Your heartless brother, who spoiled your park, is helpless," the Count of Saint-Pol told him smoothly, "flanked on three sides by Duke Charles of Burgundy, Duke Charles of Guienne——"

"We are both Charleses, both dukes! That is good, that is good! It is good, isn't it?"

"Excellent. But not the whole of it. By sea Louis is bottled in by Edward's ships. That is good too. Now Guienne can trade again with England. The English love your wine."

"So do I," said Charles. "Probably there's enough to go round, though."

"Plenty for everybody, Your Grace. You need export only enough to pay for the glorious war that is coming, and when you are victorious you will be King of France."

"I should like to be a Most Christian Majesty. I am just as good as Louis."

"Better, Your Grace," they said. Everyone in the ducal court assured him that, with him at their head, or at least with the use of his name, this time surely they would humble the Spider King. But first, to be thorough, the danger that a crown prince always presented in historic crises of this sort would have to be forcefully removed.

Duke Charles did not immediately understand the soft, murderous suggestion. "Must you do that?" he asked when it was explained.

"King Edward did not hesitate for the good of England. Neither

329

must you, for the good of France. The greatest kings are never soft."

"Nay, who calls me soft!"

It was no easy task to penetrate the maze of security measures with which Louis protected the royal family: guards, watchmen, soldiers, spies, spies spying upon spies. Nor was the attempt made at once, for everyone knew the suspicious nature of the king. He would not relax his vigilance, but others lazier, with less to lose, lulled by the passage of time, inevitably would.

News of the gathering of all the old traitors around his brother's ducal court reached the king. He wrote friendly letters, entreating his brother to explain why he was not satisfied with the rich appanage of Guienne, offering one, two, then four more provinces in addition to all he already had. Charles of Guienne did not even answer, but the herald who had waited in vain for a reply, reported that an army was openly gathering in Guienne and ships were sailing constantly from Bordeaux to Portsmouth and from Portsmouth to Dunkirk: Guienne, England, and Burgundy were in communication by sea! Slowly, deliberately they were weaving the noose that would strangle him; there was no need to ask why his brother was not satisfied.

He drove himself and his generals to prepare France for civil war, the saddest of all his wars, since this would be between him and his own brother. Olivier often set the antimonium cup before him at supper these nights; always he drank it. Still he could not sleep, and the barber at his own expense—which he could well afford, for he was amassing a fortune—hired harpers to play softly outside his apartment, which he now occupied alone. Charlotte had never seen him in a seizure. In his present state of tension he was desperately afraid of one. He told her, which was true, that the nursery was safer for her and the children. It was barred as heavily as Cardinal Balue's cell. He seldom permitted her to venture out with them even to the palace gardens. He remembered how once, long ago, a tile had inexplicably fallen from a roof and missed him by inches. She complained that their health was suffering. "They're alive," he replied sharply. They would not be if Saint-Pol, Alençon, Nemours, and some of his other vassals succeeded in making his brother king. The Duke of Guienne, with astonishing naïveté, was publicly boasting that he would be Most Christian Majesty within a year. He had placed Count Jean d'Armagnac in command of the army of Guienne. At that Louis could hardly believe his ears, but it was a measure of the peril.

The king sent to Scotland, Italy, Savoy, Switzerland, for soldiers to augment his army, offering such wages as no soldiers had ever earned before. Thousands joined him. But there were thousands in Guienne too, and more thousands in England, veterans of the Wars of the Roses. Old memories of the brutalized Butchers tormented him. And there were more thousands in Burgundy.

He appealed to the pope to judge between him and his brother. The

330

pope replied with a suggestion that Cardinal Balue be released from his cage, which His Holiness understood was four feet wide, six feet high, and eight feet long. Furiously the king retorted that Balue had been caged only a few months, was now comfortably housed in a dry commodious cell in the Châtelet in spite of persistent gossip to the contrary, and challenged the Holy Father to appoint a commission to investigate, adding sarcastically that his cages were not like Italian cages: far roomier. He tore up the letter, of course, and had a less offensive, more diplomatic one written. But he did not release the cardinal, and the pope did not take sides.

One of the diplomatic things in the letter to the pope made history. Louis had ordered mass prayers for peace at high noon every day. Henceforth every Frenchman, whoever he was, would stop whatever he was doing when he heard the midday bells, bow his head, and recite three Ave Marias.

Organized prayers for peace on a national scale had never been known before, far less commanded by royal edict. Louis was assaulting the gate of Heaven itself, clamoring to be heard. If one prayer was good, how much better and louder and more efficient sixteen million prayers would be, all uttered simultaneously!

Not everyone prayed in a realm so divided, especially the great lords. But the little people, as always, wanted peace; the threat of another, longer, more terrible war, with hideously improved new weapons, was dark and heavy. In their thousands in the shops, in their millions in the fields, wherever church bells could be heard—and that was everywhere— the little people of France pulled off their caps and paused and prayed the first *Angelus*. The beautiful national custom was destined to survive long after the emergency that created it was forgotten, the generation that first uttered the prayer dust, and the king who commanded it a legend.

Louis did not pray the first Angelus.

His hat was on his head, his rim of leaden saints rattled as his whole body shook, not with sickness but with fury. His face sweated in the fierce heat of a forge where an executioner was heating torture irons. He did not hear the church bells of Paris, for he was deep underground in a prison dungeon, and the screams of the man as the irons were applied drowned out all other sounds.

It was routine work for the executioner, who was employed, like his father before him, by the governor of the Châtelet prison. Sometimes he was careless, but not today, for never before had the king shown any interest in witnessing the interrogation of prisoners. "Will I kill him before he speaks?" the executioner asked in an aggrieved tone. "Not I, Your Majesty. We don't get the credit we deserve as professional men. We have legal standing. We have a guild. We have to study, like lawyers and surgeons. This work is an art, Your Majesty. I learned it as a boy; I am expert. He will not even lose consciousness. He will talk, and when he goes to trial there will be no ugly marks, since I never touch the face—"

"Silence!"

"I was only explaining—"

"Be silent. I must not miss a word he says. You too, over there, be silent!" The prison chaplain was praying too loudly.

"I always pray, Your Majesty. Sometimes they go very unexpectedly."

"God has good ears. Let *me* hear what he says!"

The man who lay spread-eagled on the rack, whose body still smoked in spots where the red-hot irons had seared the flesh, was a burly young gardener employed in the palace gardens. He had always been steady and dependable. Louis, whose spies shadowed even the gardeners, had reported that his habits were regular, except perhaps that he drank on Saturday nights. Since he was always sober by Monday, the king had treated the matter lightly. Charlotte liked him. He was a genius with roses.

This morning she had taken the children into the garden for one of the rare outings that the king now allowed. The gardener had suddenly left the bush he was pruning and turned his knife on the dauphin.

A seemingly half-idiot assistant who worked with him—he had complained about the stupidity of this helper—suddenly underwent a startling change of character. He jumped up, shouted with crisp authority, and threw himself between the knife and the child and, though he suffered a slight wound, succeeded in holding the assassin till help came. It was astonishing how soon help arrived. Charlotte had thought the garden all but deserted. In seconds it swarmed with the king's spies.

In minutes the gardener was stretched on the rack.

"Why did you do it? Who put you up to it?" Louis demanded. He was utterly unmoved by the torture of the man who had tried to kill his son.

"I am already dead," the gardener groaned. "I won't tell."

Louis smiled unpleasantly. Dead he already was, for the king had decided. But not before he revealed who had hired him. "Touch him more firmly, Executioner." Again the searing of flesh and the screams. He was a powerful man. The executioner expertly adjusted the wheel of the rack, putting more tension on the ropes lest the prisoner writhe too freely and spoil the precision of the iron as it sought out the tenderest spots.

"Well, fellow, this can hardly be pleasant for you. Why did you do it? What made you turn on my son? Have you a son? Suppose I should turn on him! You would be here to watch. Well?"

"No son," the man groaned, gritting his teeth. "Damn you, king! God damn you to hell!"

Louis shrugged; the priest prayed; in the background Olivier le Daim watched with a curious light in his small sharp eyes. The king nodded to the executioner, who again applied the iron.

When the shrieks subsided the king said: "Now will you tell me?

332

What was the reason? Drink? Money? A woman—" The man's face altered slightly. Louis was at his ear in a bound. "No one shall harm her! I swear it on my saints! No one shall know. You did it for a woman? Nay, that is understandable. You wanted to be rich and buy her pretty things? Tell me like your own father confessor! Let me put an end to your pain. I can. I will. I swear it on my saints if you tell." His voice was full of understanding; his face seemed very kind.

The tortured man nodded. It was a woman; he did want to buy her pretty things.

"You should have come to me. I like women too. I could have given you money. I still will, if you tell me who paid you. Tell me who paid you."

"He's gone."

"Who was he?"

"You won't burn me again?"

"On my saints I swear it. Whisper to me. Who paid you?" The king bent his ear close.

It was an emissary, the man confessed, an emissary who then disappeared, an emissary of the Duke of Guienne.

The king drew in his breath in a long, satisfied hiss, "Ah-h-h! I am not surprised." He rose and stood back from the man, who turned his face and looked hopefully toward him.

"Now kill him," the king said.

The executioner raised a white-hot iron to plunge it into the prisoner's bowels.

"Liar!" the man screamed. "Liar! Liar! Liar!"

Olivier le Daim darted from the shadows behind the king's back. "No! No! Not in the belly! You'll ruin everything! Your Majesty, you promised me!"

The priest laid a restraining hand on the executioner's arm. "Your Majesty, for the records of the prison, wait! This man has not been tried. Your Majesty's laws are so well known—the courts are so strict nowadays—"

"You want a trial? He shall have a trial! Court's, eh? The king is a court, the court of last resort. Prisoner, you have confessed high treason. Priest, mark down the proceedings of this trial for your prison records. Confessed prisoner, do you know the law of high treason? Listen to the law. To compass, contrive, devise, plot, or imagine the death of the king, the queen or their eldest son and heir—have I more than one?— that is high treason. That is the law. Do you know the punishment for high treason? Listen. The traitor shall be drawn on a hurdle to the place of execution and there be hanged by the neck, but not till he be dead, and while yet alive be disembowelled and his body divided into four quarters, the head and quarters to be at the disposal of the king. Now you are fairly tried. You are guilty. But the king can be merciful. I promised you would not be burned again. I promise to put an end to your pain.

The king does not lie. Executioner, execute him quickly before I do."

The doctor cried: "Your Majesty has forgotten your promise! Your Majesty has forgotten me!"

The executioner, confused by the orders and restrictions, hesitated how to dispatch the prisoner and picked up a hatchet.

"Oh, no, oh, no!" Olivier pleaded.

"Nay, hold," Louis said. "I promised my doctor something."

Olivier whispered, "He will spoil a beautiful specimen."

"Then you do it."

"I am a surgeon, not a hangman, Sire!"

"Pasque Dieu, you two fools. Get on with it."

"I will show him how," Olivier said.

The king nodded assent. The priest crossed himself with a shaking hand.

Under Olivier's direction the executioner carefully stuffed rags into the condemned man's throat and held his nostrils shut till he died of suffocation. "Depart, O Christian soul—" intoned the priest.

"Well, I certainly never did that before," the executioner said. "I don't think it hurt at all."

"I doubt if it was pleasant," Louis said.

Olivier asked, "May I have him now?"

The king rose to go.

"I don't care."

"What—what is to be done with the body?" the priest interposed. He feared he knew not what black magic and necromancy. Olivier's reputation was not good.

"I shall dissect it, Your Reverence."

"You must not."

"To know the body is a surgeon's business. How can I cure the living unless I study the dead?"

"It is contrary to canon law," the priest said.

Louis asked slyly, "Are you sure, good father?"

The chaplain fumbled in his thoughts. He was of peasant stock, a simple man in a thankless post. People avoided him on the street. His duties in the Châtelet had never required study of the monumental compilation of legislation that made up the corpus of canon law, nor was he wise enough to interpret it. "It is certainly contrary to custom," he said stoutly.

Olivier, seeing his prize slipping away, said in exasperation, "You cut up dead bodies of the saints, and very awkwardly sometimes, and scatter them all over the world; but you stand there and tell me that I, a surgeon, shall not dissect one body of a dead criminal in the interest of science!"

"Softly, Olivier," the king said. "We shall leave this decision to an expert. If my memory serves me, Cardinal Balue is still in residence in this place. Go to him, Olivier, and get his opinion. Would you like to go too, good chaplain, if you think Monsieur Le Daim is a liar?"

"I meant to suggest no such thing," the priest said in a frightened voice. "Naturally, if the cardinal permits I must have been wrong in my objection."

As they left the dungeon Louis remembered something. Looking at the still corpse on the rack, he murmured: "It's a pity he didn't tell me the name of his woman. I should have sent her these."

Deliberately he placed a copper penny on each of the dead man's eyes. "There, fellow. I promised you money. I always keep my word."

Chapter Forty-eight

Olivier le Daim had his prize. For weeks he was busy in his dark study, where the door was always locked and from which issued an odor of alcohol, aromatics, and death. He had never been liked; palace attendants now crossed themselves when they walked by his door—whatever unholy thing he was doing should not be allowed. Some of his evil reputation passed by association to the king. But his mood was exalted. How superior this fresh specimen was to the rotting debris he had snatched from graves!

"The things I am learning, Your Majesty! The things I have already learned! Medical history will remember you."

"Eh?"

The dead gardener had ceased to interest the king. He had served his purpose the instant he identified the king's brother as the power behind the attempt on the dauphin's life. Louis feared there would be other attempts as long as Charles of Guienne lived. He doubled the guards around Charlotte and the children; he doubled his efforts to prepare France for civil war. Absorbed in his military activities, he had forgotten his doctor.

"What was that you said, Olivier?"

"What I have learned, Your Majesty. Men have galls, just like ferrets!"

"Very likely, very likely," the king said idly. "Mark it down. Keep clear records of everything always. By the way, how did you convince the cardinal?"

The doctor hesitated slightly. "I made a little promise in your name. I said you would release him. His Eminence immediately remembered nothing in canon law that forbids dissection of a body, though he was

335

adamant on the subject of desecration. As if I would desecrate so beautiful an object!"

The king's conscience did not trouble him, nor was he especially interested. "You promised, I did not." Nor did he care whether human beings had one gall or a dozen. He was too occupied even to worry about his health.

Suddenly, for the first time since the king had known him, the doctor fell ill. He had prepared a new medicine for the king. If ferret gall was beneficial in the falling sickness, was it not reasonable that the fresh gall of a healthy human in the prime of life would prove even more beneficial? Much medical reasoning was based on equally far-fetched analogy, like the administration of extract of mummies, which never decayed, to preserve the body from decay, a standard remedy. But lest the new preparation poison his master, Olivier tried it first on himself. It did not work; it gave him cramps and made him retch; he destroyed it.

He used his obvious illness as an excuse for a further venture. He wished, he said, to leave the court for some weeks.

"I cannot spare you," the king said, "though I feel well at the moment."

"But I am sick, Your Majesty."

"So is France. Stay here."

"I had thought that a little trip to the south would restore me. Many beneficial herbs are available there which cannot be bought in Paris now that the Guienne border is closed."

The king looked at him oddly. "Where do you propose to go?"

"Guienne, Your Majesty."

"Bordeaux?"

"Perhaps."

"You and your beard and your elegant dress are well known by now, Monsieur Le Daim," the king reminded him.

"No one would recognize one more humpbacked beggar, without a beard, clothed in rags and"—he looked away—"with a chin that will not invite close scrutiny."

The king said heavily, choosing his words, "Your health is, of course, of great importance to me and to France. On second thought I feel that I have no right to forbid you to go."

"Thank you, Your Majesty," the barber began in an excited whisper. "I plan—"

"Keep your plan to yourself! But take my good wishes with you for the success of your mission, which I call God to witness you state is the gathering of some herbs."

"And I shall bring them back to prove it, I swear by all the saints."

Louis detached the purse from his belt. "Take this to speed your journey."

The barber took it without hesitation. "No doubt I shall have to hire assistants to help me gather the herbs."

336

"I do not wish to hear the details. I am extremely busy."

He had heard no evil, spoken no evil. Before the whole court of heaven, if some literal-minded angel should accuse him, he could say: "Prove it! I stand on the letter of the law! Prove wherein by word or deed I plotted the sin of Cain. The thing was done without my knowledge."

During the time that Olivier was gone, the threat of war edged ever closer. Louis's couriers could not get through to his brother in Bordeaux. Letters from Burgundy ceased. In England the victorious Edward made a royal progress through his realm, giving great feasts—he was a tremendous eater—in the cities that had supported him, sitting in bloody judgment on citizens of cities that had opposed him. The sixteen great nobles were already executed; now he turned on the lesser leaders. "And his was the white-rose badge!" Louis muttered. How red it was now. Louis disliked gluttons on principle and hated all Englishmen by instinct, but he grudgingly admitted that Edward had known how to bring peace out of civil chaos.

Olivier's long absence frightened the king. He told himself that he missed the deft and gentle razor, or the watchdog alertness with which the barber stood guard over the smallest details of his health. Once he imagined he had a chill, and called for the antimonium cup, thinking to treat himself in secret, and poured into it a draught of wine. But his mind was busy with other matters, he used the wrong wine, or he let it stand too long; it tasted bitter—poison must taste like that—and it purged him painfully next day. Then he admitted to himself that what he really feared was that Olivier had been recognized and caught. He did not suppose Olivier would stand up well under torture. He trembled at what he might confess to an executioner.

One night there was a familiar scratching on the secret door of his audience chamber. Dressed in rags, a stubble beard already growing back on his chin, Olivier entered the room. He placed a soiled little cloth bag smelling vaguely of common mint on the king's writing table. "The herbs I promised Your Majesty. Thanks to your kindness I am now in the best of health."

So was the king's brother, as far as the king knew. He had asked his best agents repeatedly for reports on Duke Charles of Guienne. News was sketchy and hard to get, but what there was, was in no way unusual.

"Was your mission a success?"

"Yes, Sire." There was a note of triumph in the doctor's voice.

"I am usually well informed, but I heard nothing of you down there."

"I will gladly relate in detail all that I did."

"No."

But Olivier could see from the king's face that he did not mean "No."

"Naturally I preferred to do nothing conspicuous that might be connected with my absence or with you."

337

"Is there any news of my brother?" Louis asked, as if he were changing the subject.

"The Duc de Guienne sups every night with Madame de Montsoreau, who is pinker and plumper than ever. Often his almoner, a Favre Vesois, joins them."

"A tidy arrangement, Pasque Dieu! One's almoner and one's mistress. She is a charity?"

"They are all good friends and boon drinking companions."

"Bad brother, bad woman, bad priest."

Next day Olivier le Daim made his official reappearance at court. On first seeing him the king crossed himself. The creature must be a witch! Overnight his beard was full-grown, glossy, black, and carefully waxed into a point as usual. Then Louis remembered with a revulsion of the stomach that the gardener had had hair like that. He could not bring himself to let Olivier shave him.

The barber laughed. "It is only the hair from a horse's tail. All barbers know that hair from the head is thin and weak; the beard is thick and wiry. No, no, the traitor went back to the Châtelet long since, and no doubt the good chaplain has given him honest Christian burial by now. I stitched him into a man again. Even the cardinal would have been satisfied. Very well, I shall stop talking."

"There was no news from Guienne today," the king said, submitting to the razor.

"If I were an astrologer," Olivier smiled, "I should say, in a week the planets will conjoin themselves into a configuration favorable to Your Majesty."

The week passed, nothing favorable happened, and Olivier went about the palace with a curiously dejected air that only the king could fathom. So be it; whatever the plan, it must have miscarried. Perhaps he would not have to defend himself in heaven. He did not thank God that his soul was clear of complicity in a brother's murder, for he was squarely on record with God that he knew nothing about it.

Then a rumor filtered up from Bordeaux that Madame de Montsoreau was ill. At the end of a week she was worse. Then the rumors flew thick and fast: she was dying, and Charles of Guienne was beside himself with grief, unable to sign the few letters and orders that constituted his only duties as head of the coalition against the king. Four weeks later she died.

Olivier said, "This is not the favorable configuration that I foresaw, Your Majesty."

"Do not mention it. I forbid you. You were gathering herbs. I have them in my writing table. Go often in public. Let people see you. Let them remember that you have been in Paris more than a month. Mention that frequently. Let no one be able to say, 'Behold the cause; behold the effect.'"

338

Louis sent a herald with a letter of condolence to his brother. Seeing the lilies edged in mourning on his tabard, the border guards let him through. But he was stopped, rudely searched, and turned back at the gates of Bordeaux. The letter would be delivered to His Grace, he was told, but His Grace would see no emissary of King Louis.

Surly and taciturn as the guards might be, the peasants were willing to talk. The Duc de Guienne was also ill, they said in whispers. He was suffering from a sickness in the stomach like that of his father King Charles VII. "Tell the king," they said, "that we pray God to preserve him from a similar ailment."

"Amen!" Louis said vehemently when the herald reported the loyal wishes of the people. "Were they praying the Angelus?"

"Everywhere, even in Guienne."

"Good. Did you stop to pray, too?"

"Sire, I confess that I rode so fast—"

"You would have been punished if you had stopped. I am glad to hear that you prayed without stopping."

It was always good news to hear that the people were loyal. It was good news that his enemy was incapacitated. The good news continued. English and Burgundian ambassadors stood by helplessly and watched the key figure in the coalition against the king grow daily weaker and thinner. Some of the great rebel lords wavered, for if Charles of Guienne should die there would be no prince of blood royal to rally round, no vestige of legitimacy to their revolt; and they did not trust one another.

And they were frightened that Louis, from a distance of a hundred leagues, seemed able to conjure away the life of an enemy. Old stories that the king was a witch revived. New stories were told of a room in the palace where no one went but the king and his doctor, a dark place smelling of death. There, it was said, they drank blood and wrought spells and invoked demons.

Duke Charles of Burgundy stormed and raged and called for immediate invasion; Edward of England said he must wait for the Duke of Guienne to recover. An invader needed a friendly faction among the invaded.

Eight months after the death of Madame de Montsoreau, the Duke of Guienne turned yellow, spat blood, and died screaming that Louis had poisoned him.

Then it was remembered that Favre Vesois, the duke's almoner, had caught and prepared a fish of great size and personally cooked it and served it to Charles of Guienne and his mistress a month before she died.

There was a hysterical cry of "Poison!" The unfortunate almoner was thrown into prison. The next morning he was found strangled in his cell.

In Burgundy Duke Charles took up the fratricidal cry, but Edward of England replied with British phlegm that he knew of no poison which took a month to prove fatal to a woman and then required eight months more to prove fatal to a man. King Edward knew chaos intimately and at firsthand. In the welter of confusion that immediately followed the death of the king's brother, he knew that no French noble, no French faction, was to be trusted. The time was not yet ripe for an invasion of the continent. He returned to the consolidation of his realm.

One by one Louis's rebel lords left Bordeaux, left one another, and returned to their fiefs. There was now no royal sheep for them to fleece. There was only the terrible Spider King.

The one thing that could have broken the coalition had happened. How Louis had compassed the death of his brother an awed Europe could only speculate; but that he had been responsible for that death, so opportune, so absolutely essential to him, no enemy doubted and many friends believed. It was noticed that he had aged greatly in appearance.

Alone, Charles of Burgundy declared war.

Chapter Forty-nine

It was war, but a Burgundian war on a single front, not the crushing encirclement of a coalition that the king had feared.

In Burgundy Duke Charles published a screaming manifesto. It reached far back to the death of Charles VII and accused Louis of poisoning his father, though everyone knew Louis had been in Burgundy at that time. It accused Louis of trying to poison him himself at Péronne, though everyone knew Louis had been alone and a prisoner at Péronne. And now, charged the manifesto, the Spider King had brought about the death of his brother in Guienne by means of poisons, witchcraft, conjury, and diabolical invocations.

"He charges too much," Louis said, grimly reading a copy of the manifesto. "Philippe de Comines did not write this. He would have been more specific. People will believe one big lie but not a mass of little ones that betray confusion of purpose." He wondered how so inept a manifesto had come out of the Burgundian chancellery. Duke Charles's incorrigible temper, probably. The duke was openly swearing to avenge the death of his ally by putting all France to fire and sword.

He was as good as his word in so far as his power availed him. He crossed the Somme and invaded France. At the little town of Nesle, which was helpless before his army, he called for a parley with the mayor of the place to arrange terms of surrender; and while the gates of the town were open he entered with his soldiers. The affrighted in-habitants, men, women, and children, fled to the parish church for sanc-tuary. The duke gave the order to butcher them all on the spot. En-tering the church on horseback, surveying the devastation, he shouted to his soldiers, "By St. George, lads, you have stocked a right good abat-toir!" His horse was red to the fetlocks.

The fate of Nesle served as a warning to other towns. When the Bur-gundians arrived at Beauvais on the road to Paris, they were met with fanatical resistance. Even the women took part in the defense of the city, and another Jeanne, like Jeanne d'Arc, wrote her name large in the heroic annals of France. Her name was Jeanne Lainé. A Burgundian man-at-arms had actually planted the Burgundian flag on the battlements. She flung herself upon him. With a hatchet she struck him down and top-pled him into the moat, hurling the Burgundian flag after him. "Jeanne Hachette! Jeanne Hachette!" the French defenders screamed, heartened by her exploit. The Burgundians, disheartened and ashamed in propor-tion, withdrew and settled down to an unproductive siege. Then Louis relieved the place with an army, and Duke Charles marched away. His prestige had suffered a double defeat: Burgundians had been repulsed, and women, *women* had helped repulse them!

The king remained in Paris at the heart of his kingdom, but he had learned to be everywhere at once. Couriers galloping over the wonderful web of roads that fanned out from Paris; cannons at intervals thundering signals by day, rocket signals of fire by night, even carrier pigeons, kept him informed. By means of them he moved his armies, not as in a mo-ment of forgetfulness he had done at Montlhéry, but like a master chess-man brooding over every piece on the board, seeing and managing the whole. While one force relieved Beauvais, another marched south to re-store order in his dead brother's chaotic province. With force marched favor. Never before had the people of Guienne had a voice in their own government. A royal emissary with the army convoked an assembly of notables. It was the king's pleasure, he told them smiling, that they elect representatives and govern themselves. The cheering provincials rallied solidly behind the king. Then the army marched farther south and be-sieged Count Jean d'Armagnac in Lectoure. The city fell. Count Jean was stabbed to death. High and Low Armagnac were confiscated to the crown.

"I should have done that years ago," the king commented with satis-faction when he heard the news. "I was soft in those days."

His agents were busy too. Shortly in Burgundian Lorraine the people revolted against Duke Charles's tyrannical governor, Peter von Hagen-bach. The burghers sat in judgment upon him, found him guilty, tor-tured and hanged him.

Charles the Terrible, till now so proud, sued for a truce. Louis gra-ciously accorded it at Senlis on October 23, 1472, after less than a year of war.

Now there was time to cut down another traitor. In the spring he cited the Duc d'Alençon to appear before parliament, which convicted him of treason and condemned him to death. Louis commuted his sentence to life imprisonment but confiscated his estates to the crown. Fall of the House of Armagnac! Fall of the House of Alençon! He was toppling like rotten castles the great edifices of feudalism.

Péronne, which had brought him so low, was now only a recurrent nightmare, lost in the triumph of the victory of Senlis. No subtle man, casting about for a master, could hesitate whom to choose now.

At the signing of the Treaty of Senlis, Philippe de Comines, handing the ducal seal to Charles of Burgundy, whose face was an apoplectic red, whispered as the duke pressed it into the wax and stamped out of the room, "Would it please Your Most Christian Majesty to grant me a private audience?"

The king smiled Yes. "I have waited for you many years, Messire d'Argenton." It was a victory even greater than the truce, for Philippe de Comines was a weathervane, and the political wind was blowing fair for France.

Philippe de Comines did not enter the service of his new master empty-handed, and set out at once to make himself useful in the office of grand chancellor which Louis immediately gave him, saying, "I am unconquerable now." Comines had some interesting correspondence relative to the Count of Saint-Pol.

"It was my duty to intercept these at the time, Your Majesty. Now it is my duty to deliver them. They are addressed to you." Saint-Pol was offering his services too.

"Pasque Dieu, that perpetual traitor!"

"It hurt my conscience that I did not turn them over to Duke Charles," Philippe de Comines said, tongue in cheek. "But happily a truce exists and it is not too late to repair my neglect. The duke always needs money. Nothing would please him more than to confiscate Saint-Pol's Flemish estates."

"Nothing would please me more than to confiscate his French estates. And his head."

The king sent an army to the north. Philippe de Comines sent the traitorous letters to Duke Charles. Alarmed at the approach of the troops, Saint-Pol fled over the border to the friend of his youth, whose equerry he had been. Louis wrote to him to have no fear; the French army were in the vicinity only to reoccupy the Somme territories in accordance with a string of old treaties, all of which he cited. Calling Saint-Pol by his French name, he wrote, "Come and see me, Louis, for I can always use a head like yours." The king's next remark to Comines was exactly what Comines expected. "No," the grand chancellor smiled, "Your Majesty will have no use for the body."

Saint-Pol prudently remained in Burgundy. Louis demanded his extradition as a French vassal.

Duke Charles replied that he would exchange the Count of Saint-Pol for René of Lorraine, a Burgundian feudatory who had rebelled and fled to France for asylum.

Louis hesitated only for a moment. René was a relative of sorts, grandson of old King René of Provence. But the tie between him and the grandson of his uncle was thin indeed. "The exchange would eliminate any ambiguity that might arise in connection with your uncle's will," Philippe de Comines reminded him. Provence was to come to Louis when old René should die.

The cynical exchange was made. Saint-Pol lost his French estates, his Burgundian estates, and his head. Another great feudal house, the House of Saint-Pol, had fallen.

René of Lorraine also died. Down in Provence his moribund grandfather painted gloomy pictures, but he did not change his will. He knew it would do no good; Louis would take Provence anyway as soon as he died. So be it. Let France grow, as it was miraculously growing under Louis XI. One day, God willing, there would be peace. No one else had ever achieved it; Louis's methods might. Shortly King René did die, and the map of France leapt south to rest upon the Mediterranean. From the Pyrenees to the Somme, from the Alps to the Atlantic, from the Channel to the Mediterranean, France!

"Now," said the king, "I must have the Rhine."

Chapter Fifty

He wanted the Rhine because a Gallic precision of mind demanded that broad, majestic river for the northern boundary of France in place of the Somme, which wandered this way and that, sometimes north, sometimes south, in a purposeless fashion, as if it shared the unstable character of Duke Charles, whose Burgundian territories it bounded, all frantic motion and no direction. There was a singleness of purpose that the king could understand in the way the ancient Rhine flowed undisturbed to the sea.

But the king did not want war to get the Rhine. It would come to him automatically when Burgundy was conquered. He did not want war even to conquer Burgundy. He had always been appalled that the fate of a whole nation could be decided by the outcome of one battle, and that one battle could be lost in one hour by one trivial accident. He had never forgotten Montlhéry, which he would have won but for the panic of Charles of Melun. True, Melun had been a coward. But even brave men had been known to desert for obscure personal reasons. Courageous warriors had sometimes unthinkingly eaten their usual breakfasts; nausea would seize them in the violent exertion of battle; they would vomit in their tight-fitting helmets and have to leave the field. Too much could hang on too little in war.

War, to the king in his maturity, was only one aspect of diplomacy. He was especially contemptuous of those solemn declarations which started wars, the ceremonial throwing down of a mailed glove, the formulistic shouting of a traditional *défi*. He would fight to get the Rhine; he would fight to annex all Burgundy, but a declared war, begun with feudal pageantry and conducted with unpredictable hazards, was not his way of fighting. Diplomacy was slower, but far more sure.

As the king grew steadily more calculating, Charles the Rash grew increasingly violent, and even without the constant secret intervention of the king seemed fated to destroy himself. Each year in his towns rebels rose against his governors. Each year on his borders there were armed clashes with neighboring principalities. He racked his rebels and beat back his foreign enemies ever more mercilessly. And thus each year Burgundy grew weaker, while France, at peace, grew stronger under Louis's firm hand. In a battle with the Swiss, which Duke Charles had expected to win without effort, the Burgundians were shamefully beaten and had to withdraw. A good many Frenchmen were inexplicably among the prisoners taken by Burgundy. The duke hanged them all and sent a furious demand to Louis that France cease breaking the peace, and accused Louis of making secret war against him. Louis replied blandly that he knew nothing about the French prisoners. They must have been there on their own responsibility; they must be volunteers. Pasque Dieu, he was not at war with his good cousin. He was cultivating his garden and devoting his time to the curing, not to the killing, of men.

And so he was, some of his time—he had always had more time than most men, whom insomnia did not rob of normal sleep. Plenty of time remained to devote to subsidizing the Swiss enemies of Duke Charles, which he was doing on a vast scale. It was expensive, of course, but it was cheaper than war. The year that Duke Charles hanged the French "volunteers," the king released to Olivier le Daim another criminal for a history-making experiment. Ever since the doctor had dissected the gardener, he had begged the king for permission to perform a new operation.

"But first I must consult my ecclesiastical expert," the king said. "I know where to find him. I am confident that His Eminence has not changed his residence." Cardinal Balue had been a prisoner in the Châtelet six years.

The condemned criminal, waiting death in an iron cage for a murder so fiendish that the chaplain thought he was possessed, daily begged to be hanged. Roaring drunk he had struck down an eccentric, but harm-

344

less, old woman on the street and hacked off her head and thrown it through a window, brandishing his meat ax, a tool of his trade, and screaming that she was a witch who had conjured a pain demon into his groin.

Olivier had examined him, inquired among his neighbors, and uncovered a misearble history of yearly increasing drunkenness. Hidden in the shadows of the cell he had listened to the poor creature groan when he had to endure a call of nature.

"It is unquestionably a kidney stone, Your Majesty!" he said enthusiastically. "I could cut it out in half a minute. Let me try! Everything fits, even the drinking, which they often do to blunt the pain."

From the Châtelet Cardinal Balue readily gave his permission. He did not have to be bribed with a false promise of release. He had reconciled himself to life imprisonment. There was not the slightest objection to the operation from the point of view of the Church, he said.

Olivier sneered. "I shall never understand! It is a sin to cut the unfeeling dead, but no sin to cut the living."

"When you get what you want you don't ask why and forget how," the king said. "But you shall not cut this man, Olivier."

"Why?" He sounded like the dauphin when Louis refused him another sweet.

The king sighed. "I'll pardon the fellow if he lives. It is quite possible that drink and the pain of the stone drove him mad, and that he'll be a good citizen again when the thing is out of him. But you shan't do the operation. People would only say I had invented a new torture and that Olivier the Devil had performed it. No, some reputable university professors shall cut for this stone."

"But Your Majesty, I have my own way of cleansing and closing wounds. They may kill the man."

"If they do they cannot blame you. Or me."

The man lived, however, nearly a month, free of his pain, blessing the king and the University of Paris, where surgeons with a skill that satisfied even Olivier le Daim cut out a pearl-white calculus two inches long. It was saved and exhibited in a crystal case at lectures. It was a historic operation. Unfortunately, the man died of blood poisoning, a common ailment that everyone knew was caused by imbalance of the humors, in no way connected with the operation.

"Aren't you satisfied, Olivier? You were right; it was a stone and the man lived till he died of something else."

"If only they had let me dress the wound! I could have saved him."

"Didn't they dress the wound?"

The doctor shrugged helplessly. "Oh, yes, Your Majesty. With cobwebs."

The king frowned. Cobwebs were a traditional dressing. But they could also be employed as an impudent jest at a spider's expense. "Perhaps there is no connection," he said in a low voice.

345

Olivier was thinking only of the experiment. "Perhaps not. Your Majesty. But I cannot consider an operation a success if it ends in death."

"Everything does," the king said.

It seemed to his intimates—and there were fewer of them every year —that fits of gloom came more frequently upon the king than in former times. They could hardly be traceable to crises in government, for there were none. Everywhere he was successful. France was united, the great feudal lords brought down a little, the humble citizenry elevated a little, the leveling process achieved that he had envisioned when as a youth he had suffered agonies from a fear of heights, a fear that was creeping insidiously back as his hair grew sparse and white. Foreign affairs were also satisfactory, his lifelong enemy frustrated and weakened by the violence of his character and his genius for making enemies. Burgundy was too busy protecting itself to threaten France. The queen blamed the king's residence for his melancholy.

"My dear lord, this is the golden high noon of your reign, but you live in a prison like Cardinal Balue—you really ought to release that poor man. Why do you shut yourself up in such a place?"

The king had retired to the château of Plessis-lez-Tours in the plain of Touraine. It was more like a fortress than like a palace. It bristled with watchtowers and resounded to the tramp of soldiers. Spies lurked in the gardens. Hidden cannon, primed and ready to fire, covered all avenues of approach. At night drawbridges were raised and iron portcullises slid down. There were mantraps in the bushes along the moat.

"It wouldn't be gloomy if you were here," Louis said. But he did not command her. She was a southern princess, still young, and she had always been fond of the sun. "But it would be impious to demand of God that a rose and a mushroom should flourish in the same garden."

"I have never said I would not join you at Plessis, Louis," she said with spirit. "I know my duty, and though pride is a sin I am proud of having done my duty always."

"God never made a better woman," the king said tactfully.

"And I'm not a rose; I never was a beauty."

Louis said, "My dear queen, how you do go on."

"And you're not a mushroom, though you're pale as one."

"I never was a beauty," the king smiled. "Do you know, Charlotte, that used to bother me? I wanted to be tall and handsome like Henri LeClercq."

Now he had coaxed a smile out of her. "That grim old warhorse! Was he ever handsome? Nay," she crossed herself, "I should not have said that. He was a good man."

As it had to the king's enemies, death had come to some of the king's friends too. The grand master had perished of a fever contracted in a swamp where, too old for such work, he had waded all day inspecting the foundations of one of the king's new military bridges. The king had suffered a bout of the fever too, with results which Olivier considered significant and which he planned to employ in the future if the need arose.

"You didn't know him when he was young, my dear. I was even younger, but, Pasque Dieu, how jealous of him I was!"

"You always showed him favor."

He looked at her as if he did not understand. "Why certainly, Charlotte. He had ability."

"Who was he really, Louis?"

"Just a great Frenchman, my dear."

"Oh, very well. But I think you know."

"It is enough to be a great Frenchman."

"Grandfather Cardinal used to make me memorize the genealogies of all my ladies. Father also set great store on family trees. I grew quite expert," she teased. "Did it never strike you that the grand master in his last days bore a curious resemblance to the old Prince of Foix?" Again she crossed herself, and so did the king. The gallant prince had also died, and his grandson was King of Navarre, friendly to France since Louis was subsidizing him too in the first difficult years of his reign. In return, however, the young king had renounced all claim to his father's fiefs on the French side of the Pyrenees. By silence, death, and division Louis had kept the secret, now locked up forever, of a combination of human accidents that might have created a threatening unification of territories in the south of France. Olivier le Daim was wrong. An operation, in one sense of the word, could be a success if it ended in death.

"The grand master looked no more like Gaston of Foix," Louis said, "than—Pasque Dieu! let me think of some horrible example—than Count Jean d'Armagnac, let us say."

"That monster? Heaven forbid!"

"Amen," Louis said, wondering what Heaven forbids and does not. But he wanted to erase Charlotte's suspicion. "And as for Jean LeClercq, he is a Comminges to the fingertips. That at least is a good beginning for a family tree, my dear."

Young Jean was happy these days. He enjoyed the king's favor and the queen's confidence; and he was proud of his appointment as military tutor to the dauphin, who threw inkpots at his Latin master but escaped at every opportunity to the castle garden to practice swordsmanship with Jean. "I shall be," the dauphin would say, drawing himself up as straight as his awkward shoulders would permit, "a great knight, like Count Jean de Montfort!"

Arm in arm the king and queen in their leisurely walk had approached their son. He was not much like Count Jean, as anyone could see, except perhaps the king. He was spindle-shanked, big-headed, and barrel-chested; he was short-tempered and self-willed. But he handled a sword well and already rode with his father's sure seat. They heard the sounds of steel on steel in an open area beyond the hedge-lined garden path.

"Let's watch," the king said, halting her step with a pressure in the crook of his arm on hers. It always took her a little aback by its strength.

"It seems like spying, Louis."

"Well, what's wrong with that?"

"I'm always afraid Charles will get hurt."

"If Montfort ever hurts the lad, Pasque Dieu, I'll cage him!"

The dauphin was not hurt. Twice, as computed by the rules of the game, Jean ran him through; then, in a quick succession of self-imposed defeats, the tutor three times lost his head before the dauphin's wild slashes. "Enough!" Jean laughed. "You have winded me, Monseigneur. Every day you get better and better. It is I who ought to find a sword master." He threw his arm familiarly across the dauphin's shoulders, who looked up at him proudly, and together they walked off the field.

Charlotte smiled. "A courtier, too. He lost on purpose."

"But Charles did very well for a beginner," Louis said stoutly. He did wish his son were more patient with his studies; Charles would not rule France in an age when the shining armor and flashing blades that so fascinated him now would be of much account. But the dauphin was young, and patience no doubt would come in time. The king prayed often nowadays that God would let him live into the manhood, at least the young manhood, of his son. It was ironical that the whole of his life had been to centralize power in the person of the king. The next king would have to be an extremely strong man to assume the enormous burden of responsibilities that a French monarch now bore.

"Does Charles sleep much at night?" he asked the queen suddenly.

"You should know better than I, Louis. Ask his tutors. He always slept well as a child when I took care of him." There was a touch of asperity in her tone.

"Now Charlotte, be reasonable. You couldn't keep him in a nursery forever. He actually has a fuzz of beard on his cheeks. He wants me to let Olivier shave him." The king chuckled heartily.

"A cat could lick it off!" she said.

Louis said soberly: "Even a simple knight's son goes to some neighboring castle away from his mother to do a stint of squiring and learn his manners in a manlier environment. How much more necessary that training is in the heir to the throne. You have not been deprived of the companionship of your son, Charlotte."

It was simple truth and immemorial custom. "No, my lord husband," Charlotte said dutifully. "But I know of no law that compels a mother to like it."

"The princesses are growing up too," Louis sighed. "Soon, I suppose, I shall have to marry them."

Charlotte brightened. "I should think you ought. There at least we agree. Anne is already thirteen."

"She seems so young," the king mused.

The queen asked, "How young was I?"

348

"Nay, that was different. Anne is my daughter."

"Isn't Charles my son?"

"Pasque Dieu, he is *my* son!"

"Louis, Louis, Louis," sighed the queen. Sometimes it seemed more peaceful in Savoy or the Dauphiny, where she spent much of her time nowadays, away from the gloomy fortress of Plessis-lez-Tours and the complexities of the king whose temperament she understood less and less every year. He always missed her, he said, and he wrote her frequent letters whenever she was away. But she suspected the tender ones were the composition of Philippe de Comines; those full of politics were the king's own. There was never time for him to write in his own hand any more; he merely signed them with his neat, minute, and extraordinarily legible signature: five firm hard letters. When she did come north to see him, he still seemed curiously remote, as if a great distance still separated them. She wondered if she had ever been close.

Having determined to marry the princesses, he promptly did; Anne to Pierre de Beaujeu de Bourbon, to tie the powerful House of Bourbon closer to the throne; and ugly little Jeanne at the age of ten to Louis of Orléans, a giddy young prince who could be counted on not to molest her since he much preferred to fly his hawks and jump fast horses across fifteen-foot ditches. But Jeanne's marriage snared the loyalty of the great House of Orléans, for it was unknightly from the feudal point of view, unpleasant from the domestic point of view, and impractical from any point of view to raise one's hand against one's overlord, king, and immensely wealthy father-in-law, who would choke you with favors if you obeyed and clap you into an iron cage if you did not. Anne wrote to her mother that she was happy. Jeanne had never been able to learn to write.

Both weddings were brilliant, and occasions for national holidays. But the queen was lonely without her daughters, and reproached herself for suggesting their marriages too precipitately. She wrote from Grenoble that she planned to return to Plessis-lez-Tours. It was a concession.

The king replied from Paris that he strongly advised her to remain in the south. There was trouble again, he said, old trouble which he did not have time to explain but which would require his attention every waking hour. "Which is nineteen hours a day," she sighed. There was no reason to go north for that.

She wrote that instead she would make a visit to the new Duchess of Bourbon, their daughter Anne.

From Saint-Quentin—how the king was moving about!—came a curt answer: "No, Madame. The duchess will come to you. Then both of you stay where you are. Guard well what I reveal—the north is threatened with invasion. There is room here only for soldiers. Send me six of your prettiest ladies-in-waiting, gay wenches, not prudes. Louis."

"I do not understand," she murmured, hiding the missive lest one of

349

her ladies inadvertently read it. She was suddenly suspicious of all her attendants. "What wantons I must have nurtured unaware!"

She showed the letter to her confessor, a grave and elderly Savoyard. "Reverend father, the king is just like everybody else!"

"Nay, Madame, his worst enemy cannot say that against His Majesty." He adjusted his spectacles and read.

"I hate him!" she said.

He scanned the letter and smiled. "I think that Your Majesty need not. True, the king has reached an age when great understanding is sometimes required, and many heartful prayers. But in my experience with such matters, which is broader perhaps than Your Majesty supposes, I have never known the man to ask his wife to supply the other woman. The request for so large a number of ladies alone should be an indication—"

"The king is thorough," Charlotte pouted. But she was appeased. The king was also secretive. She would be the last to learn if he wanted them for himself.

Pursing his lips, the confessor said slowly: "Alas, I think I understand. This is another result of the imprisonment of the cardinal. He wants the women for Zem Zem."

Word that the king had caged a prince of the Church, he explained, had traveled all over Christendom, and beyond. "In Turkey," said the confessor, "the Sultan Bazajet heard of it and, I regret to say, congratulated His Majesty on what he termed a fearless action. Less regrettably, the Grand Turk sent him many priceless holy relics from Constantinople, it being the nature of Turks to make costly presents, which we would call bribes, to persons from whom they expect favors."

The queen smiled. It was Louis's nature too.

"The Grand Turk also sent to His Majesty his brother Zem Zem, chained in golden chains, suggesting that if the king could cage a cardinal he would no doubt be willing to cage Zem Zem, who was a threat to the throne of Turkey much as the late Duc de Guienne was to the throne of France."

"Neither the cardinal nor the Turk is caged," the queen said.

"There is no doubt that His Majesty removed the golden chains at once."

"He says that Zem Zem is a very personable young man, cultured, lettered, not at all black, and a great favorite at court. He treats Zem Zem most hospitably."

"So," said the confessor, tapping the letter with his spectacles, "it would seem. I suggest that you remind His Most Christian Majesty that Christian hospitality does not extend to the encouragement of heathen polygamy."

"My poor ladies," said the queen. "Be assured, Your Reverence, I shall keep them safely by me."

Louis had other ladies for his purpose by the time he received the queen's refusal, and they were not for Zem Zem. That handsome young heathen was doing very well on his own, happy in safe exile, occupied in the organization of a fleet of ships that soon were plying the Black and Mediterranean seas. Amid all his worry and military activities Louis found time to think of French trade. In exchange for keeping Zem Zem in protective custody, he had extracted from the sultan a commercial treaty that gave France precedence over all European nations. Duke Charles of Burgundy cried, "For shame! Now the Spider trades with the heathen!" Edward of England grumbled, "Unfair!" The Spider had thought of it first.

Duke Charles knew nothing of trade but he knew its importance to his treasury. His Flemish merchants made continual representations to him that Louis was negotiating fabulously profitable monopolies and that if the process continued Burgundy would be bankrupt. In desperation the duke turned to diplomacy, since that seemed to be the new way of getting along in the world.

He had a heavy hand in contrast with Louis's finesse, but subtlety from him was so unexpected that it almost succeeded. It was also of help that the English king was a bluff, unsubtle ally.

A Burgundian spy got through to the cell of Jacques de Nemours, the last of the traitors among the great French lords not yet pardoned or hanged. Three times a rebel on three separate occasions, Nemours was deemed by the king not vicious but weak, unreliable. He caged him.

Through the bars the spy whispered hopeful words of freedom. "You have only to sign a letter, my lord of Nemours. It is already written. Quickly! The pen is already inked!"

"Where are you from?"

"Your master."

"What master?" It was a naïve and revealing query.

"Your late good Burgundian master and friend, Duke Charles. Quickly!"

"How do I know you are not from the king?"

"That Spider is doomed if you sign this."

"I am afraid."

"Do you want to be free?"

"Dear God, yes!"

"Then—here!"

Nemours scrawled his name. "What does the message say?"

"You promise to open your city of Saint-Quentin to the Spider's enemies."

"Whom is the message to?"

The spy was disappearing into the shadows.

"Edward of England. Be of good heart."

"Good God!"

Too late the conversation came to the knowledge of the king. "Clumsy, tardy, traitorous agent! You should have intercepted the letter!"

"Your Majesty, I heard it only by accident—the Burgundian was disguised as a guard—his escape so well organized—"

"Heard it by accident, did you? I'll have your ears looked into!" An executioner cut them off and punctured his eardrums with the hot iron cautery, so that he was deaf thereafter.

"His escape was organized, was it?" The prison governor was dismissed and retired in disgrace with loss of pension. The guards were sent to the galleys to row for ten years in the king's new merchant fleet. "Prisons are lazy, miasmic places," the king remarked. "Let them pull on an oar for a while and breathe some fresh air and get some healthy exercise."

But he did nothing to Jacques de Nemours, for that would have revealed that he knew. Nemours, indeed, was suddenly treated better. The king visited him. "You are a trifle thin, Monsieur de Nemours. Pasque Dieu, I must fatten you ùp!" He strode away from the cage. Not once had he blinked his eyes as he peered through the iron bars.

"Fatten for what?" Nemours cried in a terrified voice. For a tortured moment, under the baleful, hypnotic glare of the king, he had envisioned a ghoulish meal with himself as the meat. He remembered all the old stories of witchcraft; the king's hatred had glowered naked on his face.

Duke Charles sent the letter to England. If ever Louis XI was to be stopped, he said, the time was now. France was not so united as might appear from across the Channel. He had documentary proof! King Edward had only to step across the narrow sea with an invading army; Saint-Quentin, the stronghold of the north, would open to him like magic. The Burgundian and British armies would join and advance together, would loot and despoil the City of Paris, where the king's treasurers were said to use shovels to pile the king's treasure. He reminded Edward that he alone had penetrated as far as Beauvais.

An Englishman versed in calligraphy, a former wool merchant and a diplomat at the Burgundian court, an immensely able man who was now a printer in the almonry at Westminster at the Sign of the Red Pale, William Caxton, verified Jacques de Nemours' signature.

Edward was impressed by Duke Charles's show of skill; the French king might be off his guard. He gave an ear too to the complaints of his London merchants, who were furious at Louis's rapid capture of most of Europe's trade. And the British nobility, many of whom could remember their fathers' lost French fiefs, pushed him to the venture. Somewhat hesitantly he agreed. He crossed to Calais with a competent army and waited for Duke Charles to join him.

Fatigued and discomfited, the duke met him after a week with a small retinue of Burgundian knights, scarcely more formidable than a personal bodyguard. He had been called away at the last moment, he said, by an unexpected incursion of the Swiss into his province of the Franche-

Comté. He had been forced to leave the bulk of his army behind to repel the invaders.

"You're having a good deal of touble with those sheepherders, aren't you?" the king asked dubiously.

They pushed on through Burgundy to Saint-Quentin in the valley of the Somme.

Louis was already there. The royal standard of France flew from the ramparts. The massed artillery of France was levelled against them.

"I had expected something more of a welcome, good brother-in-law," Edward said, "and something more of help from you."

"Louis is a liar, a coward, a cheat! His cannon are dummies! He's done this before! He could have had no warning. Send your *défi!* Saint-Quentin will tumble down like Jericho!"

Edward grinned uncomfortably and turned heavily to his most trusted counselor. "My good brother-in-law here must have ridden too long in the sun; he speaks a bit wildly. You crowned me king, my lord cardinal. What do I need as king," he nodded in the direction of Saint-Quentin, "to bring those high walls tumbling down like Jericho's?"

Adopting his mood, Cardinal Bourchier answered, smiling: "You need first, of course, to be Joshua. Then you need the manifest will of God, which I do not consider here manifest. This looks more like the will of King Louis. You would also need such ancillary reinforcements as seven priests with seven trumpets in a circumambient march seven times for seven days around the city—"

"Charles," the king said, "you have made me look a fool in front of all Europe. Even His Eminence is laughing at the impossibility of this thing."

"Brother-in-law, you swore by St. George!"

"I shall keep my oath," Edward scowled. But he had crossed the Channel at great expense and personal discomfort, without his favorite cook, expecting a strong ally and a weak enemy. He had found just the opposite. Now he could look forward only to extricating himself from the situation with whatever remnant of dignity he might salvage from compromise. He sent a herald with his *défi*, but he chose the herald carefully from among his least fiery messengers. He gave him special instructions out of Duke Charles's hearing. "If the king receives you pleasantly," he said, "let him know that England is not averse to an amicable settlement. There are altogether too many French cannon and too few Burgundians here."

The king received Edward's *défi* while seated at a table under a cloth-of-gold canopy on a large greensward just outside the city gates. Behind him stood a few attendants; he seemed otherwise unprotected. But the herald could see faces lurking in the shadows of tree trunks and bushes, and everywhere there was the sulphurous smell of slow matches burning in the hot August air.

The herald rode up, hurled down the glove, and spoke in a powerful voice the words that challenged France to war.

"Good lad! Brave lad!" cried the king. "I have heard it many times but never so well spoken." He jumped up from his chair and picked up the glove. "It is France's fault that it did not ring properly. The grass is too thick. I should have chosen harder ground. But your voice rang lustily, Herald." With a pleasant smile he returned the glove. "Now that your mission is done, and done so nobly, come sit with me and drink a cup of wine. It is a hot day."

The king wore a long rich cloak of marten skins. The perspiring herald wondered how a man could endure it on such a day. "Come sit with me," Louis repeated.

"It is not customary, Your Majesty."

"My dear boy, nothing ever is till somebody starts it. Drink to France and I shall drink to England. Since we are going to kill each other, it will cost nothing to be polite."

Olivier le Daim set out two silver goblets. The herald shot a glance at the humpback, hesitated, and sat down. He observed with uneasiness that a hedge now hid him from view of the English army. The king raised his cup. "To England!"

"Without offense, Your Majesty, may I suggest that we exchange cups?"

The king smiled, chuckled. "Hear him, Olivier? Hear him, Philippe? This is a man! I like you, Herald. I know what you are thinking. How stoutly you come to the point! No, no, you must not drink out of my cup. I might have foreseen you would want to exchange, and poisoned my own. But I will drink out of yours." He reached over, drank half of the wine, and set it before the herald again. "Well, Englishman?"

The herald drained it. "To France, Your Majesty!" Then he was silent for a moment.

The king laughed. "You see, my friend, you are still alive and so am I. What a handsome tabard you wear, by the way." He touched it with a finger on which blazed the largest emerald the herald had ever seen. "But the texture, Pasque Dieu, coarse as wool. It wears longer, of course, but for your mission today—Olivier! Come here!—I should have thought your king would dress you more becomingly. Olivier! Show my guest some of that velvet I was speaking about this morning." He lowered his voice and whispered to the herald, "I was saving it for the queen, but you shall have it!"

It seemed to the herald that the King of France was receiving him very pleasantly. He felt he could deliver Edward's message that England was not averse to an amicable settlement. There would be no harm in accepting the proffered velvet also. It seemed handy; Olivier le Daim showed it to him. It was of soft silk pile, wonderfully light and luxurious, such as only great lords could afford. "There are some thirty yards of it, Your Majesty," the doctor said.

The herald started to say something. Louis held up his hand. "Nay,

354

nay; I know, I know. Not here. Your squire will find it in your tent to-night, war or no war. I like you."

"But Your Majesty—"

"Nay, more? Of course! You need money too to have it made up by a tailor. Comines, give me your purse!"

"I think it contains only about a hundred écus, Your Majesty," the grand chancellor said.

"Mine contains exactly two hundred écus, eight sous, two deniers," the king said. "That is two hundred pounds, eight shillings, tuppence. Will that, and the purse of my chancellor, pay a tailor's bill in England, Herald?" He placed his purse on the table beside Philippe de Comines's. It was a small fortune.

"I do not know how to thank Your Majesty. I am not a rich man."

"Under your tabard, lad, under your tabard with them! It is nothing to what I am prepared to do for your master King Edward, whose humanity I have admired so long, if he will consent to treat with me in the interest of peace and our common good."

"Sir, I think he could be persuaded."

"He has had heavy expenses. It must have cost fifty thousand écus to transport his army to this place. Duke Charles deceived and deserted him, but I will be his friend. I will pay whatever it costs to take all those good brave Englishmen back to England. Their blood should not be shed in an adventure that even Burgundy abandons. Nay, more; your king must have heavy expenses in England too. I will help my brother king. Tell him that every year I shall send him thirty thousand, forty thousand— England and France must be friends. Who can put a price on friend-ship?"

"I am not, of course, empowered to negotiate with Your Majesty."

"Tell him," Louis said soberly, "that I want peace. Tell him my heart, not my guns, speaks now. If he forces me to fire upon him, I shall do so reluctantly. But you must tell him too that I am prepared, well pre-pared, for a war that I do not want."

Edward agreed to parley. The experts met and began to haggle over the terms. Crestfallen, Duke Charles left Saint-Quentin with his futile little band to rejoin the Burgundian army who were still fighting against the Swiss. The Swiss seemed to have inexhaustible resources; they were burn-ing and ravaging the whole province of the Franche-Comté.

The leaders of the British expeditionary force were treated with the same generosity as the herald. Every day long tables were set up on the greensward. Boars were roasted to tempt the islanders; whole sheep and beeves and deer turned on great spits over pits of embers, sizzling and browning and wafting a hungry hospitable aroma into the English camp. Jolly fat Frenchmen in cooks' aprons with baskets full of bottles and sweetmeats went unarmed among the English tents, distributing samples, coaxing the reluctant to follow their leader and come, taste King Louis's cheer! They came by scores, and the humble foot soldiers who were not invited ate their hard campaign rations sulkily. But Louis remembered them too. A mule train of fresh French provisions and barrels of beer arrived to cheer them. No army of invaders was ever so treated.

The king had canopies set up over long tables on the greensward to shield the English nobles and officers from the heat of the sun. Obsequious servants set heaped trenchers of meat before them and filled their cups with vintage wines that most of them had never tasted, and washed their hands and dried them on linen napkins. Jugglers and minstrels entertained them. Every man was a king. Then one day, to vary the entertainment, all the servants were replaced by comely French lasses, laughing, bantering familiarly with the Englishmen, consenting without too much reluctance to meet milord of this or milord of that and walk with him under the trees when the feasting palled and the sun went down.

Matching wits with Philippe de Comines in the conference tent where the treaty was taking shape, Cardinal Bourchier raised outraged eyebrows at the king's newest temptation. "Upon my soul, my lord grand chancellor, never since Jael drove the nail into Sisera's head have women been used thus in war! Certainly never on such a scale. For the sake of all the good wives these gentlemen left behind them, I must bring our negotiations to a speedy close. That will cost—for the extra ships—hm-m, hm-m, your king spoke of fifty thousand pounds—there will have to be many extra ships to get the men home in a hurry—let us say eighty thousand."

"Seventy-five," countered the grand chancellor. "Surely not every Englishman is married."

The cardinal agreed.

The question of a yearly payment to the English king then arose. Bourchier wanted to call it a tribute; Comines wanted to call it a gift. They compromised on the wording, and into the treaty was inserted a clause that called for an annual *pension* to Edward. The amount was fixed at fifty thousand pounds.

The treaty was signed and sealed.

Europe cynically dubbed it "The Traders' Truce."

King Edward was vastly pleased. But Louis, who had supped often with him and suffered agonies of apprehension from the quantities of food he had been forced to consume to match Edward's appetite, uttered frantic prayers of thanksgiving when he watched the English army march away. "Pasque Dieu, one day that man will gorge himself into the grave!"

He knew the English king now as a man, and saw his weaknesses. Edward was cruel, but self-indulgent, grossly gluttonous, and fundamentally lazy. So long as he received his fat pension to spend on his pleasures, he would never exert himself; France would be safe. Louis placed him first on his list of foreign investments.

The menace of invasion had passed, but the menace to his health remained. He went on a rigorous fasting diet. He drank Olivier's bitter draughts. He prayed. In a letter that eventually found its way into the royal archives for history to boggle at, he made a princely donation to the Abbey of St. Claude to obtain, by the intercession of the saint, *le bon et parfaict estat de mon estomac*. The good and perfect state of his stomach was increasingly on his mind.

He returned to Paris, ordered the head of Jacques de Nemours struck off in a public market place, and retired to his fortress at Plessis-lez-Tours. The last French traitor was dead, the last great feudal estate confiscated. The last foreign enemy but one was conquered, and that one was isolated, without a friend, attacked on every side. A little more time, and Burgundy too would fall.

Now he must fulfill an oath to God, for he had vowed at his coronation that if God would deliver to him all France and permit him to unify it, he would honor the Blessed Virgin as no king had ever honored Her before.

This he now did.

Chapter Fifty-one

The king's religion had always been of a special stamp, intense and practical, like his nature. Under his surface orthodoxy ran a deep vein of superstition, as it did in millions of his subjects. He never scoffed when he saw crosses of garlic hung up on peasant doors to keep away werewolves, for he too employed a talisman, wearing his emerald openly now to keep out a disease that no one had ever been able to cure and that might be caused by demons. His reverence for the saints was coupled with a conviction of the need for reciprocity, as if they and he were partners in a treaty: those who helped him could expect liberal donations to churches that bore their names; those who failed him might have their images ripped from his cap and stamped upon. Heaven was a greater France, God a greater king, and the demons, he supposed, must be very much like the rebel French lords.

Now God had permitted him to bind the French demons. Now he fulfilled his oath to God. In an unprecedented gesture of devotion he conferred letters patent of nobility upon the Holy Virgin, creating her a French countess, granting her a territory, and taking it back to hold in fief as her vassal.

No one laughed, though most devout men of the Church shivered a little without knowing why. Some protested that the action was a sin.

Bewildered, Louis asked, "A *sin!* Pray tell me in what?"

They answered, "In the indignity."

But he replied that he could conceive of no greater honor, and he challenged them to discover a single instance in his whole reign when he had ever before alienated so much as an inch of French ground or bent his knee to hold it in fief from an overlord. Yet that was what he was doing now. That was the honor he reserved to the Mother of God alone.

They remembered the grotesque and beautiful legend of the Jongleur de Notre-Dame. Perhaps it was an honor. But it was hard to understand, and queerly sinister.

Sinister too was the way he kept to himself in his grim retreat, where even the queen had to be announced. It was remembered how in former times he had supped with her at a public tavern. There was gossip when Olivier le Daim engaged a staff of assistants, who disappeared into the mystery of Plessis-lez-Tours and reappeared only on rare occasions, their lips sealed, their purses heavy, seemingly afraid to express an opinion even about the weather.

Olivier reported to the king, "It is whispered that Your Majesty is sick."

"Wait till they say My Majesty is dead!" he snapped.

Soon the doctor was able to report that they were saying that too. The rumors arose on several occasions. Then the king would show himself for worship in the cathedral unexpectedly, unchanged as far as anyone could see except that each time he looked older, as if a year for him were two years in the life of an ordinary man. It was believed that he was turning vain in his old age: no one had ever worn such a profusion of fur. People rather approved. It seemed like a welcome mellowing in the iron discipline that the king had always imposed upon himself and now imposed upon all France. If Louis XI had made France safe, he had also made France dull.

Suddenly, in the winter of 1477, the king, France, and the whole world shuddered at a terrifying apparition in the sky. It was a comet, less brilliant than the one that had appeared in 1456 when Louis as dauphin had fled to the court of Duke Philip the Good, a fugitive from the fury of his father; but sinister, portentous, and inexplicable, as they always were. In the dull vacuum of their well regulated lives, ordinary Frenchmen almost welcomed it, since it gave them something to stir and drain their emotions. The king, remembering the seizure that had accompanied the first comet, drew his furs tighter around him and prayed. He had felt the warning chill and fallen often lately. Dear God, now he would fall again!

Olivier tried to cheer him. "When you caught the grand master's fever you did not fall, though you had experienced the chill. I have a plan. The warning has not yet come. Trust me. Before it does Your Majesty must catch a quartan fever and then you will not fall!"

"Try anything. But hurry. I am afraid. I lost the Dauphiny when the other comet appeared."

From the fortress Olivier and his doctors fanned out through the town and countryside, knocking on doors, inquiring at hospitals, prisons, monasteries, homes, searching everywhere for a victim of a quartan fever. The king wanted to sup with him, man, woman, or child, it did not matter. But at once. Tonight!

The hour was late, the request strange, a comet hung in the sky. People drew back in consternation from Olivier and the mysterious doctors. Many sick persons got out of their beds protesting vehemently that they were well. One or two invalids, too ill or demented to fear, were rejected. The sickness had to be of a definite sort, a recurrent fever that attacked the victim every four days.

No one could be found.

Swathed in his heavy cloak, rubbing his emerald against the flesh of his head, the king spurred furiously out of his retreat and spent the night wading in the swamp and breathing the pestilential air under the bridge where Henri LeClercq had caught the fever that killed him.

But in spite of all his efforts Louis did not contract a fever, nor did he experience the warning chill, nor did he suffer a seizure. But his strange behavior had been observed, the strange request of the doctors was remembered, and even the queen, who was in Savoy, heard of her husband's growing eccentricities.

She could not explain them. "But he isn't a witch, and he wasn't invoking demons under that bridge," she said flatly. "I am going to join him." Perhaps that would help put a stop to the ugly stories.

"Nevertheless," the king mused, "that comet meant something."

"It might have meant something good," Olivier said dubiously.

"You do not believe that."

No one did. The doctor sighed. The comet faded in a day.

The next day, from the city of Nantes, a courier came galloping on a frothing horse that was near dead from exhaustion, cruelly cut with whip and spur. There was tremendous news.

Duke Charles, having suffered a series of humiliating defeats at the hands of the Swiss, had seen them push out of the Franche-Comté and penetrate to the heart of Lorraine, the narrow, critical province that connected the northern and southern components of his vast Burgundian territories. If Lorraine fell Burgundy would be split in two. There was superb strategy in all the operations of the Swiss as well as inexhaustible supplies of money, mercenaries, arms, and provisions. Everyone knew they came from France but no one could prove it.

The sheepherders, whom the imperious duke had found so contemptible but now could not beat, had taken the city of Nancy, capital of Lorraine. In a blinding snowstorm, with an inadequate force, Duke Charles rashly set out to retake it.

On Sunday, the 5th of January, in an overwhelmingly one-sided battle, the little Burgundian army was dispersed, taken prisoner, or slaughtered. The duke himself was killed by an unknown enemy. Next day one of his pages found his master's mangled body, stripped of its beautiful black armor, naked, frozen, half buried in a snowdrift.

"Now, *now*," cried the king, "I shall have the Rhine!" He was trembling for joy. "Ring bells! Fire salutes! Shoot off fireworks! Light bonfires! Declare a holiday! Broach a barrel of the king's wine on every street corner!" He seized the arm of the grand chancellor and danced with him around the room.

Haltingly, heavily, Philippe de Comines danced, his eyes on his shoes. He too was a Burgundian; once he had served the duke.

"Step higher, step higher, Philippe! Thou'rt a laggard partner. Are you weeping for your late rash lord? Nay, nay, I am better! I won, he lost. I am alive, he is dead. I am great, and so are you, and he is gone, and I shall have the Rhine!"

"Your Majesty," Olivier le Daim cautioned him, "you are overexciting yourself."

"Get out, you ape!"

The doctor slunk away. He went to call the queen, whose presence was always good for Louis, since he held his emotions in check when she was near him. When he heard the rustle of her skirts as she entered the room, regal, poised, and calm, the wave of wild enthusiasm passed.

"Tell her, Grand Chancellor. I cannot trust myself."

Philippe de Comines bowed deeply, smiling. He was all diplomat and courtier again, the little prick of conscience quickly healed. "His Majesty has had glorious news, Madame."

"France has had glorious news," the king corrected.

"Burgundy has fallen, Madame, and there is every indication that France will be able to annex it, barring certain unpredictable eventualities such as the development of the imperialistic policies of the Habsburgs of Austria and the likelihood of a rising sentiment for independence in the Flemish Netherlands—"

"Charlotte," the king interrupted, "the chancellor here will take ten minutes to tell you what I can say in a word: my last enemy is dead, and Burgundy has fallen to pieces, but I must not yet rejoice because the rush for the spoils will now be on."

"You will get your share," the queen smiled.

"My *share?* What is that?"

The rush for the spoils was a rush for the hand of Duke Charles's only child, his daughter Marie. Had she been ugly and old, she would still have had plenty of suitors, for she was the richest heiress in Christendom. To the intense embarrassment of Louis XI, Marie of Burgundy was nineteen, exceptionally beautiful, romantic, like her father, and proud, like all the Burgundian nobility. Fastidious, vivacious, and exquisitely mannered, she embodied in her person all that was best in a feudal princess. And, like the queens of England, she could by law inherit the entire patrimony of her father. Marie was Burgundy itself. Whoever should marry her would gain in the sweetest manner imaginable sovereignty over an empire that countless wars and rivers of blood had not yet won.

The king set his heart on arranging her marriage with Charles the dauphin. But Marie was not a tractable princess, nor did she have a genius for political alliances. There was a man among her swarm of suitors to whom she felt strongly drawn, regardless of the consequences. The daughter of Charles the Rash had inherited, along with his auburn curls and flashing eyes, a heedless strength of will that did not appear on the softly feminine surface. The man she loved, and who returned her love, was Prince Maximilian of Austria, son and heir of the Holy Roman Emperor. He was brave, literate, and handsome as she was beautiful. His lineage was the oldest in Europe and the most revered. Had they been of humble birth, their humble neighbors would have said, "God made them for each other." In the place of such a prince for such a princess, Louis XI resolved to substitute Charles his son.

Queen Charlotte shook her head dubiously. "Politically I see the advantages, my dear, but you must not leave Marie entirely out of your calculations. She is ripe to wed long since, and probably even anxious, unmaidenly so. Our poor little Charles is ten years her junior."

"That does not matter in princes. And he is big for his age."

"And his appeal is like yours, Louis, rather out of the ordinary. The Austrian prince is so tall and comely."

"Those are not the real values, Charlotte. Duke Charles was tall and comely too; where is he now?"

"A woman doesn't think like a man, my dear."

"Then women don't think straight. I've always known they didn't."

But he tried to see his son through a woman's eyes, illogical as he knew them to be. He had to agree that Charlotte might have found an argument against the dauphin.

"I understand that Prince Maximilian writes her poetry too, in elegant Latin," Charlotte said.

"Then, Pasque Dieu, the dauphin must study his Latin harder. I suggest Ovid. He shall learn to write poems like Ovid, full of love and lips and longing. I have read Ovid."

"I never considered him quite proper," the queen said primly.

"From what I hear he's just the thing for Marie."

He called his son. "Charles! How is your Latin? Have you read Ovid?"

"I am still on Caesar's Commentaries, Sire."

"Good, good. The Gallic heir must learn the Gallic wars. How have you progressed?"

The dauphin said honestly, lowering his big head in embarrassment, shifting his grotesquely bowed legs, "I regret to confess, Sire, that I am still on the first line, *Gallia est omnis divisa in partes*—All Gaul is divided—"

"Do not go on, son. I've always hated that line." He wondered, when the printer that Caxton had just sent him from England came to print the Commentaries, whether anyone would notice if he changed the *est* to *erat*. "Gaul *was* divided, but not now. Tell your tutor to teach you to write love poems like Ovid's."

"I don't like love poems. I like war stories."

"Don't hurry the boy, Louis."

"Madame, I have hurried for fifty-five years!"

He did not abandon the project of marrying the dauphin to Marie. She was in residence in Ghent in Flanders. He determined to send her an emissary armed with jewels, presents, and promises, to advance the suit of his son.

"If I were the princess I'd want to know how my future husband would look," Charlotte said.

"But you didn't."

"I wasn't nineteen."

"Hm-n," Louis said. "Very well."

He sent for the *enlumineur* from the Bibliothèque du Roy. "Maître Fouquet, paint my son. Make him whatever is necessary to steal the heart of a woman. Can you finish the portrait in a day?"

The embarrassed artist replied: "The dauphin is an interesting subject, Your Majesty, and I am greatly honored. But I confess I am confused by Your Majesty's gracious command. There are many ways of painting a person's likeness."

"All the better. Your hands are free."

"And, of course, there are many kinds of women. Whom—what kind of lady does Your Majesty have in mind?"

"Very pretty, much courted, a little rash, nineteen, probably sensuous. Paint to appeal to a woman like that."

"It—will take more than a day, Your Majesty."

The king narrowed his eyes. "You need not be absolutely literal, Maître Fouquet. Paint the great spirit of the lad. He shall have to appear a little older, of course. Make him something like Jean LeClercq. Nay, paint Jean LeClercq himself and make him something like the dauphin. Charles will have more time to study his Ovid if he doesn't have to stand there while you look at him and paint."

"It is a difficult assignment," the artist said, "but I shall try."

Next the king cast about for a persuasive emissary. He regretted that he was unable to employ Philippe di Comines, but the grand chancellor, with all his ability, was out of the question. Marie of Burgundy hated the man who had betrayed her father and gone over to his enemy.

"Olivier, can you go on a diplomatic mission of enormous importance to France?"

362

"Once I did, Your Majesty, when I gathered some herbs in Guienne."

"This is entirely different. No herbs. Nay, wait! Perhaps herbs! For a love potion! Well?"

"The action is fleeting, Your Majesty."

"How long?"

"A day."

"Long enough to sign a marriage contract?"

"The subject would not give marriage a single thought, Your Majesty."

"Then no herbs."

He revealed his plan to snare Marie for young Charles.

"I am ill equipped as a simple chevalier, Your Majesty. Burgundy sets great store on titles."

"Confound you, take the countship of Meulant! Very well, my lord count. Are you satisfied?"

The barber pushed his advantage. Louis was more and more dependent on him. "I should also be a military man to mingle on equal terms with the chivalry of Burgundy."

"How well they teach doctors to bleed! Leech, be my governor of Saint-Quentin. You shall not reside there for I need you here. But take the title and the revenue."

Olivier le Daim, Governor of Saint-Quentin, Comte de Meulant, set out at the head of a brilliant escort with a pack mule of costly presents and a competent portrait of Jean LeClercq in a dauphinal cloak of state, the only resemblance to the king's son that the artist could introduce into the protrait.

Marie refused to see him. She and the imperial prince spent all their time together, riding out every day—she was a fearless horsewoman—while he flew hawks and she bent a bow at pheasants, hitting them too. The French delegation lingered a week in Ghent, the laughingstock of the town. Then when she discovered that people were openly insulting him in the streets, sneering at his hump, and the outrageously elaborate garb he wore to try to hide it, she took pity on him and granted him an audience.

She remarked graciously that the dauphin was far better looking than reports she had heard of him, refused the presents, and stated that, despite all objections from any quarter whatsoever, she would marry the man she loved. The doctor left Ghent in disgrace, with dogs barking at the heels of his escort and street urchins trying to steal the gold tassels off his shoes.

He knew he was beaten. It took no doctor's eye to mark the difference between bent little Charles and the tall, quick-witted prince whom popular admiration already dubbed "The White Knight of Austria."

But he had learned something that might blunt the edge of the king's wrath at his failure. He had pricked up his ears at the princess's words "despite all objections." He had found out who, besides Louis, was objecting to the match.

It was the stubborn, freedom-loving Dutchmen. Philippe de Comines had been right. There was a growing sentiment for independence among them. Now that one tyrant was gone they did not propose to fall under the yoke of another, neither Louis of France, so dangerous and close, nor the Holy Roman Emperor, to whom three hundred German princes bordering on the Netherlands swore allegiance. Why, they asked, could not Marie marry a Dutchman?

To the queen's delight Louis decided to wait on events. If the dauphin could not woo the princess, he, the king, would woo the Netherlanders, and they would block the marriage. He lowered imports on Flemish goods and offered startlingly profitable opportunities for Flemish craftsmen to come to France and set up factories. New industries in fine ceramics and optical glass arose. Frenchmen would learn the techniques and the factories would remain even if later he expelled the original craftsmen.

To a degree the policy was successful. Shortly the Dutch took matters into their own hands. They kept the princess in protective custody in Ghent; Maximilian was permitted to see her only in the presence of others. In her distress she promised to make any concession demanded of her. The representatives of Flanders, Hainault, Zeeland, Brabant, and Holland presented her with a document they called the Great Privilege. It was their privilege, not hers. If she would renounce her right to sign treaties or wage war or levy taxes without their consent, she could marry whomever she chose. She signed at once and flew to Maximilian's arms.

"*Par le Pasque Dieu!*" Louis swore in wonderment at the news. "She lost everything!"

"Oh, I don't know," smiled the queen.

"Now I must fight Maximilian, I suppose."

"Is that necessary any more? Burgundy is broken up into harmless little countries now."

"No, no, Charlotte. I am not afraid of Burgundy. But I must have the Rhine. Charles will need it. Every French king, every Frenchman, will need it always."

"I hate to think of your declaring war, Louis."

"Who in the world said I was going to?"

But powder poured out of the arsenals, the cannon wheels began to turn, and the king's armies pushed through Burgundian Picardy and entered Burgundian Artois. Maximilian fought bravely in defense of his young bride's inheritance, but the French whipped him soundly at Guinegaste. Maximilian could not support a war. His Burgundian troops were spiritless. His Austrian father sent no help, for he was far away, immersed in the futile paper affairs that clouded the twilight of the Holy Roman Empire. The prince pawned his wife's jewels; he was already bankrupt. Simultaneously, as they had for Duke Charles, uprisings occurred to embarrass him. After Guinegaste he fled into Flanders, and Louis called the

French army home. Flanders revolted. After Flanders, he fled into Gelderland. Gelderland revolted. In his fortress at Plessis-lez-Tours Louis sat grimly smiling. He had stirred up an inferno of chaos in the Netherlands.

While the Netherlands seethed and erupted, Louis turned his attention to ordering further the already great order in France. It came to his notice that one of his judges had cut off the ears of a Parisian Jew who had been convicted of clipping coins. A Lombard in Provence, guilty of the same offense, had had his tongue pierced.

"Why weren't they punished alike?" the king asked.

He was told that the laws were different in every French province.

"Why?"

They had always been different.

"I command that you punish these criminals equally. See to it!"

There was only one way to equalize the punishments. The Jew whose ears had been cut off now had his tongue pierced; the Lombard whose tongue had been pierced now had his ears cut off. But the busy king had no time to mete out such equal punishments in every litigation in every province of France. He was also building roads, bridges, canals, churches, improving his system of posts and increasing the strength of his armies. To guard against inequalities in the future, he ordered a Digest compiled of all French laws, ordered them unified, reconciled with one another, simplified, and sent as a guide to every judge in the realm.

The university professors to whom he delegated the task of compiling the Digest protested that the mechanical difficulties alone involved in copying so many laws would take years.

"Print them, then!" He already had one English printer. He sent to Italy and Germany for more.

Like the silkworkers, the ceramics workers, and the glass workers, printers now came to France, attracted by wages better than anyone else would pay, for the king subsidized the entire industry.

But there were further difficulties in the compilation of the Digest. There were not enough professors, most of whom also taught philosophy. They complained to the king that he was pushing them beyond their capacity.

"I do not understand philosophy," the king said, "and I don't think anybody else does. Pray, gentlemen, stop teaching it till you finish my Digest. That will give you more time."

To the scandal of Europe the magnificent French universities were, for some time, the only Christian centers of learning where philosophy was banned. To every objection the king replied, "My son will need laws, *clear* laws, when he comes to reign." The dauphin was still on the first line of Caesar. And the king had observed in himself an alarming new symptom. He had hurried all his life; now he must hurry to its end. He had given the professors time; he prayed for time from God.

For no reason, with no warning, and with no aftereffects except his perpetual terror of a seizure, he would suffer sudden spells of dizziness. It seemed to him also that things were a little fuzzy when seen with his right eye, and that sounds were a bit dull in his right ear. He had never confided the secret of his falling sickness to the queen; now pride and force of habit kept his new weakness secret also from everyone except Olivier le Daim, whom he had not stripped of his countship nor deprived of the revenues of Saint-Quentin. The doctor was more necessary to him than ever now.

To the doctors of his great medical school at Valence in the Dauphiny, where the wind of the Renaissance was blowing bold ideas over the Alps out of Italy and surgeons were more progressive than in Paris, he delivered the bodies of four executed criminals for dissection and study. He promised four more each year. He bade the surgeons discover why the right side of a man was weaker than the left. Pasque Dieu, one half wore out quicker than the other! He suggested that they count the ribs. Perhaps the fault was Adam's, in which case he supposed nothing could be done.

The queen noticed his habit of turning the good left ear when she spoke and smiled at his notion that he was hiding his defect. It was only natural, she knew, for elderly men to grow a little deaf. She merely spoke a trifle louder when she walked with him in the gardens of Plessis, passing her arm through his in the intimate Italian gesture that had shocked him at first, years ago. Her proud and prudish king!

Walking with her one day in the spring of 1480, while telling her the good news from Flanders, he started to say, "I had to plow the Dutch field before I could reap the harvest." In the middle of the sentence she felt his arm grow limp. He stumbled, fell, and lay still.

She had thought they were alone, but there was no privacy for her even in the garden. Suddenly Olivier le Daim came running up. He pulled her roughly away. "Go, Your Majesty! Leave him! Leave him to me!"

She shook off his hand angrily and knelt beside the king.

"No, no, Your Majesty! I beg you! He will torture me! He has always threatened to if I let you see him like this! Oh, God, do go!"

"Be quiet, Olivier."

She raised the king's head and looked into his face. He appeared to be sleeping. His body was limp and motionless. She spoke to him but he did not answer. His breathing was deep, and his cheeks puffed out at every breath as if the sleep were profound, like the sleep of a laborer after long hours of heavy toil. His face was a little flushed.

"Louis!"

Olivier was kneeling too, observing the king sharply. He took the pulse and found it firm.

"What has happened to him, Doctor?"

"Not what I feared," Olivier muttered.

"What did you fear?"

366

"The king has suffered a stroke of apoplexy, Your Majesty."

Charlotte crossed herself and prayed, weeping.

"I do not think it is severe. I am sure it is not fatal."

"Oh, treat him, Olivier!"

"I will, I will. Be of good heart, Madame. I will cure my master." But his voice shook, and he did not feel the confidence he tried to inspire.

He made a signal which Charlotte did not see, and instantly they were surrounded by guards. There had been even less privacy than she had thought in the garden. Now she was glad. Olivier le Daim spread his cloak, and they placed the king's yielding body upon it.

"Gently!" Olivier growled at the men. "Gently, by God, or I'll cage you!" They knew he could; they knew he would.

"Oh, please be gentle," Charlotte pleaded.

The doctor took two guardsmen's pikes and ran their sharp points needle-wise, skillful as a sempstress, through the rich heavy velvet of his cloak and used them as poles for an improvised litter. They carried the king gently into the castle.

* * *

After that there was great silence and mystery surrounding the dark fortress of Plessis-lez-Tours. Emissaries arriving from the Netherlands were met by Philippe de Comines, who received their complaints that Flemish trade was ruined, begging the King's help against Maximilian, whose presence they blamed for the trouble. Philippe de Comines said the king would take the matter under advisement. Emissaries from Marie also arrived with a petition to the king, addressing him as cousin and praying for aid against her rebellious subjects. Philippe de Comines told them too that the king would study the merits of her plea.

Thus, though Louis lay helpless, paralyzed, speechless, his policies marched triumphantly forward, his enemies weakened one another, others fought his battles.

A faithful circle of intimates guarded his secret. But no one could still the rumors to which the king's long and longer absence from public view gave rise. Olivier le Daim searched in vain to find and punish a barber from whom he had bought a pint of human blood, a common admixture to tonics that all doctors prescribed. It could always be legally purchased as a waste product from any barber, who got it from the universal practice of bleeding for a multitude of common ailments. Recognizing Olivier, the barber had apparently gossiped and then, rightly fearing punishment, fled. But the stories were started, the damage was done. Many people believed that the king, tiring of human form, had changed himself into a giant spider. Others, whispering on dark street corners and over their wine in taverns, held to the theory of a vampire bat, which seemed to account more adequately for the doctor's purchase. Even the university professors laboring over the Digest, who were less superstitious than most people, asked, If the king is alive why is he afraid to be seen?

For nearly a year there was no answer. The ugly rumors grew.

Finally Philippe de Comines told the king, "I have had to let a story leak out to the people that Your Majesty is not in good health."

Louis was propped up in bed against a mass of pillows, a fur cap bordered with all his saints on his head. Little by little under Olivier's care he had regained the use of his limbs, though the right side of his mouth drooped and his right arm was still so weak he could hardly use it.

"Why ever tell anybody anything?"

"A deputation of the clergy arrived yesterday inquiring whether they should pray for Your Majesty."

"Don't they always? Pasque Dieu, command them to!"

"They wanted authority for special prayers for your health."

"Did you authorize them?"

"I did, Your Majesty."

The king sighed. "I wanted the prayers all along, but to get them I had to admit that I was sick." It was a difficult decision. "I am glad." He blamed his apoplexy on Marie of Burgundy. "If I had sent a woman ambassador to that confounded female, I wouldn't be in this trouble!"

Philippe de Comines said in alarm, "But Your Majesty, there's no such thing as a woman ambassador!" The stroke must have affected the king's mind.

"Well, why shouldn't there be? Once there weren't any cannon, either."

Now that the secret was out, he employed every stratagem of which he was capable to counteract it. Signing his name with infinite patience, steadying his right hand with his left to keep the letters hard and firm, he addressed requests to neighboring sovereigns for beasts of the chase, as if he were still an enthusiastic hunter: stags from Sweden, horses from Spain, dogs from England, falcons from Switzerland.

He no longer dared keep a prince of the Church in prison. A cardinal's prayers were potent things, like heavy guns. Late one night he sent for Cardinal Balue. Expecting instant sentence of death the cardinal approached and knelt at the foot of his chair, while Louis glared at him. The king rested his cheek against his fist, his elbow on the arm of his chair, seemingly judicious but actually hiding the droop of his mouth which he could not make straight in spite of all his efforts.

"Will you pray for me?" the king demanded.

"I have always prayed for you," the cardinal said simply.

"Why?"

"In ten years one forgets and forgives many things, Your Majesty."

"Will you pray harder if I let you go?"

Balue blinked. He did not immediately understand.

"Your Eminence, I asked you a question. If I release you will you pray harder?"

The cardinal said confusedly, "Indeed, I shall; of course I shall; it would be the most natural thing in the world—"

Louis did not want anything natural. He wanted the supernatural help

368

of the cardinal's high-caliber prayers. "Will you pray for my health?"

"Certainly, Your Majesty." A priest would do that for anyone.

"You are free. Now go. I do not want you in France."

Hardly knowing how to act after ten years of solitude, Cardinal Balue spoke trembling, awkward words of thanks.

"Do not thank me. Pray for my health, or I'll clap you into a cage and never let you out!"

The cardinal fled to Rome, and all the world soon knew that Louis XI was still alive, still formidable, still able to bargain and threaten.

At the same time the king permitted his universities again to teach philosophy. The reaction of his clergy against the ban had been universal. Did he plan to forbid religion too? Religion and philosophy were inseparable. They were not inseparable in the king's mind, but he needed the prayers of his clergymen. The Digest would have to wait.

Visits from the queen particularly distressed him. Along with the old fear of heights, great sensitiveness about his appearance had returned: he was ashamed of his drooping mouth and held a handkerchief against it. He used the word "hideous."

"My dear lord," said the queen, "that is not only not true, it is nonsense. You are better and stronger every day. Soon you will be riding again."

"In front of people? Oh, no, Charlotte. It's hard enough for you to see me like this."

But he walked with her more in the castle garden and spent much time with the dauphin, who had got to *quarum unam incolunt Belgae* in the Commentaries.

"Yes, Charles, the Belgians still live there, this side of the Rhine. We shall have them when we get the Rhine. They belong to France."

He nearly got the Rhine. In the ruin of their commerce and the disruption of their provinces, the Netherlands were ready to forget their fear of him, forget their desire for independence, and turn to the only protector strong enough to restore their prosperity and security. They were ready to make any concession. There was already a faction among them who argued that if the ambitions of Louis XI were as pretentious as Charlemagne's, so was his power.

Then, on March 27, 1482, "that confounded female" tricked him again. Marie's horse stumbled and fell over on its side. She foolishly kept her seat, refusing to jump, and the animal pinned her leg under its belly. She suffered a cruel wound in her thigh. Too fastidious to permit a surgeon to treat her, she resolutely bore the agony of infection. She died of blood poison. Maximilian immediately quit the Netherlands he hated and went to the court of a German prince who was friendly and feudatory to the Empire.

The Dutch traders now saw themselves in a somewhat different position. They still wanted peace, but they were shrewd enough to know that they were in a better bargaining position, for the revolts in their provinces would now subside. They approached King Louis two days before Christmas with a treaty of friendship and commerce. They offered much, but not their independence and not the Rhine. Wearily Louis signed. He had lost one enemy; he needed two to pit against each other. In other years, he knew, he would have contrived a scheme; but his stroke had sapped his energy and he lived in constant fear of death.

The Dutch emissaries found him in a stifling hot room before a great fire, withered, white, almost invisible in his depth of furs. He signed the treaty with great difficulty. He knew he could no longer hide the fact that he was failing. He no longer tried to. Charlotte had been wrong. He was growing weaker, not stronger.

The treaty gave him Picardy, Artois, the Franche-Comté, the duchy and county of Burgundy. An empire. But the Burgundain provinces along the Rhine and the great river itself he knew were lost to his reign. But perhaps in the reign of his son—he could hope!

When it was time to swear on the Bible that he would keep the treaty, he found that he could not raise his right hand. It was exhausted by the effort of signing his name.

"If I touch the Scriptures with my left hand, gentlemen, I pray you to excuse me. My right is a bit feeble," he said.

Then, recollecting that an oath sworn by the left hand might some day be declared void, he exerted a great effort of will, gritting his teeth, trying to raise his right hand. He could not.

At length he succeeded in moving his right arm sufficiently to drag his elbow over the book. He swore to keep the treaty.

Consciousness of advancing weakness and public exhibition of it unnerved him. He wrote to Ferdinand, King of Naples, broadly reminding him that he had old claims on the Neapolitan throne which had come to him through the testament of his Uncle René of Provence. But it was not his intention to press those claims. Not if Ferdinand would send him a certain Calabrian hermit whose reputation for sanctity had impressed him. He needed the prayers of Francis of Paola.

Francis was a friar of the Franciscan order of monks, who were known as The Minors, "the less." Dissatisfied that their strict Rule was not strict enough, Francis had founded a separate order, The Minims, "the least." His Rule was so strict that superiors of his Houses were not called abbot or prior or guardian or rector or minister, but Corrector, and the monks of his Rule must abstain perpetually not only from meat but also from eggs, milk, butter, and cheese.

"They should live longer," Louis approved. So, he still hoped, would he. He had more than normal fear of death since every seizure all his long life had been a little foretaste of it. But greater even than the fear of death was his fear of what would happen to France if he died while the dauphin was so young.

Francis of Paola came—he would have come as readily for anyone, even a lackey, if the lackey had stood in such need of prayer as King Louis XI, for despite his Most Christian title his life, as the record had grown, was by no means the most Christian in the world. No one denied he had founded a new kind of national State and that nations were racing to copy it. But he had used any means, however extreme, to build it, and his concept of national morality had nothing in common with his concept of individual morality. Individual Frenchmen could sin; France never.

Francis of Paola had started his journey at once, but he could come to Louis no faster than the wind that blew his ship from Naples or the mule that bore him up from Montpellier to Plessis-lez-Tours. It was a weary wait for the king. Time dragged. He fretted about the hourglasses. They must be clogged. He had the sand taken out, cleaned, dried in ovens. Replaced, it ran just as slowly.

In his fear of death and his anger that Francis, Olivier, his emerald, his doctors, his saints, nobody, nothing was doing anything to save him, he schemed a scheme to save himself. He remembered his coronation and the holy oil that tradition held, and he firmly believed, a dove had brought from heaven. That was tangible!

He dispatched a herald to Paris with a demand that the *Sainte Ampoule* be delivered to him forthwith. He was going to anoint himself. Once more. From head to toe.

The horrified clergy of Notre-Dame hid the precious relic. The herald, fearful of death if he returned without it, disappeared.

Francis of Paola arrived. The king threw himself at his feet. Though his posture was humble his voice was full of reproach: "You should have hurried. I might have died." He explained his plan to reanoint himself, "but you shall do it now," and complained that the custodians of the *Sainte Ampoule* had disobeyed him. He ordered Francis to assert his great ecclesiastical authority and put them firmly in their places.

Francis of Paola said, "First let me teach you that you cannot snare the mercy of God."

Pasque Dieu, thought the king, a visionary!

Francis of Paola slipped into the routine of the royal chapel with quiet sureness, as if he were in his home. The king had expected threats, a raking inquisition of conscience, from the founder of the strictest Rule on earth. But Francis spoke to him, as if to a child, with a simplicity like Friar Jean's. It was disturbing to the king not to be questioned and reassured on every detail of his life: he had prepared elaborate justifications for every broken commandment. The great man did not catechize him. "You are asking yourself the questions, Louis. Answer them truthfully, to God."

"I have always employed persuasive emissaries, like Your Reverence."

"Come with me." He led the king to the altar and pointed to the cross with its image of the Crucified.

371

"Do you ask me to be your emissary, Louis, when you have a greater One?"

He was not very reassuring. To the king's admission that he feared death he merely said: "You were not afraid to be born, and death is but another birth. Do not be afraid."

Louis was. But it was a comfort to find a friend who ate more abstemiously than he, slept even less than he, and who, for all his lack of finesse in dealing with the Almighty, had a reputation for being headed straight for sainthood. The king would steal into the oratory at odd hours of the night. Francis of Paola would be there praying—the king knew he was not asleep for he hid and peeked and saw Francis's open eyes. Good, good! He wasn't lazy! His prayer would get through if anyone's would! Louis of France would live!

In April of 1483 an agent brought him early news of the death of Edward of England.

"How did he die?"

"At table, Your Majesty."

The king laughed. "I knew he would! I knew he would! What was he eating?"

"A mess of sprats."

The king laughed again. "Fish! Cheap fish! All he could afford. I cut off his pension a year ago." He had intended merely to weaken the English king, whom he deemed a litttle too powerful. The death was unexpected. But it was good for France, for neither of Edward's sons was old enough to reign. There would be a British regency now.

"I outlived the great glutton. The news is good. The news is good."

But somber news soon followed. Both British princes were murdered in the Tower, and Richard III had usurped the English throne.

"Nay, that is bad, the man with the withered arm! I do not like slayers of kings' sons." Louis suffered a great depression of spirit. The murdered Prince of Wales had been exactly the age of the dauphin. "Poor hapless lads." But still the news was good for France. Usurpers usually had trouble with their subjects. The War of the Roses would probably flare up again.

Olivier tended him, Francis of Paola prayed for him, and he surrounded himself with a profusion of relics, but still he grew weaker. Suddenly he was aware that, without his summoning them, the royal family were gathering at Plessis: his daughter Anne, his daughter Jeanne, their husbands. The queen and the dauphin stole in and out of his room now without being summoned. It was a bad sign.

"I will trick you all; I will get well," he said scowling. "Olivier! Do you want to be a duke? Make me strong again! Physic me! It is not my desire that there be a French regency too!" But the king's stomach had not been able to tolerate medicines for a long time. Olivier le Daim gave him sugar pills and weak infusions of harmless herbs that he made taste bad simply because the king thought them valueless if they tasted good. The doctor had substituted a pewter replica of the antimonium cup. The king's failing sight did not detect the difference.

He clung furiously to life but he prepared for death also, for he always tried to protect himself on all fronts. He arranged for a regency. It was a model of exactitude, full of checks and balances, brilliantly foresighted. "Principal of all its provisions," he dictated from his bed to Philippe de Comines, "is that my daughter Anne shall stand *in loco parentis* to the dauphin," and he added to the grand chancellor: "No woman is wise, Philippe, but Anne is the least foolish of them all. See to it!"

He commanded that sketches be made of his tomb. Seeking to flatter him, the artists depicted his effigy crowned, in armor, supine like a Crusader king. "Fools!" he rasped, hurling the sketches from the bed with his left hand, "Doesn't anybody know me after so long? Show me kneeling in a simple cloak, head bare, in prayer. And my dog. Place Pégase beside me."

One of the dogs that had come from England when he had first tried to hide his illness was a hound that bore a faint resemblance to Pégase who had been killed by the snow leopard in the Alps. To the king's dim eye, influenced by old memories, the resemblance was exact. He named the hound Pégase and insisted that it sleep on the hearth in front of the fire in his room.

No one protested that dogs had never before been placed on kings' tombs. Louis XI's whole reign had been one long series of startling innovations. Dutifully they drew the dog in the sketch of the tomb that he approved.

"Now carve it! Pasque Dieu, I want no changes when I die. No changes in anything. Do not dally. Show me a notarized receipt for payment to three—nay, six—sculptors every day. Bear me out to see it when it's done. And make me comely."

The hammers pounded, the marble chips flew. That was the middle of August.

But they never bore the king out to see his tomb. On the night of Sunday, the 29th of August, 1483, he said to Charlotte, "My dear, is it raining?"

"No, Louis."

"It must be raining. Go to the window and see."

The queen went to the window.

"No, my dear. It is not raining."

"Pasque Dieu, how can you tell? It is dark. Hold out your arm. I hear water falling."

Charlotte sighed, held out her arm. "My dear lord, there is no rain."

He said impatiently: "No one will tell me the truth any more. I am not afraid of rain. Why don't you admit it is raining? Very well, I shall see for myself."

But he could not rise. The struggle to do so wrought a change in his sunken features. His mouth drooped lower. She rushed to the bed, but he had already fallen back against the pillows.

"It is a cloudburst," he gasped, "a flood! Save the guns!" His diction was thick, almost unintelligible.

He had heard a growing roar as of a waterfall in his ears. It was especially strong in the deaf right ear. Pasque Dieu, he was regaining his hearing! He would trick the world! He would live!

The royal family gathered round the bed. Olivier le Daim said in a shaken voice: "It is another stroke, a thunder stroke of apoplexy. I am powerless."

Chapter Fifty-two

During the night, as the king lay dying, sometimes his lips would move. The sorrowing circle around the bed could not make out the words. Nor could Louis see their human faces.

The room was full of the ghosts of future kings.

"Nay, Charles!" the scarcely moving lips were shouting to his son, "Not into Italy! Adventure not beyond the engirdling Alps. They hold the south. Look north! The Rhine! Get France that northern border! Pasque Dieu, you do not hear me; you ride on. You silly prince!"

To Francis I, in a fine short cloak: "The blood is already mixed? Where are my son's sons? Those aren't the Valois legs, though those could be the Valois shoulders. Shame on you for that woman! But you rule *du bon plaisir*. I made that possible for you."

To Henri IV in his stiff circular ruff: "Protestantism? What is that? Good lad, you give it up, whatever it is."

The power of the kings was growing. "Mine, mine! I planted the seed. Without the seed there is no flower. Flower of the Lilies, grow!"

Louis XIV: "The greatest bears my name! The king and state are one. That should simplify things. Pasque Dieu, how long you wear your hair! Have you a scar? Do you fall too? You will not tell. But you can tell *me*. You strut away on high red heels—you must be short too. I wish I had thought of high heels."

Louis XVI: "So many named Louis! I am not forgotten!" A chopping block and a guillotine. "Nay, that is a neat device." But horror! It is the head of the king that falls.

A confusion of governments—the vision was faster and less distinct. "My sight is a bit feeble but I hear guns, French guns, everywhere in

374

Europe." Strange men in drab garb wielded authority, consulting their parliaments. "Nay, I understand parliaments, but where are the kings?"

The map pulsed and shuddered, its outlines twisting like serpents, but the Alps and the Pyrenees stood firm. "It is getting so dark. Dear God! Dear guns! Dear mountains! Guard poor kingless France till the people learn, if the people can, to rule themselves."

Parliaments regularly elected, codifying the laws, equalizing justice everywhere in France. "Mine, mine again! My work lives on, though the kings are gone! Or are they?" Firmly on every parliamentarian brow, on the brow of the people triumphant, rested the crown of Charlemagne!

"The people in power? How do they fare? The map! The map! Let me see France!"

The vision faltered, faded.

"Depart, O Christian soul—" intoned the voice of Francis of Paola.

"Nay more, more! Does France get the Rhine? Let me see the map!"

The map of France shone clear. Northward it leapt to engulf and sweep beyond the Rhine.

"Pasque Dieu, the people got what the kings could not! But more! Don't cheat me! It is not the end—"

"Out of this world," came the voice of the priest, "depart."

The king's lips had ceased to move.

But in death the drooping corner of his mouth had twisted up into a satisfied smile.

Nor Is It Yet
THE END